Looking Forward Through the Rear View Mirror

Stephen P. Bye

Hardcover ISBN: 978-1-63492-958-5
Paperback ISBN: 978-1-63492-957-8

Published by BookLocker.com, Inc., St. Petersburg, Florida.

Printed on acid-free paper.

This is a work of historical fiction, based on actual persons and events. The author has taken creative liberty with many details to enhance the reader's experience. The characters are purely fictional.

Library of Congress Cataloguing in Publication Data
Bye, Stephen P.
Looking Forward Through the Rear View Mirror by Stephen P. Bye
Fiction: Coming of Age | Fiction: Humorous | Fiction: Satire
Library of Congress Control Number: 2018907062

BookLocker.com, Inc.
2018

First Edition

This is dedicated to everyone, especially to Karen, who listened patiently to my storyline over the many years that I composed this novel. A special thanks goes to Megan, who contributed her insightful editorial support. I also want to express my appreciation to all those who provided inspiration, far too many to acknowledge individually

Preface

This work of fiction began over eight years ago, when my objective was to entertain readers by introducing eclectic personalities and integrating them into humorous scenes, which evolved into a collage about people and life in the mid-1960's. Although the characters are fictional, the story is based upon an assemblage of interactions with a few thousand people encountered over my 67 years. Some readers may believe that the characters are simply caricatures, but I can assure you…they are not.

I chose 1965 as the year for this tale. For some readers, this will create flashbacks in history, refreshing your memory of a unique period for politics, major events, music, television shows, sports, and movies. For others, it may arouse your curiosity and motivate you to investigate topics that you may have never known. The titles of several songs are connected to specific scenes or conversations, and I hope that you will investigate the lyrics, as several are linked with the dialogue or background in specific ways. Buried in the humor, I created metaphors for you to discover and correlate to more current times. In a few cases, I have taken the liberty to embellish a scene in an attempt to convey humor, to create a parody, or to establish a distinctive point of view.

The names of many characters were chosen by using sophomoric humor, by modifying the names of famous people, or by simply turning letters around in a key word. Hopefully you will simply chuckle (or groan), but will detect a connection with the character's background or stereotypical occupation or personality.

I selected a typical Midwestern city of approximately fifty thousand people as the setting for the story to reflect a myopic or parochial perspective on social issues, religion, and political philosophies that was generally exhibited in a community that may have been more sheltered than what you may have encountered… or possibly more progressive. Nonetheless, it is my recollection of a slice of a culture in 1965, and does not represent any personal beliefs, biases, or political agendas.

The main character, Scott Spykstra, is a naïve young teenager, who struggles to understand a broader world outside of his sheltered family surrounding. After becoming a golf caddie at a private country club, he encounters scores of people who are very diverse. As he begins his coming of age journey over the summer of 1965, Scott tries to interpret what he hears and feels. He desperately wants to look forward in his personal development, but is conflicted with the core values and the simple life imbedded in his upbringing over his past fourteen years.

As the vignettes unfold, I trust that they will create a few special connections for you, as well as to generate a few laughs along the way.

Chapter 1

So much had happened since eighth grade graduation. The summer had been eye-opening...no...life changing. The path of my sheltered life had been widened by a series of events and the future now seemed much more intriguing. I slouched down in the back seat of my parents' Plymouth and stared into the rear view mirror, attempting to link everything that had occurred over the past few months. I began to search for some sort of logical explanation to the grave newsflash that I had heard on the car radio early Friday morning when I was groggy...sleep deprived from the prior night's escapade. I initially thought that the report of the shooting was a dream, but as the radio broadcast was updated, the bulletin shocked me, as if I had been struck by the actual bullet. I was wide awake and my spine began to tingle until I started to shiver. I had never known anyone who had been shot, let alone an apparent killer...a murderer who I had spent nearly every day with over the past few months...a murderer who helped me see the world in a new and different way.

It would be a long trip back home today...the drive from Balsam Lake to La Crosse would take five hours. I gazed out of the window at the trees. The leaves were still full of life, but soon they would be changing...red, orange, yellow, then eventually brown, dead and fallen scattered on the ground as the bitter winter approached. I closed my eyes and recalled a spring morning in mid-April, when it all began to unfold.

I laid in a fetal position in bed and couldn't open my eyes. Sweat consumed my five foot-eleven frame, drenching the bed sheets. I was panicked, having skipped every ancient history class for the entire year. The final exam was scheduled in a few hours and I had no idea where to even find the classroom. Eighth grade graduation was only four weeks away and flunking the class would surely dictate a summer school sentence or worse, a repeat of the semester. The class bell rang and I faintly heard a woman's voice call my name. I desperately wanted to answer, but couldn't generate a sound. I heard my name called again. "Scotty...Scotty."

Presuming it was Sister Maureen, I finally mumbled a feeble response. "I don't know how I missed your history class for an entire semester, Sister Maureen. Please don't punish me," I pleaded. "I'll do anything to make up the class and still graduate!"

I slowly opened my eyes. My mother, Elsie, was leaning directly over my face. I barely got a few words out of my parched mouth. "What about my ancient history class exam?"

She put her cold hand on my forehead. "Do you have a fever? You must be hallucinating. You don't even have an ancient history class. Up and at 'em!"

"My name is Scott, not Adam."

"Up and at 'em, Scotty. You need to get ready for church. You're serving Mass this morning for Father Jesus Chevy."

I fumbled to turn off the alarm clock, which I mistook as the class bell in my nightmare. Still disoriented, I asked, "What day is it, Mom?"

"It's Wednesday, Scotty dear. This is Holy Week and your Easter vacation starts today at noon. Get dressed and brush your teeth. Dr. Dreiling warned you how cavities start."

I didn't need another lecture about cavities, as I hated the visit to the dentist. The drone of the drill and obnoxious fumes were enough to make anyone ill, much less when clumsy Dr. Dreiling ruptured a nerve in a tooth.

"I put out clean boxer underwear and black socks." Mom gestured toward my bed. "You need to wear your black trousers. The altar boy cassocks are too short and you don't want your pant legs or white socks showing. Be sure to ask Sister Maureen again to buy a cassock that fits you. Now get dressed while I go fix you something to eat."

Black pants and black socks always seemed too formal to me, as I preferred white socks and tan trousers. I was the tallest server by at least three inches, but I doubted that Sister Maureen would ever fulfill my request. I closed the door and turned on the radio and spun the dial to a new station...KORN 1490, where the amateur disk jockey, Colonel Cobb, played the top rock and roll songs. He was a flake, often botching the title of the song or the name of the artist. As usual, he didn't disappoint me.

> *KORN PLAYS ALL THE POPS AND*
> *WE'RE REALLY POPPIN'. I'M*
> *TELLING YOU NOW THAT THE*
> *NEW NUMBER ONE SINGLE THIS*
> *WEEK IS "I'M TELLING YOU NOW"*
> *BY FREDDIE AND THE STEAMERS.*

I left to brush my teeth and when I returned to my bedroom, Cobb was spinning "Ferry Cross the Mersey."

> *THAT WAS "FAIRY CROSS THE*
> *MERSEY" BY ANOTHER BRITISH*
> *BAND, GERRY AND THE PLAYBOYS.*
> *THAT PIXY MUST SURE HAVE*
> *SOME MAGICAL WINGS.*

After dressing quickly, Colonel Cobb introduced a new song.

> *HERE'S A NEW TUNE ON OUR*
> *CORN STALK THIS WEEK CALLED*
> *"COUNT ME IN" FROM JERRY*
> *LEWIS AND THE PACEMAKERS.*
> *JERRY IS THE SON OF GARY LEWIS,*
> *THE COMEDIAN.*

Mom shouted, "Scotty, breakfast is ready! I have poached eggs, bacon, and toast on the table and they're gettin' cold. Hurry dear!"

I did not want to be called dear, or even Scotty. I preferred Scott or Spike, the nickname my buddies had created, shortening Spykstra, my last name. I hated Mom's constant drill sergeant routine and became annoyed when she misinterpreted the news or mangled certain words. For example, she pronounced Father Jesus with a 'J' instead of an 'H', as if he was indeed the Lord God Almighty, and his last name, Chavez, calling him Chevy, as if he were a car. To keep it simple, I referred to him as Father JC.

When I joined Mom for the daily ritual at the breakfast table, her tiny radio was tuned to WZZZ, which was programmed for more news and also played classic songs from the forties and fifties. I referred to WZZZ as the sleep station, which also aired delayed broadcasts of the comatose Chicago Cubs, my favorite baseball team. *The Paul Harvey News and Comment* program had just begun and Mom never missed it. Her favorite feature was 'The Rest of the Story'. She even mimicked Harvey's classic sign-off, 'Good DAY', in her daily conversations.

Paul Harvey reported on the planned test of a nuclear bomb in the Nevada desert later that day. I immediately thought of the bomb shelter signs in the school and the drills we practiced in class. "Mom, can someone really survive a nuclear blast by hiding under a wooden desk?"

"The government says you can and we should trust everything that they tell us."

My ears instantly perked up when Harvey described the first indoor baseball game hosted by the Houston Astros at the new Astrodome, which he referred to as 'The Eighth Wonder of the World'.

Mom chimed in. "I can't believe a major league baseball game is being played inside a building. Won't pop-up flies hit the ceiling? AND, how can they ever grow grass in there? I'll betcha that the Astrodome will be demolished someday and replaced with an outdoor stadium, since fans needed fresh air. I don't like the new team nickname...the Astros? Do they really mean asteroids? I prefer the old name, the Colt.45s, a cute herd of forty five little ponies.

I corrected her, although she probably wasn't listening. "The Colts are a professional football team in Baltimore. Houston's former baseball team was called the Colt .45s, a type of pistol. Astro is short for astronauts."

"I don't think so. Why didn't they just name them the astronauts then…or the spacemen?"

Typically, I paid little attention to her babbling as she commented on the news. I also detested poached eggs, so when she stepped out of the kitchen, I buryied them at the bottom of the paper trash bag, where she was unlikely to find them. I knew that she often rooted through the garbage searching for S & H Green stamps or grocery coupons that Dad carelessly discarded.

Paul Harvey was still jabbering and then sounded off with his patented 'good-DAY'. A commercial jingle then played promoting Mayer's Chevrolet and Grandma's Donut Shop, when Hunter Chetley, the WZZZ newsman, came on the air to report more news.

> *THE UNITED STATES AND SOUTH VIETNAM BEGAN 'OPERATION FACT SHEET', A FORM OF PSYCHOLOGICAL WARFARE, BY DROPPING LEAFLETS BY PLANE OVER CITIES IN NORTH VIETNAM, ADVISING CIVILIANS TO TURN AGAINST THEIR COMMUNIST GOVERNMENT.*

"Scotty, those communists have been plotting to defeat us for fifty years. Why didn't anyone listen to General Patton at the end of World War II? We're now asking the North Vietnamese to surrender after reading a pamphlet? I betcha most of 'em can't even read English!"

"Mom, the pamphlets they're dropping are probably printed in Vietnamese." As she faced toward the sink to wash some dishes, I shook my head. I began to realize that my Mom's myopic perspective on life seemed to be influenced by the limitations of her ninth grade education.

*ON TUESDAY, THE U.S. HOUSE OF
REPRESENTATIVES VOTED TO
APPROVE THE TWENTY-FIFTH
AMENDMENT TO THE
CONSTITUTION, DEALING WITH
PROCEDURES TO FILL A VACANCY
IN THE OFFICE OF PRESIDENT. IT
INCLUDED A PROVISION
ALLOWING FOR THE VICE-
PRESIDENT TO BECOME
PRESIDENT IN THE EVENT THE
CURRENT PRESIDENT DIED,
BECAME DISABLED, OR WAS
DETERMINED TO BE
INCAPACITATED.*

"Scotty, judging from all of the insane policies Lyndon Johnson has been implementing, he should be removed for incompetency. Hubert Humphrey can replace him as President. I don't endorse his liberal policies either, but at least he's from Minnesota next door. You can't trust those Texans…they all talk weird."

I decided to ignore her.

*ON SUNDAY, PRESIDENT JOHNSON
SIGNED THE ELEMENTARY AND
SECONDARY EDUCATION ACT
INTO LAW NEAR STONEWALL,
TEXAS. THE CEREMONY TOOK
PLACE IN FRONT OF THE SCHOOL
LBJ ATTENDED AS A CHILD AND
HIS FIRST SCHOOLTEACHER WAS
A SPECIAL GUEST. THE NEW LAW
GIVES THE FEDERAL
GOVERNMENT POWER OVER THE
OPERATION OF ALL PUBLIC
SCHOOLS IN THE COUNTRY.*

Mom was getting more vehement. "See what I mean, Scotty? Someone should find his report card from that teacher to see if LBJ ever got past the first grade. What right does the government have in taking over local school policies? Our mayor and the city officials are certainly capable of running our educational system here. Pretty soon, Johnson will take over our Catholic schools too!"

"Maybe, the nuns could sure use some new ideas."

> *YOU WILL RECALL EARLIER THIS WEEK WE HAD REPORTED THAT TASS, THE SOVIET NEWS AGENCY, ANNOUNCED PROOF THAT AN EXTRATERRESTRIAL CIVILIZATION HAD BEEN DISCOVERED BY ASTRONOMERS IN MOSCOW, CLAIMING IT HAD BEEN DETECTED FROM A VARIABLE PATTERN OF SIGNALS. YESTERDAY, AT A PRESS CONFERENCE IN MOSCOW, THE ASTRONOMERS CONCEDED THEIR CONCLUSIONS WERE PREMATURE AND UNSUBSTANTIATED BASED UPON RESEARCH FROM OTHER SCIENTISTS.*

Mom held up her finger, suggesting she had a discovery. "Scotty, do you think the Russians were picking up the radio broadcast of the baseball game from the Astrodome in Houston?"

"Who knows?"

Chetley was unrelenting.

> *THE MISSISSIPPI RIVER CONTINUES TO FLOW OVER ITS BANKS. THE NATIONAL GUARD HAS BEEN CALLED TO HELP WITH*

*THE SANDBAGGING. LATER
TODAY, PRESIDENT LYNDON
JOHNSON WILL FLY OVER
SEVERAL CITIES, INCLUDING LA
CROSSE, TO VIEW THE
DEVASTATED AREAS IMPACTED
BY THE FLOODS.*

Mom interjected with another brainstorm. "Dear, LBJ is using the flood as an excuse to come here to run our schools. Say, don't they have a shortage of sandbaggers? LBJ's is full of hot air...they should hook a hose to his mouth to fill those sacks faster."

"They're asking kids at school to volunteer to help with the sandbagging, so my friends are thinking about it. Mom, I don't know about the President's intentions, but I'll take out the trash bag to the garage before I leave for church."

I was tired of hearing the news and Mom's comments. Growing up in a small city of fifty thousand people, the 1965 events reported throughout the world, or even within the United States, seemed far away to me. Except for the report on the local flooding, it was difficult to comprehend how the other news had any impact on my life.

"You're so thoughtful, Scotty dear."

Mom then ordered me to bundle up before heading outside. "Sonny Cloud, the weather guy from WZZZ says it's cold out there. Put your ear-muffs, stocking cap, and mittens on. Be sure to turn on the flashlight on your bicycle too. Good DAY!"

Before I opened the outside door, she yelled at Dad. "Milton, Milton, it's time to get up. I have hot breakfast on the table and its gettin' cold. You need to hurry, honey!"

I hustled to the garage and dumped the trash bag in the metal garbage can, rearranging the contents. I maneuvered my one speed black bike out of the garage into the darkness and flipped the switch to the flashlight that Dad had welded to the handle bar. As soon as I was out of Mom's sight, I tore off the winter gear and pulled out my blue Chicago Cubs baseball cap, tugging it down over my forehead. I quickly picked up the pace for the eight block jaunt to St. Stephen's Church.

I arrived with ten minutes to spare before Mass started. Francis Farmer, my altar boy partner, was already dressed in an oversized black cassock and a white cotta that hung down below his knees. Forgetting that Francis had an acute stuttering problem, I queried him on the status of the Mass preparation. "Hi Franny…what do we need to do?"

"G…G...Goo…d M…mmm…mor… nin. S…Sco…ot. I…I…d…d …d…i…nnn…see…F…F…aaa…t…ter Ju…Juce…y…yet."

I patiently listened to Franny's stuttering. Franny could barely finish a sentence; much less recite the prayers. I was curious why Sister Maureen had allowed him to become a server. How had he ever passed the test to recite the Latin prayers? Franny weighed no more than seventy pounds and was less than five feet tall. He wore the smallest cassock in the closet, which still dragged on the floor. He wore thick glasses, so when I stared directly at him, his eyeballs seemed three inches in diameter. Most kids called him Google Eyes or Goggles, but he preferred Franny. The nuns called him Francis.

I took charge. "Franny, fill the cruets with water and wine. I'll light the candles." Franny mumbled an indistinguishable response and followed my instructions.

After opening the closet and sorting through the cassocks, I began to panic. The largest one was a size twelve, at least four sizes smaller than I needed. I tugged my arms through the sleeves of the tiny cassock and futilely struggled to stretch the fabric. After attaching every third button, I still couldn't fold my arms across my chest, feeling as if in a straightjacket. I glanced down at the cassock, which barely covered my knees. It look like I was wearing dress.

I grabbed a scepter to light the candles and frantically searched every cabinet drawer for matches. Not finding any, I picked up the telephone and called Father JC in the sacristy. In a Spanish accent, he cursed, explaining he would light the candles himself. I dashed across the sanctuary to the sacristy, where he was waiting, signaling me to pull the cord for the bells to start the Mass.

As we reached the center of the sanctuary, I attempted to genuflect, although the snug robe restricted my motion. Halfway to the floor, the cassock tore down the rear seam. As I knelt down as the Mass prayers began, the cassock split again. I occasionally heard Franny mutter something, but it was comical…he stuttered in Latin too.

As Father JC went to the pulpit to deliver the sermon, I slowly lowered myself into the server's chair, but the cassock tore one more time. As I listened to his boring homily, I closed my eyes, my mind drifting to the meaning of a few Catholic terms. Was a Low Mass named after a bunch of midget priests or only those with deep voices? Were High Masses named for tall priests or those who sang Gregorian chants in soprano? I reflected on the word pastor, which spelled backwards, is rotsap. Was it a mere coincidence that our pastor's name was Father Rotsap? My mind diverted to the pews…was that word selected so people seated in them were allowed to fart?

Franny nudged me with his elbow. Apparently I had fallen asleep and was snoring too.

After the sermon, our task was to prepare for the Offering. Franny's only responsibility during the Mass was to carry the cruet set to Father JC from the Credence Table to the altar. As he shuffled across the sanctuary, Franny suddenly tripped on his cassock. The glass cruets shattered on the marble floor, with the water and wine each forming a puddle. To make matters worse, Franny slammed his nose and chin on the floor. Blood streamed from his mouth and nostrils, creating a pattern in the pool of wine. His eyeglasses flew across the sanctuary and came to a rest under the server's chairs. I quickly retrieved them, noticing both lenses were cracked and one bow was broken. Franny struggled to attach his glasses to one ear, hanging at an odd angle. Except for Ethyl Buffont, the school nurse, the congregation seemed oblivious of the incident, apparently frozen in solemn prayer. She rushed toward the sanctuary to aid Franny. Nicknamed Mrs. Buffoon for her excessive weight, she easily picked Franny up with her muscular forearms, rested him on top her large bosom, and carried him into the server's room.

When the Mass ended, Father JC closed the sacristy door and reprimanded me for falling asleep. He ordered me to clean up the wet floor, so I decided to use my shredded cassock. I meticulously picked up all of the pieces of broken glass and deposited the soaked cassock in a trash can.

I dashed to the school, which was adjacent to the church. I couldn't find Franny in his classroom, but tracked down Mrs. Buffont in the school office. She explained that Franny had two chipped teeth, a cut lip, and a broken nose, but decided to ride his bike home.

As I was leaving, Sister Maureen bolted into the office, her nostrils flaring. She obviously was not happy. "Mr. Spykstra, I understand there were problems at the Mass this morning."

"Yes, Sister. "Franny tripped and fell on his face. The cruets broke…the water and wine spilled all over the sanctuary floor."

"And what else?" Her eyes widened.

I could feel my heart beating faster. "There were no matches and I couldn't light the candles. Then I had to wear a very small cassock, which ripped at least three times."

"I sent the large cassocks to the cleaners. What happened to your cassock?"

"It ripped in several places, so I decided to use it as a rag to wipe up the floor, as Father JC ordered me to do."

"A rag? Cassocks are sacred! We have them all blessed before they're even worn. They're expensive too…the catalogue lists them at six dollars, so please bring me the money tomorrow, Mr. Spykstra."

I had always been intimidated by Sister Maureen, so I started trembling. Somehow, I blurted out a timid excuse. "But Sister Maureen, I had to wear one which was four sizes smaller than I need. It's not my fault that it tore in several places!"

"I don't want to hear any excuses. Bring the money tomorrow." Her nose was two inches from my face. Her beady eyes could pierce steel and she had horrible breath.

"Yes...yes, Sister." I couldn't believe that I was being punished, but couldn't protest any further.

I didn't know how to ask my parents for six dollars. Without even listening to what happened, Mom could easily get enraged, even for innocent indiscretions, like the time I broke a glass. Dad would always side with her too. They would be angry.

Chapter 2

Through my blurry eyes, I studied my watch, comparing it with the clock on the dashboard. I had only been sleeping for twenty minutes since we left Balsam Lake. I shut my eyes again, trying to recall what prompted me to volunteer for the altar boy program in the sixth grade. Mom was so proud of me, constantly bragging to her friends and relatives for my service to God. She was very religious, having converted to Catholicism in her mid-twenties.

My best friend, Steve Vale, and I were the first of the server group to master the Latin prayers, so we were often paired for server duty. The best assignment as the lead server was to ring the bell, which had become a competition among the altar boys. Franny and the other wimpy servers would weakly ring the bell only once. A few others clanged the bell loudly, as if there were a fire in the church. A couple servers were able to spin the clapper, making a whirring sound lasting for several seconds. The boys in our class voted for the most creative bell ringer, who was honored with the 'bell-shit' award each month. I never won the vote, as I merely rang the bell with two or three solid shakes, mostly with concern of being punished by Sister Maureen or Mom, if I got too inventive.

During the Communion service, the server held a paten, supposedly to catch any loose fragments of a host when the priest placed the flat piece of bread on the communicant's tongue. I actually never saw any wafer particles, although the priest always cleaned the paten after Communion as if there were. Communion was always the most entertaining part of the Mass when the parishioners knelt along a long rail. Many of them had unusual features like protruding nose hair, warts, pimples, bushy eyebrows, scars, yellow teeth, and discolored tongues. Sister Maureen's teeth were so horrible, they could have been a model for the periodontal disease picture displayed at Dr. Dreiling's office. Looking down the rail line, some of my friends made funny faces, causing me to choke up, desperate to suppress a laugh.

I was surprised at the number of people who chewed the host. Years ago, at my First Communion, the nuns scolded anyone who chomped down on the Eucharist, as it was akin to eating a Jesus sandwich. One day, Sister Maureen became hysterical when Father Rotsap dropped a host on the floor. She rushed to the spot, drawing a circle on the floor with some chalk, as if marking off a crime scene. After Mass ended, she returned with a toothbrush to collect all of microscopic host fragments.

One day, I began to notice the cleavage of a well-endowed woman, who often wore open dresses during the summer. I was mesmerized by her bouncing boobs when she strolled to the communion rail. The servers called her Mrs. Jugs, which seemed to be an unusual name. I even saw Father Rotsap, bending down to improve his sight angle for a closer view of the hollow between her breasts.

Sister Maureen asked me to join the funeral crew, where my responsibility was to carry the twenty pound cross. The class clown, Matt O'Connell, nicknamed OC, was also assigned to the funeral unit. When the servers retreated to the sacristy during the sermon, OC would gently close the door and don the priest's vestments. He proceeded to parade around the room, exposing his bare buttocks, claiming a fracture was developing in the Catholic Church. OC also took a few slugs from the wine bottle, adding water to it later, so no one suspected. His capers didn't seem proper, given the solemn mood in the church, but no matter how many times OC performed his antics, we went into convulsions with fits of laughter.

During the Novenas, the four servers split up, facing each other across the sanctuary. OC never wasted any time making funny faces. Once I started to giggle, I quickly masked it by coughing repeatedly. Twice, I needed to escape to the server's room to avoid an embarrassing outburst. On one occasion, OC was my partner for a Mass celebrated by Father Rotsap, who had a hearing problem. I struggled to remain my concentration, as OC substituted silly words into a few Latin prayers. OC also confessed to urinating in the water used in the cruet one day. As an acolyte, he purposely ignited Franny's cotta on fire, prompting Father JC to strip off his heavy vestment to smother the flame. I never knew what OC had planned for his next prank.

Another server responsibility was to light the incense at funerals, Novenas, and for the Stations of the Cross during Lent. One night, OC decided to load an entire box of incense on top of ten charcoal pellets in the censer. The smoke became so intense in the server's room that Sister Maureen called the fire department. OC was put on probation and sentenced to paint the first floor walls in the convent during a nuns' retreat, under the supervision of the scatter-brained school janitor. Never to waste a once in a lifetime opportunity, OC explored the inner sanctum of the convent where few outsiders were allowed to enter. He later admitted to plugging one toilet with paper and swiped the nuns' underwear from the laundry room. As a parting gift, he planted a dead mouse inside a heating vent. The stench became so unbearable, a fumigation company was hired to inspect the building. It took two days to find the rodent and the nuns were forced to sleep in cots in the basement of the school. That night, he snuck into the school and pulled the fire alarm, forcing the nuns to evacuate in their bathrobes on one of the coldest nights of the year. He was the coolest guy in our class.

OC later organized a party and charged a quarter to view his collection of the nuns' panties and brassieres. The panties were white or black, and according to the reports, resembled men's large boxer shorts. A couple panties apparently had evidence of brown skid marks, although OC later confessed he had actually used brown shoe polish. I declined the invitation to attend his private showing, concerned of being caught as a co-conspirator. OC was certainly entertaining, although I was leery he would lure me into trouble.

Chapter 3

I awoke with my head resting at an awkward angle with a pool of saliva forming a pattern on my blue knit shirt. I twisted my head to unloosen the kink in my neck and peered out the car window. We passed one farm field after another, interrupted only by red barns and white farmhouses. Driving on the narrow two-way highway, we approached a farmer driving his tractor on the gravel shoulder. Dad steered our car across the yellow center line, blaring the horn, as he mumbled something under his breath. In turn, the farmer stuck out his hand and extended his middle finger. Mom was horrified, turning her head away in disgust. It reminded me of the time OC first offered me some not so helpful advice last year.

On the playground in seventh grade, I had observed OC walk up to Linda Allen, holding up his fist, extending his middle finger toward her. Later when I asked him what it meant, he told me that it was code for sending a surreptitious romantic message to a girl, calling it 'Love Potion Number 1', altering the digit of The Searchers' song from 1963. Naturally shy, I had always lacked confidence to speak with girls, but one day, I decided to use OC's signal to reveal my secret crush on Carrie Simpson. I figured that I had done it wrong because she immediately looked away and ran off. It certainly didn't help with my insecurity when Carrie and her friends avoided me after the incident. When OC later admitted that the 'Love Potion' signal really meant 'go to hell', I really felt embarrassed.

I cleared the thoughts of my shame as our car neared a highway billboard, featuring an attractive blonde lady in a red dress. Her shapely figure triggered my fixation on images of women's bodies and I began to visualize what she might look like without clothing. I soon felt guilty about my dirty thoughts, recalling one of my most humiliating encounters ever.

At the end of school one day, Sister Seaxburh, our music teacher, asked me to carry a box of books to her music room. She was a young, attractive woman, and I had recently developed an infatuation with her. I even researched the background of Saint Seaxburh, a female saint from the seventh century in Medieval England. Perhaps her name alone had subconsciously tempted me with romantic thoughts. As I walked behind her, I thought of OC's underwear caper and imagined the color of her panties. Through a stream of light cast through a hallway skylight, I could vaguely see the outline of her shapely body. My vison was interrupted when she suddenly stopped and pointed to a table where she wanted me to drop the box.

"Thank you, Mr. Spykstra." Her smile seemed engaging.

"Yes, Sister Seaxburh. I hope you have a pleasant evening." Instead of turning to leave, I stood still in my tracks, hoping she would need help with something else.

Sensing my hesitation, she asked, "Is there anything I can do for you, Mr. Spykstra?"

"Ah, yes...can you meet me in the janitor's closet and strip naked? I will take all my clothes off too." I still cannot determine whether I actually responded or was just hallucinating.

"I'm sorry, Scott. Did you say something?" Her eyebrows were raised reflecting some curiosity.

Feeling numb, I thought that I was going to faint. My head was spinning and I couldn't even look at her. I struggled to utter a word..."Oh...I...I...I hope you have a nice day, Sister Seaxburh." I pivoted and quickly raced down the corridor. I did not want to gaze back, but when I reached the end of the hallway, I couldn't resist. She hadn't moved an inch and was just staring at me with a bewildered look on her face.

Outside, I gasped for breath in the cool air and cut across West Street in mid-block. I was dumbfounded by my apparent absurdity. How could I have even concocted that evil thought, much less find the courage to admit the sin in my next Confession? I slapped myself across the side of my head, wondering where these thoughts were coming from. Why was I so enamored with female nudity?

I once saw Mom's bare hinder for a split second through a small gap in my parents' bedroom door from a reflection in her dresser mirror. Otherwise, I had never seen a naked woman, or even a picture of one. After two young neighborhood boys had confessed seeing their mothers in a bathtub, I probed for more details. My curiosity backfired though, when one kid snitched to his mother, who then called Mom. The incident ultimately resulted in a belt whipping from my Dad and two weeks of silent treatment in the house. I never determined who actually ratted on me, but just prayed the whole incident would soon be forgotten.

A real breakthrough came one day at my friend Gomer's house. His parents had purchased an encyclopedia set and had recently received the 'H' volume. Gomer nervously paged through the book, until he came to the section entitled Human Body, which had a photo of a naked woman. Although the photo was black and white, my eyes were glued to the image. I bookmarked the page with a small piece of paper and every time I visited Gomer's house, I sneaked volume 'H' from the bookcase for another peek when no one was watching.

Our neighbor, June Morgan, also stimulated my obsession with nudity. Nearly every sunny summer day, she would arrange her chaise lounge in her driveway, only thirty feet from my bedroom window. Mrs. Morgan, a striking blonde, wore a one-piece bathing suit, complimenting every inch of her thirty-two year old body. Every twenty minutes, she shifted positions to ensure her tan lines were perfectly blended. Closing the door in my bedroom to avoid suspicion from Mom, I stared at her for several minutes. I even used my cheap dime store binoculars to zoom between her legs, hoping to spot any stray pubic hair. One afternoon, I spotted a few black ones when she tugged up the side of her swimsuit. I was mystified as to why it was black, while the hair on her head was blonde. When Mrs. Morgan turned over to her stomach, the split between her boobs was prominently displayed, and the outline of her nipples were magnified after dousing her bathing suit with cold water in attempt to stay cool in the hot sun. I was equally obsessed with her hinder, which was perfectly rounded. To further my fascination, I strategically placed a finger over my eyes to obscure her bathing suit, creating the illusion that she was naked. I often wondered if she was aware of my spying, or if she was purposely attempting to arouse a young man's fantasies.

I had no one to share my compulsion with. I didn't have a brother and could never ask my Father about women or sex. I even resisted revealing my naivety to my closest friends to avoid ridicule and embarrassment. Was this captivation normal or only my unique obsession?

Chapter 4

As we stopped at a traffic light in a small town, I studied the design of a white bank building, reminding me of the game of Monopoly that I often played with my best friends...Steve Vale, Nick Kanack, and Tony Pfeiffer. They had all adopted nicknames from television characters on *The Andy Griffith Show*. Steve was Gomer, Nick was Goober, and Tony was Barney.

We made several amendments to the rules of the Monopoly game, based on suggestions from Goober's Grandfather Sol. The winner was determined by the team holding the highest dollar amount after a designated time period, usually between eight and ten hours. Each property was acquired with a loan for one-hundred percent of the purchase price, based upon Grandpa Sol's prediction that banks would someday adopt high risk mortgage programs for real estate in exchange for charging premiums in the interest rates for those types of loans. With an aggressive lending environment, there was no reason to buy houses incrementally, so hotels were added as soon as a monopoly was attained, again without any cash equity required. Grandpa Sol also expected that lenders would be extremely accommodative for key borrowers in the decades ahead, so no team could ever go bankrupt. After all of the properties were acquired, monopolies were quickly created through a series of trades or direct purchases, as each team was permitted to buy a property from their opponent at a negotiated price, usually well in excess of the stated price on the actual deeds.

Since there were so many spaces and cards related to the taxation of the wealthy, Grandpa Sol concluded that the creators of the original Monopoly game had adopted the socialistic philosophies implemented during the Great Depression years. For example, he explained that the two hundred dollar stipend collected when passing GO, was effectively a form of public assistance, since there was no actual job cited for the players. He also prophesized that more citizens would rely upon government welfare programs in the future, using FDR's socialist agenda and LBJ's Great Society vision, as examples.

Since the capital account of the teams easily exceeded the amount of cash printed for the game, there was no reason to use the Monopoly bank, so the accounting records were kept on a piece of paper. We believed that we were also espousing a futuristic monetary experiment, as Grandpa Sol suggested that the use of cash would be totally eliminated someday. Under our rules, when income was received or expenditure incurred, a credit or debit was entered into the player's account. I was designated as the accountant for both teams, based on my math aptitude and honesty.

Grandpa Sol also predicted that prisons would become privatized someday, so the Jail and Go-To-Jail spaces were each sold for two hundred dollars. The jail landlord was obligated to pay a twenty five dollar referral fee to the owner of the Go-To-Jail space. Due to future municipal fiscal problems, Grandpa Sol anticipated that cities would someday monetize their parking lots and meter income by selling those assets, so the Free Parking space was sold for two hundred dollars and the rent set at twenty five dollars. No houses or hotels were permitted on the Jail and the Parking properties, although we discussed an amendment for future games, based upon selling the air rights.

Half of all fees, taxes, and payments governed by the defined spaces, as well as the Community Chest and Chance cards, were aggregated in the form of a lottery. Anyone landing directly on the GO corner space automatically collected the funds. Grandpa Sol had also expected that lotteries would become an important factor for municipalities to raise revenue in the future.

We also planned to allow an increase in zoning densities, allowing more hotels, since more costly skyscrapers were being erected in exclusive real estate locations in the U.S. For example, each property on the second street, starting with St. Charles Avenue, could have two hotels with rents doubling. Properties along the third street, beginning with Kentucky Avenue, would have three hotels with triple rents and the fourth street would have four hotels, quadrupling rents, resulting in the total maximum rent for Boardwalk at eight thousand dollars, for example. The inexpensive properties along the first street would continue to allow only one hotel, however. Although more computations would be necessary, Gomer had also recommended that we apply a factor of 2.3 to the original deed prices, rents, fees, taxes, and income based upon the increase in the rate of inflation since 1935, the year in which the original game was introduced. The base income tax would then be four hundred-sixty dollars, up from two hundred.

I recalled the time we played marathon Monopoly during our Easter vacation, while listening to music. Gomer brought out his record player and a stack of LP records. "Last week, I bought *The Beach Boys Today* album. There are some great songs, including "Do You Wanna Dance," "Good to My Baby," "When I Grow Up," "Help Me Rhonda," and "Dance, Dance, Dance.""

The album was nearly done playing when Barney finally arrived and a simple conversation about our summer plan turned into one of the most pivotal moment in my life. "Sorry to be late. There was a long line at the labor office. I needed to get a new work permit to caddie again this year at the Mississippi Valley Country Club."

Irritated with Barney's tardiness, Gomer ignored him and pressed, "Let's begin the game. Barney, we rolled the dice and you're Goober's partner."

I was curious about caddying. "Barney, what does the caddie deal involve?"

"My brother, Jimmie, and I first started caddying at a golf club in Kansas City. After we moved to La Crosse early last summer, I went to the Mississippi Valley Country Club and discovered they had a caddie program too. Between the two courses, I made three hundred dollars. I never knew much about golf, but they taught me what to do. You carry a bag or pull a cart, keep score, rake the traps, search for lost balls, and order drinks for the golfers. It's easy and some of the golfers are actually nice and most of the players tip us too"

"Are you paid based upon the time you're there?"

"No, the player pays for each round. The pro shop sets the caddie fee based upon whether you're an A, B, or C caddie. I'm a B caddie and the rate is two-seventy-five for eighteen holes."

"What if there are no golfers who want a caddie?"

"That can be a problem. There are some days when I don't get a loop, but I play cards, listen to the transistor radio, or just talk with the other caddies."

"That doesn't seem too great." Relaxing at home or hanging out with you guys seems more appealing.

"But the caddies also get to play the course once every month for free."

My ears perked up. "Mississippi Valley is a beautiful course compared to the crappy La Crosse Municipal Golf Course I've played a few times with Dad."

Goober jumped in. "Our family belongs to the MVCC. My Dad asked me to caddie for him, but it was boring and I like to sleep late. My Grandma gives me spending money, so I don't need to work. This summer, I plan to hang out at Boone's Boat Club, where our boat is docked. A few cool girls have already asked me to go water skiing. Gomer, you earn some money from your paper route, right?"

"Yeah, I'm set with spending money, so I wouldn't be interested."

I noticed that The Beach Boys album had ended and asked Gomer to fire up another record. "How about a Dave Clark Five song?"

"I only have a couple of their 45s, but I don't want to keep changing the records. I'll put on *The 4 Seasons Gold Vault of Hits.*" The album contained many familiar tunes including "Let's Hang On," "Ronnie," "Ragdoll," "Dawn," "Bye Baby," and "Big Man in Town." Barney's voice had not yet changed, so he even mimicked Frankie Valli with soprano licks on a few songs.

Within a ninety minutes, Gomer landed on the last available Monopoly property, Baltic Avenue. After engaging in intense trade negotiations, I lost track of time and suddenly checked my watch. It was already six o'clock, the exact time Mom always served supper every evening. I jumped from my chair and tossed on my jacket, explaining to my friends that I was late for dinner.

On my run home, I thought more about the caddie job. Even though Barney would be there, the thought of interacting with older caddies and adult strangers gave me some apprehension. What if I made mistakes and was embarrassed? I wasn't sure it was worth the risk.

Despite sprinting home, I arrived ten minutes late. Upon entering the house, Mom screamed at me. "The food is getting cold, so your Dad started eating already. I went to the trouble to make your favorite supper tonight. The next time you're late, I'll send you straight to your room all night and you can starve!"

I surveyed the serving dishes on the table…round steak, mashed potatoes with thick, brown gravy, boiled carrots, and croissant rolls. I agreed with Mom…it was my favorite meal.

As we ate, Mom appeared to calm down. "Scotty, do you remember that we're having the Knudson's for dinner on Easter Sunday. I'm making rump roast."

A perfect menu, I thought…a rump roast in honor of Mrs. Knudson's big rump. I had forgotten our family Easter tradition dinner with my parents' old friends, Clara and Olaf Knudson and their daughters, Francine and Bertha. I hated to entertain the Knudson sisters, as I had absolutely nothing in common with them. They were interested in classical music, theatre, and poetry. Last year, I convinced them to play Monopoly, although they were only interested in playing by the real rules. They forced me into bankruptcy when I couldn't pay the two dollar rent on Mediterranean Avenue. As guests, Mom allowed the girls to watch anything they desired on television. Last year, they wanted to see a Leonard Bernstein symphony concert, so I missed the final round of the 'Azalea Open Golf Tournament.' This year, I surely didn't want to miss the opening game of the NBA Finals between the Celtics and the Lakers that was scheduled to be on TV at one o'clock.

"Mom, I can't wait to count the number of pimples on Bertha and Francine's faces."

"You have zits too, Scotty dear. You should let me pick them after dinner. The Knudson's are nice friends and they're arriving around noon, so you'll have fun with their daughters. What did you and your friends do this afternoon?"

"Goober, Gomer, Barney and I started a marathon Monopoly game. That's why I was late."

"Who is Barney?"

"He moved here from Kansas City last summer. His real name is Tony Pfeiffer, but we named him Barney, after Barney Fife, the deputy on *The Andy Griffith Show*. We started late because he needed to obtain a work permit to caddie at the Mississippi Valley Country Club."

"Scotty, you should consider signing up to be a caddie. You have played golf a few times and I bet you can earn some money to help us pay for your high school tuition."

"I'll consider it, although Barney said you might just sit around all day and not get a job."

Mom interrupted my dinner. "Scotty, you need a haircut for Easter. Dad can clip you when you're finished eating and then he needs to finish up our tax returns."

"Mom, the guys were discussing taxes during our Monopoly game this afternoon. Goober's Grandad says the federal government is taxing too much."

"Yes, your poor dad slaves away for only four hundred dollars a month. What are we paying in taxes this year, honey?"

"With our exemptions and a couple deductions, our taxable income is about forty-one hundred dollars. The tax table says we owe nineteen percent, so we'll pay the IRS around seven hundred, seventy-nine dollars. A guy at work said they should move April Fools' Day from April first to tax day on April fifteenth, because only fools pay taxes." He chuckled. "I heard a comedian on TV say that tax day should be moved to Halloween because the IRS is out to trick everyone on the tax forms and their agents can then wear robbers' masks as a costume." He laughed again and looked at us for a reaction, but Mom was busy cleaning the pots and pans in the sink and I was stuffing my mouth full of steak and mashed potatoes. Dad continued, "So Scott, you could really help us with income from a caddie job."

"I'll talk to Barney about it again." I scraped up the last remnants of gravy on my plate.

Dad stood up and retrieved the electric clippers from the closet. He had no barber training and I always looked as if I had been scalped. "Jump on the stool under the light so I can see."

"Dad, can you leave my hair longer this time?"

"Elsie, what do you think?"

"A little longer, but not like the hairdos of those Beatles!"

I could go without a haircut for a year and my hair would still be shorter than the Beatles' cuts. Dad didn't keep his promise. The clippers pulled my hair as he pressed down, finishing in only two minutes. I peered down at the hair scattered under the stool and slowly rubbed my hand over my head. I couldn't grab any hair, so I quickly found my baseball hat in my room to hide the damage.

Returning to the kitchen, I decided it was time to ask for the money for the altar boy cassock. "Sister Maureen told me to bring six dollars for a cassock that fits me."

"Six dollars! Why? They should be paying you for all the times you serve. Don't they share money with the servers for the funerals and weddings?"

"Father Rotsap takes all the money for the server's fund."

"I have a good reason to call Sister to give her a piece of my mind."

"Please don't, calling her will only cause trouble for me. Can I use the money in my bank account?"

"Okay, but paying for a cassock is not right. You're going to lose a lot of interest too."

"Thanks, Mom. I gotta go. See you around ten."

"Be home by nine o'clock. Your father has to go to work tomorrow."

I raced to Gomer's house, panting to catch my breath.

Gomer was agitated again. "We all agreed to be here by seven and you're ten minutes late!"

"My Mom ordered my Dad to give me a haircut after dinner." I slowly took off my baseball cap and the guys burst out in laughter.

Goober knocked off my cap and rubbed my buzzed head. "That's a haircut? Did your father use a chainsaw?"

"No, a hatchet with a dull blade."

Gomer was curious. "Spike, why can't you just go to a regular barber?"

"Because a haircut costs a dollar."

"Spike, if I were you, I would use my allowance to pay for a haircut."

"Gomer, my parents believe in thrift. You know, save for a rainy day."

"My bank account has a balance of fifty cents, so if a storm strikes, I'll drown. The Serendipity Singers have a song out now called "Don't Let the Rain Come Down," so I'll remember to sing it on a dark, cloudy day. Since we're talking money, let's get on with our Monopoly game. It's my turn to shake."

Goober landed on a Chance square and read the top card. "I've been elected Chairman of the Board and it says I have to pay everyone fifty dollars. Now, why would a CEO pay anyone? I've heard that executives make a lot of money, so a CEO should be the one receiving the payment! Grandpa said some socialist created this card or else it was a misprinted!"

Gomer took his turn and landed on the Luxury Tax space, smacking his head in annoyance. "Seventy-five dollars! We may own a few properties, but we're dead broke. Spike, what's our account balance?"

"A negative thirty-four hundred dollars."

"See what I mean…taxing people with negative assets."

"Grandpa says that socialists created luxury taxes to punish rich folks. He also is adamant about a repeal of the income tax, which was established by an amendment to the Constitution in 1913. If there had to be any type of taxation, it should be limited to tariffs on all imported goods, which was how the government was primarily funded before 1913. Hand me the dice." He rolled two fours, counting off eight spots from North Carolina Avenue and landed on the GO corner square. "Credit us two hundred for reaching GO and all of the money in the lottery pot."

The amount in the lottery was three hundred eighty bucks. "That's five-hundred eighty for your account."

Goober pounded the dice on the table and rolled four, which put his race car on the Income Tax square. He counted again to be certain. "I hate this tax…two hundred dollars gone because of bad luck."

I reminded him that the tax amount is the greater number of two hundred dollars or ten percent of the total assets.

"But Spike, our fund balance isn't positive, so the government should pay us ten percent welfare payment based upon our negative account!"

"Goober, the value of all of your properties and the hotels adds up to thirty-eight hundred dollars, so ten percent of that is three-hundred eighty."

"That's not fair! We might land on that space every time around the board and the taxes can quickly add up to thousands of dollars. If you guys are lucky to miss it, you won't have to pay anything. The rule should be changed, so that if someone lands on the tax space, they're exempt from paying again for at least ten turns around the board."

"The IRS has established a seventy percent marginal income tax, but clever people can set up by a bunch accounting schemes to pay far less."

"Our family pays a huge income tax every year, but we get no benefit. Grandpa Sol says the system is rigged to keep the powerful politicians in office. Lyndon Johnson and Congress want to provide even more public assistance under his Great Society plan."

"Yeah, my Dad says LBJ is nuts." He shook the dice in his hands and threw them on the table. "Eight, I'm on the Reading Railroad, which we already own."

"Gomer, the name is actually pronounced red-ding. It's a short line railway company still operating today in Pennsylvania. From what I've read, they are in some financial straits."

"Goober, Pennsylvania is in financial trouble?"

"Maybe, but the Reading Railroad is certainly having distress with too much debt. The same path the USA is following. Your turn, Spike."

I landed on a Chance space and selected the top pink card. "I win ten bucks for second place in a beauty contest."

"Must have only been two contestants."

"Gomer, you're so ugly, they named a candy bar after your face and called it a Nut Buddy." I laughed at my own joke as I glanced down at my watch. "Guys, I need to go home."

"Can you all meet at ten o'clock in the morning to pick this up? Mom ordered me to go to Confession tomorrow before Holy Thursday services start, so I can play until around one o'clock. See you guys at ten."

I hurried home, not wanting to receive another lecture about being late. I walked through the side door into the kitchen and found my parents on the davenport in the living room watching *The Dick Van Dyke Show*. I said a quick good-night, went into my room, and shut the door.

I had been thinking about the caddie job all evening, but was still nervous about meeting the other caddies. How bad could they be? Plus, it would surely help to have some spending money to buy more baseball cards. Mom had allowed me buy only one pack every week for a nickel. She confiscated the chewing gum, citing the cavity threat, although I was only interested in collecting the cards anyway.

Starting two years ago, I received a weekly allowance of twenty-five cents. Growing up in the Great Depression, my parents were adamant regarding thrift, so every three months, they would accompany me to the First National Bank to make a deposit. Since I was always too shy to talk to the tellers, Mom made the deposit for me. The teller would empty the change from my yellow piggy bank and run my passbook through a machine. I always examined the interest credited to the account, normally was three or four cents. My parents constantly reminded me of the importance of accruing interest, and over time I had nearly twenty dollars in the account.

I pulled my Magic 8 Ball out of the desk drawer and began to engage it about the caddie opportunity. After cross-examining the gadget for ten minutes, I was satisfied the responses were mostly positive, so I reluctantly decided to caddie at the Mississippi Valley Country Club for the summer.

Chapter 5

On my walk to St. Stephen's, I rehearsed my confession, reciting the Ten Commandments out loud to be certain I had covered all potential violations. I contemplated adding my naked women fantasies to my list of sins, but I couldn't match that specifically to any Commandment, so decided it was not relevant. What a relief!

I opened the heavy wooden doors of the Church and counted at least five people lined up on both sides of the two confessionals and about thirty more parishioners scattered throughout the pews, silently kneeling in prayer. It was eerily quiet. I spotted OC stroll in the side entrance and line up on the right side of Father Rotsap's confessional. I lined up on the left side, behind an elderly gentleman and three women. The line moved slowly and twenty-five minutes passed when OC entered his booth.

The light went out above the left cubicle, signaling the old man had finished his confession. I had already begun to perspire, and as I slowly opened the creaky door, my heart raced even faster. I knelt down on the worn cushion in the dark compartment and my kneecaps started to throb. Through the mesh screen, I could easily see the outline of Father Rotsap. He had forgotten to close the window, so I clearly heard OC begin his confession.

"Bless me Father for I have sinned and my last confession was…ah…um…two years ago."

"Why so long, my son?"

"I didn't have any sins to confess, so I didn't want to waste your time."

"Continue, my son."

"I yelled at my parents about fifty times and I took the lord's name in vain."

"How often?"

"Just a guess, but between ten and twenty times."

Without pausing, Father Rotsap delivered OC's penance. "Say five Our Fathers and five Hail Marys. Is there anything else?"

"Well, I found a few girly magazines under my brother's bed. I tried reading them, but my eyes drifted to the pictures of the naked women. I just couldn't control my eyeballs."

"How many magazines did you see?"

"Five, six, well…maybe more like nine or ten."

Your mother or sisters should not see those magazines. For your penance for THESE sins, go home and bring them to the rectory immediately and I'll be certain the magazines are properly destroyed."

"Yes, Father."

"Is there anything more?"

OC seemed hesitant to respond. Father Rotsap probed again. "What else?"

"This is difficult to tell."

"I am here to listen, my son."

"I snuck into the Hollywood Theater last week to see a movie called *The Pawnbroker*. I know it was condemned by the Legion of Decency, but I was curious of what was in a C movie. In one scene, a woman exposed her breasts, but otherwise, the movie was pretty boring."

"Oh boy, I loved that scene too." Father Rotsap coughed repeatedly for a few seconds. "I meant, I read the reason why the Legion of Decency banned the movie for Catholics." He paused for a few more seconds. "For THIS penance, you are forbidden to ever see a condemned movie again. Also, NEVER divulge what we discussed here in the confessional…please."

"Yes, I promise."

"Go in peace my son."

Father Rotsap closed the other window and immediately turned in his chair toward me. He cleared his throat and coughed, signaling me to launch into my confession.

"Bless me Father for I have sinned. My last confession was four weeks ago. I talked back to my parents once. I lied four times and I took the Lord's name in vain, but only twice." I had actually never sworn, but decided at the last second to embellish my list of sins to seem more credible.

Like a broken record, Father responded. "Say five Our Father's and five Hail Marys, my son." He took a deep breath and slammed the window shut.

I vaulted from the kneeler and pushed the confessional door open so hard that it slammed against the wall, breaking the still silence in the church. Everyone turned to stare at me, so I put my head down and counted off fifteen pews toward the front before I knelt down to recite my prayers.

Hoping to get a peek at OC's girly magazines, I briskly exited the side door of the church and stationed myself in front of the rectory. I waited impatiently for several minutes, checking the time repeatedly. I finally gave up, needing to report as an altar boy for Holy Thursday services. As I was putting my cassock on, OC bolted through the server room door, gasping for breath.

"OC, what are you doing here? I didn't see your name on the server list."

"Steve Vale called me to substitute for him. I had to dash home after confession and deliver a package to the rectory."

"I know. I heard your confession."

"No, Father Rotsap heard my confession."

"Father Rotsap forgot to close the window, so I heard everything you both said."

"Well then, was my penance fair?"

"NO! Why does HE get to destroy all those girly magazines?

"Because he is a priest, I guess. My brother will be mad when he can't find them. You won't tell him, will you?"

"Absolutely not. Boy, priests must hear some interesting stories in confession."

"Scott, I've never told anyone, but I actually heard a lady's confession once. One Saturday morning, my parents were mad at me and kicked me out of the house. I didn't have anywhere to go, so I came to the church and went into the priest's confessional compartment to sleep. After a few minutes, I heard the door open and a lady immediately began to confess her sins."

"What did she say?"

"She started with the usual stuff…some minor boring stuff about cursing and a few lies, especially concerning her golf scores. I nearly fell off my chair when she admitted kissing another woman on the lips several times. Then, after she mentioned masturbating twenty-five times, I flew out of there before she expected to hear a penance!"

I had no idea what masturbating meant and could not admit my ignorance to OC. "Wow! Who was she, a nun?"

"I'm not telling, although I guess she likes to beat around the bush a lot. Also, I discovered the nuns have lied all these years. A priest can really see the person through the screen in the confessional. That's almost as bad as the threat the nuns made in the first grade, when they told us the dead guy nailed to the cross on the wall, didn't obey the Ten Commandments."

"Did anyone see you run out of the confessional?"

"I don't think anyone else was in the church, at least I didn't see anyone."

I had never heard of two women kissing, except perhaps a peck on the cheek. As soon as I got home, I looked up masturbation in my dictionary, but unfortunately, it wasn't listed. I concluded that it must have some reference to an expert on baiting a hook for fishing, although perplexed how that could relate to a sin.

My thoughts swung to Father Rotsap's reaction to OC's movie confession…he had obviously seen it too. I wonder how he disguised himself in a public theatre. He clearly wanted to look at OC's girly magazines and I also recalled Father peeking at Mrs. Jugs' boobs at the communion rail. His repetitive penances, regardless of the list and severity of sins, suggested that he never listened to anyone's confession. It reinforced my hunch that reciting sins to a priest was a hoax, cooked up by someone to clear one's conscience. Mom had always demanded that I confess my sins every month, but I decided to never report a few harmless indiscretions to a priest ever again.

Chapter 6

My radio was tuned to KORN, where the local weather, news, and sports were broadcast at the top of the hour. The rookie newsman, Hamilton Radio, was a real hayseed, who always seemed to botch the information. He was wrapping up a story of a barge accident on the Mississippi River where a seaman was missing.

> *IF THEY'RE HUNTING FOR THE SEMEN, WAS THE SPERM LOST TOO?*

Radio continued with the weather forecast.

> *TODAY WILL BE PARTLY CLOUDY AND PARTLY SUNNY WITH SOME CLOUDS. I DON'T KNOW WHAT THE CURRENT LA CROSSE TEMPERTURE IS, BUT UNCLE SEYMORE CALLED FROM COON VALLEY AND THE THERMOMETER ON HIS BARN READ THIRTY-SEVEN DEGREES. WINDS ARE OUT OF THE WEST, GUSTING TO TWENTY MILES PER HOUR FROM THE EAST. IT SHOULD BE A GREAT DAY FOR FLYING KITES. TONIGHT WILL BE DARK AFTER THE SUN GOES DOWN, SO REMEMBER TO TURN YOUR LIGHST ON. THE LOW TEMPERATURE WILL BE THIRTY-ONE DEGREES, SO COVER YOUR FLOWERS AND STUFF WHICH CAN FREEZE, LIKE YOUR FLOWERS. I'LL RETURN AT SEVEN O'CLOCK WITH MORE NEWS AND WEATHER.*

AND REMEMBER, WHEN IT'S
NEWS, IT'S NEWS TO KORN.

The radio engineer quickly spun a tune, sparing the listeners from more of Ham Radio's lunacy. Appropriately, the first song was "Everybody Loves a Clown" by Gary Lewis and the Playboys, followed up with "Cathy's Clown" by The Everly Brothers. I instantly turned up the sound knob when "Twist and Shout" began to play, seconds before Mom burst into my room. "How can you listen to trash sung by those creeps with hair as long as most girls? They wear those tight pants and high-heel shoes too! Even Ed Sullivan had The Beatles on his show. Their songs are not even music. Scotty dear, aren't you going to the golf club today?" Mom could change the subject and tone of her voice in a millisecond.

I was tempted to tell her that The Beatles had the top five songs on the hit list, but decided not to have a confrontation with her. I would never get the last word, and even if I did, she would never agree with me.

"You want to sleep or listen to junky music? I'll make some hot oatmeal for you. Its thirty-three degrees out. I made your lunch…a peanut butter sandwich, some chips, and an apple. I wrote your name on the sack. What are you going to drink there?"

"Barney said they have a pop machine. I have a dime and a nickel in my desk drawer. They may have a bubbler around too if I need some water."

"Scotty, keep your money in a safe place. You can't trust anyone these days. Better wear your brown sweater." She pointed to my bottom dresser drawer.

I found my brown sweater in the closet. "Mom, I need to go…the bike ride should take fifteen minutes."

"Don't forget your lunch. Did you take your money?"

"Yes, I should be home before five."

I opened the garage and wheeled my bike out the door. I carefully wedged my lunch bag under the seat, jumped on the pedals and began the two mile ride to the golf course. I passed blocks of modest houses and through a small commercial strip on the first half of the route. As I neared the country club, the size of the homes increased, as well as the dimensions of the perfectly landscaped lots. I turned into the golf club entrance at one minute to seven and cut across the vacant parking lot toward the caddie shed. I spotted Barney, OC, and Franny, along with several other kids.

Barney greeted me. "Park your bike behind the cart storage building." Mom constantly warned me of bicycle thieves, so I chained my bike to a wire fence using my padlock. I followed Barney to the side of the pro shop building. "Most of the guys put their lunch on top of the pop machine, so throw it up there." I stepped on a bench to reach the top, carefully positioning my sack lunch in back, where it seemed more secure. He then gestured toward the bulletin board, where a torn section of yellow paper was delicately hung in place by a rusty nail. "Here's the caddie sign-up sheet. There's a line between the A, B, and C caddies. You'll be a C caddie at first. You can't sign up on the list until seven o'clock though."

I check my watch, which read five past seven. "Then I can sign up now, right?" I studied the sheet. Several names, which were barely legible, were scrawled on the paper. I spotted a dull golf pencil with teeth marks lying on the concrete sidewalk. I picked it up and carefully printed my name at the bottom of the C list.

"What happens if the caddies arrive before seven o'clock? Do they line up in order?"

"Andy Bumgardner decides the order. He runs the bag room most days and assigns the caddies. If he's not around, he'll ask the older caddies about the order."

"Doesn't sound too fair to me."

"Andy's policy isn't fair. It doesn't matter much for C caddies anyway, because they never reach far down the list most days."

"How am I going to advance above a C caddie if I don't get a job?"

"There are a lot of caddies early in the year, but some will stop coming after a while. Come here every day and ask Andy if you can help out and he'll notice you. Another guy, Benny Roombach, runs the bag room when Andy isn't here. Did you bring your work permit?"

"Here in my pocket."

"Give it to Andy later. Let's go to the caddie shack."

The caddie shack resembled a shed. It had a roof, but there were only three walls and no windows. It was dark inside as apparently, there was no electricity service. The wooden structure was crudely built over a cement foundation, with several holes in the graffiti covered walls. It was furnished with two old picnic tables, four rusted metal milk crates, and three pine fruit boxes. Every square inch of the table tops revealed carvings of initials, vulgar words, and a few crude drawings of shapely naked women. The area around the shack was primarily hard pan dirt with a few patches of grass. The shed was shielded from the main parking lot by a grove of mature oak trees. A rusted metal basketball backboard was bolted to a nearby tree, although had pulled away from the trunk by several inches. The rim was also bent forward and there was no basket netting. An expansive grassy area, seemingly having optimum football field dimensions, was situated to the north, and bordered by several expensive homes.

"Barney, where's the bathroom?"

"In a cubbyhole room under the clubhouse, but watch out for the rats. The club occasionally supplies toilet paper there, but I suggest you bring your own. Don't ever take a whiz around the caddie yard. If the people in the nearby houses or members see you, they'll call the pro shop or the club manager and you'll never caddie here again. Some of the caddies run over to the gas station down the street, although it's not much better."

A dark green 1957 Chevy, equipped with wide white-wall tires, rolled into a parking space identified with a hand-written sign that read CADDIE MASTER. The driver screeched the brakes, down shifted, and popped the clutch. He got out of the car and then adjusted his sunglasses. "How ya doing today, chumps?"

An older caddie responded. "Andy, you're looking pretty cool in that car. Did you get any last night?"

"Bronco, come over and sniff the seat!"

"And see your cum stains? No way!"

Andy had a wide smile. "I know you're jealous."

Barney motioned toward the car. "Spike, the Chevy is Andy's pride and joy. You're going to have to kiss his ass to get ahead around here, so volunteer to wash his car soon. Let me introduce you to a few guys. Bing, come over here. Scott is my buddy at St. Stephen's. His last name is Spykstra, so we call him Spike."

Bing had a welcoming smile. "How ya doin', Spike. Welcome to the Club."

"Hi, how long have you caddied here, Bing?"

"This is my fifth year."

"Spike, his real name is Bobby Crosby, but we call him Bing…you know…like the singer who also hosts the clambake golf tournament at Pebble Beach in California."

Andy suddenly appeared. "Okay you scum-sucking rookies, let's hit the course and we'll teach you clowns something about caddying. Bing, grab a bag from the storage room. Jake, you can play too. Is Rutt here today?"

Jake spotted Rutt crossing the parking lot. "There he is…must have been in the can."

"Come here, Rutt. Did you just take a shit?"

"A giant one! Can't you smell it way over here, Andy?"

"Rutt, I know you don't wash your hands, so go find Lars Dix's clubs. He deserves to have some crap on his grips and be sure you hold every one of his clubs. Bronco, I'll need you to help out too."

I studied Andy more closely. He was short...about five-foot eight...and stocky, with a body-builder physique, evidenced by his large forearms. His hair was shaggy, like he cut it himself. He had a ruddy complexion with a scar on his left cheek and forehead, so I assume he must have gotten them in a few fights. According to Barney, he was graduating from Lincoln High School next month and had enlisted with the Marines at the end of the summer, following in his father and grandfather's footsteps.

Andy had a deep, gravelly voice, like a frog's. "Fools, line up by the fence near the first tee. That's where you will always wait for your player. The first thing you need to do is count the clubs in the bag. The legal limit is fourteen, so tell the player if there are more. Next, arrange the clubs in the slots. The wood clubs and the putter go in the section closest to the strap. The irons from 3 to 7 go in the middle section. The 8 and 9 irons plus the wedges go in the last slot. Some of you may have trouble reading numbers, especially you Catholic dopes. Hopefully, there will be another caddie with you who can help. For you other dumb shits, a putter is the club with a flat surface and the woods are the clubs with the large heads, like my dick. Woods usually have covers on them marked 1, 2, 3, 4, or 5. The number 1 wood is called the driver, which most golfers use to tee off. When your player asks for a driver, don't run off and call a taxi...they want the wooden club marked with a 1. A better idea is to hand the driver to the golfer when he leaves a green on the way to the next tee box. You might put the head cover in one of the pockets in the bag so you don't lose it, so be sure you put the cover back on the driver when you're done with the loop. The 3-wood is also called a spoon and the 2-wood is sometimes called a brassie."

Bronco interrupted. "So don't run off to the kitchen when the player asks for a spoon, or if he mentions the brassie, don't look in the bag for a trumpet or a trombone. The old guys here still call their irons a mashie and they're not talking mashed potatoes. If they ask for a niblick, don't go licking or nibbling them on their neck...they want a wedge or a 9-iron."

"Good points, Bronco. Always get a scorecard from the box and grab a pencil too. We don't have pencil sharpeners out there on the course, so make sure the pencil has some lead. Some wimpy men and many women use the new silly carts which have slots for each club. Some of you look pretty stupid, so don't hoist the cart over your shoulder. You'll have to pull the little cart like a sissy, although some of you look like you'll fit the part perfectly."

OC raised his hand. "What's a loop?"

"It's a circle...something round...like a zero. About where your IQ tops out!"

"You said we should put the head cover back on the driver after the loop."

"A loop is eighteen holes. You should remember loop because it rhymes with poop. If we ever let you out on a caddie job, I'm going start by lining you up with a horrible player. I call those poop loops."

OC looked puzzled. "What if the player quits after nine holes? Should we put the head cover back on since he didn't finish the loop?

"Are you a Catholic kid?"

"Yeah. I go to St. Stephen's."

"Figures...what's your name?"

"Matt O'Connell, but they call me OC."

"From now on, we'll call you Zero. Before I forget, have all of you turned in your work permits?"

I dug the paper from my pocket and handed it to Andy, who searched for my name. "Spykstra, huh?"

"Yes, Bum."

"Rookies don't get to call me Bum...it's either Andy or sir!"

I nodded, but didn't feel good about my first real encounter with him.

"Let's move over to the first tee. Spykstra, take Bing's bag. Zero, you can carry my clubs. Rutt, take that little runt with the goofy glasses," pointing to Franny. "Jake, pick out the biggest loser of the litter. Now…your player will normally pull two golf balls out of their bag, so make sure you know the brand and the number on the ball. Right away, ask your player if he needs his balls cleaned."

OC raised his hand again. "I heard there are some weird guys who play here, but I'm not washing anyone's nuts."

"I'm glad you mentioned that, nut-head! Here's a ball washer." He pointed to a box mounted on top of a four-foot tall pole. "You place the golf ball in the notch and move the wooded handle quickly up and down. Zero, I bet you have a lot of practice in the shower with that motion, right?"

OC clenched his hand in a fist near his crotch and moved it quickly up and down. The group howled with laughter. I didn't understand the joke, but played along with a smile.

"Relax, Zero…we don't need to see any cream on your jeans. Now, notice the benches we have on each tee? Caddies can't use them, but you might catch a peek at some snatch if a woman sits down on one at the right angle."

Franny slowly mumbled a few words, apparently asking Andy if snatch was a golf term.

"Mumbles, when you go home tonight, ask your mother. What the hell is wrong with you? Can't you talk?"

"He stutters", OC added, defending Franny.

"Stutters, eh?" He laughed and winked at Rutt, mimicking Franny's stuttering pattern. "D…D…D…id…u…j…j…just escape from the astronomy lab with those thick glasses?"

OC quickly defended Franny. "He just has bad eyesight."

"Bad eyes? How will he be able to see a golfer's shots?"

"He can see far away, just not up close."

"Well then, how will he be able to keep score? Jesus, Rutt...where did these idiots come from?"

"Like creeps from that old movie, 'Creatures from the Black Saloon'."

"That's lagoon, you dumbass." Andy seemed impatient. "Let's tee off. Jake, you're first. Rutt is second up and Bing is third. I'll play last."

Jake carefully placed his golf ball on a tee and took three practice swings. He surveyed the fairway, apparently to plot his route. He rested the club on the ground, adjusted his cap, took two more practice swings, and checked his belt, tightening it a notch. He peered down the fairway again and tugged again at his cap.

Andy was pissed. "Jake, we only have an hour."

"Sorry, Andy. I'm just making sure that I'm set. I haven't played since last year."

"If you screw around anymore, I'm going to come over and break your arms. You'll have plenty of time until you hit your next shot then."

Jake took a vicious swing, letting out a loud grunt, and topped the ball just ten feet. The caddies roared with laughter.

Andy wasn't amused and pointed down the fairway. "Jake, take these two dildo twins with you out there and teach them how to forecaddie." I assumed that Dildo must be the last name of the two kids who looked alike.

"Right away!"

Bronco, you play golf, right? Take Jake's place."

Without taking a practice swing, Bronco drove the ball straight down the fairway.

"Good shot, just what we needed. Rutt, tee off now and don't screw around."

Rutt quickly teed up his ball and took a fast swing, which was short and choppy. His rapid swing resulted in a good connection, but the ball flight suddenly veered far to the right.

"Shit, a banana ball!"

Andy shouted, "That curved so much, that's worse than a banana ball…it's a badnana ball!" He threw his arms to the right, as they watched the ball sail into a grove of maple trees. The ball caromed off a tree trunk, landing thirty yards further to the right in another fairway.

"If there are two caddies in your group, one should move up the fairway to help track the tee shots. The caddie on the tee should signal with an arm angle the direction of the ball flight. If the ball goes out of bounds, the forecaddie will cross his arms in an X above his head. That's a two shot penalty and the golfer should then play another shot from his current spot. Regardless, most of the players assume their ball is in bounds and when they can't find it, they'll covertly drop another ball, like one member does through a hole in his pant pocket. Golf is based upon the honor system, but if your guy cheats, never tell the other players. If you're keeping score, ask your player what they had on the hole, even if you know exactly how many shots they had."

OC raised his hand again. "If we know exactly how many strokes they had, why would I write down another score? Isn't that cheating?"

"Yup, most of them are dishonest. But you're paid by your golfer, so suck up, no matter what they do. Most guys have excuses for being shitty golfers. When they hit a bad shot, tell them the ball took at bad bounce, a sudden wind gust changed the ball flight, or someone moved in the middle of their swing to distract them…be creative. Most of these clowns tell their friends they had a lower score than they actually had. If they tell you to put down a 6, even though you know they had a 7, ask them if they had a 5. You'll be surprised how many players will agree with you. On the other hand, a guy playing alone or with his wife might tell you to record a higher score than you know he had."

"Andy, why would someone do that?"

"To jack up their handicap to receive more strokes when they play in a tournament or match play. Those cheaters are called sandbaggers."

"Sandbaggers? I understand, just like when I packed sandbags during the flood, and lied about how many I filled to get a prize! Andy, what is match play? Do golfers compete to see who can hold a lighted match the longest?"

"Zero, you are so unbelievably stupid! Don't you know anything about golf? Match play is a golf game where the winner is determined by who wins the most individual holes. Bing, you're next to play."

Bing was left-handed and had a fluid swing, blasting his drive down the center of the fairway. Andy then hit his ball, which took a violent left turn past the white stakes. Jake signaled with his arms crossed. After lecturing everyone on golf etiquette, Andy didn't have a choice but to play another tee shot. "I hate that damn hook. The ball is out of play, so I have to re-tee for my third shot."

OC waved his arms. "Andy, a bird chirped in your backswing and must have distracted you. It was a great hit, but that gust of wind blew it out of bounds."

"Zero, you may be dumb, but at least you remembered something I said. Now, shut up while I concentrate." Andy also hooked the next drive, ending up under several pine trees. He flung his driver thirty yards behind the tee. "Zero, pick up that club and let's go!"

"Andy, why didn't you throw the club ahead of the tee? It would make more sense, since we have to walk forward."

"I'll toss the club anywhere I want, so shut up and fetch it!"

We started walking down the fairway with Andy providing more instructions. "The caddies must walk two feet behind the player's right side, although Bing's caddie should walk on his left side since he's left-handed" I instantly switched positions. "Balance the bag on your shoulder so it's parallel to the ground and adjust the strap so it's comfortable. Put your hand over the irons, so they're re not rattling as you walk, and never drop your bag on the concrete where the irons can bounce."

Andy rushed over to help Franny. "Mumbles, your bag is dragging on the ground. You're about as handy as a pay toilet in a diarrhea ward!"

The bag was obviously too heavy for Franny. Andy jerked the bag away and let the strap out a few notches. Franny struggled to heave it around his shoulders and lost his balance. The bag fell and the heads of the irons crashed down on the concrete path.

"Mumbles, you are a worthless piece of shit. Get out of here and don't ever come back."

Tears streamed down Franny cheeks as he bolted away. I was tempted to follow him.

"Andy, better expect a call from Franny's mother, especially when he asks her about snatch."

"Zero, are you shittin' me? He'll really ask her that?"

OC nodded.

"We don't need no sissies around here anyway. Bronco, take this shithead for your caddie. What's your name, shithead?"

"Theodore Sullivan III."

"The third, eh? Third rhymes with turd, so Teddy Sullivan the Turd?"

"No, it's pronounced third! Third rhymes with bird. My first name is Theodore."

"Bull-shit! You're Teddy Turd around here now!"

OC, the two forecaddie Dildo twins, and I began to search for Andy's ball. OC spotted it between two trees, where Andy measured the angle for his next shot. He pointed to an area fifteen feet to his right, where he instructed us to stand. "Keep an eye on this shot." Andy swung the club voraciously and the ball careened off a tree directly toward us. After we dove on the ground, Andy shouted, "FORE!"

OC jumped to his feet holding up four fingers. "Yes, there are four of us here that you nearly killed."

"F-O-R-E." Andy slowly spelled out the letters. "Fore is the golf term for look-out. If your golfer drives a shot toward another person, yell FORE as loud as you can. And if you hear someone else screaming FORE, hit the deck."

"Why did you yell fore after the ball stopped?"

"It's never too late to scream it. At least you can tell someone you yelled fore and lie when you did."

Andy sauntered over to his ball and bent over to inspect for damage. "Zero, this is a Dot 4. I was playing a First Flight 2 off the tee. I told you that you need to know what golf ball your player is using? That's another two shot penalty for hitting the wrong ball, you idiot!"

OC shrugged his shoulders. "The fore-caddie spotted the ball, so that's his fault," he said, pointing to the innocent victim.

"Zero, he wasn't responsible to know what ball I'm playing. It was YOUR duty. The golfer is ultimately responsible for identifying the correct golf ball, but he will blame you and come to the pro shop to chew me out and demand that I fire your ass. Now, spread out and find my drive."

OC found Andy's First Flight 2 ball resting two inches behind another nearby tree. Andy was more irritated. "Crap, I can't play this. I have to declare an unplayable lie and drop the ball two club-lengths away. Let's see how many shots I've taken…three off the tee…two penalty shots for playing the wrong ball; and another penalty shot for the unplayable lie. I'm already hitting my seventh shot."

Bronco sauntered over to evaluate Andy's progress. "Andy, do you need an adding machine to keep your score?"

"Shut up, dork. You might be an A caddie, but I can still assign you a poop loop with old Mrs. Fecey."

"I'm only kidding, Andy. I know you're giving instructions."

Andy chopped his ball on the fairway, but was still two-hundred yards from the green. "Give me the spoon, Zero."

"I'm not a waiter, get your own silverware!"

"Zero, what did I tell you earlier? The 3-wood is called a spoon. Now hand me the 3-wood!"

Andy lashed the ball toward the green. It bounced two times, hit the pin, and dropped straight down into the hole. The caddies cheered loudly, while Andy took a bow. "A quadruple bogie eight...that's a snowman!"

"Snowman?"

"Zero, an eight...a circle on top of another circle. Haven't you ever made a snowman? When you write the 8 on the scorecard for a player, add a line straight down from the top of the lower circle, so it resembles a big butt-crack. That will signify how shitty the player really is."

I scanned the area, watching Rutt hit another acute slice, banging a large tree. I followed Bing and Andy to help search for Rutt's ball, which we ultimately discovered on the fringe of the 12th green. On his next shot, he swung downward, excavating a deep, foot-long divot, as the ball flopped into a sand trap. Andy inspected the damage. "Damn you Rutt...you should know better. Replace that divot pelt and stomp it down so the seams aren't even visible. Sod Greenman will kill me if he sees this!"

"Andy, who is Sod Greenman?"

"Zero, he's the head greenskeeper. His real name is Stoddard Greenman."

With his next swing, Rutt whiffed, but splattered the green with sand. Andy examined the putting surface. "Jesus, Rutt, now look at this mess!" Andy turned the rake over to the flat edge, carefully dragging it over the green. "We need to get all of this sand off the green." He then took a towel and snapped at the clumps. Finally, he got down on his knees, brushing the green with his hands repeatedly and blew the last specs off with his mouth. "Rutt, pick up the ball before you hurt yourself and show the caddies how to rake a trap. I need to get over the 1st green."

Bronco's second shot was buried in a trap, while Bing's ball had landed on the green. Bing pulled the divot repair tool from his pocket and leaned over the damaged turf, gathering the caddies around him. "Watch me now…insert the tool around the edge of the divot a few times and then step on the spot. Make sure you grab a divot tool before you go out on a loop. There's a box of them next to the scorecards on the 1st tee. Andy forgot to mention to grab a few extra golf tees too."

"Hey Bing, I have an idea…I can use the divot tool to pick out my boogers", OC said jokingly.

"Zero, you're the real tool!" Bing placed a white plastic marker behind the ball. Grab a ball marker from the 1st tee too." He tossed the golf ball over to me. "Clean it!"

I caught the ball, spit on it, and rubbed it on my shirt.

Andy punched me on my forearm, knocking the ball out of my hand. "What the hell are you doing, retard?"

"Cleaning his golf ball."

"Do you think a player will want to touch the ball after you gobbed on it? The golfers may not wash their hands after taking a piss or shit, but they certainly won't want to hold a ball with your slobber on it. You need to have a wet towel with you. You'll find those on the 1st tee next to a bucket of water."

I didn't know what to say, but thankfully, OC interceded. "Andy, there's a lot of crap to remember…scorecards, pencil, divot repair tool, tees, ball-markers, wet towel, your player's golf ball brand. What else?"

"Zero, you need to remember your player's name. Rutt, can you recall a group of rookie caddies who were this dim?"

"No, Andy. This crew is the worst."

Bing decided to intervene. "Rutt, I recall when you were a rookie, your player asked you for a tee and you asked him if he wanted ice in it. Can you remember the day your player asked for an iron and you suggested he buy wash and wear clothes? How about the time when your player asked you to meet him next to the range and you went into the kitchen in the clubhouse to find him?"

"Shut up, Bing! Bronco, play the trap shot."

Bronco asked Teddy Turd for a sand wedge.

"A sandwich? I don't see a delicatessen shop around here."

"Turd, are you kidding me? It's the club with an S on it, you meatball!"

Bronco blasted the ball onto the green and it rolled to a foot from the hole. He scooped up the ball, claiming his putt was good.

Bing walked around at several angles to line up his twenty-foot birdie putt. "Spike, stand beside the hole and press the flag around pin with your hand, so it doesn't flutter in the breeze. After I strike the ball, pull the flagstick out."

I grasped the flag so it was tightly wrapped around the pin. After Bing stroked the putt, I struggled to pull the pin, which stuck in the base of the hole. The ball hit the flagstick and bounced two inches away. I finally managed to jerk the pin out, damaging the grass edging above the cup.

"He said PULL the pin! I know you're dumb, but are you deaf too?"

I had an excuse this time. "Andy, it was jammed in the cup."

"You took a gouge out of the edging too! Jesus, I'm happy we have another mutant with us today, so you losers learn another lesson. Make sure the pin is loose when you grab it and bring it up straight, so you don't damage the cup edging. Bing gets a two shot penalty for hitting the pin while putting on the green, even though it was his caddie's fault. Instead of a birdie 3, it's a double bogey 6."

Everyone was laughing at me. I was so humiliated, that I decided at that moment to quit and walk off the course. I took a few steps toward the clubhouse, when a hand gripped my shoulder. An older rookie caddie, wearing a tattered army jacket and a red bandana, stopped me in my tracks. I looked directly into his steely blue eyes, as he whispered to me. "Hang in there, kid. These assholes are not as tough as they may seem." He winked and turned away.

I inched towards Bing's golf bag, as he handed me his putter. "You made a mistake, but don't worry. New caddies always screw up, although Andy won't let you forget it."

I was grateful that OC spoke up again to lighten the mood. "Golf has too many damn rules. Did the Catholic Church have a hand in making them up?"

Andy answered. "Some old, stupid golfers from Scotland dreamed up the rules. Now, who's got the scorecard?

"I do," OC shouted raising his hand.

"Write down an 8 for me. Bronco had a par 4. Bing had a 6 because of his caddie, and Rutt gets a 9-X."

OC scribbled the scores. "Okay…9-X, 4, 6, and an 8. What's a 9-X, Andy?"

"Zero, an X is when a player quits or records a bad score on a hole."

"But you had an 8, which is a bad score, so why not add an X?"

"Screw yourself Zero, write down an 8."

"Should I add the asshole crack?"

"Hell no, but you can draw a real thick line pointed up at a forty-five degree angle to resemble my large cock with an erection. All right losers, let's skip over to the ninth tee. I need to be at the shop by eight o'clock. The first tee time is eight-thirty. In a few weeks, the tee times begin at seven, so you'll need to be here no later than six-thirty. Rutt, you and I will just walk along now. Bronco and Bing will still play. Let's change the caddies up. He instructed a younger kid wearing a green, red, and white stocking cap to carry Bronco's bag. "You look like a stupid elf with that silly hat."

"My Mommy told me to wear it because it was cold outside."

"Tell your Mommy it's my business what you wear here, Sugarplum. So what's your name?"

"Dewey Doolittle."

"Doolittle, eh? Sounds like you may be too lazy to be a caddie. We'll just call you DooDoo for now."

DooDoo leaned on the golf bag, which nearly crumpled in half.

"Jesus Christ, DooDoo! Don't put your weight down on the bag. It isn't designed to hold you up. You may have broken the bag supports."

I was relieved that Andy signaled for the kid with the army jacket to take Bing's clubs from me. "Sergeant Bilko, what do they call you?"

"Jesse James."

"Like the outlaw? You look a little old for a caddie…what are you doing here?

"This caddie job is part of my probation. I've been expelled for fighting in the tenth grade and spent five years in reform schools and three in the Wisconsin State Prison in Waupun. I enjoy beating the crap out of jerks like you. I was just released last month for burglary and first degree assault."

I moved a few steps closer, not wanting to miss this conversation. I had never known anyone who had been in prison, although Jesse's comment to me on the first green suggested that he was not as ruthless as he appeared to the others.

"Jerk, eh? Any time you want to spar asshole, let me know. I didn't receive these scars playing with dolls. I've been boxing down at the city gym for three years now, so you better call your dentist before you meet me. Actually, with your teeth, I'd be doing you a favor. And never wear your army issue coat or that bandana here again. Got it?"

"Andy, I'll put up with your bullshit for now because I need to comply with my probation terms, but don't insult me or I'll find out where you live. By the way, I've done a little prizefighting, learning the ropes in the joint."

"If I hear one complaint, you're history. I'll make sure you return to your cell, convict. Our caddie coveralls are white, different from the striped ones you've been wearing on the chain gang." He glanced at the ground for a few seconds, apparently recalling more caddie instructions. "Oh, I forgot to mention the caddie dress code to you losers. Did all of you buy your clothes from a rummage sale or dress wearing a blindfold this morning? From now on, always wear tee shirts, white tennis shoes and socks…no boots or regular shoes either.

OC interrupted again, "Andy, so we don't need to wear underwear, shorts, or pants, eh?"

"Caddies wear white coveralls, so I couldn't give a shit what you wear underneath. If you morons pass the caddie exam, we'll give you a green cap, but don't lose it."

Andy had apparently run out of things to say and seemed disinterested. "You guys play out the hole. I'm headed to the pro shop. Rutt, you take over."

Bronco and Bing both laced their drives well down the fairway. As Bronco knocked his wedge shot safely on the green, a large piece of turf landed ten yards ahead of his divot.

Rutt instructed Doolittle, "DooDoo, hand Bronco the putter now that his ball landed on the putting surface. Replace the turf in the divot spot, stomp it down, and clean off the wedge with your wet towel."

After Bing proceeded to roll his ball on the green, Jesse handed him the putter and replaced the divot without being prompted. "Nice shot!"

The caddies gathered in a circle around the 9th green.

Rutt pointed to the flagstick. "DooDoo, tend the flag while Bronco lines up the putt." Doolittle tromped across the green and positioned his foot directly in the line of the putt. "Careful where you're walking, Big Foot. Never, ever, put your clodhoppers in a putting line or a player will wrap his club around your neck. Check where all the balls are lying before you step on the green."

DooDoo now held the flag straight out, using both of his hands.

Rutt shoved Doolittle away. "Tending the flag means tending the flagstick, you retard!" Rutt demonstrated the proper technique. After Bronco and Bing putted out for pars, Rutt threw the flagstick toward DooDoo like a javelin, barely missing his head, imbedding it at a thirty degree angle in a sand trap.

"That's all, you knuckleheads. Andy will hand out an exam in the caddie yard and the senior caddies will also have another little test for you later."

I returned to the caddie shack, where Barney was relaxing on a crate. "Barney, I don't think this is going to work out. Except for Bing, the senior caddies are a bunch of jerks and Andy is the worst. He made me feel like a complete loser after I made some mistakes on the course."

"Hang in there, Spike You can make it. Just give it a few weeks."

"Even if I ever get out there to caddie, my player will probably fire me on the first hole."

"The players are not all creeps."

I sure hoped he was right.

Chapter 7

OC was wheezing heavily as he trotted into the caddie yard.

"Sounds like you're going to die, OC!"

"Barney, must be the cigarettes." He coughed a few times.

"Don't let Andy catch you smoking on the course."

"Why? Everyone who's cool smokes these days. Cy Clone, the WIZZ weatherman, even chain smokes while he's live on TV!"

The twin brothers ambled into the caddie yard. Up to this point, neither had said a word to anyone in the class.

Barney addressed them as they entered the shack. "Are you two brothers?"

I couldn't tell if Barney was joking or serious.

"We're identical twins. I'm Tom Bunker and he's Ron Bunker."

I then realized that I was wrong about their Dildo last name. I wondered why Andy had called them dildos since their name was actually Bunker…maybe just another option for look-alikes.

"People usually have a hard time telling us apart."

No kidding, I thought. The Bunker twins were carbon copies of each other. My eyes darted back and forth between the two of them. Thankfully they were wearing different colored sweatshirts, Tom in grey and Ron in blue…or maybe it was the other way around.

"Do you guys ever play jokes on people?"

"Our favorite thing is to wear our Dad's huge trench coat and pretend our bodies are joined together. You cannot believe the stares, especially when we kiss each other. At school, we fool our teachers constantly by switching desks. I wear Ron's clothes so often that even I get confused who I am most days."

"Are you Ron or Tom?"

"Yes!" They both answered simultaneously.

Our attention turned toward the door, as we heard a whimper. DooDoo limped into the shed, blood streaming down his shin from a gash in his left knee.

"What happened to you?"

He sobbed and his voice trembled. "I tripped and fell on the driveway. I want my Mommy. I'm going home!"

OC explained to Barney what happened out on the course during our training. "Andy gave the kid some crap about his name. But that's great…with DooDoo gone, that's one less caddie to compete with."

Jesse walked in and immediately took off his army jacket and threw it on one of the picnic tables. His right forearm featured a tattoo with crossed swords and the word KILLER carved beneath. A lady's face was imprinted into his upper left arm with SWEETHEART etched above. I couldn't take my eyes off of them. Why would someone do that to their body?

Bing was the first senior caddie to return to the shack. "Cool ink, Jesse. A few men golfers have tattoos too, but I bet Andy won't risk assigning you to a lady golfer. Better keep 'em covered. They probably have a rule here about those. So, your name is really Jesse James?"

"It's actually Dean James, but call me Jesse."

Bing extended his arm for a handshake. Jesse grabbed his thump around his own and clasped his hand tightly around Bing's. "Where did you learn that grip?"

"From the Negro guys at Waupun State Prison."

"Cool! My name is Bing. I've been here for a few years. Be careful of Andy and his stool pigeons…Rutt, Bronco and Buddy."

"Got it, thanks."

OC tapped Jesse's Killer tattoo. "I just wanted to touch a tattoo, man. Can I try that handshake too? I'm OC."

"Okay."

"Smooth, Jesse!"

Even though Jesse had briefly comforted me on the golf course, I was too timid to introduce myself and when Barney tried to add his welcome, Jesse ignored him.

A few minutes later, Bronco, Rutt, and Jake arrived in the caddie yard, along with a short senior caddie, who they called Moose. Rutt screamed out instructions. "Mutants, line up over there." He pointed to the grove of trees twenty feet away. "We need to test your tee digging skills. We'll mash a golf tee in the ground and all you have to do is remove it with your teeth. You'll have thirty seconds and if you fail, you'll have to keep trying until you do. If you don't want like it, then scram and don't ever come back here again. Bronco has a watch with a second hand, so he's the official judge."

Bing interceded. "Spike, you're first up." Bing pushed the tee down in a grassy area, stomping it down with the flat portion of his tennis shoes, so the tip was barely visible.

Rutt motioned to the ground. "C'mon Bing, that's not deep enough. Let me stomp on it."

"You can have your turn later, Rutt."

"You're too soft, Bing. Maybe you should dig a tee too!"

"Maybe you should dig a booger out of my nose, shithead!"

"Any time, fuzz nuts. Meet me over by the tennis courts after this is over and we'll see who's a shithead."

Rutt was now nose to nose with Bing. Jake stepped forward and separated the two of them. "Relax guys, we have to start the initiation."

Bing put his hand on my back and pushed me toward the ground. "Spike, down on your knees and hold your hands behind your back. Bronco, I mean John Cameron Swayze...are you set with your watch?"

"Yup, I'll say go when the second hand strikes twelve."

Nearly two minutes passed, when Bing nudged Bronco. "What's wrong Bronco? Too tough for you?"

Bronco shrugged. "I didn't hear a bell when it reached twelve."

"The watch doesn't ring when it hits that number. Otherwise, you'd hear it go off every minute!"

Bronco still seemed confused. "Okay… three… two…one…GO!"

I pounced on the tee, locking my front teeth around the tip, but couldn't get a very solid grip. I pressed my nose further into the grass, which smelled like urine. Sinking my front teeth into the dirt further, I pulled backwards, like a steam shovel to get some leverage, chomping down on the tee until it came free. I shot my head up to display the tee in my mouth and then quickly spit it out. I closed my jaw, grinding chunks of dirt lodged between my teeth. Clearing my throat, I desperately tried to generate saliva to flush out the grit, but could only spit out microscopic bits and shreds of grass.

Bronco checked the time. "Only twenty seconds…not bad for a sissy. Now let's see what Zero can do." He found a section of hard pan dirt, and stomped on the tee three times, the last one with the edge of his heel. The top of the tee was a quarter-inch below the surface of the ground. Upon Bronco's signal, OC burrowed down in the dirt like a wild badger and popped up with the tee in only ten seconds. He chunked out a mouthful of earth. "Anyone have a toothbrush?" He couldn't stop grinning. I could see pieces of dirt were wedged between his teeth. He got up and lit a cigarette with a lighter he pulled from his back pocket and exhaled a series of smoke rings in celebration.

In a squeaky voice, Moose interrupted. "Zero, your mouth was designed for tee digging. Maybe you'll have a future as an archeologist. Chang and Eng, you twins are next. Bronco and Rutt, you can do the stomping honors for a dual tee dig contest."

Rutt was puzzled. "Moose, who are Chang and Eng?"

"Chang and Eng Bunker...they're the original Siamese twins from Siam in the 1800's. Didn't you read about them in history class? Incredible, another set of Bunker twins!"

"They look more like Tweedledee and Tweedledum to me."

"Rutt, this is hard for people to believe, but the Siamese twins were actually married.

"To each other?

"No...they actually fathered TWENTY-ONE kids. Eng had eleven and Chang had twelve."

"That's impossible! All with one woman?"

"No...they married two women who were sisters. Instead of a 'ménage à trois', they could have called it a 'ménage à quatre.'"

"Huh?"

"You should have taken French in high school, but I know that you wouldn't have even passed English without my help."

"The only thing I need to know about France is a French tickler. Now, let's get this twin tee dig started!"

I was trying to follow their conversation. I had thought about taking French in high school, but picked Spanish instead. The only thing that I liked about France was French fries.

Rutt picked a spot in the grassy area and pushed two tees into the turf. Bronco jumped up and down on them four times to be sure they were well imbedded. "Boys, anyone interested in a side bet for a buck to see who wins?"

Rutt was always eager to gamble. "Bronco, I'll take the kid in the grey sweatshirt. Is he Chang?"

"You're on! So I have Eng?"

"Ying...Yang...Ching...Chang...who in the hell gives a damn what their names are? I have the kid in the grey sweatshirt. "On your mark...get set...GO!"

Tom and Ron ripped the grass around the tees as if they were sheep. They came up for air a couple of times to spit out the dirt and pieces of turf. Tom surfaced in twenty-two seconds, three seconds ahead of Ron.

"You owe me a buck, Rutt!"

Blowing his snot into a crumpled dollar bill, Rutt carefully folded it, and hurled it at Bronco. "Nice doing business with you, chump. Now, let's move on, I've been waiting all morning for the jailbird to do this." Rutt scraped a pile of soft dirt to form a crudely shaped bowl, pouring Bronco's pop carefully over the dirt to create a mud-pie. He pushed the tee deeply into the center of the murky mess and then kicked a little more dirt on the pile so the tee wasn't even visible. "Moose, give me your pop. I need a little more mix."

Jesse didn't say a word and quickly dropped to his knees. He put his hand to his mouth and pulled out a bridge holding false teeth, extending them for Bing to hold.

"Sorry pal, but I don't hold anybody's fangs."

Jesse grinned and tucked them into his back pocket.

Bronco began the countdown…"Five…four…GO!"

Jesse's face was quickly immersed in the mud, apparently using his tongue to locate the tee. The seconds ticked by and he didn't seem to be making much progress. Rutt shoved Jesse's head down, submerging his face further into the goop. "Pretend you're eating out your slut girlfriend and maybe you'll get lucky."

Not understanding a word of it, I waited for another other caddie to provide an explanation.

Bronco was counting. "Fifteen seconds…now twenty…twenty-five…twenty-six…twenty-seven…twenty-eight…twenty-nine…thirty…thirty-one…thirty-two."

Jesse popped up, his face caked in mud, displaying the tee on his tongue.

Rutt seemed jubilant. "Too bad, loser…that took more than thirty seconds. You have to do it again, just like your next stint in jail."

Bing corrected him. "Hold on. I counted twenty-eight seconds on my watch. Bronco cheated him by starting too soon after he said go! I have a second hand on my watch too."

"Bull shit! Crosby, you're feeling sorry for this derelict. Are you sweet on him or what?"

Jesse jumped up, wiping the mud from his face, and slowly took a few steps toward Rutt. In a flash, he punched Rutt in the nose and followed up with a left upper-cut to his jaw, lifting him off the ground. Rutt landed on his back, unconscious. I was stunned, having never seen a violent fight up close. Jake and Bronco knelt over Rutt and tried to wake him. After a few seconds, Rutt regained consciousness and rolled over on his side. He coughed violently, spitting out blood as three teeth fell to the ground.

Moose ran to the bag room to inform Andy, who raced to the scene. He wrapped a towel around Rutt's nose and mouth. "I'm going to catch hell, you turds! What happened?"

Bing piped up. "Rutt forced Jesse James to dig a tee out of the mud and smashed his head into the crud. He was being an asshole, so Jesse clocked him."

"James, you're on probation. Get out of here and don't return for two weeks. Rutt's nose is broken and he should go to the hospital. Bronco, you have a driver's license don't you?"

"Yeah, but I don't have a car here today, Andy."

"Here's the key to my car and BE CAREFUL. I don't want bloodstains on the seats, so keep the towel around his face. I know the mileage on the odometer, so you better bring the car straight back here."

Bronco and Moose escorted Rutt into Andy's car and he collapsed on the seat. Bronco struggled to start the engine, so Andy scurried over to check. "Are you sure you know how to drive?"

"Of course, Andy"

"I'm going to inspect every inch of the body when you return and if I see even one scratch, you're a dead man." Andy watched intently as Bronco navigated the car over a curb, wincing as the under-carriage brushed the concrete. Seconds later, after hearing a blaring horn and the squeal of brakes, I expected a crash, although there was only silence. Andy blew out a sigh of relief. "God damn him!"

I couldn't believe everything that just had transpired over the past ten minutes. There was a neighborhood bully who constantly picked on me a few years ago, but Andy, Bronco, and Rutt were much worse. Initially I was annoyed that Bing made me go first, but now realized he was actually giving me a break on the initiation.

I trudged to the shack with Barney, as the senior caddies forced Teddy Turd to dig his tee. "Some tough guys they have here."

"Spike, they're trying to intimidate you rookies. Rutt's had a rough life. His dad is an alcoholic who hits him all of the time. His mother died years ago, so his older sister helped raise him. They live in a boathouse down on the river because his dad is a commercial fisherman."

"What's his real name?"

"Shep Ruttledge."

"Shep, eh? Sounds like his dad treats him like a dog. How about Bronco?"

"His name is Jeff Broncovich. He's stupid and hangs around Buddy and Rutt. He's been a caddie here for three years and is a senior at Jefferson High too. He's a decent athlete...a linebacker on the varsity football team and a wrestler too. He's a brown nose though, so you'll see him kissing a lot of butts, especially Andy's."

"And the little wimp, Moose? How has he survived here?"

"There's a story going around that Moose does all of Rutt's homework and even takes some tests for him. His name is Lionel Trane. He's afraid of being struck in the eye with a golf ball, so he wears some ridiculous protective goggles. He's very bright. Who else would know anything about the Siamese twins? The women golfers love him because they think he's cute and feel sorry for him to lug the big bags. Can you believe it?"

"Is Jake a good guy?"

"Yes, his last name is Schnaeker. He keeps to himself and doesn't say a lot. He's a great caddie. You can learn a lot from him. He's a body builder, so he won't take any crap from Rutt and Bronco. He'll be a senior at St. Anthony's`. Andy likes him too."

"And Bing?"

"Well, you saw how friendly he is. He's a real honest guy and takes everything seriously. He won't bullshit you."

"Anyone else?"

"There's another asshole senior caddie named Buddy. He lives on the north side. His dad owns an auto repair shop and Buddy works there a couple of days a week. Andy is his cousin and they hang out together. His real name is Felix Greco. Have you ever heard of Buddy Greco?"

"Is he a wrestler?"

"He's a famous jazz singer, so the nickname of Buddy stuck with him as a kid, I guess."

We settled into a picnic table on the right side of the shack, seated across from one another. My finger traced the outline of one of the naked ladies etched into the wood. "Spike, there will probably be some new caddies coming over the next few weeks too." He lowered his voice to a whisper. "I shouldn't tell you this, but there's another contest, which is even more challenging than the tee digging. I can't tell you the details, or I'll be in trouble with the senior caddies."

"Come on, please tell me! Doesn't the club have some responsibility?" I shuttered to think what could be worse than the tee digging.

"They treat the caddies as independent contractors and what goes on is not their concern, unless it involves the members. Andy is an employee, so he keeps his distance, except for when he has to train the caddies. He gives orders to Rutt or Buddy to run the caddie yard."

"Does the head golf pro interact with the caddies?"

"Only when he takes one for his round."

Andy strolled up to the caddie shack with some papers and a box of pencils. "First, here's a sheet listing the caddie pledge of allegiance. I will ask to you to recite them at any time, so memorize them. I have a written test for you rookies too. There's only thirteen questions and you need to get nine correct to pass. Zero, you'll be happy to know there are mostly multiple choice questions and two fill in the blank. Now, no talking and spread out so no one is tempted to cheat. You'll have ten minutes to complete the test."

OC raised his hand. "Let's see…no talking, no cheating no guessing, no smoking, no farting…what else?"

"Shut up, Zero! Let's see how dumb you really are!"

I grabbed a seat on the bench to write on the table and scanned the test.

Question 1: The maximum number of golf clubs a player can have in the golf bag is:

    A) There is no limit.
    B) As many clubs which can fit in the bag with a weight limit of 30 pounds.
    C) 14.
    D) The number is assigned based upon the golfer's handicap.

Question 2: Andy Bumgardner is:

    A) The toughest guy on earth.
    B) A lover of many beautiful women.

C) A model to all caddies.

D) The most handsome man in La Crosse.

E) All of the above.

Question 3: When carrying a golf bag down the fairway with a left-handed player, a caddie should:

A) Keep abreast and to the right of the player.

B) Keep two paces behind and to the left of the player.

C) Keep two paces behind the player to be able to smell the golfer's farts.

D) Keep two paces in front of the player, so he can smell your farts.

Question 4: What must a caddie pick up on the first tee?

A) A sharp pencil.

B) A wet towel.

C) A divot repair tool.

D) Ball markers.

E) A blank scorecard.

F) All of the above.

Question 5: When caddying for a lady golfer, a caddie should:

A) Keep a rubber in your pocket in case she gets horny on the course.

B) Position yourself on the right place around the green to see some ass when she picks her golf ball out of the hole.

C) Place the bag at a lower angle when she selects her club to increase the probability of seeing her tits.

D) Trade jobs with another caddie who is assigned a male golfer.

E) All of the above.

Question 6: When asked to keep a scorecard, a caddie should always:

A) Write down the player's names identified on their bag tags or ask for their names.

B) Ask each player their score immediately after completing each hole.

C) Add the scores immediately after completing each nine holes.

D) If a player records an 8, draw a line down the top of the lower circle to resemble a butt crack.

E) All of the above.

Question 7: If a player has an 'AB' (anal breakdown or shit attack) on the course, a caddie should:

A) Sprint to the clubhouse or nearest restroom to get a roll of toilet paper.

B) Like yelling FORE, scream POOP as loud as possible.

C) Tell the player that he has a crappy lie.

D) Suggest the player wear black trousers next time to camouflage the stains.

E) Write a suggestion here:

Question 8: A trap is:

A) A metal spring gadget used to catch wild animals.

B) Areas on a golf course filled with sand.

C) Where police catch speeding cars.

D) When a woman schemes to marry a guy.

E) All of the above.

Question: 9: A green is:

A) Another name for a booger.

B) A color.

C) An area of a golf course mowed tightly with a cup and a flag.

D) When a stoplight signals GO.

E) All of the above.

Question 10: Caddies are like Marines because:

A) They're prepared to go into the bush.

B) They will not leave anyone behind.

C) They 'improvise, adapt, and overcome' obstacles on a golf course.

D) They shout OORAH, when their player makes a great shot.

E) All of the above.

Question 11: A tee is:

A) A drink in England.

B) An undershirt.

C) A gadget to hold a golf ball.

D) A letter in the alphabet.

E) All of the above.

Question 12: A ball is:

A) What a player hits on a golf course with a golf club.

B) A fancy dance.

C) Having sex with a woman.

D) One testicle.

E) All of the above.

Question 13: What's your actual name? (Fill in F):

A) Shithead.

B) Mutant.

C) Meatball.

D) Chump.

E) Retard.

F) All of the Above; My name is:

OC was the first caddie to finish the exam. "Boy, the quiz was sure tricky. I circled B for Number 7. The toughest question was Number 5, so I selected number A. I always keep a rubber right here in my wallet."

I wondered why anyone would keep a rubber band in their pocket. "OC, I thought Number 5 was a trick question, so I circled D. For Question 7, I inserted 'Hand the player a diaper'. I hope Andy likes that idea."

Andy collected the exams and immediately scanned OC's sheet. "Zero, now I know you are a sex maniac, I'll ask the attendant in the women's locker room to put up a sign warning of caddies packing rubbers and walking around with bulges in their pants."

Bronco now addressed us. "Listen up, rookies. We have one more test for you which will be next Saturday morning at seven o'clock, so be here on time. I recommend you bring a supporter, you know…a jock strap. You all take gym class, right?"

"What's the reason for a jock strap, Bronco?"

"We have a traditional football game between the rookies and the senior caddies and the game gets pretty rough."

"Well, why didn't you tell us to bring a cup too?"

"Oh yeah, I forgot…be sure you bring a cup."

I assumed that there was some connection with Barney's hazing warning and the reason to wear a jock and a cup, but I did not want to think about it for another second. I was still unsure if I would even return next week.

Barney escorted me toward the corner of the golf shop building and pointed to the large wooden sign hanging over the pro shop. "See that sign?"

"Yeah, it says GEORGE PALMER-PGA PROFESSIONAL. Is he related to Arnold Palmer?"

"No, but George is the king around here. He gets pissed any time someone asks him if he's related to Arnold Palmer. By the way, he may ask you to shag some golf balls for him, so jump at the chance. He won't pay you, but at least he'll know who you are."

"What should I call him?"

"PRO, only the name, PRO."

"What's shagging?"

"My brother Jimmie said that in England, shagging means having sex. But here in La Crosse, it means retrieving golf balls when a golfer practices hitting shots. You'll also get to know the ass pros."

"Ass pros?"

"The three assistant golf professionals. Sam Paganica is the lead assistant...a practical joker whose nickname is Pags. He says his last name is based upon the original game of golf played by the Romans with sticks and a leather ball filled with feathers. Last year, PRO hired Robert Condor, who played on the PGA tour for a couple of years and you must call him Robert or Mr. Condor. We heard his name was Bobby Comdon, when he played in high school in Milwaukee. Then he won two amateur state championships and shortened his name to Bob. After he qualified for the PGA tour in 1962, he legally changed his name to Robert Condor. What a phony!"

"Never heard of him. I guess that some people don't like the name their parents gave them. Most movie stars have stage names. Did you know that John Wayne's name is actually Duke?"

"That's his nickname...his real name is Marion Mitchell Morrison. Back to the ass pros, Condor has a real bad temper and when he misses a shot, he will blame you for anything. If you ever caddie for him, don't even breathe before he plays the shot. The members hang around to hear his stories while he was on the tour, especially when the chicks lined up at his motel room. He still goes out and tries to qualify for a few PGA tour events, so he practices constantly and plays in money games with the big gamblers when he's in town. Over the winter, PRO hired a hot babe named Sally Van Dyke. She has a great body and each boob looks like an enlarged golf ball with one big dimple." Barney extended both hands out as if holding them. "Some of the men have a running bet on how large her boobs really are. The highest guess is thirty-eight, and her cup size estimate is all the way up to double D. Someone will need to steal her bra from the women's locker room to determine the winner. The men hang around the pro shop just to watch her knockers flop around. Pags says PRO hired a beautiful woman as part of his marketing theme, 'More money from a big breasted honey'. We don't know yet if she will use a caddie, but it will be a challenge without getting a boner. Now you know the line-up in the golf shop, except for the starter and the course ranger."

"What's a starter?"

"The guy who calls the group to the first tee. We have a couple of starters who only work during peak hours. The main starter is P.A. Lloyd. He told me last year that he's a retired insurance agent and was raised in London. He's a real funny guy and has a lot of stories. He tries to convince the lazy golfers to take a caddie. His unique English voice projects as a natural megaphone, so he doesn't even need to use the PA system. The other starter is Howie Fuchs, which is spelled F-U-C-H-S. Be sure you say the pronunciation right...FOOOKS. Howie is kind of forgetful, so he's not around as much anymore. Some members purposely mispronounce his name. If there was ever a reason to change a last name, there's a great example, so just call him Howie."

I stared at Barney, not understanding what was so unique about his name. "And the ranger?"

"The ranger drives around the course to make sure everyone is moving along at a proper pace. We call him 'The Lone Ranger,' but his real name is John Reid. He loves to chew tobacco, so watch out when he spits. He can schmooze the members but give them a kick in the ass when he has to. We heard he was a real asshole when he won a few state football titles at Jefferson High in the forties. Supposedly, he was an all-state guard and line-backer and went on to play at Fordham University. PRO says he played too long without a helmet."

"Does he have a wife named Lona?"

"Lona Ranger...very funny!"

Just then, the PRO rolled his red sports car into the parking space marked as RESERVED FOR GEORGE PALMER, PGA PROFESSIONAL. He swung his door opened and pulled his lanky frame from the bucket seat. He surveyed the group of caddies, just as OC lit a cigarette. PRO shook his head in disapproval.

"Barney, do you think Andy called him about the fight."

"Spike, you can bet on it. He's pissed and it's not about OC's cigarette."

PRO stood six-foot four and weighed about one hundred-ninety pounds. He had a dark complexion, appearing to have a mid-summer tan. With thinning dark brown hair, he was strikingly handsome. A snappy dresser, PRO was attired in dark grey slacks, a bright red golf shirt, white shoes, a white belt, and red socks.

"Spike, he dresses impeccably every day. He must have a huge wardrobe because he never wears the same clothes twice. He's a talented merchandiser and models the clothes displayed in the pro shop so the members will purchase his stuff. He also stocks fashionable women's clothes. He demands a high quality of service and that's why he promoted Andy to run the bag room. Andy knows every member and the make of their car. He has their golf clubs set up when he sees them drive into the parking lot. He may be an asshole, but he sucks up to every member, even though he hates most of them. PRO knows Andy will whip the caddies in shape too."

After a few minutes, I heard PRO screaming at Andy about the fight. Five minutes later, Andy ambled into the caddie yard, kicking an empty pop can off the side of the shack and cursing under his breath. He was clearly upset.

Buddy had just arrived. "I heard a fistfight broke out earlier. I only wish I was here to help Rutt. What are you doing here, Andy?"

"Vicki Dix called PRO to report the fight. I told him that the rookie caddies are horrible, so he told me to spend a few days down here whipping them into shape." Andy picked up a milk crate and slammed it against the wall. He repeatedly stomped on the pop can and launched it toward a white house bordering the vacant field. Andy had a powerful arm and the aerodynamic flat can sailed directly toward the large picture window of the home, embedding in a crack in the siding, inches above a green canvas awning.

"YA WHOO! What a throw, Andy! That's the Dix home, right?"

"Yeah, Buddy, but I missed. I was aiming for the picture window."

Seconds later, a lady and a man came around the house to check out the noise. The woman stalked around the yard, peering at the house from several angles.

"Andy, I bet they can't see the pop can from the ground. Where they're standing, the awning may be blocking it. Anyway, there's no way they can know it came from here. The house is over sixty yards away!"

The woman turned toward the caddie yard and shook her fist at us, extending the middle finger of her right hand.

"Andy, she shot us the bird! Can you believe that?"

I could not understand why she offered the 'Love Potion Number 1' signal to the caddies.

The man seemed dismayed. He put his hands on his hips and then raised them up, as if baffled by the event. He put his arm around the lady and escorted her toward the house. Before they turned the corner, she raised her hand again with the 'Love Potion' sign.

Three minutes later, Pags trotted into the caddie yard. "Andy, what the hell happened? VD called accusing the caddies of hitting a golf ball or throwing a rock at their house as revenge for her complaint. She threatened to file a police report...unbelievable!"

"Vicki Dix...VD...what a bitch!" Andy managed to extract as much saliva he could muster and hurled a spit gob to the ground. "That's how I feel about her."

"Andy, don't look now, but the fuzz are over in the backyard. VD is picking up a few rocks from the grass and pointing at us."

"Buddy, there are hundreds of rocks in the perimeter edging of the grass. So what!"

"The cops are taking down some notes."

The lady stomped the ground repeatedly, apparently desperate to make her argument as the officers escorted her around the yard. They had another brief conversation and strolled around the front of the house, glancing up again at the roof.

A few minutes later, a police car slowly entered the golf club lot and parked near us. Two officers, the same ones who had been in the couple's yard, got out of the car. As the cop moved closer, I read the name SERGEANT CONSTABLE on his badge.

"Hello boys. We had a complaint from the neighbor that something crashed into their house. Did you see anything?"

Andy didn't waste a second to answer. "Not a thing, Officer Constable. We've been here for an hour and didn't see anything, but we heard a noise. We thought a bird had collided with their picture window. You know, birds sometime fly into glass."

Buddy jumped in. "I didn't see anything either, but the lady seemed real upset, as if we caused a problem. She shook her fist at us with one of her fingers extended. She was at least sixty yards from here, but I thought it was her middle finger. I'm not sure what she meant."

The cops stared at one another. "Did you other boys see or hear anything?"

OC piped in. "No sir. Most of us only got here a few minutes ago. I sure wish we could be of assistance."

"Okay, but if you see or hear anything involving their house, you'll be sure to call the police department, right?"

"Yes sir. Right away. Thank you and have a good day, officers."

"And one more thing. We heard there was a fight here a little earlier and someone got hurt pretty bad."

I peered at the ground and there were a few seconds of uncomfortable silence.

Moose entered the conversation. "Well, yes...there was an alteration between two older caddies who despise each other. One accused the other of cheating in a poker game last night and they began to exchange punches. One kid may have a broken nose and lost a couple teeth. Another caddie drove him for the hospital and the other kid left."

"You kids are caddies, eh?"

"Yes, we are loopers."

"Loopers?"

"A caddie loop is eighteen holes, so they call us loopers. Hey, loopers rhymes with troopers!"

"Very funny kid. We don't want any more trouble here. Let's go, partner."

As the cops exited the parking lot, Andy let out a deep breath, relieved they had escaped more trouble. He winked at Buddy and addressed the caddies. "So we're perfectly clear, none of you didn't see a thing, correct?"

One by one, all of us nodded affirmation.

Andy looked satisfied. "Let's start some poker action. Who's in?"

OC shot his hand up. "What are the betting rules?"

"Zero, the most you can lose on a hand is a quarter. It's the dealer's choice of the game and there's no credit here. It's all cash on the barrelhead."

"I haven't played cards a lot...mostly 'Crazy 8's' or 'Go to the Dump' with my Grandma. You'll have to help me with the rules. What's higher, a flush or three-of-a kind? And how does a straight rank?"

"Don't worry Zero, we'll help you."

"Andy, I only have seventy-five cents with me, so I can only play a few hands."

"All-right then, Zero, Jake, Buddy, Moose and I are playing. Any of you other chumps want in?" He was peering straight at me.

I could only stammer. "N...n...n...not right now...maybe next time."

"You may not have a next time based upon your performance earlier this morning."

My stomach started churning again and I glanced at Barney.

Barney whispered. "Forget it. Don't ever jump into a card game with them, they all cheat."

Andy took charge of the card game. "Let's go suckers. I'm dealing first and we're playing five-card draw with nothing wild. Ante-up boys with a nickel. Hey, we don't have a pot to hold the money." He pointed directly at me. "Hey you...we need your hat."

I reluctantly took off my faded baseball cap and handed it to Andy, who inspected the blackened lining from my sweat stains.

"Jesus, this cap is disgusting." Andy picked up the five nickels from the picnic table and threw them into the cap. Andy held out the deck for Buddy to cut and quickly dealt one card at a time, starting with OC on his left. I positioned myself behind OC, who held his cards very close to his jacket. I couldn't see his hand, no matter what angle I chose. OC appeared nervous, rearranging his cards every few seconds.

"Zero, you're first to make a bet."

"Andy, do aces count as one?"

"Are you kidding? In a poker game, aces are the high card, you fool. By the way, you can ask for up to four cards."

"Okay, aces are high then. Well...uh...I don't know what to do?"

"Zero, why don't you fold and drop out?"

"Would I get my nickel returned?"

"No, meatball. Your ante is on the line when you begin a new game. Do you want to put up a nickel on your hand?"

OC picked up a nickel and placed it on the top of his left hand. "Now what, Andy?"

"I mean place a bet on the cards you're holding in your hand!"

"Andy, I'm not making a bet. My cards suck."

Andy rolled his eyes and shook his head. "Anyone interested to bet their hand?"

Jake flipped five pennies into the pot. "I'll bet five cents."

"Jake, you turd...you're betting with pennies? I don't want your stinking pennies!" He picked the coins from the hat and threw them into the field. "Put a nickel in the pot."

"Right-O, chief."

Moose quickly matched the bet, as did Andy and Buddy. Andy stared at OC. "Are you in or not?"

"I guess I'm in. Where do I put my nickel?"

"In the pot, right there in the baseball cap!" OC carefully placed the nickel in the cap. "Don't touch it, just drop it in!"

OC fumbled around with his cards again and finally announced his intention. "Give me two cards."

"Are you sure, moron? When you're ready, give me your discards and we'll exchange them."

"Can I trust you to give me two in return?"

"Sure, I'm the dealer. Hurry up! This shouldn't take us more than a minute to play a hand, especially with only five players. We'll give you a break for a couple of hands, but we'll penalize you for slow play and you'll forfeit your bet."

"Doesn't sound fair."

"Life in the caddie yard isn't fair. Besides, you can quit any time."

"No, I need to learn. I appreciate you teaching me."

OC traded two cards with Andy. Buddy, Jake, and Moose exchanged cards too and Andy declared he was drawing three. I noticed that Andy pulled a card from beneath the deck.

"Zero, you can now propose another bet to raise the pot."

OC was again shuffling his cards again.

"Zero, are you going to raise the pot?"

"I didn't know your toilet was too low."

"I take that nonsense as a pass. Bronco, what's your bet?"

"Pass."

"Moose?"

"I'll bet five cents."

Jake hesitated for a few seconds. "I'm in too."

Andy matched the bet. OC fidgeted again for a few seconds and threw in a nickel as well. Buddy surprised everyone by matching and raising the bet another nickel.

Moose, Jake, and Andy each threw in another nickel and stared at OC.

"My turn?"

"Yep, call or fold, Zero."

"I have a question. If I have five cards in order, is that better than five hearts?"

"Yep"

"I'll call and raise you all another nickel."

Andy stared at Buddy, curious if he heard Zero correctly. "Did you say you were raising the bid?"

"You heard right."

"Okay, wise ass, we're all in. Let's see your hand."

OC beamed. "I have five hearts, a 6 7 8 9 and a 10. Is my hand a straight or a flush?"

Andy's eyes rolled and he threw his cards at OC. "You have a straight flush, Zero! Unbelievable! Can you guys believe that? Just 'Crazy 8s', eh?"

"And 'Go to the Dump' too."

"Zero, I'm going take you down to the dump and throw you in a pile of garbage. Then, I'll teach you what a real flush is when I stick your head in the toilet. You cheated, so we're not paying you!"

Andy picked up all of the coins in the hat.

"What do you mean? I won fair and square!"

"Zero, don't ever play games with me! I'm keeping your money to teach you a lesson."

Buddy was quick to accuse OC too. "Zero, I saw you cheat, so shut up."

OC was at a loss for words for once in his life. He picked up Andy's cards and threw them down, revealing two jacks and two aces. Barney and I walked a few paces away. "Barney, Andy was the one who cheated. I saw him deal himself the card from the bottom of the deck twice."

"Well, now you understand how the rigged game is played around here."

"Yeah, but I didn't realize they were so desperate to save a quarter."

"It doesn't matter how much money is involved. Andy can't stand losing."

Bronco rolled up in Andy's car, honking the horn repeatedly. Andy sprinted to the car, circling it three times to inspect for damage. "Hey knucklehead, you drove over the curb going out and the bottom of the car scraped the pavement. What the hell were you doing?"

"Well, I wasn't used to your steering wheel and the gas pedal is pretty sticky. And I forgot I had to use a clutch to change gears. My Dad has an automatic transmission on his Imperial, so I'm not used to a manual transmission. There's no damage, though."

"You better hope not!" Andy dropped down on all fours on the ground to inspect the under-carriage. "What happened to Rutt?"

"He'll be fine, except he lost three teeth. I got him checked into the clinic and tried to find his dad. The hospital was calling a dentist. I doubt that Rutt has ever been to one."

Pags stuck his head around the corner. "I need three A caddies NOW! Buddy, Moose, Rutt, get your asses up here, pronto!"

"Rutt isn't here, he's at the hospital."

"Okay, Jake, you're up then. I need two more caddies for a double too. "Andy, do you want a loop?"

"Nope...I'm going home."

Pags pointed to Bronco and Bing, can both of you take 'em?"

Bronco quickly responded. "Who are they?"

"Chatem, Dix, Sliek, and Cook."

Bronco nodded, "What the hell...we'll be right there."

As Bronco and Bing scurried away, Barney explained the golfers' names. "Those guys are all lawyers, so we call 'em Cheatem, Dickhead, Slick, and Crook.

"Do you guys make up nicknames for all of the members?"

"Yeah...most of 'em."

I was getting hungry and strolled to the soda pop machine and dug fifteen cents from my pocket I carefully placed the dime and the nickel into the slot, and pressed the cola button. I punched the button five more times but to no avail. I banged on the other pop button options repeatedly, although nothing came out. I kicked the machine as Pags came out of the bag room. "Careful there, pal, or you'll hurt yourself."

"Pags, I'm a new caddie. I put fifteen cents into the pop machine and nothing came out."

"Sorry kid, it's been acting up lately."

"Can you give me my money back?"

"The bottling company owns the machine. They're the only one who can give you a refund."

"Well, who can I talk to?"

"The guy comes here a couple of times a week to refill the machine. I'll tell the shop to put you on a list for a refund. What's your name?"

"Spykstra...Scott Spykstra."

"Okay, Scott. We'll let you know."

He didn't sound convincing. "Thanks anyway."

I climbed up on the bench to find my lunch bag stored above the pop machine. There were only three sacks left and none were mine. Someone had stolen my lunch. I felt betrayed and slowly trudged to the caddie shed to confide in Andy. "The pop machine stole my money and someone ripped off my lunch!"

"Boo-Hoo! Here, take my hanky and have a good cry." He picked up a dirty rag off the floor and threw it at me.

Pags returned to the caddie yard. "I need a B caddie. Pfeiffer is up on the sheet."

"That's me!" Barney exclaimed. Heading away, he turned to me and OC. "Thanks for coming out. Do you like it so far?"

OC was quick to answer. "I love the place. I can hardly wait until next week."

I certainly didn't agree with his enthusiasm. "Maybe you didn't pass the test, OC."

"I bet I got at least nine questions right."

Teddy Turd stayed silent, sitting on a milk crate in the corner of the shack by himself. OC, who was always friendly, engaged him. "Turd, what's your story?"

"My father ordered me to come here to caddie but I didn't realize some of these guys were such jerks. My knees were shaking when Andy yelled at me. I nearly fainted when I had to dig that tee out of the ground. And then the fight...I've never seen anything like that before."

"Well, you got through the tee digging, right?"

"Yes, I closed my eyes and said a prayer. It was a miracle the tee came right out."

"Bing set up your tee right after the fight, so everyone was too preoccupied with Rutt and Jesse, so consider it a miracle."

It was getting noticeably colder, when Pags appeared again. "Guys, we're not expecting any more golfers today, so you can take off. Thanks for coming out. See you later."

I was disappointed. I fumbled with my bike padlock and finally sprung the lock open. I jumped on the pedals and only made it twenty feet, when I heard Pags call my name. "Scott, that's your name, right? I have something for you. Can you come over here?"

I slammed on the brakes, parked my bike, and quickly sprinted up to the bag room, sensing I had my first loop. My heart sank as Pags handed me a broom instead. "Sweep the driveway in front of the building and the aisles between the bag racks. There's also a big pile of towels that need to be returned to the laundry room in the clubhouse. Go around to the other side of the men's locker room entrance and you'll see a door marked for deliveries. Open it and you'll see a sign for the laundry room. Drop 'em in there."

My shoulders slumped. "Sure, happy to help you out. Where's the dust pan?"

"We don't have one. Just improvise with something. There's a stack of magazines in the shop which may work."

I crisscrossed the pavement to sweep up as much sand and grass as I could, creating a six-inch pile. I opened the golf shop door and saw some magazines on a table. I picked up the one on top and felt a hand rest on my shoulder. I whipped my head around to see PRO standing over me. "What are you doing, kid?"

I was petrified. "Well...uh...Pags said I might use a magazine to pick up the dirt I swept up." He signaled toward the driveway.

"He said WHAT?"

"I could use a magazine from the golf shop. You know, as a dustpan to sweep up." I glanced over at Pags, expecting him to come to my rescue.

"Pags, did you tell this idiot to come in here and steal a magazine for a dustpan?"

"No, I told him to improvise." He motioned to me, "Moron, why did you come in here to use one of our expensive magazines? These are for the members. I don't believe they will want to read a magazine full of dirt."

My heart was in my throat. "Well, I'm sorry if there was a misunderstanding."

"Get the hell out of here! Caddies aren't allowed in the golf shop...EVER!"

I trembled as I closed the door, hearing laughter from the pro shop. I found a cardboard box and ripped the side to collect the dirt. I hastily swept the bag room and gathered at least twenty towels. I crossed the parking lot to the rear of the clubhouse, and located the service door. I found the laundry room and threw the towels into a large hamper. As I pivoted to leave, I was startled by the locker room attendant. "Whoops, I nearly ran into you. Say, aren't you Barney's brother, I mean Tony's brother?"

"I'm Jimmie Pfeiffer...Tony is my brain-dead younger brother."

"I met you a couple of times over at your house. I'm Scott Spykstra."

"Oh yeah, what are you doing here?"

"I just started here as a caddie today. Pags told me to drop off some dirty towels from the bag room."

"Where's that slime ball Andy?"

"He went home after PRO banished him to the caddie yard."

"No shit? Andy must have really pissed him off."

"Well, from what I saw today, it doesn't' take much for PRO to get upset. Pags asked me to sweep up and suggested I use a magazine from the pro shop as a dust pan and the PRO ripped me a big one. The staff got a good laugh at me."

"They love to give caddies crap. Don't worry, there's a bright side. Now they know who you are."

"Yeah, I'm the butt of their jokes."

"They call me Jimmie Clean, since I have to sanitize everything in the men's locker room. I have to scrub toilets after they dump their smelly logs in them. Some of them don't even bother to flush. What a bunch of pigs! The richer they are, the worse they act. I'll tell you a few stories sometime. I need to get back in the locker room. Someone probably sat on a toilet seat wet from pee. See ya, Scott."

"So long."

I sprinted to the caddie yard, realizing I hadn't locked my bike. I held my breath and rounded the corner of the building, relieved to see it. On my trip home, I reflected on the day's recap, rehearsing how I would describe it to my parents. They will ask about everything, but I certainly couldn't mention the initiation, the fight, or the bullying of the senior caddies.

Chapter 8

I rolled into the driveway, jumping off my bike near the garage door, which was surprisingly unlocked. I could never understand why anyone would steal anything stored in there, except perhaps, our '58 Plymouth Belvedere. It was a shiny rust color and had a unique push button transmission. I parked the bike, careful not to rub against the car and scratch the finish. Dad inspected the car daily, so he would banish me I my bedroom for weeks if he detected any slight blemishes.

Elsie was hovering the moment I came in the house and smothered me with an onslaught of questions. "How was your day? Did you get a caddie job? Were any of your friends there? How was your lunch?"

She might go on to ask twenty more questions, so I quickly cut her off. "I didn't get out on a loop today, since there weren't many golfers out on the course. I met a lot of great caddies and a couple kids go to St. Stephen's with me. Caddying is going to be a lot of fun once the season goes along. And your lunch, it was great, as usual." I lied.

"Scotty, I was so afraid you wouldn't be warm enough. Are you sure you didn't catch a cold? Come here. Let me see if you have a fever." She rubbed her hand over my forehead.

I pulled away. "Mom, I feel fine, but I'm a little hungry."

"Have an apple, but only eat one. You shouldn't spoil your appetite for supper."

"What's for dinner?"

"Herring and clam chowder. We can't eat meat on Holy Saturday."

I had forgotten that it was a day of abstaining, it seemed like just another dumb rule instituted by the Catholic Church.

"I know, but herring stinks and I can't stand clam chowder."

"Try a little bit anyway. I'll heat up some frozen fish sticks too."

When she left the kitchen, I grabbed some saltine crackers out of the cupboard and stealthily stuck them in my pocket, just a second before she returned. "How many caddies were at the golf course?"

"Maybe fifteen, eight of them were new caddies. They gave us a class and taught us all of the rules and etiquette. Barney showed me around and introduced me to most of the older caddies, which was nice. I ran into his older brother, Jimmie, who works in the men's locker room." I didn't want her to ask any more questions, so I changed the subject. "I'm going to my room and change my clothes."

My stomach was growling like a truck engine. I scarfed down the last cracker, when Mom burst into my room to announce that supper was ready. I tore off my sweatshirt and jeans and put on a comfortable tee shirt and sweatpants and sat down at the kitchen table. "Hi Dad, what did you do today?"

"Mom and I went grocery shopping and I went over to BML Mart to buy a Baja Marimba Band album. They have a big shipment on sale, although the records were slightly warped. Then I watched *Wide World of Sports* and took a nap. Mom said you didn't get a caddie job today."

"Most of the golfers ride in gas powered carts or use pull-carts, so only a few needed a looper. There were several senior caddies there today…they get first dibs."

"What's a looper?"

"Another name for a caddie."

"Scotty, here are your three fish sticks."

"Can I have some bread to make a sandwich? Do you have any tartar sauce?"

She opened the breadbox and took out two slices of white bread. She combed the refrigerator and displayed a jar of mayonnaise out on the table. "Scotty dear, you need to be in bed at nine o'clock tonight. Easter Sunday services will be crowded and we need to be there early for a parking spot."

"The guys are getting together tonight to finish the Monopoly game."

"That's not a good idea. Their parents are probably planning to attend early Sunday services too."

The phone rang and she answered. "Hello, yes…he's here, but we're still eating supper. He'll have to call you later." She slammed the phone down. "Don't your friends know not to call during the dinner hour?"

"Who was on the phone?"

"Barney."

"Mom, we're all meeting at seven o'clock."

"Elsie, let him go with his friends."

"All right, but be home by eight-thirty."

I gobbled down the fish sandwiches and dashed out the door towards Gomer's house. When I got there the guys were already set up in the basement and listening to a Beatles record. Before starting, we agreed to end the Monopoly game at eight-fifteen. Goober and I could not overcome Gomer's uncanny streak of luck with the dice. Their team finished with $22,567 compared to our $15,246, so I paid Barney a quarter for winning the game.

"Barney, after you went out on your loop today, Pags asked me to sweep up before I left for the day."

"That's good!"

"Not really. He told me to use a magazine from the pro shop as a dustpan. But when I took one, PRO ripped me up and down. Pags just sat there without defending me."

"That's not surprising. No one wants to be on PRO's bad side."

"Any chance you think he'll forget what happened?"

"Maybe."

Barney didn't sound too reassuring. On my walk home, I weighed the pros and cons of heading back to the golf club next week. The negatives seemed overwhelming.

I arrived home just in time and went straight to my room to listen to WPUK, which featured my favorite disk jockey, Ralph Upchuck, better known as The Duke of Puke. The Duke was famous for non-stop comedy routines and hilarious promotions. He annoyed conservative adults, like my parents, many of whom believed rock 'n roll music depicted the devil's message. I didn't want to miss the start of his show, which always featured a vomiting sound, when he immediately shouted, 'The Duke of Puke is on the air to throw-up some great tunes!' His sign-off to each show included another patented message, 'We're all headed to the dumps,' which was followed by the sound of a long fart, a big sigh, and a toilet flush. The community leaders tried to promote a boycott of the advertisers on his program and complaints were filed with the FCC. However, as the critics became more vocal, his popularity rose dramatically. In fact, the station owner, a large media outfit from Philadelphia, planned to syndicate his program on a national basis.

Mom shouted from the living room, "Scotty, turn off that racket and go to sleep."

Without protest, I shut off the radio, flicked the switch on my bedside lamp, and closed my eyes.

Mom woke me at seven-thirty. I lay in bed, contemplating why I had ever decided to become a caddie. I pulled the pillow over my head, my thoughts now turning to the challenge of high school. I remembered it was Easter Sunday and shifted my focus on the task of entertaining Bertha and Francine Knudson this afternoon. I squirmed, feeling my heart beating faster, with what seemed like many impossible missions to conquer.

Mom abruptly invaded my room again. "Out of bed now!"

As usual, Mom had tuned the radio to WZZZ. Hunter Chetley delivered the eight o'clock news.

> *THE MISSISSIPPI RIVER*
> *CONTINUES TO RISE TO RECORD*
> *LEVELS. ALL ROADS LEADING TO*
> *FRENCH ISLAND HAVE BEEN CUT*
> *OFF. THE MUNICIPAL AIRPORT*
> *THERE IS OPEN, ALTHOUGH ONLY*
> *ACCESSIBLE BY BOAT. BE SURE TO*
> *GIVE YOURSELF A LITTLE EXTRA*
> *TIME TO MAKE YOUR SCHEDULED*
> *FLIGHT.*
>
> *IN A SPEECH YESTERDAY,*
> *PRESIDENT LYNDON JOHNSON*
> *SAID HE WAS OPEN TO PEACE*
> *TALKS TO END THE VIETNAM WAR,*
> *BUT ADDED THAT THE USA WAS*
> *DETERMINED TO SACRIFICE LIVES*
> *TO DEFEAT THE COMMUNISTS.*
> *JOHNSON PROMISED THAT THE*
> *U.S. WOULD NOT WITHDRAW*
> *FROM SOUTH VIETNAM UNTIL*
> *THEIR INDEPENDENCE AND*
> *FREEDOM WERE GUARANTEED.*
> *MEANWHILE, THE SOVIET UNION*
> *ANNOUNCED THEY WERE*
> *PREPARED TO SEND TROOPS, IF*
> *REQUESTED BY THE NORTH.*
>
> *IN WASHINGTON, AN ESTIMATED*
> *FOURTEEN THOUSAND STUDENTS*
> *MARCHED TO THE WHITE HOUSE*
> *TO PROTEST THE WAR,*
> *ALTHOUGH LBJ WAS AT HIS*
> *RANCH IN TEXAS. A PETITION*
> *ENTITLED 'A DECLARATION OF*

PRINCIPLE, 'SIGNED BY SIX THOUSAND STUDENTS AND FACULTY FROM THE UNIVERSITY OF WISCONSIN, WAS PRESENTED TO GEORGE MCBUNDY, THE PRESIDENT'S NATIONAL SECURITY ADVISOR. A FEW HUNDRED PRO-WAR DEMONSTRATORS GATHERED ON THE OPPOSITE SIDE OF THE WHITE HOUSE, CARRYING SIGNS SAYING 'STAMP OUT STUDENT COMMUNISTS' AND 'PEACE THRU SURRENDER IS DEFEAT.'

IN ANOTHER STORY, THE AMERICAN SOCIETY OF NEWSPAPER EDITORS CONCLUDED THEIR ANNUAL CONVENTION IN WASHINGTON, DC YESTERDAY. IN A POLL, EIGHTY PERCENT OF THE EDITORS RATED PRESIDENT JOHNSON'S RELATIONS WITH THE PRESS AS FAIR OR POOR.

IN SPORTS, THE CHAMPIONSHIP SERIES OF TH NATIONAL BASKETBALL ASSOCIATION KICKS OFF TODAY IN BOSTON, WHERE THE CELTICS WILL HOST THE LOS ANGELES LAKERS. BOSTON IS SEEKING THEIR SEVENTH CONSECUTIVE NBA CROWN. AND THAT'S THE WAY IT IS. HAPPY EASTER!

Next, Richard Bore, the WZZZ morning music host, introduced Irving Berlin's "Easter Parade" sung by Bing Crosby.

Mom started up. "Those long-haired University of Wisconsin radicals protesting the war should all be expelled."

"Mom, we're learning about our first amendment rights to free speech in civics class. Those students aren't violating the law if they're demonstrating peacefully."

"They're violating the law by trampling on the White House lawn! And since we're talking about free speech, remember you have to allow Bertha and Francine Knudson to watch any program they want today."

After Church, the Knudson's arrived promptly at noon. Bertha and Francine voted to watch "Way of the Cross", a documentary film tracing Jesus' path on the way to his crucifixion, followed by *Profiles in Courage, Wild Kingdom, College Bowl*, and *20th Century*. I couldn't wait until the Knudson's left at six o'clock.

In homeroom the next morning, Sister Maureen reminded everyone the African Pagan Baby Fund Drive had just ended. She announced that Mary Henderson and Matt O'Connell had achieved the highest contribution for the girls and boys respectively. Mom was convinced the charity for adopting orphans babies was a scam and refused to donate.

"Mr. O'Connell, you have collected enough money to name your pagan baby. What name have you selected?"

"Sister, I name my pagan baby Jose Pagan." OC enunciated a 'J' instead of an 'H' for José."

"You're naming it Pagan?"

"After the San Francisco Giants baseball player."

I raised my hand to help explain. "Sister Maureen, the baseball player's first name is José pronounced with an H, and his last name is pah-GAAN! He plays third base for the Giants."

"I see…very well. Mary, what name have you chosen for your pagan baby?"

"Maureen."

"A lovely name."

I rolled my eyes. What a suck-up!

The bell rang for class, when OC had an idea. "I've decided to pick a new name for Sister Maureen. I'm calling her Sister Moron."

"You should have picked Moron for the name of your pagan baby."

"Yeah, only it would have a complex forever."

I reflected on what OC had just said about choosing a name for a baby. When it came to boys, it seemed that some parents decided to select male names using the father's name or one from older generations. Catholics were always encouraged to select one for a patron saint. I wondered if someone's name, first or last, could influence a person's behavior later in life. Perhaps the name Scott or Spykstra had something to do with my anxieties. Maybe I could change it someday like the assistant pro, Robert Condor did.

Chapter 9

As I recall, I couldn't sleep the night before the hazing threat. My mind was racing in fear attempting to imagine every potential scenario that the senior caddies had planned for us. After hours of tossing and turning, I finally gotten into a deep REM sleep. I had a vivid dream where with the rookie caddies were dressed only in their underwear and hooded sweatshirts. We trudged down a long golf course fairway leading to a distant building, resembling the clubhouse of the Mississippi Valley Country Club. We never seemed to get any closer to the building, as golf balls pelted us from all directions. Rutt and Andy ordered us to jump into a sand bunker filled with snakes, hundreds of them, slithering over every inch of the trap. I couldn't put my feet down without stepping on one. I leapt from the trap as several snakes flew after me. As I peered over my shoulder, I could see that Andy and Rutt were laughing and waving good-bye.

The clock radio popped on at six o'clock. The first sounds I heard were screams from Colonel Cobb.

WAAAAAKE-UP...YOU KORNBALLS!

"Nowhere to Run" began playing through the speaker...it seemed appropriate. I was dreading the day ahead at the golf course. I pushed the snooze button and turned over to my side, trying desperately to delay the inevitable. Not a minute later, Mom opened the door to my room.

"Rise and shine! Time's a-waistin'! Up and at-em!" She crossed the room to open the blinds opposite my bed, a flood of sunshine blinding me. "It's thirty degrees out, Scotty dear, so make sure you dress warmly."

I swung my legs out from under the covers and dropped my bare feet onto the cold wooden floor. Stumbling into the bathroom to brush my teeth, I headed to the sink and threw some cold water in my face. I rubbed my hands over the top of my head to shape the hair, forgetting Dad had shaved it too close. I stared into the mirror surveying my reflection. It was shorter than Curly's haircut from The Three Stooges. On my chin and cheeks, I also noticed a few stray strands of blond hair, which were actually longer than the ones on my head."

Returning to my room, I searched frantically for my cup and supporter, remembering the senior caddies' strict instructions to bring a jock strap for the touch football game. "Where is the damn thing?" I opened my closet door and located my gym bag stashed into the darkened corner underneath my pressed shirts and black slacks hanging above. I unzipped the small blue satchel and groped inside, finding it stiff and shriveled up in a ball, the cup intertwined in the straps. I took a whiff of the jock and gagged...it smelled like a dead animal. I slowly put each leg through the straps of the jock, adjusting it for a more comfortable feel. I assumed the cup would create a problem for the bike ride, so decided to carry it in my pocket. I pulled on a red and white University of Wisconsin football sweatshirt, which Mom had ordered from a catalogue as a birthday present last year.

"Mom, what's for breakfast?" I asked as I walked into the kitchen.

"Toast with strawberry jam and cold cereal."

I scanned the back of the cereal box, which contained six baseball cards for Roberto Clemente, Vada Pinson, Eddie Matthews, Bob Allison, Willie Davis, and Dick Groat. I didn't care for cereal much, but treasured the free baseball cards. I shook the box, which was nearly empty. Maybe one more breakfast and I could cut the cards out.

I ate quickly as WZZZ played the Perry Como song "Hot Diggity Dog Ziggity Boom." Noticing the time, I vaulted from my chair and rushed to the door. "Thanks Mom!"

"Have fun today, honey. Good luck!"

I adjusted the jock-strap one more time and started peddling my bike. My heart pounded harder with every block I passed, thinking about the upcoming initiation. Barney refused to disclose any details, no matter how many times I begged him. I turned into the golf club lot and coasted the last thirty yards, the pit in my stomach was almost unbearable. I secured my bike with the lock and walked to the sign-up sheet. There were already four names on the list. Feeling disappointed, I looked around for something to write with. I found a broken pencil lying on the concrete again and scrawled my name on the bottom of the C list.

"Hey Barney, what happened to the seven o'clock sign up rule?"

"I don't make the rules around here."

Within a few minutes, Buddy, Bronco and Rutt arrived, along with three new caddies. Rutt's right eye was still black from the fight, and he had tape across the bridge of his nose to secure it in place. He was missing three of his front teeth and he had a slight lisp as he directed the new rookies. "You three new dummies, line up over there near the trees. You other rookies can stay here for now."

The rookies lined up on their knees. Moose secured the tees, while Rutt and Buddy took turns grinding them further into the ground. I heard a shrill whistle and a kid with red hair sprung up suddenly and sprinted away. After several seconds, the two remaining rookies signaled their success by holding the tees in their mouths. Expressing their approval, the senior caddies gave them a round of applause and escorted them to the caddie shack.

Moose announced, "These two rookies are better than you losers. Now, let's proceed with the real contest. Do you enjoy races?"

OC responded quickly. "I am open to all races, religions, and creeds."

"Zero, you will certainly find some faith with this race, so you better start praying. We call this the hole-in-one competition."

"Moose, is this a relay race where we drop balls into cups along the course?"

"Not exactly." He turned towards Rutt. "There's are only seven rookies here and we're missing the convict. Shouldn't we wait until we have the whole bunch?"

"The outlaw is suspended, so we'll deal with him later."

They herded us into the golf cart storage area, located under the pro shop building. There were three dozen white Executive Walker golf carts stored there, as well as some old golf equipment and two round miniature wood putting greens covered in felt.

The senior caddies started chanting, "Hole-in-one...hole-in-one...hole-in-one."

Rutt wanted to run the show and shouted instructions at us. "Rookies, take off your pants, but you can leave your shirt, socks, and shoes on. Did any of you remember to wear a jock strap? If not, you'll need to take off your underwear too. I brought six jocks from the high school locker room in case you want to rent one for a dollar. Who needs one?"

The two new guys and Teddy Turd instantly shot up their hands. Teddy was on the verge of tears, his voice cracking. "Can anyone lend me a dollar? I only have a quarter."

"Too bad, Turd. We don't operate on credit around here."

A new kid, with the name 'RUSTY' stitched on his left jacket pocket, spoke up. "I don't have a dollar either."

"What's your name?"

"Rusty...Rusty Steele."

"Well Rusty, why don't you STEAL one?" The senior caddies laughed at Rutt's lame joke.

"You're about as funny as a submarine with screen doors."

"Yeah, I'm a funny guy."

The other new rookie interrupted. "I don't have any money either."

"What's your name?"

"Lance."

"Lance? Okay, Lance, drop your pants." As Lance slowly unbuckled his belt, Rutt burst out in another big hoot, apparently proud of his rhyme.

Barney wanted to help, so he handed three bucks out to Rutt. "You guys can pay me back next week."

Rutt snagged the three bills from Barney's fingers, stuffing them into his back pocket and handed a jock strap to Teddy Turd. "Let's see you put on the supporter, cry baby."

Teddy shuffled over to the corner and faced the wall, slowly lowering his trousers. He was wearing bright yellow underpants, peppered with brown polka dots. He peered down at the supporter, apparently confused how it was supposed to fit. He awkwardly struggled to pull his left leg through one strap and then the right leg through the other. When he pulled it up, his butt crack was errantly covered with the pouch section of the jock. The caddies roared in laughter.

Teddy's face was bright red. "How does this work?"

Rutt was amazed. "You put the jock on backwards, meatball! I'll tell you what, I'll refund your dollar if you give me your cute underwear. Those camouflage boxer shorts can probably disguise poop stains."

Teddy shook his head.

OC went over to him, pulling his own pants down slightly to show how the jock fit. "Turn it around so your hot dog fits into the pouch. You do have a hot dog, don't you?

"Yeah, my peenie."

The group exploded in laughter again. Rutt wasted little time. "Peenie? Peenie the weenie? Well, put peenie the weenie in your bikini," pointing to the jock assuming Teddy didn't know what a bikini was either.

Teddy nodded and proceeded to reverse the supporter, tucking himself into the sling. Lance and Rusty, who also faced the wall, dropped their underpants and quickly slipped into their rented jocks.

"Why are you all facing the wall? Aren't you proud of your equipment? I must say, all of you do have some nice white butts. Turd, your left cheek is a little droopy though."

Teddy rubbed his hand against the left side of his face.

Bronco entered the discussion. "Not your face…Turd. Your left butt cheek is lower than the right one. Look in the mirror sometime. Tell your mother you need a butt lift."

"A butt lift?"

"Yeah, they put a big straw up your anus and blow air in there."

"Bronco, what the hell do you know about butt lifts?"

"Rutt, I read about the procedure in a magazine. The story was right after the pictures of UFOs?"

"Bronco, the crap coming out of your butt are unidentified flying objects."

Moose was eager to proceed with the contest. "Since we have an uneven number of caddies for teams, one team will have three guys, and the other team can have four for the relay race. The winner will be determined from the first third rookie to complete the race. Zero, Lance, and Rusty Steele are Team One. Spykstra, Chang, Eng, and Teddy Turd are Team Two. Now, each of you has a cavity, right?"

OC looked puzzled. "My dentist, Dr. Dreiling, filled my cavities last week."

"I've never had a cavity." Teddy informed the group.

Moose corrected them. "We're not referring to your teeth…we mean your butt-hole. Here are the rules. First, you'll pick up a golf ball from the concrete block in the crack of your ass. Then, carry the ball over to the artificial green and drop the ball in the cup. Don't use your hands at any time, except to lift the flag pole. If the golf ball falls out or you miss the cup, you need to start over. If you can manage to drop the ball in the hole, I'll place a new golf ball on the block for your teammate. There is no time limit."

We stared at one another in bewilderment.

OC turned in circles. "Moose, you gotta be shittin' me!"

"No, we all had to go through the same initiation."

Teddy began to cry. "I can't do this. You guys are homosexuals!" He quickly pulled on his boxers and pants over his jock. As he ran for his bicycle, he stumbled, falling on the gravel. After jumping on his bike, he began peddling as fast as he could, but lost his balance and tipped over in the parking lot. He popped up again and finally rode away.

Bronco was confused. "I've been called a lot of names, but never a homosexual. What's that, someone who has sex in their home?"

Rutt responded. "A homosexual is a name for someone who is strange, like Moose. Now, can we get to business? Teddy Turd didn't have a chance in hell to be a caddie anyway. Shit, he left with our rented jock too. Moose, you didn't even tell the rookies the best part of the contest."

"The losing team has to clean all of the golf balls with their bare hands."

"You gotta be shittin' me!" OC exclaimed again.

I stood frozen in shock.

"Yup, there is a distinct possibility you will get some shit on your hands, unless you prefer to clean the balls in your mouth."

Lance turned and vomited.

"Don't you like in our contest, Lance? You must have eaten blueberry pancakes this morning!"

"I'm staying."

My head started to spin. Who would create a punishment as humiliating as this? I studied all of the rookie's faces. Their eyes were nearly popping out of their heads I could not have imagined anything more horrible. I stared at Barney, who turned away, unable to look me in the eye.

Rutt realized that the teams were now even. "You meatballs can decide your team order. Line up behind the concrete blocks. Team One will have Dot balls and Team Two will use First Flight. Maybe we should call them Team First Flight, huh? Now what should we name Team One?

"The Dots?" Bronco suggested.

"How original? There are two miniature putting greens set up over there. Team Dots can have the one on the left."

To get it over with, I elected to go first for Team First Flight, while OC wanted to start for Team Dots.

I glanced at OC. "Bad luck!"

"Scott, don't squeeze too tight. You may never see that ball again!"

I lowered myself onto the cold concrete block, snuggling my butt over the cold First Flight ball. I achieved a firm grip by forcing more weight down on the ball. I wiggled around, hoping it wasn't lodged in too deeply.

OC shrieked. "WHEEEEEE! It's freezing!"

Moose counted down, "Ready…on your mark…get set…GO!"

I lifted up from the concrete block and shuffled toward the green with my legs uncomfortably bowed out, as far as I could extend them. I carefully lifted the flag stick, lowering my hinder as close to the hole as I could squat. I prayed that the ball was centered over the hole, forcing it out with a loud grunt. I heard the beautiful sound of the ball landing in the bottom of the cup. I tagged Tom Bunker, who grasped his First Flight ball off the concrete block and hobbled off.

Meanwhile, OC had problems. He had taken too much time to wedge the ball in his butt. His face was contorted, expressing his struggle to secure the ball in place. He finally managed to reach the green, when the ball slipped out, bouncing to the gravel portion of the cart room. He squatted down, desperately trying to snatch the ball out of a depression, while his teammates screamed out conflicting instructions. OC finally kicked the ball to a flat area on the concrete, where he successfully captured it by sitting down on the floor. The Dot golf ball protruded out from his hinder and then popped out, rolling into the gravel again. Everyone was overcome with laughter, except for OC and his teammates. I was so focused on OC's adventure that I had forgotten to watch my own partners' progress. Tom Bunker aced his turn, while Ron hovered over the cup, executing a perfect drop.

Moose held up his hand. "Team First Flight is the winner!"

OC still could not capture his ball and threw his hands up in defeat. "Screw this! What do I have to do now?"

Rutt evaluated the situation. "Zero, you're a goddamn joke! You are so incompetent, you can clean all of the First Flight Team golf balls yourself. Your teammates still need to complete the contest though."

OC carefully picked a First Flight ball out of the cup with two fingers. "Aw, this ball has some turds stuck to it. Who didn't wipe their ass?" He held the ball up to his nose and took a whiff. "HEEEW...ICK!" He gobbed on the ball and rubbed until it was perfectly clean. "What should I do now, Moose?"

"Clean the next one."

He closely inspected the next ball in his hand. "There's green crap on this one! Spike, what the hell did you eat last night...pickles?" OC managed to extract as much saliva as possible by clearing his throat five times and hawked on the ball again. He tossed it over to Moose. "Zero, clean the last one without any spit."

"No problem, Moose." OC reached inside his shirt and stuck his left hand under his right armpit and then proceeded with his right hand under the left. He rubbed his hands together and worked over the third golf ball.

"Pretty creative, Zero."

While OC was busy cleaning, Steele had finished his circuit successfully and Lance was crouched down, camped over the hole. Unfortunately, he lost his balance, quickly catching himself with his right hand on the floor, just a split second before the ball dropped in the cup.

"You can't use your hands, that's a penalty!"

"Come on, Rutt, give me a break! The ball dropped in the cup before I used my hand. What did you guys see?" He pleaded for help from Bronco and Moose.

As expected, they agreed with Rutt. "The judges vote that you broke the rules, so I invoke the penalty."

"What penalty?"

"Lance, clean OC's ball in your mouth. Zero, tie a towel around Lance's head to cover his eyes."

OC stared at Rutt for a few seconds in disbelief.

"I said NOW, Zero." OC stood behind Lance and complied.

"Lance, Moose will place the ball in your mouth and NO spitting. You'll have to swallow anything left in your mouth, after the ball is cleaned, okay?"

"Yeah, I can hear."

"Open your mouth." Moose popped the ball in and Lance instantly started to gag. He rolled the ball around in his mouth for ten seconds and blew it out. He took a deep breath, and swallowed hard. Moose picked the ball up in his glove hand and examined it. "Looks clean to me. You can take off your blindfold now." Moose tossed the ball over to Lance when I noticed it was a Dunlop brand. Apparently Moose actually had a conscience by exchanging the Dot ball with a clean Dunlop ball before putting it into Lance's mouth.

Rutt winked at Lance. "Don't ever screw with us again. Steele can clean the ball that was up his ass with his hands. That's enough entertainment for one morning. Now we can tote bags for some real assholes today."

OC interjected. "Bronco, you told us last week to wear our jocks and cups for a football game between us rookies and the senior caddies."

"There's no football today, maybe a little later in the summer, if you meatballs are still around."

I desperately wished that all of the hazing was finished. I wasn't sure if I could handle any more. I motioned Barney over. "I understand you couldn't risk warning me, but this was awful."

"I had to go through the initiation last year and I was on the losing team, so don't give me any lip."

"I can't wait to see the senior caddies force Jesse to do that."

I was relieved to have survived the golf ball race, but feared that more rites of passage lie ahead. I certainly wanted to play football with the senior caddies for a chance to get even. My wish fortunately came true later in the summer.

Chapter 10

OC initiated the conversation with the new caddies, initiating a sense of bonding. "Hi guys, I'm OC, although the asshole senior caddies call me Zero." He pointed to me. "He's Scott, but we call him Spike. He and Tony Pfeiffer, I mean Barney, go with me to St. Stephen's. Barney caddied here last year and he's a good guy."

"My name in Lance Allott."

OC hesitated a second. "Your name is Lancelot Allott?"

"Just call me Lance."

I now recognized him. "Didn't you play on the St. Robert's football team?"

"Yeah, I was the center and Rusty Steele was our quarterback."

"Lance, I played fullback and linebacker for St. Stephen's."

"You had a good team there, but we got tapped by the referee on the last play to lose the championship."

"Lance, do you know the ref who called the penalty?"

"Andy somebody."

"Andy Bumgardner, and he's the caddie master here."

"Really? He's a real turkey. He penalized me in the first half for protesting his call and the bullshit flag on the last play of the game was a joke. We deserved to win!"

"He may have bet on the game."

"Does he play football with the caddies?"

"I doubt it. He keeps clear of the stuff down here and lets the older caddies do his dirty work. Last week, he got into trouble with PRO. He was banished to the caddie yard because of a fight, but he'll be back next week. Have you caddied before?"

"My Dad and Rusty's father play golf at the La Crosse Municipal Golf Course and we've caddied for them a few times. We met Bobby Crosby there one day and he told us to come out here to try it. I don't see Bobby here today."

Barney spoke up. "Bing wanted to avoid the initiation. He does not condone hazing, but doesn't want trouble with the senior caddies either. Andy makes every new caddie go through a training class and take a test."

"Crosby says we may have enough experience, so we may not need to."

"Good luck convincing Andy of that."

Rutt approached the rookie caddies. "Congratulations clowns, the senior caddies voted you into the program, although it was a split decision. Don't ever tell anyone about the hole-in-one race. And we mean NO ONE! Is that clear?" He pointed his finger at all of us for an acknowledgement.

Rusty reluctantly muttered, "Crosby said that we didn't have to take the written test, since we caddied at the municipal golf course."

"Yeah, and I'm really Timmy from the *Lassie* TV show! Dream on fools! Andy's not going let you caddie here just because you say you have some experience. Who did you caddie for anyway?"

"My Dad taught me everything. He was a caddie at a private country club in Philadelphia that was real famous. It's called Mary something, and the pins were unique in some way."

"Special pins, eh? Were they curved with a couple of red stripes around the top? Were there gutters along the sides of the fairways too?"

Moose overheard the conversation. "Rutt, he's referring to the Merion Golf Club in Philadelphia. They've played a few US Open and US Amateur golf championships there. They have baskets on top of the pins instead of flags."

"Are they Easter baskets? Do their caddies dress up as Easter bunnies and the golfers play with eggs instead of golf balls? Is that where they came up with the scramble golf format?"

"Rutt, the baskets are designed with some light wood."

"Moose, you know everything. By the way, I've got some arithmetic homework you need to finish for me tonight."

"Arithmetic? I had arithmetic in second grade."

"I'm actually taking Math III, but I'm in the advanced class."

"Rutt, you mean third grade math?"

"Who needs math? The golfers here can't add their scores right and most of them seem pretty successful."

OC had been quiet for a while. "Rutt, you mentioned Timmy from *Lassie*. Do you watch that?"

"Sometimes, so what?"

"Do you ever get close to the TV when *Lassie* comes on and cover up the L with your finger? *Lassie* turns into assie! It's very funny!"

Rutt shook his head. "Zero, you are SO clever. Do you have a sleeping bag?"

"Sure."

Rutt kicked OC in the crotch. "Now your bag is wide awake!" OC squirmed around on the ground, shrieking in pain. I tried to help, although he rolled further away in the grass.

Bing Crosby arrived in the caddie yard and hurriedly approached Lance and Rusty. "So, you survived the tests, eh?"

"You didn't mention the tee digging or the hole-in-one contest."

"The race is a rite of passage around here. I couldn't warn you, but it's over now and you're in. When you have more seniority here, you can make up the rules."

"Bobby, Rutt said we will need to take a caddie test!"

"The test is a joke. Any idiot can pass it. Some of the questions are about Andy anyway, so answer as if he is King Shit on Turd Island."

"We believe you, but don't give us any more bull crap."

Bronco had just spoken to Benny Roombach in the bag room. "Benny said there's going to be a lot of loops today because the gas pump is broken and they can't use the golf carts."

A minute later, Benny was standing in the door of the shack, carrying a sheet in his hand. I need three A caddies and a B caddie. I'll take Bronco, Buddy, Jake, and Pfeiffer."

Ten minutes later, Benny was back. "I've got two players who'll need C caddies, so I'll take Spykstra and O'Connell. Get your rear ends up here. Bing and Moose, you can take the two other golfers."

OC was curious. "Benny, who are we caddying for?"

He seemed irritated. "Their names are Jerome Misor and Harry Ott. Misor is President of First Intercontinental Bank and Ott is the chief credit officer."

Moose was also curious. "Who do Bing and I have?"

"Water Mellon, the President of MellonMade Enterprises and Hank Kerchev, his head marketing guy."

"Yeah, Walter Mellon is a bit seedy, but I'm going to take him anyway. He's in the fast lane."

"A perfect match for you, Moose, since you operate in the last lane."

"Benny, I'm definitely never taking a banker. They're the cheapest players who belong here. They view a tip as if someone robbed their bank. They're so cheap, they squeak when they walk!"

"Okay, whiney...you can have Mellon. One of his companies designs women's clothes, so maybe he'll let you model one of their new dresses with your cute figure."

Benny escorted OC and me into the bag room. "Grab a coverall! Where is your cap, O'Connell?"

"Um…I must have left it at home."

"Damn you…we told you to always bring it! There's an old one lying on the shelf. It's a little faded and ripped, so pull it down as far as you can and find some coveralls."

"Here are some cool white ones."

"They're all white ones, dumbbell. Now find one that fits. Spykstra, do you wear a size sixteen?"

"Yes, sixteen is the same size for my altar boy cassock at church, only they're black."

"A cassock? Are we in Russia?"

I found a pair of coveralls that fit perfectly.

OC quickly dressed. "Benny, I'm a real caddie now!"

"O'Connell, you look more like a clown with that stupid cap! Now, let's locate their bags. The board shows where all of the clubs are stored. O'Connell, Misor's clubs are in bin 173, so go find them. Spykstra, Ott's clubs are stored right behind us in bin 14." Benny pointed to an old brown leather bag, resembling wrinkled skin of an old lady, who had too much time in the sun. "Yank Ott's bag down off the rack."

I had trouble securing the handle and tilted the bag so it would fall into my hands. Suddenly, the bag tipped over and the clubs crashed to the concrete floor.

"Nice job there, fumbles!" Benny bent over to pick up the clubs to inspect for damage. "You're lucky, Spykstra. Ott's clubs must be at least thirty years old. I haven't ever heard of this brand…Hot Shot? There's a lot of dents in them. He must have hit a few rocks with them over the years. His name is Ott, so let's call him Odd Man! So, you have an odd job today! HEE…HEE…HEE. Check out these woods! The strings are coming off the head…and how about these head covers…someone's old mittens?"

OC returned holding a pink golf bag with floral colored head covers. "I've got Misor's clubs."

"Whose bag is that?"

"Mr. Misor's bag...from bin 173."

Benny inspected the name on the bag tag. "O'Connell, those are Mrs. Misor's bag from bin 172. Would a man have a pink bag with flowers?"

"Oh, I just thought he might be a little different, you know? I have a cousin who plays with dolls and girly stuff. He likes the color pink too."

"The senior caddies call you Zero, huh? So genius, find Mr. Misor's red and black bag in bin 173."

A minute later, OC dragged Mr. Misor's bag across the concrete floor. "The bag ain't got no strap."

"Here, take the strap from Mrs. Duetsch's bag." Benny whipped it at OC's feet. "Hook it to Misor's set!"

"This is white...it doesn't match Misor's red and black bag. That reminds me of a riddle, Benny. What's black, white, and red all over?"

"A newspaper."

"No, it's a nun with a bad nosebleed!"

Benny wasn't laughing. "Get to the first tee or I'll kill you. Bing and Moose, these pathetic losers need your help."

I hoisted Ott's bag over my right shoulder, and immediately felt the narrow strap cutting into my skin. "Benny, I need to adjust this. The strap hurts and it feels like the bag has rocks in the bottom."

"Baby, here's something for your tears." Benny threw a wet towel in my face from a foot away. He inspected the strap. "There's only one more notch to let out. You'll have to deal with the pain. Ott likes to ride in a cart, so he couldn't care less how much the bag weighs or how bad the strap is."

OC and I followed Moose and Bing to the first tee. "Do you rookies remember what to do? Grab a wet towel and pick out a few tees, a ball marker, and a divot tool. Moose, grab a scorecard and a pencil. You can keep score today."

P. A. Lloyd dramatically announced the next tee time pairings in his British accent. "On the tee, the nine-forty-five group...Peter Long, Hugh Cox, Dick Harden, and Lars Dix. Long, Cox, Harden, Dix. In the hole, the nine fifty-five starting time...Misor, Ott, Mellon, and Kerchev."

Bing couldn't restrain his laughter and was nearly choking, tears running down his cheek. Moose wondered why he was crying. "What's up Bing?"

"Moose, don't you get it? Long Cox and Harden Dix! Pags has been trying to get those members in a group for three years. Unbelievable! Spike, did you hear the names of that foursome?"

"No, I was distracted. I was checking to see what's in the bottom of Ott's bag."

"Spike, don't ever open the pouches in a player's bag unless he instructs you to. He'll accuse you of stealing something!"

"Sorry, I had no idea."

OC was quick to come to my defense. "Scott didn't know that. Andy never mentioned that rule in our caddie class."

Suddenly, Harry Ott stood in front of me. He sported a thick, droopy black mustache, resembling Julius Wechner from the Baja Marimba Band. I had seen his picture from the record album jacket that Dad had just purchased from the BML Mart. "Find anything interesting in my bag, kid?"

I stuttered for a few seconds. "Well...uh...uh...uh...Mr. Odd, I wanted to see if there was something in the bottom of your bag. It's a little heavy and difficult to balance. I honestly didn't take anything out." I could feel my face turning red.

"My name is OTT...Harry OTT. The pro shop keeps telling me I should take a caddie. If you're a typical looper, I'll never hire one again. You had better do something today to help my score!" He glared at me with his piercing eyes without blinking once.

I suddenly became dizzy. Had I really called him Mr. Odd? I had a lump in my throat and sensed a trickle of sweat down my back. I offered to shake Ott's hand, although he ignored my gesture. "I hope that you have a good round today, sir. My name is Scott...Scott Spykstra. This is actually my first caddie job."

"It might be your last caddie job too." Ott continued to glare at me. He jerked his putter out of the bag and stomped over to the practice putting green.

Bing tried to console me. "You'll be fine."

Before I could respond, the other players arrived. "Howdy boys, I'm Walter Mellon. You guys are our caddies, huh?"

"Good morning, Mr. Mellon. I'm your caddie. My name is Lionel, but everyone calls me Moose."

"Moose, eh? I can't guess how you got the nickname. Can you tote my heavy bag for eighteen holes? I certainly don't want to carry it myself if you break down."

"No problem. I can handle your bag, sir."

"Moose, what's up with those goggles? Do you pilot one of those old open cockpit bi-planes?"

"No, I just don't want to take a chance that a ball could hit my eye and blind me."

"Lionel, you may not be able to see my blinding shots today. I'm a big hitter, if you haven't heard." He snapped his putter from the bag, unzipped one of the pockets, and selected two golf balls. "I might need to putt today, so I'll be right back. Don't steal anything while I'm gone."

"Yes sir. I'll keep guard for suspicious persons too."

Hank Kerchev introduced himself to Bing with a handshake. "Hello, I'm Hank Kerchev. Nice to meet you. What's your name?"

"Bing."

"Bing, huh? Is that a nickname?"

"My name is Bobby Crosby, but everyone calls me Bing...after the entertainer Bing Crosby, you know?"

"I've seen him on TV and in a few movies."

Jerome Misor strolled up to Kerchev. "Hello Hank, how have you been? Here's a sleeve of Po Do golf balls with the initials of First Intercontinental Bank stamped on them. I have one for Walter too. Here's a ball marker and some tees. How's business been since we last played?"

"Great! Walt will fill you in on the details of a new women's line we're planning."

"I'm anxious to hear. You know, we absolutely have to be the lead bank lender for your company. I invited our chief creditor officer to play with us today. His name is Harry Ott. When are we up?"

Kerchev checked his watch. "We have about ten minutes."

"Terrific! We had to take caddies today since there's no gas available for the carts. I hope I can walk eighteen holes. I've gained a few more pounds over the winter and I haven't gotten much exercise. HO...HO...HO! Which one of you boys has my bag?"

"I do Mr. Misor. My name is OC. I'm a new caddie and I'm honored to carry your clubs today."

"I haven't had a caddie in years. The last one lost five balls and they were expensive ones too...a quarter each. So, I expect you to have an eagle eye today. What's your name again...Ollie?"

"No, it's OC...the letters O and a C. It's short for O'Connell."

"Ollie, what's the story with your cap there? Is that a cap or a hat? I hope there's no wind today, because it will be in Illinois before you know it's gone."

"Can I wash your balls sir?"

"No thanks...I had a bath last night."

Misor instantly walked away, spotting Mellon on the practice green. Mellon slapped him on his butt. "Hey Misor, how's my favorite banker? You must have pulled a few strings to hand out these expensive golf balls. They're pretty unique with FIB stamped on them."

"The initials for First Intercontinental Bank."

"Jerry, how original? Perfect for an honest golfer, like me. Where did you find the ball markers...in a box of cereal?"

"Only the best for you, Walter. Great to see you. How was your winter?"

"Perfect! I spent three months in Phoenix. I bought a new pad at a golf club resort. There are three golf courses there with a giant clubhouse. My house has four bedrooms and five bathrooms with a private pool and a spa. All of the gals can't wait to strip their clothes off when they see the pool and hot tub."

"Sounds pretty special. How does your wife, Ada, enjoy the house?"

"Ada? She doesn't even know I bought it. I only bring our models down there."

"Isn't Ada curious why you spend so much time away?"

"Sure. I tell her I'm on some business trips. I call her every few days and send her some new clothes and gifts, so she's very happy. I also send her to a resort in California for two weeks. Do you need some marriage counselling or something?"

"No, Helen and I have been happily married for twenty-three years now. Our kids keep her busy and she enjoys the curling club in the winter and her social circle in La Crosse. I take her to Chicago for a couple of weekends every year to see a show."

"What a lucky lady, Misor. I have a new line of women's wear she might enjoy. You might even love them too. I'll tell you about it during our round."

"I can't wait to hear more. Can we help expand your lines of credit?"

"Let's not get ahead of ourselves, Misor." Mellon examined him from head to toe. "It looks like you've added a few pounds over the winter. That's a colorful outfit you're wearing…green and orange plaid slacks, a purple and grey argyle sweater and red golf shirt. Did you dress in the dark this morning? Your old brown shoes have seen their better days too. I like the pink cap though. What's the lettering say…'Best Dad'? Wow, your kids must have hunted everywhere to find that one. Let's check out your socks now. C'mon, pull up your trousers."

"Okay, but only if you promise me all of your bank accounts."

"I heard your commercial on the radio that I can get a toaster for opening a new savings account. I could use one for my Arizona pad. Let's see 'em."

Misor tugged his pants.

"Jerry, I knew it! One yellow and one white. By golly, you've got the full rainbow in colors today. One more thing…I want to see your belt."

"Okay, Walter, and then we're playing golf."

Misor lifted up his sweater, revealing a white belt, although he also wore a pair of clip-on suspenders with dollars signs on them.

"Jerry, you are a true banker, always thinking money. And you don't even need a wallet…you can stuff your cash under that big belly hanging over your pants. You're conservative too…a belt in case the suspenders fail."

"You're a real comedian, Walter. I nearly forgot to introduce you to my chief credit officer, Harry Ott. Harry, say hello to Walter Mellon."

"Nice to meet you, Mr. Mellon. I joined First Intercontinental Bank in March, but I've gotten up to speed on all of your business lines. Mr. Misor has filled me in on the history of your relationships with FIB."

"There's not much history there, only a loan on two of my cars and the house here in La Crosse. Nice to meet you, Ott. How's your golf game? You must be damned good if you can play with those shitty clubs."

"I recently joined the MVCC, although I was member of the Goose Lake Country Club in Duluth. My handicap was fifteen there last year."

"How long did it take to grow your big black mustache? That must come in handy in bed, if you know what I mean. You remind me of Junius Wrecker of the Badja Mexico Band I saw on TV the other night."

"I believe you have those names wrong. It's Julius Wechner from the BAJA Marimba Band. My wife even thinks I look like him."

"Oh…yeah…that's what I meant. Do you play the xylophone on the side too?"

"No, but I can play the organ."

"I like to play with my organ too." Mellon coughed three times. "You say you're a fifteen handicap, eh? I usually shoot around eighty-five, but I don't keep a regular handicap. Since par for the course is seventy-two, the difference is thirteen, so I'll give you a shot on both nines. Misor, you're a twenty handicap, right?"

"Right, but I've only played once so far this year."

"Misor, I'll be a gentleman and give you four shots each side. Hank is a real stick with a six handicap, so he'll give you fourteen shots and Ott nine shots for the round. Let's play Low Ball-High Ball.

Hanky and I are partners, so how about ten bucks a hole with carry-overs for ties?"

"Walter, I was expecting to play for ten cents a hole per team with no carry-overs."

"A dime? You gotta be kidding! All right, I'll compromise on a dollar per hole. I don't want to deprive your wife a weekend in Chicago. But let's add a buck for closest to the pin on par threes and a buck for a sandy."

"What's a sandy?"

"Well Mr. Ott, Sandy Easey is a nymphomaniac dancer down at Dizzy Izzy's. I had her down in Phoenix one weekend and I was never as tired after that trip...blue balls too."

"Tell me again, what's a sandy bet?"

"Well, Sandy IS a nymphomaniac and she also IS a dancer at Izzy's, but a sandy on a golf course is a one-putt par or birdie after playing out of a sand trap."

"There's a lot to remember."

"Ott, you would never forget Sandy if you spent ten minutes with her. But if you're worrying about tracking the golf bets, we have four smart caddies to help. Which caddie is keeping score today?"

Moose raised his hand.

"Good, he's my caddie, so I'll keep an eye on the scores after every hole."

Ott flipped his putter at me. I deflected it, striking Moose in the head, knocking his glasses crooked.

"Ott, are you trying to hurt my caddie? If there's anyone who can hurt my caddie, it will be me! We're up on the tee now. I might as well go first, since I will have the honors pretty often today." Mellon took two practice swings, twirled the clubhead three times, and solidly connected with his tee ball down the middle of the fairway. "I didn't quite get all of it, but it'll do." He spun the club in a circle above his head signifying his accomplishment. "Hanky, let's tee off by teams, so you're next." Kerchev took one practice swing and smacked his drive down the right side, ten yards past Mellon's ball.

Misor was next to play. He took a minute to stretch his legs and rotate his hips, when Mellon called out. "Hey Misor, we don't need to watch your exercise routine. We're here to play golf." He leaned over toward the caddies and whispered, "And to take your money."

With a thunderous grunt, Misor launched a left hook, which caromed off a grove of trees, well out of bounds. He immediately pulled a ball out his pocket and rested it on the tee. "That was my warm-up shot. I'll hit my mulligan now."

"Not so fast, pal. You're playing your third shot. There's no mulligan allowed in a money game, especially with the petty stakes we're playing for."

"Okay, Walter, but next time, we'll be certain all of the rules are set before we tee off."

Misor took another whack. The ball dribbled fifty yards from the tee box.

"Jerry, you're in play now. Maybe you can still make bogey! HEE...HAW."

"Crap! All right, Harry, now you can go ahead."

I heard Ott murmur to Misor that he never played for such huge money stakes. Ott was visibly nervous. His practice swing was so fast, even Misor had to counsel him. "Harry, relax, where's the fire? Slow down! Think about that old spiritual song...swing slow sweet Harry Ott."

Ott wound up like a top and whiffed, striking the turf two feet behind his ball, tearing up a twelve-inch piece of sod. "That was a practice shot."

Mellon yelled. "No it wasn't!"

"Yes, I always do that on my first practice swing."

"Maybe in Duluth, but not here in La Crosse, Harry baby."

Ott mumbled something under his breath. He took two more practice swings, nearly as fast as the others. He swung mightily, clipping only the top of the ball, which landed twenty yards from the tee. Ott slammed his driver to the ground in frustration.

"Harry, your ball didn't even reach the ladies' tee! You know what that means?"

"No, Mr. Mellon...what?"

"You have to drop your pants to play your next shot, since your ball isn't past the red tees. But don't worry, women won't see you since they're not allowed on the course until two o'clock."

"I refuse! It's below my standards."

"That's our rule around here, Ott. Jerry, you should know about the policy from all of your short drives. Tell your partner to drop 'em. We need to get a peek at his sexy underwear!"

Misor whispered into Ott's ear. After hesitating for a few seconds, Ott threw down his driver. "Jerry, if you insist, but only this one time!"

The other golfers near the tee were closely observing the debate, while P. A. Lloyd drew closer, perhaps expecting to referee a fist fight. "Boys...take it easy now."

Mellon shouted over, "Relax P.A., don't get YOUR panties in a wad too!"

Lloyd pointed downward below his belt. "Mr. Mellon...my underwear fit me just fine." He pivoted and shuffled back toward the tee.

Ott finally unbuckled his belt and dropped his trousers, sporting a pair of white boxer shorts with red dragons. Cat-calls erupted, the loudest of which came from Mellon. "Ott, your legs haven't seen the sun in years!"

"Mellon, speaking of the sun, why don't you stick it where the sun don't shine?"

I couldn't believe the tone of the conversation. I looked toward the older caddies for their reaction and saw them chuckling. Fearing Ott's temper, I stared down at his golf bag.

"I'll bet your wife loves the fire coming out of your undies. Whew!"

Ott was boiling now. "Shut the hell up! My wife's name is Mary."

"Mary Ott? Really? I traveled to Washington last week and stayed at a motor inn with her name. Is she building a motel chain?"

He took a few steps toward Mellon with his fists clenched and threw down his cap. Misor quickly stopped him. "Cool down Harry, he's just having a little fun with you."

Mellon put his hand on Ott's shoulder. "Harry, I prefer a little drama on the golf course and appreciate a guy with a little spunk."

Ott now screamed at me. "Caddie, hand me my 1-iron!" His trousers were wrapped around his ankles and his white boxers sparkled in the bright sun. He clubbed his shot perfectly, landing a few yards short of Mellon's drive.

"Nice shot there, Harry. A 1-iron is a tough club to hit. You play better with your pants off. You should take them off for the rest of the round, 'cause Hanky and I are gonna beat your pants off anyway."

"We'll see, Mellon." He pulled up his grey trousers, tucked in his black golf shirt and adjusted his matching black sweater.

"Ott, at least you dress well compared to what your boss wears. Jerry, I didn't know the circus was in town."

OC heaved Misor's bag onto his shoulder and the strap instantly loosened. The bag crashed on the concrete cart path with a thud and the irons clanked loudly.

"What the hell did you do, Ollie? My clubs are brand new!" He snapped up a club. "There's a nick in my 9-iron for Christ's sake!"

"Sorry, Mr. Misor. Your bag didn't have a strap, so we found a replacement. The strap must not have been properly secured."

Misor plodded ahead to locate his ball. He proceeded to hack away, bunting his ball only fifty yards at a time. After three more shots, his ball was finally near his opponents' drives.

"Jerry, you're hitting your sixth shot already. Why don't you pick up? The way you're playing, we will take forever to play the 1st hole."

"Not a bad idea, Walter. I'll save my energy for the next one."

Ott was ready to play. "Caddie, give me the baffing spoon." I couldn't remember what he was referring to, so I ruffled through the clubs, pretending to look for it. Ott suddenly jerked the 4-wood from the bag. "The baffing spoon is the 4-wood, nut head. Who trained you to be a caddie?"

I was speechless.

Ott connected solidly, but the ball never got more than ten feet off the ground. Everyone watched in amazement as the ball bounced straight toward the hole, deflected off the left grass bunker onto the green, disappearing into the cup. Misor congratulated Ott. "A birdie! Now that's a shot to crow about!"

"Hold on, Misor! That was a par. The whiff on the tee counted as a shot. So Ott had four shots, if you can count that high."

"Yeah, I guess you're right, but it was a par after all. Still, a great shot there, Harry."

Mellon twirled his club again and nestled his 6-iron ten feet from the pin, while Kerchev flared his ball into the greenside sand trap. After Kerchev's next shot landed two feet from the hole, Mellon signaled his approval with a thumbs up sign. "Nicely done, Hanky. That putt is good by me."

Ott was furious. "Mellon, you can't give your partner a putt!"

"Hanky always makes those, so don't get upset. Now, let me see if I can knock in this birdie putt. Moose, take a peek at this line. Maybe your goggles have X-ray vision."

Moose knelt down and squinted. "Maybe a cup to the left of the hole."

"Is that a D cup or an E cup?"

"I'd say a tea cup, Mr. Mellon."

"You've been so helpful, Twinkles. I'll have to guess, close my eyes, and pray." Mellon proceeded to spin his putter before settling over the ball and proceeded to feather it into the center of the cup for a birdie.

Mellon instructed Moose to write down the scores. "I had a 3 to win the low ball against Harry's 4. Hanky had a par to win the high ball and also had a sandy par save from the trap. "Good hole there, partner."

Ott raised another objection. "Mellon, isn't the 1st hole the number one handicap? My net 3 tied the score for low ball."

"Moose, what handicap is the 1st hole?"

"The 9th hole is the number one handicap, Mr. Mellon."

"Sorry Ott, but good try. You're down a buck a piece, plus Hanky receives a dollar for the sandy from all of us."

Misor threw his cap to the ground in protest. "Walter, I thought we were playing a dollar per team."

"No, a dollar for each player."

OC snagged Misor's hat and handed it to him. He appeared worried. "Harry, we need to play better."

The first two hundred yards on 2nd hole was roped off for irrigation maintenance and temporary tee markers were placed far forward. The hole was lined with mature trees on both sides of the fairway, so Moose and I walked down the right side to watch the drives.

"Spykstra, I unbuckled Misor's bag strap on the first tee. It's a trick we always play on the new caddies...works every time. You're lucky, I tried to unhook Ott's strap, but it was too brittle."

"Moose, did you hear Ott talk to himself the entire hole?"

"What was he saying?"

"Hail Marys."

"What's a Hail Mary, a pick-up line in a bar?"

"No, it's a Catholic prayer. Maybe it is has some connection with golf."

"We need to watch the drives now, ready?"

Mellon sliced his drive into the trees. Kerchev and Ott followed with perfect tee shots, while Misor duffed his shot again.

I heard Misor cussing from across the fairway. "Shucks, I've never played this bad...EVER!"

Mellon was eager to help. "Jerry, you play like you dress...utter disarray. Maybe you should take your pants off too."

Violating a caddie commandment, OC offered advice to Misor. "Keep your head down, sir. I'll keep an eye on your shot...just relax."

"I can't relax when I can lose a lot of money. All right, I'll close my eyes and think about something pleasant...like walking into my bank vault." Misor then clubbed a 3-wood left of the fairway.

"Great shot, Mr. Misor, but the ball went right into the creek!"

"Creek? Damn it!"

"I can try if you carry a shovel in your bag, Mr. Misor."

I followed Moose into the grove of trees to help find Mellon's ball. We found it wedged between the roots of a large oak tree, blocking his shot directly to the green. I headed back to the fairway toward Ott's tee shot. "Nice drive, Mr. Ott."

"Shut up and mark off the distance to the hole."

I was confused. "The distance to the hole?"

"How many yards to the pin?" He seemed pissed.

Moose came to assist me. "Spykstra, I'll help with the distance." Moose motioned for me to position myself parallel to the white post on the left side of the rough. "That post is the one hundred-fifty yard marker." We walked ten paces from Ott's ball back to the line opposite the post. "Spykstra, tell Ott that he has one hundred-sixty yards to the middle of the green."

"Mr. Ott, one hundred-sixty yards to the pin."

"The pin seems closer. Okay, I'll trust you since I've only played here twice before." Ott selected a 6-iron and knocked it straight at the pin. I watched the ball disappear over the green, splashing into a pond. Ott slammed his club down. "Jerry, I can't believe I blasted a 6-iron over the green on the fly. The ball must have travelled at least a hundred-seventy yards!"

"Harry, you were only one hundred-forty yards out. You should have used an 8-iron at the most."

Ott glared at me. "On hundred-sixty yards, huh? Were you deliberately giving me the wrong yardage so your buddies can win more money?"

"No sir. The distance was one hundred-sixty yards. Moose told me."

Moose shook his head. "Nope, I said subtract ten yards from the post marker, not to add ten yards."

I was stunned. Why had I trusted Moose? I quickly apologized to Ott. "I can't believe I made a mistake. I'm truly sorry."

"You'll be sorry all-right!" He whipped his 6-iron at my head. I barely ducked in time as the shaft whizzed past my ear.

Misor came to my defense. "Harry, haven't you ever made an addition error?"

"No, never. That's why you hired me."

"Hmmm…you're absolutely right."

After retrieving Ott's 6-iron, I turned to track Mellon's second shot. He was positioned much closer to the fairway from the spot where his tee shot had landed. Mellon shouted that his ball was on the green in the regulation two shots.

Ott had marched thirty feet ahead of me, so I hurriedly caught up with him as he bent over the edge of the murky pond. "Caddie, you cost me a shot and a lost golf ball. Royals are expensive in case you don't know."

I spied a ball three feet from the edge of the rocks and asked Ott to use his 1-iron to retrieve the ball. I knelt down and cornered the ball with the club, meticulously dragging it toward the edge of the pond. My foot abruptly slipped, and I lost my balance, plunging into three feet of frigid water. My feet began sinking into the mud and I shouted. "Help…Help!"

Kerchev and Mellon were laughing. "Quick, throw him a life preserver…man overboard! We have an episode of *Voyage to the Bottom of the Sea* playing right before us."

Misor quickly added, "Or *Sea Hunt* with Lloyd Bridges?"

Fortunately, Bing rushed to my aid by extending a rake for me to secure. As he pulled, I sensed both of my shoes loosening, sucked off by the thick sludge. My right foot soon released from the muck, followed by the left. I looked down to see my shoes and coveralls layered with brown mud and ugly green algae crud.

"What a nightmare! Thanks Bing."

"Holy cow! Don't walk on the greens for a while. See if you can peel some gunk off your shoes!"

Ott was not amused. "Caddie, did you find my golf ball?"

I couldn't believe I had held on to the ball during all of the commotion. I rubbed the algae off on with a towel to identify the golf ball. "This one is a Dot 2 and has a gash in it!"

"Shit, I should put a gash in your forehead!"

"Ott, you can drop your penalty shot right here. In case you don't know the rules, you're playing your fourth shot. We're playing this as a par 4 today, just so you know."

"Mellon, I certainly know the rules, so quit lecturing me."

"No problem, Harry. Knock it in."

After Ott nestled his chip shot two inches from the hole, Kerchev was accommodative. "Good shot Harry. Take it away!"

Mellon interrupted. "Wait a second Hanky. Ott needs to putt that!"

Ott was pissed and tapped the ball in the hole. "Mellon, I'll remember that. I had a bogey 5."

Mellon and Kerchev easily putted in for par 4's. Misor picked up again after his ball finally ended up in a sand trap.

"Jerry, instead of your ugly pants, you should have worn your swim trunks if you had planned on spending so much time in the water and on the beach today."

"Walter, the temperature is too cold for the beach. Maybe next month after I bring the boat out."

"By the way, you're down two bucks each. Ott, do you want to press us?"

"Hell NO!" Ott stomped away.

As we approached the next tee, I could see most of the fairway roped off for construction too and the hole was set up to be played as a par 3.

Mellon addressed Misor and Ott. "Shit, is the whole course torn up today...this isn't even golf! Jerry, maybe Sod Greenman set it up today so you could break eighty on the front nine." He snickered.

"That's not funny, Walter. I'll find my groove soon."

""Feelin' Groovy" huh...sounds like a good name for a song. Look, since they're playing this as a par 3 today, the closest shot to the pin wins a buck, but the ball needs to be on the green. And to help you with the yardage, here's a plaque marking one hundred-forty yards to the center. I'll even show you what club I picked." Mellon displayed his 9-iron. After his signature clubhead twirl, he lofted a high arching shot which clipped the top of the pin stick, coming to a rest near the front of the putting surface. As if shooting a rifle, he pointed the butt of his 9-iron at the pin, and pulled an imaginary trigger with his index finger. "Pow...that was a direct hit!"

Playing next, Kerchev's ball landed on the green, took one bounce, and rolled straight into the hole. Mellon stuck two fingers in his mouth, producing a loud whistling sound and then started to applaud. Mellon encouraged the caddies to join in the celebration, although I stopped clapping immediately when Ott seized my right wrist in his giant fist.

"What the hell are you clapping for?" Ott's face was beet red as he released my arm from his grip.

"I'm sorry, but Mr. Mellon wanted us to."

"Do I have to remind you who you are caddying for?" He pointed at his face.

"Caddie, don't mind him. That's a fine shot, Hanky. How many aces for you now?"

"To be honest, I've lost count."

Misor and Ott seemed paralyzed, staring at each other in bewilderment. "Harry, let's change our batting order. I'll hit first. Ollie, hand me a 6-iron." Misor tuned away in disgust after pulling his shot to the left toward the woods.

Ott watched the ball intently. "Wait a second, partner. The ball bounced off a tree and rolled on the green!"

"I'll take it, that's my lucky ball."

Mellon instantly informed Misor of the situation. "Jerry I hate to disappoint you, but even if you make your putt, you can't even tie the hole. There's no one strokes given here. This is the seventeen handicap hole."

Ott yanked an 8-iron from the bag. He took five practice swings and set up for his shot. Trying to regain his concentration, Ott hovered over the ball for what seemed like an eternity. A split-second before he swung, Mellon started choking, causing Ott to shank his ball into some thick evergreens.

"Mellon, you distracted me on purpose!"

"A big bug flew into my mouth and I couldn't stop!"

"Bug, my ass."

"Did I hear you had a bug up your ass?"

Ott stormed off the tee box in the direction of his shot. "Caddie, by some miracle, did you happen to see where my ball landed?"

"Yes sir, right in the middle of those green shrubs."

"They're all green, numb nuts!"

I couldn't figure out how Ott knew my testicles were still numb from the frigid pond. "Sir, your ball went in right here." I pointed to a section of thick evergreen shrubs. I sprawled on the ground and lifted a few branches. "There it is, a Royal 4."

"My ball is unplayable. I'll have to take a penalty to play my next shot." Ott carefully measured two clubs lengths from the spot where the shot landed, inserted a tee in the turf, and dropped his ball.

Mellon came closer to check. "Anywhere is fine, Ott. Why don't you just pick up and take a bogey?"

"I play by the rules. It's a gentleman's game... apparently no one ever told you."

Misor inspected Mellon's ball position. "You're off the green, Walter. I'm closest to the hole, so I win a dollar from everyone."

"Jerry, did you forget that Hanky's ball is in the hole!"

"Technically, he's not closest to the hole. MY ball is!"

"Ask your partner for an interpretation."

"Harry, whose ball is closest to the pin? Mine, right?"

"Kerchev had a hole-in-one. Nice try, Jerry."

"Harry, we'll discuss that on Monday at the office. At least we get strokes on the next hole."

The caddies all walked together down the 4th fairway to follow the drives. I was curious about Mellon's question about a press. "Moose, what's a press?"

"A big factory machine, a defensive strategy in basketball, a publishing business, a weightlifting motion, a large laundry apparatus, a fruit compressor, or media coverage…take your pick."

I could not correlate any of those descriptions with golf, but was more interested in Mellon's shot from the trees on the 2nd hole. "Moose, wasn't Mellon's drive on the 2nd hole behind the tree? It looked like he had a clear line to the green when he struck his ball."

"I don't know. I was helping you with the distance to the green for Ott's shot and before I turned around, Mellon's ball was in the air."

All of the players and caddies walked together again, when Misor asked Mellon about his business. "Walter, Hank said you were working on some new women's clothing ideas."

"He did, huh? Jerry, this line is pretty confidential, but I'll tell you if you keep quiet. We're bringing out a line of lady's panties…see-through panties and edible ones."

"Edible panties? You mean panties which can be eaten? They might be a little dry and would surely give someone cotton mouth. Who would ever buy them?"

"Misor, we're researching this now and based upon your question, it doesn't sound as if you would be a customer."

"Walter, Helen buys her own undergarments. I once bought her a negligee that she returned the next day. She thought the gown was too short, even though it hung below her knees."

"Ott, are you interested? I saw your dragon underwear, so maybe you have a little more adventure in your sex life with your lady."

"I beg your pardon, sir! It's none of your business what Mary and I do in private. If you are planning to operate in the sexual perversion business, our bank will not to be associated with your company. In fact, I don't need to play another hole with you either, Mellon. Let's go, Jerry."

"Let's not be too hasty, Harry."

"Jerry, in case you didn't understand, he wants you to nibble on your wife's panties while she wears them. I've had enough from this buffoon!"

"Ah, I guess you're right, Harry. I'm sorry Walter. We cannot associate with customers who are involved with questionable business practices."

"Okay then, I assume you and Jerry won't be participating in our panty taste tests with your wives."

"You're damn right!"

"Then I won't be by your bank on Monday to pick up my toaster. Oh, you owe Hanky five dollars and me three dollars for the first three holes. And since you're forfeiting the rest of the round, you owe another fifteen bucks each for the next fifteen holes."

"Bull shit, Mellon. You forfeit! I saw you kick your ball from behind the tree on the 2nd hole, where you recorded a 4. You cheated and you're now 'DQ'd.'"

I wondered why he was referring to Dairy Queen.

Mellon pointed to everyone in the group. "Who else saw my alleged kick out?"

I noticed Moose staring at the ground, when Ott confronted him. "Hey runt, you're Mellon's caddie, you had to see him cheat!"

"No, I wasn't watching."

Ott screamed. "You are his caddie! How could you not be watching him? Christ, I don't care, Mellon. I saw you cheat and I'm not paying you a thing! I'm reporting you to the board!"

"Go right ahead. I'm Vice-President of the Board and head of the rules committee. Hanky is President-elect for next year."

"I don't care if you're Vice-President of the United States. I'm still filing a complaint and you're going to have to pry the money from my billfold."

"Ott, have a nice walk to the clubhouse. And Jerry, don't forget to pick up your golf ball from the fairway. I know you would lose sleep if you left it out there."

I stared at OC, bewildered over what we had just observed. We dropped our golf bags and sprinted to pick up the golf balls. Misor and Ott departed so quickly through the woods that I didn't even see the direction they went. Neither OC nor I knew a short-cut back to the pro shop, so we elected to retrace our path over the first three holes, collecting several strange looks from the golfers we passed.

As we walked along, I contemplated my first caddie job. I had always held bankers in high esteem, but these guys were fools. Misor was a sniveling sap, while Ott seemed like a hatchet man, with his cold personality and lack of compassion. Mellon had the reputation of an honest businessman, however, in the hour I spent with the foursome, I concluded he was a callous man with no moral compass.

We finally reached the pro shop, where Benny was waiting. "What the hell happened out there? Spykstra, look at you! Have you been rolling around in the mud with a bunch of pigs?"

OC spoke up. "Our guys got in a fight over their golf bets and women's panties. We thought a rumble would break out right on the 4th fairway."

Benny looked surprised. "From what they told me, you guys should be on probation. They said you were the worst caddies they've ever had. For some reason, they still paid you though. Here are the envelopes with some money in them. They asked what your rates were and I told them two-fifty for eighteen holes. Ott made a calculation on his scorecard and threw it in the trash barrel over there."

OC peered into his envelope. "There are a couple of coins in there. What the hell, only forty-five cents." I opened my envelope and counted forty cents, double checking in case a nickel was stuck in the seam.

We walked over and rummaged through the garbage and Benny picked the scorecard out, handing it to me to decipher the math. "Ott divided two-fifty by eighteen, which was 13.8¢ per hole. Then he multiplied by three, which is 41.4¢. He gave me a negative tip of 1.4¢!"

OC grinned. "I got a tip of almost a ten percent from Misor!"

Benny clapped. "Well boys, welcome to the Mississippi Valley Country Club."

Chapter 11

I'll never forget my first caddie loop, which turned out not to be a loop. It cemented my initial memories through interaction with successful businessmen...men who had charisma but flawed character, and others who were simply fools. My second caddie assignment was just as memorable, although vastly different. OC and I were tasked to caddie for older Jewish golfers, who were distinctive in so many ways.

OC and I trudged solemnly back to the caddie shack, where the Bunker twins were still hanging around.

"Why are you guys back so soon?" Tom Bunker asked.

"Our bankers quit on the 4th hole after they had a fight with the other players. We got stiffed too. My player only paid me forty cents, but OC got forty-five."

"What's with all the mud?"

"I had a little accident fishing a golf ball out of the pond on the 2nd hole. At one point, I thought that I was going to lose my shoes in the muck, but thankfully Bing pulled me out."

I lumbered over to a crate near the front of the shack and plopped down hard just as rain started to fall with a steadily pitter-patter on the tin roof. There was so much crud caked on my sneakers that I couldn't even find the laces. I inched forward and stuck my shoes out in the rain, slowly diluting the mud.

Tom Bunker studied the gray storm clouds that had rolled in. "The weather sucks. I can't imagine any more golfers coming out here. C'mon Ron, let's blow this pop stand. We'll see you bums next week. Let's saddle up." They rode away quickly.

OC stood up. "I'm taking off too. I've got some stuff to do at home."

"OC, we can't leave until Benny tells us. Why don't you go ask him?"

Just then, Benny popped his head around the corner of the building. "I need four caddies. The Jews are coming!"

"The jewelers?" OC asked, apparently not hearing him clearly.

"No, the Jewish members. They always play a few holes in the afternoon. They need caddies since there's no carts available."

OC shook his head. "I already got jew'd by a cheap banker. I'm not getting jew'd again, especially by actual Jews. They might even take my forty-five cents or try to sell me something. I've heard about their penchant for bartering!"

"Zero, don't ever say the word 'jew'd' around here again!"

"Who are these guys?"

"Ben Lipschitz."

OC cut him off. "Lipschitz…you're kidding! Did he get that name by kissing a turd?"

"Lipschitz owns BML Mart."

"BML Mart, eh? His middle name must start with an M, so B.M. Lipschitz? I heard they sell some real crap there, so that makes sense."

"Very funny, Zero. Abe Goldman is bringing a guest, Ezra Epstein. Goldman owns Goldy's Diamonds, AG's Tie Land, and Old Abe's Tavern. The fourth player is Izzy Cohen…he runs Dizzy Izzy's, the nightclub out on Highway 61."

"Dizzy Izzy's has topless dancers! I want to caddie for him. He won't even have to pay me if he gives me a pass to his club."

"Let me see what I can do for you, Zero."

"He may jew," he took a breath. "I mean, screw with you Benny…so let me ask him for the pass."

139

Benny surveyed the caddie yard. "Where are the other caddies, Spykstra?"

"They took off. They figured that with the rain, no more golfers would come out to play."

"No caddie can EVER leave without letting us know. Didn't we tell you the first day? Now, you two losers are each going to take a double."

"A double?"

"Yeah, two bags each, Zero. The rate for a double is three bucks for nine holes."

"How much does a triple pay?"

"There's no such thing as a triple, only singles and doubles."

"How about home runs?"

"I'll tell you what, Zero. If you get the runs, you can go home!"

"Will the Jews make us wear those funny beanies? Aren't they called yams?"

"They're called a yarmulke, but sometimes yams for short. Ask Lipschitz about them. BLM Mart advertises them to guys with bald spots on the top of their heads."

"How much do they cost? Maybe I can jew," he took another breath, "I mean, jaw the Heeb down to buy a father's day present. My Dad is losing his hair fast. A yam will look better than the stupid comb-over weave he tries with hair spray."

Benny glared at him. "Don't say Heeb either!"

"Okay, but Jewish people give me the heebie jeebies."

Benny rolled his eyes. "They're going to play around one-thirty."

OC checked his watch. "One-thirty, that's ninety minutes from now!"

"If you take off, you'll be in deep shit."

"Benny, I'll have enough shit to deal with if I'm caddying for a guy named Lipschitz, but you better get my Dizzy Izzy pass."

Ignoring OC, Benny turned to address me. "Spykstra, get yourself a new set of coveralls."

I started to explain what had happened, but he turned and walked to the bag room.

OC looked surprisingly excited about our upcoming loop, considering how the last one turned out. "Spike, three bucks for only two hours work, AND, I'll get to see titties at Izzy's!"

I had never even met a Jewish person, although Mom had mentioned that they were mysterious and spoke a strange language called Hebrew. My parents and their friends had often spoken about getting jew'd, so I interpreted the word simply as getting cheated, not realizing until now that it related to people of the Jewish faith.

The time quickly passed and Benny finally called us for the round and positioned their golf bags on the rack outside the pro shop. He pointed to a little red and black plaid bag. "Zero, here's Izzy's bag."

OC examined the equipment. "What the hell, there's no strap on this bag!" He picked it up by the handle. "This must only weigh five pounds. There's an old driver, a rusted 7-iron, a woman's 5-iron, a bent 9-iron and a left-handed wooden putter in here. Benny, why does he need a caddie?"

"He's nearly blind. He can't see more than ten yards."

"How old is he?"

"At least eighty-five. He can't walk very well either."

OC's mouth was wide open. "He might die on me out there and I'm not giving him mouth to mouth, even if I get the pass!"

"The pass is in his locker. He'll deliver it to me after the round."

"Unless he dies first. Where is he anyway?"

"I saw him wandering around the pro shop."

OC picked up a tan bag next to Izzy's. "Whose clubs are these? The plastic strap is half-torn off. There are six clubs, but it's a hodgepodge, a miniature 5-iron and a left-handed 3-iron." OC turned the bag around. "The tag says Abraham Goldman."

"Zero, you seem pretty feeble. You can take Goldman's bag too and can carry a bag in each hand. They can't weigh more than five pounds each."

"No problem, Benny. I can lift at least a hundred pounds. But what happens when they hit shots in the opposite direction?"

"Go back and forth or tell them to take turns playing one ball…and one more thing, don't ask Goldman what kind of beer HE BREWS at his tavern!"

I located Lipschitz's black bag. It appeared brand new, with several large pockets on the side. "Benny, he has a new set of Power-Built clubs. He must be a good player!"

"He's a hack! The clubs are a demo set from the pro shop. His shitty set of clubs is missing from the bag room and he's holding us responsible to replace them. He even hired an attorney, so we're letting him use this set for now. Keep a close eye on his shots or he'll demand that you to pay for any lost balls."

I checked the tags on the rest of the bags and couldn't find Epstein's name, when Benny pointed to a set of clubs resting on a pull cart. "It has a built-in seat that Epstein apparently uses between shots while he reads his book."

"A book?"

"Yeah, I believe Lipschitz called it a tank. Epstein's an assistant at the Synagogue who's planning to enroll in a seminary to become a Rabbi."

"To raise rabbits?

"Zero, you're an idiot. A Rabbi is like a priest, but in a Jewish church, called a Synagogue. A Rabbi also gives circumcisions on little boys' weenies."

"He decides their size?"

"Zero, why don't you ask him?"

"Maybe he can extend my schwantz! Did you say Goldman owns a jewelry shop? That makes sense...a Jew selling jewelry.

"He also owns AG's Tie Land."

"He imports Oriental rugs and cheap junk from Thailand, that little Asian country?"

"No. Its spelled T-I-E and L-A-N-D! His company designs ties that men wear around their necks when they dress up, you moron!"

"Oh, you mean neckties. I get it! Now, where is Izzy?"

A little old man emerged from the pro shop. He was only five feet tall and wore bright red trousers with a sparkling gold jacket. He wore a white cap, with DIZZY IZZY'S printed on the front, with the shape of two women dancers embroidered below. OC held out his hand to shake. "Nice to meet you Mr. Izzy...err...Mr. Cohen. I've planned to visit your club for a long time."

"I'm not Izzy, my name is Abe Goldman. Izzy is right behind me."

I turned to see Izzy bump into the door frame and nearly lost his balance. Goldman quickly grabbed his shoulder and steadied him. "Izzy, didn't you see the door?"

Izzy tried to respond but coughed several times and spit up a big chuck of gunk on the concrete. He kept hacking until Goldman slapped him on the back, sending his false teeth flew flying out of his mouth and coming to rest on OC's left tennis shoe.

OC was disgusted, but managed to balance them on his foot to keep them off the pavement. "I am not touching those things with my hands!"

Izzy regained his breath and stopped choking. Goldman snatched the set of teeth and handed them to Izzy. "Thanks Abe. I must not have put enough stick-um on these suckers this morning." Izzy carefully inserted them in his mouth, pushed them in position, and chomped down a couple of times. "Good enough to eat out now! Where's my clubs?"

OC rushed over to Izzy. "Right here, sir. I'm caddying for you today. My name is Matt O'Connell...they call me OC though."

"Ozzie? Like in the *Ozzie and Harriet's* TV show? How is Ricky's latest record doing?"

OC shrugged. "I don't know offhand, but Ricky Nelson had a number one song about four years ago called "Travelin' Man.""

"I remember that one." Izzy began to sing off-key.

After Goldman asked my name, he contemplated for a few seconds. "Your initials are SS, huh? That's not good." He asked me what my middle name was and I timidly responded, "Orville."

"Orville? So SOS, eh? Are you in distress?"

"Well, I am a little nervous about starting High School in the fall."

He immediately began to pitch me on a unique deal in his jewelry shop to buy some special cuff links and even offered to engrave them with my initials. I told him I needed to make some money caddying before I could splurge on luxury items, Goldman kept going. "The price might be higher in a couple of days. There was a customer in the store yesterday who was interested in purchasing them on a lay-away plan, but he couldn't make up his mind. We have a great sale on necklaces ending in three days. When did you last buy your mother or girlfriend a special gift?"

"I don't have money to buy gifts.

"Well, good luck finding a girlfriend."

"I sure could use a little luck in that department."

He shook his head and walked toward the course with Izzy. I then saw two men emerge from the clubhouse. Both were dressed in long black coats and wore baggy black trousers which were three inches too short, exposing their white socks. I picked out Epstein right away, holding a book in the crook of his right arm. He wore a large black hat with a wide brim, and had a straggly black beard. As he drew closer, I noticed that he only had a right arm and could hear him chanting in a strange language.

The other man, who I suspected was Ben Lipschitz, approached me directly. "Good afternoon, young man. My name is Ben and here is my guest, Ezra Epstein. Who's pulling his cart today?"

"I am…my name is Scott. I have your bag too."

"Both of us?"

"Yes sir. There are no other caddies available."

"Let's make the best of it then. We're playing the back nine today. Ezra is a Gabbai, also referred to as a Shamash, and he helps run our synagogue. He will read scripture from the Tanakh throughout the round. When he reaches his ball, you will select the proper golf club and hold the book while he hits his shot. Be sure to insert the ribbon in the page he is reading from in case it closes. After he has played his shot, take the club from him and place the Tanakh back in his hand with the page open. Don't speak to him unless he asks you for something. If he happens to mention fishing, please don't ask him to show you the length of the largest fish he caught or how he bates his hook."

I tried to envision how a one-armed man would show the size of a fish, and then recalled OC mention of masturbation in the confessional. Epstein must be a master baiter too, if he can bate a hook with one hand.

I grabbed a scorecard, although Lipschitz snapped it from my hand and tore it up. "You will not need a score card. We do not count our shots since we don't believe in sports competition. We are here to enjoy the peace of the garden."

As we trudged toward the 10th tee, I tried to imagine how peaceful the garden was when they drove the noisy gas carts, which often backfired.

Abe helped Izzy to the 10th tee box and motioned OC to follow. "Put a tee in the turf for Izzy and balance a golf ball on it."

OC pulled out an old, dirty ball from Izzy's bag. He tried to clean it in the ball washer, although it didn't seem to help. "This ball is really old, but it's the only one in the bag."

"No problem, Ozzie. I can play a grey ball. The ball is round, right?"

OC held it in the air. "Maybe, but it doesn't have any dimples." OC reached into his bag again and grabbed a tee, rubbing it in his fingers. I was standing close enough to see it had the shape of a naked lady. "Mr. Cohen, can I keep this tee as a souvenir?"

Ben held his finger in front of his mouth. "Shhhh! Mr. Cohen does have ONE vice."

Izzy took a feeble practice swing with the driver and imbedded the head in the turf, a foot behind the ball. The club flew out of his hands and landed near OC's feet, who hesitated a second, picked up the club, and handed it back to Izzy. "Keep your eyes peeled on the naked lady tee, Mr. Cohen, and whack her a good one!"

Ben censured OC and ordered him to shut his mouth.

"I meant for Mr. Cohen to whack the ball. I'm sorry, I will go to confession soon."

"You're Catholic? Now I understand your lack of morals."

Izzy shuffled his feet in position, slowly bringing the club back awkwardly, and swung quickly. He managed to tick the ball slightly, which rolled between his feet. Izzy looked around, "Abe, where did my shot go?"

"Between your feet, Izzy."

"How many feet?" Izzy shaded his eyes, gazing ahead of the tee box.

"Between your shoes."

"Choose? Choose what?"

Izzy obviously couldn't hear well either. Abe was frustrated. "Caddie, retrieve the ball and tee it up for him again." OC crawled along the ground carefully and replaced the ball.

He wound up and whiffed again. "Where is the ball?"

OC mumbled in my ear. "Yikes, we'll be here until dark at this pace!"

On his fourth attempt, Izzy swung and amazingly, the club head squarely connected with the ball. The shot rolled out one hundred-fifty yards. Izzy looked around the tee box, assuming he had missed again. He looked down at his feet. "Where is it?"

Abe shouted. "Great shot, Izzy."

"Thanks. I aimed right for her hinder, a real hinder grinder, eh?"

Ben nodded to me. "Mr. Epstein will tee off now. Caddie, please set his golf ball on the tee."

I unzipped the large pouch in his bag and selected a ball with the word Shalom stamped on two sides. I pulled the cover off the 3-wood, since there wasn't a driver in the bag.

Ben snagged a 1-iron from Epstein's bag and handed it to me. "He uses the 1-iron for his drives."

"There must be a mistake, sir. This is a left-handed club and he doesn't have a left arm."

"Mr. Epstein swings back-handed."

I stretched out my right hand to hold the Tanakh, simultaneously offering the club to Ezra with my left hand. Attempting to balance Ben's bag, I juggled the book as it shifted back and forth, my pinky finger and thumb pressing on the binding to hold it steady. It fell to the ground with a LOUD thud, closing with the ribbon hanging out. Ben's bag tipped over, the clubs bouncing on the concrete path, reminding me of Andy's warning on my first day of caddie training. I braced for another lecture.

The players gasped and Ben bellowed. "The scared Tanakh has fallen to the earth!" They lifted their heads to the sky and fell to their knees.

OC instantly grabbed the book and handed it to me. "The book only touched the ground for a second. Maybe no one up there saw it. The clubs look fine though."

Ben sneered at OC. "Who cares about the clubs, they're a demo set!"

I fumbled around, flipping pages, hoping there was some evidence of the page the book was open to. Goldman swiftly snapped the Tanakh out of my hands. "Sonny, I saw the page he was reading from. I will insert the ribbon to the proper page."

"Thank you, sir."

I turned to watch the Epstein hit, and with a perfect tempo, his drive arched perfectly down the middle of the fairway, landing nearly two hundred yards out. No one said a word. Lipschitz motioned to me to exchange the book and golf club with Epstein, which I accomplished this time without error.

After taking a few steps off the tee box, Izzy stumbled and fell on the grass, so OC helped him up. A few seconds later, OC carried Izzy on his back, his arms were wrapped around OC's shoulders with his legs anchored around his waist. Izzy seemed happy. "Wheeee! A stripper named Big Beauty carried me like this ten years ago. She was six feet tall and we made up a special harness with stirrups, so I could hang on better. We made a lot of money from the customers riding her too."

Lipschitz and Goldman hacked their drives only forty yards. I followed Lipschitz to his ball, although he waved me away. "I'll use my driver all the way to the green." Without taking any practice swings, Lipschitz and Goldman merely whacked their balls a few yards at a time, as if they were playing field hockey. They even played the other's golf balls twice without even noticing. Despite their poor play, the two weren't upset, seeming to be perfectly happy enjoying nature. I now understood why they didn't keep score...who could count all of the swings, much less add their scores up correctly in the end?

OC lowered Izzy to the ground next to his golf ball and handed him the driver again. "Thanks Ozzie, now point me in the direction of the green."

"Do you want to use the naked lady tee again?"

"Yes, I'll pound her hinder again." Izzy shuffled his feet and swung, making another solid connection. The ball rolled to within fifty yards of the green.

Goldman was incredulous. "I've never seen you strike the ball that far before, Izzy."

"I've got the hinder grinder working. Ozzie lines me up with the naked lady. I'm going to call her Fanny."

Meanwhile, Epstein pulled out the folding seat on the cart and sat down; occasionally glancing up to watch Goldman and Lipschitz hacking away. Epstein was reading aloud from the Tanakh in a very low voice, although I did not understand a word. As I selected a 7-iron, he finally stood up and crept toward his ball. Epstein crisply connected as I watch his ball climb quickly, landing merely ten feet from the pin.

"Excellent shot...sir...I mean Mr. Rabbit...err...Mr. Epstein." My voice faded away as I realized my mistake. Epstein said absolutely nothing, resting the club against the cart. He pulled out the seat, and sat down. I handed the book to him and he immediately began to mumble in Hebrew again.

We all finally reached Izzy's ball. "What club should I use now, Ozzie?"

"Let's try this crooked 9-iron. I'll tee the ball up for you again."

Izzy's shot rolled up on the green. "I cracked her good, right on Fanny's crack too! Where did the ball go, Ben?"

"On the green."

"Hooray! What green?"

"The 10th."

"The 10th green? Ben, what happened to the front 9?"

"We started on the 10th hole today, Izzy. Abe and I are done playing this one. Izzy, you can putt first, since Ezra is closer to the hole."

Izzy seemed confused. "Closest to the whore? I didn't see any of our strippers out here."

"The HOLE, Izzy. H-O-L-E!"

"I forgot we were playing golf. I can't see the cup from here. Show me where it is." OC grabbed two irons from the bag and rested them in a V-shape angle behind the hole, "Mr. Cohen, putt the ball toward me." He waved his hands in the air wildly. Izzy lined up on the opposite side of the grey ball, hitting it left-handed. It travelled across the green and came to a stop just before the cup, hovering over the lip.

"Too bad. That's an elevator…you got shafted!"

A blast of wind suddenly erupted from the west, sweeping the ball right into the cup.

OC yelled and threw his hands up into the air. "Yahoo!"

Izzy glanced around, what happened?"

"You made the putt Mr. Izzy and you didn't even need to use my guide irons. You made a six!"

"I had sex…with the hole? Was it good for her?"

Goldman was ecstatic. "Mazel Tov! Izzy, it was in all the way!"

"Yep, it was a HARD one. And, as they say, never up…never in."

Epstein now concentrated over his ten-foot putt, whispering a few words. With a delicate putting stroke, the ball curled into the hole for a birdie. As I picked his ball out of the cup, OC applauded but stopped abruptly, seeing the other players' heads were tilted upward toward the sky.

Abe and Ben proclaimed, "Shalom."

OC leaned over to whisper to me. "Shalom must mean birdie in Hebrew, huh?"

I told OC that Epstein was playing a Shalom ball, concluding that it must be a hot new brand. I asked OC where we could buy a couple of sleeves."

"Just buy one long sleeve shirt and you'll have two sleeves, although Epstein probably only buys shirts with one sleeve, right?"

"OC, I guess you don't you know how golf balls are sold. They come in a pack of three balls, called a sleeve."

The group had taken nearly forty-five minutes to play one hole, when they made their way to the 11th tee, a par 3. I selected a 9-iron for Epstein, whose shot soared high into the sky. It landed on the far edge of the green and spun, coming to rest five feet from the pin. Again, there was silence. Epstein sat down and read again.

Izzy was next to play, so OC asked him if he needed his driver. "This is a short hole, Mr. Cohen, so do want your driver?"

"Not yet, he's waiting in the parking lot for me to finish."

"Okay, what club do you want?"

"I wanted to buy the Carousel Club in Dallas. Jack Ruby couldn't run the business from his prison cell. It became even more famous after he shot Oswald, so I would have made a killing there!"

Goldman interjected. "Izzy, he wants to know what golf club you like."

"I like The Mississippi Valley Country Club."

"What golf club in your bag, Izzy?"

"My putter?"

"Izzy, you need to hit a shot over a hundred yards. You use the putter on the green."

"I can see green everywhere, except for the blue patch over there." He was pointing to the lake on the 9th hole.

"Kid, give him the driver." OC pulled out the driver and set up the golf ball on the Fanny tee. Without any practice, Izzy smacked the ball, which miraculously landed in the cup on the fly. Goldman and Lipschitz jumped up and down and danced. Epstein didn't witness the shot, still quietly reading from the Tanakh.

Goldman was euphoric again, slapping Izzy on the back of his shirt. "Izzy, Mazel Tov! You have a hole in one!"

"I should have brought another shirt if I have a hole in one."

"It's an ace, Izzy!"

"An ace? We're playing poker now?"

"No, you don't understand. Your shot went into the cup!"

"Shot? We're hunting too?"

"We are not hunting today, Izzy."

Ben and Abe both topped their shots, although the balls managed to roll down the hill toward the green.

OC escorted Izzy toward the pin and pointed down. "See Mr. Cohen, your ball is in the hole. Nozzle Top!"

"I'll be damned, how did my ball land in there?"

"It was the greatest shot ever."

"Greatest shot ever? The best shot ever was Annie Oakley."

"Annie Oakley? I thought you were going to say peppermint schnapps was the best shot ever, Mr. Cohen."

"Pepper Schnops...the plumber? The only shot I saw from him was his butt-crack when he bent over to repair a toilet at my club. Where are Abe and Ben's balls anyway?"

"If they're normal, they're hanging between their legs. But if you meant golf balls, they're are on the apron."

"Abe and Ben are wearing aprons? Why, are they cooking something for dinner?"

OC muttered under his breath. "Not dinner, but I think they're out to lunch!"

Goldman and Lipschitz knocked their balls around the green a few times and finally picked up. Epstein had been patiently waiting and made his putt for another Shalom birdie.

I whispered to OC. "A magic brand for sure!"

Goldman held up his pocket watch. "Guys, we won't be able to play nine holes today. Let's skip over to the 18th hole. Izzy, does that work for you?"

"Sure, I'm ready to go to work."

OC pointed to the side of his head and drew little circles in the air. "Scott, Izzy is goofy. He's lost his marbles. I'm worried that I won't get the Dizzy Izzy pass. He doesn't seem to know what planet he's on."

OC intercepted Goldman near the tee "Mr. Goldman, Benny Roombach told me I would have passes for Dizzy Izzy's if I caddied for Mr. Cohen. He doesn't even need to pay for my caddie fee."

"I take care of Mr. Cohen's affairs. I didn't hear anything on that arrangement."

"Mr. Cohen seems a little senile to me."

"He's just suffering from a hardening of the arteries."

"Maybe, but I betcha his major artery is never hard anymore."

"Keep that secret to yourself, sonny."

OC strolled over to ask Ben Lipschitz a question. "Mr. Lipschitz. I hear that you're selling yams at the BML Mart. I might want to buy on for my Dad because of his bald head. How much do they cost?"

"Yams? We don't sell vegetables at the BML Mart.

"I know, but where can I buy a beanie like you wear on your noggin?"

"It's called a yarmulke."

"Benny called it a yam. Of course, I knew you don't wear a vegetable on your head."

"I'll have to inform Benny. Now, let's tee off. Izzy, you can shoot first."

"I thought you just said that we're not hunting today."

"We're not, but you have the honors with the eagle."

"I shot an eagle? That might be a crime!"

"Forget about hunting. You have honors!"

"Honors? Well, I'm honored to have the honors."

OC teed up the ball on the Fanny lady tee for Izzy. "One more time, Mr. Cohen." He knocked another crisp shot at least a hundred yards down the fairway.

"Nice swing, Mr. Cohen."

"Oh yes, I often sit on the porch swing out on the veranda." He pointed toward the clubhouse.

Goldman instructed OC for silence. "Shhhh!"

I selected a 1-iron again for Epstein, who swiftly rapped his ball in the fairway. I reflected on Epstein's job title, a Shamash…no wonder he could smash a golf ball so far. Lipschitz hit next, and chopped another grounder thirty yards. Goldman followed suit. As they walked off the tee, Goldman asked Lipschitz the date of his grandson Seth's bar mitzvah.

"Soon, but the date isn't set yet."

OC picked up the conversation. "There's a new tavern coming to town called Seth's Bar? Will HE BREW beers there too?"

Goldman rolled his eyes. "Sonny, a bar mitzvah is not a tavern. It's a very sacred ceremony celebrating a young man's commitment to adulthood and his Jewish faith. Ben's grandson, Seth, has studied the Torah for years and has memorized the Hebrew passages he needs to recite."

"The Catholics have something like that called Confirmation. The best part was to pick another middle name. My real name is Matthew Oliver O'Connell and to make sure I had some special initials, I chose the name Owen. So, my initials spell MOOO!"

"Sonny, that name makes sense if you were a cow. Catholics don't seem too religious and you've confirmed that with your jokes."

"Catholicism is a joke! The looney nuns drive us crazy with all of their weird practices? But you're right, some of us aren't very religious. By the way, can you send me a pass to Dizzy Izzy's?"

"No."

"Why not?"

"How old are you?"

"Eighteen."

"I don't believe you. You can't even be fourteen. Do you even shave yet?"

OC rubbed his chin. "Sure, I shave all the time." OC instantly started singing the "Look Sharp, Be Sharp" and the "How Are Ya Fixed for Blades" jingle that played on the TV prize fights a few years ago.

Goldman shook his head. "Nice try." He took the 5-iron from OC's hand and bounced another forty yard grounder.

OC was tired of running around with their bags. "Mr. Goldman, I have an idea. Have you and Mr. Cohen ever considered playing the same golf ball?"

"The same brand?"

"I mean alternate hitting the same ball. You don't keep a score anyway and wouldn't be as tired only hitting half as many shots. Having a partner might be more fun. You might try the Shalom ball, which works pretty well for Mr. Epstein. And with your ability, you need all the help you can muster."

"Sonny, that's the smartest idea I've heard from you today. Let me ask Izzy next time. Why don't you catch up to him? He's walking toward the lake."

OC intercepted Izzy a few steps from the water, "Let's head over there, Mr. Izzy. You don't want to take a bath?"

"I love baths, especially bubble baths. You can fart in the water and no one can smell it."

"You wouldn't like the water there. It's kind of scuzzy."

"My first strippers were scuzzy, although the customers weren't gawking at their heads, so it didn't matter."

"Let's walk over here and I'll use the Fanny tee for your shot again, okay?"

"Sure." Izzy rolled his next shot a hundred yards. "I'm pretty beat. I'm going to retire, even though this is the best golf I've played in a long time."

"By the way, can I have a pass for your Dizzy Izzy Club for caddying for you today?"

"Talk to Mr. Goldman. He takes care of all of my affairs."

"I did and he said I wasn't old enough. But I promise not to use them until I'm eighteen. Please?"

"Ask Mr. Goldman."

The group finally reached the green. Goldman and Lipschitz had both given up as well, so Epstein was the only person still playing. His ball was lodged in a sand trap, so I handed him a sand wedge. Epstein closed his eyes and swung quickly, sculling a line drive shot directly at the other players. The ball struck Goldman on his forehead, caromed onto the green, bumped the pin stick, and fell into the cup.

Goldman slumped to the ground…unconscious. Lipschitz instantly leaned over to take his pulse. "He's still breathing. Caddie, run to the pro shop and call an ambulance! NOW!"

OC raced to the pro shop, just as a man hustled to the green from the clubhouse. He immediately lifted Goldman's eyelids and assessed the emergency. Abe's eyes soon blinked a few times. The man identified himself. "I'm Doctor Dinh Dong. Don't say anything, mister. You just had your bell rung. Try to relax, they've called for an ambulance."

Izzy questioned Lipschitz. "Did John Wilkes Booth just shoot old Abe?"

"Ezra's golf ball smacked him in the head." He pivoted to address me. "Sonny, please escort Mr. Cohen over to his white car over there. I can see Izzy's driver standing next to it." I grabbed Izzy's arm and slowly walked him to the parking lot. As we neared the car, Izzy muttered, "I'll take my driver now…his name is Joe Ferr." The driver opened the rear door and helped Izzy into the seat.

By the time I returned to the green, Epstein was apparently saying a prayer in Hebrew, bending up and down over Goldman. An ambulance rolled up the driveway and right on to the grass. Two attendants jumped out and sprinted toward the green. A small crowd, which now numbered twenty people, had gathered around after hearing the commotion. The attendants rested Goldman on a gurney, shoving it into the ambulance.

Doctor Dong motioned to Lipschitz. "He still seems to be a bit dingy. The ambulance can transport him to the hospital as a precaution."

Lipschitz informed Epstein, "Ezra, I'll go with him to the hospital and call his wife when we arrive. I'll let you know what happens later." Epstein nodded slightly.

As Benny Roombach came over to observe, OC questioned him. "Benny, Mr. Goldman was going to give me the Dizzy Izzy pass and now he can't."

"Why didn't you get them from Izzy himself?"

"Izzy never told you he would give me the pass, did he? You're as nutty as he is! Izzy would not know a pass from his ass. Okay, then give me my three bucks for caddying."

"No can do. I can't pay you without authorization from the player. The player has to sign for your fee and he's on the way to the hospital now."

"Izzy can sign for me."

"He's gone too. I guess you're out of luck, Zero."

I questioned Benny about my caddie fee too.

"Spykstra, Mr. Lipschitz is in the ambulance."

"I'll ask Epstein then."

"He's Lipschitz's guest, so you struck out too, Spykstra."

OC was upset. "Just as I predicted…a Jew screw job!"

"Zero, you're suspended for a week."

"Screw you too, Benny. I didn't even say I got jew'd!"

"You're still on probation. Now get out of here after you clean their clubs."

We stripped off our coveralls when we reached the bag room. "OC, Epstein had a weird expression when I handed him the sand wedge in the trap. What club would he use other than a sand wedge?"

"I don't know, but the Jews wandered around in the desert for forty years, so he should know how to play out of the sand."

"And then he skulled the shot."

"What would you expect? He WAS wearing a skull cap."

"On the way home, I'm stopping at the sporting goods store to buy a Shalom ball. Epstein scored another birdie on the last hole, so he was three under par for three holes."

"Why don't you just take a couple of balls from his bag?"

"That would be stealing."

"You weren't paid, so it wouldn't be. I would take a golf ball from Izzy's and Goldman's bags, but they aren't even worth a nickel, although I did keep the naked lady tee."

"They were a bit odd, but they seemed honest. I'm sure we'll eventually get paid."

"Scott, I did learn a few things from the Jews and I even talked in Hebrew…I said 'Nozzle Top'. I think it meant good shot, but doesn't make sense to me. Of course, nearly everything that Izzy said today didn't make a lot of sense either."

I took a detour on the ride home to stop at Flog's Sporting Goods to buy a Shalom golf ball and headed directly to the golf section. There were four or five brands of golf balls, Dot, First Flight, Royal, Acushnet, and PoDo, but nothing labeled Shalom. A young clerk apparently saw me searching through the displays and came to assist. His name, Pat Flog, was embossed on a small plastic tab pinned to his shirt. "Can I help you find something?"

"I'm looking for a sleeve of Shalom golf balls. I think they're a new brand."

"Never heard of them, at least we don't carry them in stock. I can check the catalogue and order them for you. Please come to the front counter."

I watched him peruse a golf catalogue, leafing through a few pages and cross referenced the directory. "I don't seem to see it listed anywhere. Let me ask my father, who owns the store. "Pop, do you know how we can order Shalom golf balls?"

"What kind? Shloam?"

"No, they're called Shalom."

"Never heard of 'em."

I told them about the three birdies with the Shalom ball that I had just seen Epstein play.

"Young man, a few customers have ordered their golf balls with a unique stamp from the factory. I'll bet that's how the ball was marked. We can order some for you."

"No thanks, so long."

I felt like a fool and now recalled the FIB logo on the golf balls that Misor had given to Mellon and Kerchev. As soon as I got home, I looked up the word shalom in the dictionary, and discovered that it was a common term in the Jewish language to convey peace or a warm greeting. These Jewish golfers really only wanted to enjoy the peace of the golf course garden and treasured their close friendships, vastly different from the foursome of bankers and executives I had started the day with.

Chapter 12

I awoke as Dad pulled the car to a stop in a diagonal parking space in a quaint downtown district. I noticed a small café directly through the windshield with a large hand painted sign…ELLSWORTH CAFE in large orange and black letters. It had the traditional friendly appeal of a small family restaurant with red and white checked curtains covering the top half of the windows. A hand-painted cardboard poster that stated WELCOME was prominently displayed on the front door. I looked down the street and saw a few businesses with the same town name, concluding we had stopped for lunch in Ellsworth, Wisconsin.

I scanned the restaurant. There were about a dozen customers scattered around the symmetrical table pattern, and three patrons stationed on stools at a red metal lunch counter. The tables were covered in bright white tablecloths, with utensils neatly placed over orange paper napkins along with black porcelain coffee mugs, clear glass salt and pepper shakers, and a red plastic cigarette tray. An older lady, wearing white apron, greeted us immediately. She had a wide welcoming smile, as if she had known us for several years. She smelled of cigarettes and I stared at her yellow teeth.

"Welcome to our Ellsworth Café. I haven't seen you before…are you just passing through our little town?"

Mom flashed a brief smile. "Yes, we're on our way back from Balsam Lake. Does this road go to Red Wing, Minnesota?"

"No it stays here, but thanks for stopping. My husband, Clarence, and I have run this place for thirty years. We're always happy to have visitors. My name is Sophie and he does the cooking. How about a table right by the window?"

"Sure." Dad glanced at Mom for her approval.

"That's fine as long as there's no smokers near us."

She led us to a square table set for four diners, adjusting the tablecloth so it was perfectly tight, and gathered up the extra place setting. A few seconds later, Sophie returned with a green water pitcher and tall pink glasses, filling them to the brim. She produced three menus covered with plastic sleeves and opened them on the table in front of us. I immediately noted a tiny paper clipped to the top of the right side that listed the daily special of dumpling soup, meatloaf, mashed potatoes, broiled carrots, and cherry pie.

"Folks, the lunch special is right there on the top. Would you like to order something to drink right away?"

Mom wasted little time. "My husband and I will have coffee. I take mine black and he'll have cream." She pointed at me. "He'll have a glass of milk and take this ash tray away...we don't smoke."

I asked for an exception. "Do you have chocolate milk?"

"We sure do!"

Mom glared at me. "No, he'll have regular white milk."

Irritated, I stared down at the table.

"Comin' right up!"

As she turned toward the kitchen, Mom began to lecture me again. "Scotty dear, you should already know you can't have chocolate...white milk will strengthen your teeth. Did you notice that yellowish tint in hers? She's probably been smoking her entire life. That's why we never want you to try it."

A couple seated at a nearby table waved and smiled. "Howdy folks...are you just drivin' through?" The old man had a scruffy, grey beard and wore a cowboy hat. He was chewing tobacco and tried to cover his mouth, but I could see him spit some juice into a tin cup set next to his plate. He reminded me of John Reid, the MVCC course ranger.

Mom seemed irritated with the interruption. "Yep." She answered curtly. I could tell she didn't approve of anyone chewing snuff either.

"Where are you headed?"

After a moment of silence, Dad offered a brief response. "To La Crosse."

"Oh…do you live there?"

Mom rolled her eyes apparently feeling interrogated. "Yep."

"I'm Esther and this is my hubby, Boris. We love to visit La Crosse. The bluffs are so beautiful in the fall when the leaves are changing colors. My nephew, Fred Fellows, lives near there in Coon Valley. Do you know him?"

Dad apparently misinterpreted Esther's question. "I know quite a few fellas. You know, La Crosse is getting to be a pretty big city. I think the latest population estimate will get over fifty thousand when they do the next census."

"Holy Moly…I don't like driving in those big cities with all of the traffic. Main Street, which is also Highway 63 here in Ellsworth, gets a lot of traffic this time of year. The city officials finally had to put one of those darn traffic signals up last year at Main and Maple."

"Uh-huh."

"Well, I hope you enjoy your lunch and your visit in Ellsworth."

Neither Mom nor Dad elected to respond. I felt embarrassed. Those people were just being friendly.

Displaying a wide grin, Sophie lumbered over to our table again. I hadn't studied the menu, since I was hankering for a cheeseburger with fries, reporting my order to Mom.

"What'll it be folks?"

Pointing to Dad she replied, "He and I will have your special and our son will have a cheeseburger with French fries."

Sophie scribbled some notes on her green order pad. "Pickles and fried onions on the sandwich?"

"We didn't order a sandwich…he wants a cheeseburger."

"So, how about a pickle and fried onions on it?"

I nodded my head.

"Will that be it?"

Mom replied. "Some ketchup and mustard. Oh, I'll take a refill of my water."

"Gotcha!"

I began to identify state license plates as the parade of cars passed down Main Street while we waited for lunch to be served. Almost all were from Wisconsin, a few from Minnesota, and one from Iowa. Sophie distracted me when she brought the water pitcher to replenish our glasses.

"So, you're driving to La Crosse, eh?"

Mom seemed to be warming up to her. "Sure are ...we left Balsam Lake around ten, but we were getting hungry, so decided to stop."

"Clarence and I have visited La Crosse twice. The fall is so beautiful there with the colorful trees on the bluffs and the Mississippi River. The traffic gave Clarence a headache each time, so we haven't gone back for several years."

'Yeah...seems like there are more cars every day and some drivers are really reckless. We nearly got in an accident last week, when some guy turned right in front of us without even stopping at a red light. Milton had to slam on his breaks and I bumped my head against the dash board."

"Anyone can get a driver's license these days. I've never needed to get one, since I can almost walk to everyplace in Ellsworth if Clarence can't drive me."

"I don't have a license either. I had a learner's permit once, but got too nervous."

"Let me see if your lunch is ready."

She was back shortly, placing two small soup bowls, filled with steaming creamy broth and one dumpling, in front of my parents. After handing out spoons, she also produced three warm buns and a bright yellow square chunk of butter, which was rock hard. I severed a few miniature slices off the block by cutting off the corners, futilely trying to adhere them to my white roll by pressing firmly with a knife. A few minutes later, Sophie returned, balancing three blue plates in her left hand and a coffee urn in her right.

"Two specials and a cheeseburger. How 'bout more coffee?"

"Yes, please." Mom must like their coffee, as she rarely uses that word. Sophie returned thirty seconds later with three small plates with triangular shaped slices of warm cherry pie.

"I sure hope you like my cherry pie. I just baked it this morning. I brought a little piece for your son, but they'll be no charge."

"Thanks…Sure smells good!"

Suddenly, a siren blared outside. I stretched my neck to get better view down the street and saw a couple of men run past the café. I checked the other direction and could see dark smoke drifting on the horizon, at least four blocks away.

Sophie shouted to Clarence, who opened the swinging kitchen door. "Oh my, Clarence! Do you hear the fire whistle back there? Better get runnin' to get your gear on!"

Clarence tore off his discolored apron and reached for a red fireman's hat on the shelf. He shuffled past our table and sprung open the door. "Dear, hopefully that's just a false alarm."

"Folks, that's the alert for our volunteer fire department. Clarence has been on the team since he was a teenager and he's the lieutenant. I told him that he should retire, as it's tough for him to get up on the ladders now. But he feels that it's his duty to our community to keep it safe."

Boris sprung up, limped outside, and peered up the street. He stuck his head back inside and shouted at Sophie. "Looks like somethin' burnin' on the edge of town." Turning to Esther, he continued, "I'm jumpin' in the truck and seein' what it's all about." He slowly plodded across the street and pulled himself into an older rust covered Ford pick-up, just as a yellow fire engine approached, blaring its horn. Clarence was in the co-pilot seat of the engine. He waved to Sophie, who was now standing outside the café, shading her eyes to see where the smoke was coming from.

She returned shortly, shouting so all the remaining restaurant patrons could hear, "I guess I'll need to cook for a while now."

We had soon finished our lunch and desert. Sophie made another trip to our table. "Anything else, friends?"

"Nope, just the check please."

She plucked the pencil from beneath her right her and quickly added up the bill, handing it to Dad. He spent a minute to double check her math. "I can't quite read your handwriting. Is that three twenty-five or three thirty-five?"

"Three twenty-five."

Dad snagged his billfold from his left back pocket and carefully counted three single dollar bills. He reached for the rubber coin holder that was stamped FIRST NATIONAL BANK on the white cover. He squeezed it in his palm and plucked out one quarter, placing it on top of the green bills.

"Thanks folks...come back again and have a pleasant drive down to La Crosse."

"We enjoyed your lunch and the pie was delicious. Good DAY!" Mom proved that she could be gracious and appreciative when she wanted to.

I nestled into the back seat of the car again. My train of thought was interrupted as Dad shifted gears and backed the Plymouth onto Main Street and pointed the car in the direction of the smoke. Within four blocks, I spotted the back of the fire engine. A large wooden shed had burned to the ground and was smoldering. The firemen were using shovels to separate the ashen planks and Clarence was pointing to some remaining hot spots. Dad stepped on the gas pedal and we soon reached the edge of Ellsworth. He pulled into to a gas station and a tall, young attendant, sporting a grey uniform and matching baseball cap, ran from the counter area to the pump island.

I rolled down the window all the way to listen to the conversation.

"Good afternoon, sir. What'll it be?"

"Fill it up with regular. Check the oil and the tire pressure too."

"Yes sir."

The attendant unhooked the hose from the pump holder, opened the gas cap, and flipped the lever up. I could now see pump dials spinning, reflecting the gallons pouring out and the total cost, noting the price per gallon was thirty-one cents. He lifted the hood and Dad bent over, apparently analyzing the oil stick. Satisfied, the attendant slammed the hood down and snagged the air pressure hose and rolled the dial to thirty four pounds. He moved clockwise around the car to check each tire. Satisfied with the inspection, the attendant plucked a wet sponge from a red bucket and began to scrub the front windshield, covered with remnants of dead bugs. Next, he yanked a squeegee from atop a gas pump and pressed firmly on the glass, generating an annoying squeaking sound with each stroke. The fuel pump had automatically stopped at four forty-one, showing fourteen and two tenths gallons of gas pumped. The attendant lifted the nozzle slightly and diligently nudged the dial to four fifty.

"Sir, I rounded it to four and a half...okay?"

"Sure." Dad pulled out his wallet and gave him a five dollar bill. The attendant had a change gadget and punched out two quarters, placing them in Dad's palm.

"Have a safe drive now and thanks for stopping!"

"Bye-bye."

As we pulled away from the station, the attendant waved. I rolled up the back window; leaving three inches of space. It was already a hot afternoon and I needed fresh air without air conditioning in the car. I grabbed the highway map from the front seat, noting that we would cross the Mississippi River at Red Wing, Minnesota to hook up with Highway 61 for the last ninety miles to La Crosse.

I was pleasantly surprised by the welcome locals of Ellsworth. Over the course of the summer, I hadn't met many members at MVCC who were as genuine and friendly as the people we encountered that day. Perhaps I had only met a minority subset of snobs who were preoccupied by their wealth or status as country club members to be polite. The gas station pump and the shed fire immediately reminded me of the caddie yard incident that cold morning back in late April. As I replayed that day's events in my mind, I closed my eyes and quickly dozed off again in the backseat.

The temperature was twenty-five degrees and I had taken Mom's advice to wear gloves, a heavier coat, and a sweater, but rejected her plea to wear long underwear. My eyes watered from the chilly excursion to the club and I was surprised to see the number of caddies who had arrived so early. Jesse, who was dressed in a leather jacket and a stocking cap, had returned from his probation. Most of the caddies were dressed in sweaters or jackets, although Rutt and Buddy only wore sleeveless cut-off sweatshirts, presumably to promote how cool and tough they thought they were.

Rutt was shivering, blowing warm air over his hands and soon started to jump up and down. "I can't stand the damn cold. The golfers won't show until noon, if they play at all today."

Buddy took a deep breath and exhaled a vapor trail directed at Jesse and studied his exhaust pattern. "Hey, my breath is actually turning into ice particles."

"That's bull shit coming out of your mouth, Buddy. Your asshole must be jealous," retorted Jesse.

"Shut up, convict!" A replay of the fight was brewing. Jesse stepped away toward the cart garage, overtly reaching inside his coat and pulled out a silver flask.

Bing interceded. "Jesse, there's no drinking allowed here. And Buddy, cool it...they will suspend all of us if there's another rumble.

Buddy dismissed Bing. "Get lost, Crosby! Rutt, let's build a bonfire in the shack, so we can keep warm. There's a lot of trash lying around plus the stuff in the garbage cans. C caddies, spread out and collect some twigs and dead branches, anything that will burn. Zero, go down to the tennis courts and bring the trash bag."

I headed for the nearby trees and picked up a few broken branches. I found a crumpled Chicken Dinner candy bar wrapper, some dirty napkins, a Kingsbury Beer smashed cardboard box, and some faded yellowish pages from a newspaper. When I returned to the caddie shack, the rookie caddies unloaded their collection of trash.

Rutt picked up the newspaper. "Let's see what's in here."

Buddy laughed. "Can you actually read or do you only look at the pictures?"

"Buddy, I can read pictures in any language. Check this out, here's an ad for an airline to join their Fin, Fur, and Feather Club. If it involves fur and feathers, it sounds like a fantasy destination vacation to chase women. The fin must represent the shape of a lady's rear end. I need to call my travel agent right now!"

"Travel agent, my ass! Let me see the paper." Buddy ripped the paper away and scanned another page. "Here's something for you, Rutt. There's an ad for a finishing school. It says they can make you poised, charming, lovely and confident. They teach posture, poise, figure control, makeup, hair styling, diction, and all the social graces."

"Buddy, I don't need that, but they could hire me as an instructor there."

"Look at this, Rutt. They're seeking law enforcement officers for highway patrol, deputy sheriff, or police department and paying a starting wage of four hundred seventy-four dollars a month. I'm going to tear the form out and send it in. They want your height and weight too."

"Buddy, the minimum age is twenty one. You're only eighteen!"

"Never too soon to be on the waiting list. Hey, here's something which will definitely help you. It's an ad for dance lessons. You danced like a penguin at the last prom."

"At least I had a date."

"But your date looked like a refrigerator with a head and arms."

"Well, I have to admit that she was frigid."

Buddy sorted through the garbage sack that OC retrieved from the tennis courts. "What do you know? Here's a Zero candy bar wrapper. It must be named after you, Zero. It's a wrapper with no candy bar inside…like your head with no brain. Rutt, let's tap some gasoline from the pump to help start the fire. See if you can strain gas from the hose into one of these tennis ball containers."

Rutt surveyed the gas pump. "The neighbors might see me, so I need a few caddies to make a circle around me to give more screening." I joined the huddle and heard the gas trickle into the can for a few seconds. "The can is only a quarter filled, so we'll need more. I'll just break the lock." Rutt found a large stone nearby, slamming the padlock six times, finally shattering it in several pieces. "Give me a few of those tennis ball containers and I'll fill them so we'll have plenty of fuel."

Buddy had already formed the foundation for a fire on the caddie shack floor. "My wilderness training came in handy to build this."

Bing was eager to provide some history. "I heard you were nearly arrested after your winter camp outing in January after some kids nearly froze to death."

"I created a survival test for our high school wilderness club, so I took a few new freshmen out in the woods and tied them to trees. I kinda forgot where I left them. You know, all of the trees begin to look the same in the woods. I gave them whistles to blow in case of an emergency and the idiots screwed up when they dropped them on the ground. They got a little frostbite and only lost a couple of toes. Our advisor kicked me out of the club, but I was ready to quit anyway."

"Real nice, Buddy! By the way, this fire is a stupid idea."

"Crosby, I'm freezing and no one else seems concerned. What about it, Rutt?"

"Let's start the fire. Who's got a match?"

No one responded.

"You gotta be kidding me. No one has a book of matches? Hey convict, you're probably a pyromaniac, you must have some."

Jesse would not even turn around to answer.

"Rutt, he may not be a pyromaniac, but I bet he's an arsonist."

"A pyromaniac IS an arsonist, you moron."

"Bing, I knew that. I was just waiting to see if any of you dopes knew the difference. No one has a match? Spykstra...run over to the gas station over there. They'll have a book of matches."

I recalled that OC had a cigarette lighter. "OC, where's the lighter you were showing off a couple of weeks ago?"

"It's right here in my pocket."

Buddy was mad. "What a jackass! Why didn't you say something sooner, Zero?"

"Well, you only asked for anyone with matches."

"Another reason to call you Zero. Now, hand the lighter over to me."

"It's an expensive lighter, so don't break it, Buddy. My uncle gave it to me as a Confirmation gift."

Buddy had trouble getting the lighter to ignite. "I've used lighters before, so relax."

"To ignite your farts? Do you need some help? Lighters are a little tricky!"

"My thumb keeps slipping."

"That's because your thumb has been up your ass all morning."

"Bing, you can kiss my big hairy ass!"

After a dozen tries, the flame finally shot out. Buddy knelt down and lit the paper near the edge of the pile, which flickered for a few seconds and died out. "Who's the idiot who put some wet stuff in here?"

"You did, Buddy!"

"The twigs and branches are too green to burn. Rutt, hand me the cans of gasoline."

Bing tried to stop Buddy. "No, it will explode."

Buddy pushed Bing aside and poured four cans of gas on top of the pile of trash and kindling, which instantly burst into flames. The caddies jumped away. The flames scorched Buddy's hand, forcing him to drop the lighter into the fire and the combustion of the lighter fluid resulted in a small explosion.

Buddy looked for help. "SHIT...SHIT...SHIT... SHIT...SHIT...SHIT! Get some water, stomp out the fire!"

The flames instantly ignited the table and the wooden crates, climbing to the roof in a few seconds.

"Let's get out of here! Holy shit, I never thought this could happen!"

Bing was frustrated. "Buddy, you never think, you goof-ball. We're all going to be up shit creek."

Zero jumped up and down. "Buddy, you lost my Dupont lighter in there. You owe me a new one."

"Shut-up, Zero. Your lighter had too big of a flame. It's all your fault!"

Rutt agreed with Buddy. "Zero, your lighter ignited the fire."

The flames had now engulfed the entire structure and the flames were extending twenty-five feet into the air, nearly touching the tree branches. Bing ordered me to sprint to the pay phone at the tennis courts to call the fire department. I didn't hesitate, but stopped running when I heard the sirens. Two red fire engines turned into the driveway from La Crosse Boulevard. In a few seconds, they stopped near the edge of the parking lot and six firemen jumped out. They connected the hose to a fire hydrant near the clubhouse and dragged the hose toward the shack, or what little remained of it. The fire captain loped toward the caddies, who had gathered near the cart room. "I'm Captain Closer, is anyone hurt?"

Buddy responded. "I may have burned my hand, trying to put out the fire after Zero ignited it." He pointed at OC.

Captain Closer ignored him and surveyed the area. "Fellas, I see a gas pump over there. Pour some water on it."

In a few minutes, all of the flames from the caddie shack were extinguished, and all that remained was a pile of rubble. After the firemen shut off the hose, the captain bent down to examine the pile and plucked OC's lighter with his gloves. "Hmmm…someone was using a lighter here." He stared at OC. "Is this yours?"

"Yes sir, it's a Dupont, but I wasn't using it." He gestured toward Buddy.

"He's lying. See, it even has his initials on it… MOOO!"

Rutt quickly added, "Buddy is right. Zero started the fire."

Captain Closer studied every caddie, one by one. "Okay, the lighter may belong to this kid, but I hope someone will tell us what really happened here."

No one said a word.

"Well, I'll leave this up to the club to investigate, but I'm keeping the lighter as evidence."

All of a sudden, I heard a lady's voice. "I saw it! I witnessed all of it!" She motioned toward Rutt. "He was siphoning gas out of the hose of the pump into a can. I'm Vicki Dix and I saw him out of my kitchen window!"

I recognized the lady as Mrs. Jugs from St. Stephen's, realizing now her real name was Vicki Dix. She was dressed in a white bathrobe and pink slippers. She had pink curlers in her hair and didn't have any make-up on.

"These caddie hoodlums cause nothing but trouble for us and our neighbors. We're lucky they didn't light our houses on fire."

"All right lady, do you want to file a report with us or the police department?"

"Yes, I certainly do. They've been throwing objects at our house too!"

A police car turned into the parking lot and two officers jumped out...the same cops who had been there two weeks earlier. Officer Constable recognized the caddies. "Didn't we warn you kids about causing problems?"

Buddy wanted to speak first. "We weren't making trouble, Officer. We were starting a small fire to stay warm. Someone threw some gasoline on the kindling, which exploded...and boom!"

Mrs. Dix showed more hostility. "Officer, I will file a complaint. I saw the caddie taking gasoline from the pump. They are hoodlums...gas robbers. This is a citizen's arrest!"

"Oh, I remember you now. I didn't recognize you at first without your make-up. You live in the house over there, don't you?"

"Yes sir, I sure do."

"Did they do some damage to your house?"

"Not that I know of, but they're probably scheming to do that later."

"Lady, this is not your property. We'll first need to determine if the country club wants us to investigate and then, we can ascertain who was responsible for the destruction of private property. We may have you come in and make a statement later."

The officer took three steps back, after she pointed her finger in his face. "I am a member at this club and our property cannot be destroyed by hoods. They stole our gas too. Arrest them, what are you waiting for?" Suddenly, water gushed from the firehose and hit Mrs. Dix directly on her chest, knocking her backwards into the rubble.

Captain Closer screamed. "Shut the damn thing off!"

A fireman reacted immediately. "It's off...it's off! We had the coupler locked down and it malfunctioned!" The fire crew dropped the hose on the ground. The cops rushed to assist Mrs. Dix, who was lying in the middle of the charred ruins, her bathrobe covered in mud and soot. As they pulled her up, her right slipper was still hanging on her foot.

Mrs. Dix was mortified. "You fools, my husband and I will sue you! You will truly be firemen when the city fires you. Give me all of your names. Your bosses will be hearing from our attorney. The mayor is a good friend of my husband too! Look at me, you assholes."

"We're sorry, lady. For some reason, the hose nozzle unlocked...it was an accident Are you all right?"

"Do I seem all right? I'll have to throw away my robe and my slippers too! Where is my other slipper? It must be under the pile of ash!"

Captain Closer kicked away the cinders and debris. "We don't see your slipper anywhere. Did any of you kids see where her other slipper is? The caddies shrugged their shoulders.

The police officers escorted Mrs. Dix to her house. As she awkwardly limped with one slipper on, the caddies were howling in laughter.

Buddy revealed the missing slipper from under his sweatshirt. "Rutt, her shoe flew right to me when she fell. If I return the slipper to VD, I can play the prince, like from the "Cinderella" story, and see if her foot fits. She can give me a big kiss and take me to the ball in her royal carriage."

"Buddy, I don't think so, but you're on the right track though. Instead of taking you to a formal gala, VD can kiss your balls in the backseat of her royal blue Imperial."

"I'm gonna keep it for a while until I think of something devious."

OC added a thought. "Devious, huh? Why don't you think of something bad?"

"What a great idea, meatball!"

"That's why people like to have me around!"

Captain Closer ignored the chatter, as he walked around searching for more clues. "Guys, roll up the hose. There's not much more we can do here."

A large black sedan with a suicide door design, sped into the parking lot. The car looked like a yacht on wheels. The driver parked it in front of a wooden sign with the inscription: '*RESERVED FOR MISSISSIPPI VALLEY COUNTRY CLUB PRESIDENT*'. I noticed the special license plates reading *LAX-MAYOR*, remembering the abbreviation for La Crosse was LAX. The driver nearly tore the car door off, as he bolted out of his seat. He quickly marched to the remains of the caddie shack.

Bing looked concerned. "Great, now we're going to get a lecture from Linus Mayer."

I recognized his name as the mayor of La Crosse.

Mayer addressed the fire captain. "What in the hell happened here?"

"The caddies were apparently cold and decided to build a fire in this structure, or whatever it was. Someone threw a can of gasoline on the kindling, which ignited and quickly spread to the roof and other wooden stuff in there. In the ashes, we found a cigarette lighter, which belongs to one of the caddies. No one owns up to lighting the fire. Let us know if you need us to investigate further. Oh, the lady who lives in the house over there said she saw one of the caddies siphoning gasoline from the pump."

"What house?"

"The white colonial with the green awnings."

"Oh no, that's the Dix's house!"

"I'm not sure, but I believe her last name was Veedee, based upon what the caddies called her."

"Holy Christ!"

"Officer Constable escorted her to their house after we had a little accident here with our hose."

"Accident?"

"Unfortunately, the coupling on the fire house broke and the blast of water knocked her down."

"I hope you're joking, Captain! Was she hurt?"

"I don't think so, but she got pretty dirty when she fell right in the middle of all the crap here. She threatened to sue the fire department. Her husband apparently knows the mayor."

"Captain, I am the mayor! Jesus, she's the biggest bitch in the city! Damn it!"

"Sorry sir, I didn't recognize you without your hair piece."

Mayer's face now turned as white as a sheet. "Holy crap! I drove over here so fast after I got the call about the fire and forgot to put my toupee on!"

"Well, we're ready to pack up here. There's no more danger, only a mess to clean up now."

"Wait a second. Did you say Mrs. Dix saw a caddie take gas from the pump?"

"Yes, she saw them from her kitchen window. She insists on pressing charges, but I told her that would be up the club."

Mayer stared at the caddies and pointed his finger at them. "You god-damn idiots! Why we have caddies here is beyond me. A couple of board members thought the caddie shack was dilapidated and recommended the club build something nice. Well, you will now have a very nice home you can't destroy…a big concrete slab!"

"Aren't you concerned if any of the caddies were injured?"

"Captain, right now, I'd prefer to whip their bare hind-ends!"

OC whispered to me. "I'd take a whippin' any day over the hole-in-one contest. I wonder if he knows the details of that ritual."

The two policemen returned from the Dix residence and walked toward the squad car, where Mayer intercepted them. "Officer Constable, what did Mrs. Dix say? Is she hurt?"

"She's pretty distraught. She threatened to sue everyone. She's extremely upset over her pink bedroom slipper, which was lost in all of the frenzy."

Mayer eyed everyone. "Did any of you worthless caddies see Mrs. Dix's pink slipper?"

OC raised his hand. "No sir, but we'll hunt around. If we find her shoe, will there be a reward?"

"A reward? After what you morons did? You've got to be kidding!" Mayer reflected for a moment. "All right, we'll give a reward of two bucks!"

Buddy tapped Rutt on the shoulder. "Only two dollars? That's nothing compared to what I can cook up later." He turned and spoke much louder to Mayer. "Who should we give the slipper to?"

"The pro shop. I'll tell the guys there. I see George Palmer driving in right now."

The little red sports car sped around the tennis courts. The brakes shrieked as the car stopped abruptly. PRO jumped out and grabbed a golf club from the front seat. He approached Mayer, who was now standing near his car. After a couple of minutes, the Mayor got into his cruiser and sped off.

PRO slowly ambled over to where the caddies were congregated. "Well, you dummies have finally proven how dumb you really are. Clean this mess up now!" He was still clutching the club in his hand. I thought he might fling the wood at us at any moment. He stormed off in a rage and smashed the club on the concrete. The head of the club shattered and flew across the parking lot. As he neared the grassy area of the driveway, he drove the jagged edge of the shaft into the ground and marched into the pro shop.

"Wow, he's pissed!"

"Rutt, how did you expect him to respond…give you a torch award? I warned you guys that this would be trouble. Thanks a lot!"

"Bing, he'll forget soon. Hey, no one got hurt except my hand."

"Buddy, Linus Mayer will always remember this!"

"Who's afraid of Linus Mayer? Shit, he's a loser. He inherited his first car dealership from his father and miraculously picked up a few others along the way. And what a joke when he got elected mayor. Mayor Mayer won the election because a lot of voters thought the combination of the title and name would be funny. Besides, he was running against Wanda Duetsch, the lady with the cleaning business. Who would ever dream of a woman running our city? I could be arrested for spitting." He coughed up a big wad of saliva, puckered his tongue and shot it toward OC, scarcely missing his head. "A guy who needs a huge car shows how insecure he really is. And the ugly rug he wears on his head…who is he fooling? Even his golf partners know he's a chump. His name Linus even gives him away…his commercials are all a pack of lies."

"Buddy, he can still fire all of us and VD still wants all of us arrested."

"Bing, let me worry about VD."

Andy pulled into his parking space and gunned the engine. "I heard the news. Nice job, you retards. Jesse James, I bet you lit the fire!"

"Not this time."

"Rutt, what happened?"

"Andy, Zero started the fire."

OC waved his hand, signaling Rutt was not telling the truth. "He's lying! I gave Buddy my Dupont lighter and he used it to ignite the stuff! Bing can tell you what happened."

"Andy, it was Buddy's and Rutt's idea to build a fire in the first place. They decided to strain some gas from the pump too."

"Crosby, you're a snitch. We're gonna take care of you."

Jesse intervened, "No one is taking the rap except Greco and Ruttledge."

"Says who?"

"My two fists. Don't you remember what happened two weeks ago?"

"Well, aren't you two turning into a couple of homos!"

Andy was irritated. "I've heard enough. I'll deal with you retards later. Rookie caddies, there's a storage garage on the other side of the clubhouse where the ground crew keeps some of their equipment. Bring some shovels and rakes to clear this and roll the trash container over to throw the crap inside."

Several of us trotted over to the garage. I found a light switch and scanned the room. There were three lawn mowers, two wheelbarrows, a small tractor, and sprinkler equipment, as well as a collection of garden tools and hoses hanging on the wall. I opened a door to a small room, which had a toilet and a sink. "OC...what a discovery! Now we know of another toilet we can use! Let's not tell anyone."

I spied a crumpled magazine on the floor behind the toilet, as OC shoved me aside to grab it. "The cover is ripped off, but I think this is one of the girly magazines that I gave to Father Rotsap!" He leafed through the magazine and a page with a blonde woman with very large breasts, fell out. "Yeah, I've seen this one before. Man, with all the white spots, I can barely see the best part."

Out of nowhere, a hand snatched the magazine from OC's hands. Andy had snuck up on us. "What in the world are you morons doing? There's no sex education in our caddie program. Besides, you'll never hold any real tits. All you can ever hope is to see are some pictures of tits and beat off dreaming that you're kissing them. Now get to work!" Andy slapped OC over the head with the magazine and took it with him.

OC, Lance, and Jesse grabbed two shovels, a rake, a wide broom, and a hoe. The Bunkers twins and I dragged the trash bin across the parking lot. The creaking sound was so excruciating PRO came out of the shop to observe, while Andy paced, grimacing at every turn of the wheels. After fifteen minutes, we finally positioned the bin close to the rubble. After sweeping up the residue, our hands and clothes were covered in soot and dirt. Andy came to inspect the premises. "Okay, bozos, that's good enough. Take the stuff to the garage and no dawdling over there. The garbage collectors can pick the trash bin up here on Monday."

Buddy surveyed the caddie yard for a spot to rest. "Do they expect us to sit on the concrete slab now? Our butts won't be comfortable. Let's steal some couches from the clubhouse. I bet they'll never miss them. Pfeiffer, your brother has the keys to the clubhouse, right? He can open the clubhouse on Monday night when the club is closed.

Bing had a better idea. "Why can't you and Rutt build a new shack complete with some chairs and couches?"

"That would take some hard work and money. Besides, we ain't carpenters." They stared at Jesse James. "Mr. Tattoo, you've probably built a few things in the joint."

I've done more things than you will ever know."

181

"I know you skipped our initiation party last week, so you need to make up for it."

"Greco, I heard about your little game. You're lucky I wasn't here. I would have stuffed the golf balls up YOUR asshole."

"Meet us here on Monday night at seven o'clock. You've probably had plenty of experience robbing places, right?"

Bing expressed his concern again. "You chumps have done enough damage to the caddie program already. Now you're scheming to swipe a couch and some chairs from the clubhouse? Where are you planning to put them?"

"Let us worry about that. Just never snitch on us again."

Chapter 13

After hearing Buddy's plan to steal the Club's furniture, I was anxious to find Barney at school the next day, assuming his brother had provided him the details from the night before. With no luck finding him in the eighth grade classroom, I went to the boys' lavatory, and heard him singing "Stop in the Name of Love" in one of the stalls.

"Barney?" Several seconds past. "Barney...Barney...what the hell are you doing in there? Setting a record for the biggest dump?"

More high pitched off-key singing continued.

Finally, I heard a flush and the door latch flip. Barney emerged with a transistor radio held up against his ear. "Spike, what's up?"

"Your voice for one thing. You need some singing lessons!"

"I'm in the boys' choir."

"Only because Sister Seaxburh needed some sopranos...she was even desperate enough to take Franny. Your voice may never change...you actually might be a girl!"

"My brother's voice just changed last year, so I may become a bass any day now."

"Did Jimmie tell you what happened at the Club last night?"

"Jimmie, Jesse, Rutt, Buddy, and Bronco found a couple of old couches in a basement storage room. They carried them to the bushes behind the cart room. Hopefully, they'll be out of VD's sight. If she discovers the caddies swiped some of the Club's furniture, she'll surely have somebody arrested. And guess who will be on the hook?"

"Buddy or Rutt?"

"Jesse. That's why they wanted him there. He's the logical suspect for an arrest, right? We'd better hustle to the music room, choir practice starts at nine o'clock."

The boys' choir sang on one Sunday every month and occasionally at weddings. The choir also sang at funerals, although I was always excused to join the server crew. The girls also had a choir and once a month, they combined with the boys', although were seated separately in the balcony of the church.

Some of the most outrageous antics seemed to occur during choir practice and that day was no exception. When we arrived in the music room, nearly everyone was seated. Barney headed to the far left side of the room, taking his seat behind Franny. I always wondered if Franny could sing without stuttering, or if he simply hummed along. In each section, there were six singers arranged in three rows with paired seats, as the music books were shared. I partnered with Goober, while Gomer sat directly behind us in the bass section. OC, an alto, was seated directly across the aisle.

I plunked down in my chair next to Goober. "Goobs, what's new?"

"I can't wait for graduation. How about you?"

"Let me tell you a little secret." I leaned in closer and whispered so no one could hear. "I'll miss Sister Seaxburh...I even dream about her."

"Must be some real nightmares!"

"More like fantasies. My bed sheets are sometimes wet in the morning."

"What? Wet dreams about Sister Sexy? My fantasy is to get into Carrie Simpson's pants."

I was stunned. Why would a friend concoct a scheme for a girl I had a crush on? I needed to change the discussion quickly.

"What's wrong, Spike? Your face is red."

"Ah, I forgot my homework at home." I lied.

"Call your Mom and have her drive it over to school."

"My Mom doesn't drive a car. She doesn't have a driver's license."

"Huh? I thought every adult had one."

I needed to move the conversation in a different direction. "I heard the nuns at St. Anthony's are a bunch of haggard witches."

"Yeah, my brother told me that the teacher line-up for the freshmen class is a joke and they all have funny nicknames. There's a Sister Drools, who slobbers a lot when she speaks, Sister Winky has a spasmodic twitch in her eye, Sister Crop Duster farts when she walks down the hallway and finally, there's a Sister Snorts, who snorts when she laughs."

"Aren't there any normal teachers?"

"There's a priest who teaches a religion class and I hear he loves to throw erasers, chalk, books, papers, or anything if anyone isn't prepared for class. A freshman football coach has some classes too."

"What's his name?"

"Mr. Baker...he teaches home economics. When a player screws up in practice or in a game, he forces them to come to the school kitchen to make cupcakes and then he smashes them in the player's face with all of the frosting. You're going out for football, aren't you?"

"Do they have two freshman teams?"

We were so busy yacking, neither of us saw Sister Seaxburh enter the room. "Mr. Spykstra and Mr. Kanack...are you interested in talking or singing with us today?"

I immediately looked down at my feet to avoid any eye contact, although Goober was eager to answer. "Sorry, Sister Seaxburh, we were discussing how much we love choir practice."

"Maybe I can find a new song with a solo part for you, Mr. Kanack."

"I don't recall Napoleon Solo ever singing on *The Man from U.N.C.L.E.*"

"I don't know your uncle, Mr. Kanack. I'm suggesting you sing a few verses by yourself."

"Why would I sing alone? I have a horrible voice."

"This is why we prepare here. All right class, open your music books to page sixteen and let's go over the song we learned last week."

I fumbled through the music book to locate the song, "Hail Holy Queen".

Sister Seaxburh held the round pitch pipe to her mouth. I imagined my lips touching hers, although my thoughts were instantly interrupted when I heard the choir singing. She conducted in front of the bass section with her baton and sang along. She then pivoted, making her way toward the sopranos. Everyone was engaged in the song, although Goober was only mouthing the words. OC had now gotten on the floor, crawling to the vacant chair next to Gomer and immediately started to sing "She'll Be Comin' Round the Mountain." I desperately tried to ignore him, but Goober couldn't hold back his laughter. Sister Seaxburh came down the aisle and clobbered Goober on the top of his head with her hymnal.

"Ouch!"

The choir stopped signing.

"Report to the principal's office right now, Mr. Kanack."

"I'm sorry Sister. I don't know why I laughed."

"Is the song funny?"

"No."

I bit my lip and bent down, pretending to pick something up off the floor. Sister Seaxburh was so angry she didn't even notice that OC was sitting in the wrong seat. As she spun to the front of the room, OC quickly darted back to his chair. I winked at Goober as he gathered his books. "Anything to bail out of singing solo, right Napoleon?"

"I need to report to Dr. Waverly for my orders to fight Thrush."

Sister took a deep breath. "Is there anyone else who doesn't appreciate the beauty of music?"

I knew at least ten guys who wanted to raise their hands, but no one did.

"Let's continue with the song. Mr. O'Connell, since Mr. Kanack has been excused, please sit with the basses today."

As OC slid into Goober's chair, I whispered to him, "Please sing the real words. You're funny, but I can't get caught laughing."

Sister Seaxburh sounded the chord with the pitch pipe again and waved her hands to conduct the choir. OC immediately began singing "100 Bottles of Beer on the Wall."

I elbowed him in his ribs. "Enough OC, please shut up!"

I was relieved when OC reverted to singing "Hail Holy Queen", but after a minute, he improvised again, creating his own lyrics. "Hail holy crapper, my throne above, O diarrhea! Hail mother of farts and bad gas, O diarrhea! Blow out all Ye cherubim! Crap with us ye seraphim! Heaven and earth resound the boom! Wipe my...wipe my...wipe my...diarrhea."

I nearly peed my pants and lifted the hymnal to hide my face, as I noted Sister Seaxburh circling the room. She took a few steps down the row separating the altos and basses, abruptly stopping next to Gomer. She whacked his hymnal upwards, smashing his nose. "What on earth is so funny, Mr. Vale? You apparently want to join Mr. Kanack in detention!" Gomer didn't say a word. "Didn't you hear me, Mr. Vale? Pick up the hymnal off the floor and take your hand away from your mouth." Gomer lifted his hand, revealing blood streaming from his nose.

Sister began to panic. "Oh my, what have I done? I need to rush you to the nurse's office!" Gomer tilted his head back, holding his red stained handkerchief over his nose. She took him by the arm and escorted him out of the room.

When they were out of view, OC jumped up. "Let's all have a *Sing-Along with Mitch,* except let's call it sing along with OC! We'll sing the "Do-Re-Mi" song from *The Sound of Music.* The basses can start out with the first verse, the tenors sing the second verse, the altos the third, and the sopranos with the fourth." He ran to the front of the choir and frantically waived his arms. He pointed to the bass group. "Let's begin!"

As soon as we finished all of the verses, OC created his own rendition. "Dough, the cash at the bank....Ray, a fish that really stings...Me, the greatest guy in the world...Fa, the start of a fart...Sow, when you plant a seed...La, a start of a laugh... Tee, a golf ball holder...which will bring us back to dough."

OC didn't care if the words didn't rhyme. He took a bow as the choir clapped loudly. "Now let's sing the hymn that Sister Seaxburh is teaching us." OC blew into the pitch pipe as if he were playing a harmonica. The choir sang in unison, mastering the song as if they had performed it for several years. Sister Seaxburh walked into the room just as the choir finished. "Boys, I'm amazed! I can't believe you rehearsed the song while I was gone. And Mr. O'Connell, I'm astonished that you conducted the choir."

"I must have some hidden talent to conduct the sound of music."

"You certainly do, Mr. O'Connell. Now, please return to your seat in the bass section, so I can hear this beautiful song again."

The bell then rang, ending the choir session. Sister Seaxburh shouted instructions as the boys filed out. "Remember the mass at nine o clock on Sunday. Be in the choir loft by eight forty-five. And don't forget to wear black trousers and a white dress shirt."

OC always had an angle. "I'll wear my white tennis shoes, since she didn't mention to wear black shoes."

"Boys, I forgot to mention to wear black shoes."

OC still had an idea. "I'll put some black shoe polish on my tennis shoes, Sister Sexy didn't say dress shoes."

"One more thing, make sure your dress shoes are nicely polished."

OC rolled his eyes. "YES...yes Sister."

The two of us strolled down the hallway and climbed the stairs to the third floor Science classroom, where Gomer and Goober met us at the door. "How did you make out with Sister Moron in detention?"

"Great! Mrs. Buffoon stuck some tissues up Gomer's nose to stop the bleeding. Then we sat down with Sister Moron and had some milk and cookies and said the Rosary with her."

OC wasn't buying it. "And then she gave you a beer to share, right?"

"After Sister Moron screamed at Goober and me for five minutes, she took out a ruler and smacked our arms a few times. We have to report after school and pick up trash around the block."

"Well Napoleon Solo, you mentioned you were going to hunt Thrush. I guess you meant hunt trash…right?"

The warning bell rang for Science Class, taught by Sister Marie, who we nicknamed Sister Wizard. "Good morning class. Today we will be dissecting a cow's heart with your lab team. Red Owl donated the hearts, which are in the cooler here. The scalpels, forceps, and rubber gloves are on the table. I will come around to help each lab team. Mr. O'Connell, can you open the windows a bit wider? The formaldehyde may cause some odors." OC leaned out one of the three open windows for a few seconds and then raised them as high as he could.

Gomer and Goober were on my lab team. "Goobs, put all your heart into picking out a big one."

Sister Wizard assisted a girls' team, who seemed reluctant to participate in the experiment. The girls were screaming and Mary Henderson was crying. "Poor little cows, how could someone slaughter them?"

OC crept over to the open window and flung a heart out toward the playground. I heard it splatter on the asphalt pavement below, where the second and third graders were having recess. The kids shrieked and two of them pointed up to our classroom. A moment later, Sister Moron burst through the door. "Sister Marie, someone just threw an animal part onto the playground from this classroom! Two kids saw a boy with a yellow shirt throw it through the open window."

"I have no idea. I was helping the girls dissect the cow's heart as part of our science class project today. I didn't see anything."

She and Sister Moron surveyed the room and their eyes focused on OC, who sported a bright yellow shirt. "Mr. O'Connell, did you throw a cow heart out the window?"

"No, I've been working with my team on our science project...see?" He held up a heart.

"Mr. O'Connell, you are the only person in the room wearing a yellow shirt."

"Maybe those kids are all color blind!"

"I don't think so. I'm asking you again, Mr. O'Connell. Did you throw a heart out this window?" She gestured to the front window in the room.

"No!" OC answered confidently.

I saw OC throw the heart from the middle window in the room, so technically he wasn't lying.

"Mr. O'Connell, do you expect us to believe you?"

"You're calling me a liar? I can't accept unjust accusations. I can't take it anymore!" He ran to the window, climbed up on the sill, and jumped.

Sister Wizard fainted, falling back onto the group of girls she had just been assisting. Sister Moron instantly spun out to the hallway screaming. "Someone call an ambulance!"

I ran to the window, observing OC climbing down a ladder below the scaffold, positioned three feet below the window sill. Earlier that morning, I had seen the janitors erecting the structure to clean the brick façade. OC leapt the last few feet to the ground, sprawled out on the grass. We watched as OC cut his finger with the scalpel, splattering blood on his face and arms. He then took a deep breath and bent his left arm behind his back, as a contortionist would do.

The janitors and Sister Moron rushed to OC's aid and a two minutes later, I heard the eerie siren of an approaching ambulance. After it pulled up, the hospital crew sprinted to aid OC. I could hear the attendant shout to his partner. "He's in a lot of pain with a compound fracture...lift him on the stretcher carefully!"

OC screeched and shouted. "I'm not guilty. I didn't do it." Then he seemed to pass out.

The other students had observed the accident and several girls began to cry. Mary Henderson turned toward Sister Wizard, who had finally regained consciousness. "He's dead!"

Goober pleaded to Sister Wizard. "Sister Marie, Father Rotsap needs to give him the Last Rites!"

"Absolutely! I'll get Father Rotsap or Father Jesus."

A minute later, Sister Moron hovered over the back door of the ambulance, genuflecting and making the sign of the cross repeatedly. The ambulance slowly pulled away on West Street toward St. Luke's Hospital.

Most of the girls were still crying, although my friends were snickering. Mary Henderson quit sobbing and managed a few words. "The poor kid is dead and you boys are laughing. You're not going to heaven!"

Goober was shocked. "Oh no! We're not going to heaven? And all the work last year for Confirmation for nothing? I protest!"

The bell rang, signaling the end of the period. The two eighth grade classes emptied from their classrooms and passed in the hallway. Barney had heard the commotion and were curious about what had happened. "We heard Sister Moron shouting in the hallway and then an ambulance siren, but we couldn't see anything from our side of the building. What happened?"

Mary Henderson interrupted. "Matt O'Connell was delirious and jumped out the window to kill himself. He was bleeding everywhere and his shoulder was out of its socket. He was screaming in pain and then he stopped breathing. He might be dead already!" She sobbed as I pulled Barney aside. "OC just pulled the greatest prank ever. I'll tell you more this afternoon."

We got seated in Sister Moron's Civics class, just as she ran into the classroom "My goodness! Mr. O'Connell regained consciousness after the attendants lifted him into the ambulance."

I winked at Goober, who raised his hand. "Did Sister Marie find a priest to give Matt his Last Rites?"

"No, but I said a few prayers over him while he was being carted to the ambulance. He should be ready for heaven. He is in God's hands now, but please pray for him tonight too. Let's pick up on our Civics class where we left off yesterday. Mary Henderson was in the middle of her presentation, which I found quite interesting. Mary, can you continue?"

"Thank you, Sister Maureen. I was presenting my essay on the Students for a Democratic Society, who held a protest in Washington D.C. last week. There were over twenty-five thousand young students, who marched down Pennsylvania Avenue from the White House to the U.S. Capitol Building to protest the troops being sent to Vietnam. The organization, also called SDS, is exercising their constitutional right granted by the First Amendment to protest peacefully for a cause they believe in."

Goober's hand shot up immediately and Sister Moron acknowledged him. "Do you have a comment, Mr. Kanack?"

"Yes Sister. The protesters aren't real students. They are dropouts who hate our government and are part of the liberal left establishment who support the communists."

"Do you have any proof of that, Mr. Kanack?"

"My Dad says reporters have researched their backgrounds and most of them have Marxist connections. They're called Vietniks, and should all be deported for not supporting our President and Congress."

"Mr. Kanack, in Civics class, we study the rights of citizens and what legal options are out there to challenge the democratic system from a responsible perspective. We are not here to judge the membership profile of SDS. Please continue, Mary."

"Thank you, Sister. Free speech is a cornerstone of our Constitution and the Bill of Rights. The Students for a Demographic Society formed their own political party with a convention. Their ranks are growing quickly and they will nominate a candidate in the next presidential election in 1968. They are questioning the direction the United States is taking by waging war on a small country, by sending thousands of young men to die."

Goober nearly jumped out of his seat, waving his hand wildly. Sister Moron reluctantly let him speak again.

"The communists from North Vietnam and Red China are taking over South Vietnam right now and the Russians are poised to invade Florida from Cuba. It's a series of dominoes. President Kennedy didn't have the guts to kill Fidel Castro in the Pig Bay fiasco. And right after Vietnam, the Red Chinese are plotting to cross the Pacific and target Hawaii and then California."

"All right, all right! We're here to discuss our civic rights and not a wild idea about a silly game. You can play dominoes with your right-wing friends after school and study political science in college."

I knew that Goober was eager to debate her further, but he slumped down in his desk, listening to Sister Moron drone along. "In the line of discussion about freedom of speech, let's discuss the career of Edward R. Murrow. Unfortunately, he died yesterday of cancer at the age of fifty-seven. Who in class can tell us about him?"

Mary Henderson was the only student with a hand raised. Sister Moron pointed at her. "Mary, you seem to be the only person here who pays attention to current events. What can you tell us about Mr. Murrow?"

"Edward R. Murrow was a champion of free speech. He was best known for debating Senator Joseph McCarthy about government spies and dissidents in the movie picture industry. McCarthy, who was a U.S. Senator from right here in Wisconsin, argued for their arrest and imprisonment for treason. Mr. Murrow wanted to bring out the truth and dispel hateful journalism in whatever form it took and also had a television program on CBS called *Person to Person*, where he interviewed many important people."

"Very good, Mary. Now, if you boys near the windows can pull the shades, I have a film with excerpts of Edward R. Murrow's past shows in the 1950's called *See It Now*. You will find the program most interesting and for your homework for tomorrow, you will write a two hundred word essay on how Murrow influenced free speech. There is a recent commercial for the Chevy Corvair recorded by the television station in the highlight reel that I couldn't delete, so please be patient."

Goober whispered to me. "She's brainwashing all of us."

The projector stared rolling. "Goober, there's Napoleon Solo! He's promoting the Corvair!" I was surprised to see that Robert Vaughn was a spokesman in the car commercial."

"Why is such a cool actor plugging such a crappy car?"

"Shhhh...let's watch!"

There were five condensed episodes of *See It Now*. I took a few notes to help me compose my essay. The projector suddenly stopped when the warning bell rang signaling the noon hour recess. I jumped up and hustled to my locker and strapped on my lieutenant safety patrol belt.

"Goobs, see you in gym class!"

"I wonder what Jim Nasticks is planning for us today?"

"HA-HA! I get it!"

Chapter 14

The first warm day of spring finally arrived, so I wore shorts and a tee shirt. There were at least a ten caddies signed up on the list by the time I arrived at the MVCC. After scrawling my name on the C caddie list, I ambled toward the caddie yard. "Barney, it seems everyone is here a little earlier each week. Is there a six AM official sign-up time now?"

"I heard its six-thirty."

"I might as well camp here overnight."

Andy rolled up and parked his car. "Mornin'...retards. Kneel and recite the pledge of allegiance...NOW!"

OC started out before the rest of us were ready. "I pledge allegiance to the flag..."

"Not that pledge of allegiance...the caddie pledge that I gave you...dimwit!" Andy was pissed.

Fortunately, I had religiously memorized the list, rehearsing it nearly every night. We lined up, raised our right hands and knelt in front of Andy and we slowly began in unison.

> *I pledge unconditional allegiance to my cool caddie master...Andy.*
>
> *Kiss your player's ass, even if it smells.*
>
> *Tightly grip your player's bag and wash his balls.*
>
> *Laugh at your player's jokes, even if they're not funny.*
>
> *Be creative to help your player cheat.*
>
> *If you caddy for a woman, do not leave her behind.*
>
> *Do not fart on the course, unless the wind is blowing hard.*
>
> *Do not use your player's golf bag as a urinal, unless there are no trees nearby.*

Do not laugh or give instruction to your player, no matter how awful they are.

Do not repeat anything heard on the course to anyone...except to Andy.

Buddy stood next to Andy, listening intently. "Not bad...mutants. But next time, say it with a little more enthusiasm! Bum, how're they hanging?"

"Hanging tough!"

"Line me up with a big tipper today."

"I'll see who's on the tee sheet, Buddy. When do you need to go out?"

"Right away. I've got some plans later." Andy gave him a thumbs-up sign and went to the bag room.

Jesse spoke up. "Bum, I want a big tipper too."

"Andy didn't hear you, jailbird. He's only assigning you to some cheap screw anyway."

"I'm not referring to a gratuity. I want a beautiful lady with big floppy disks."

"Floppy disks?"

"Greco...big floppy tits...a woman with big bazookas!"

"There are six women members who might qualify, but you won't be assigned to a lady today, since women aren't allowed on the course until two o'clock."

"Who made that rule, Greco?"

"Linus Mayer and all of the other male board members."

"The men are fools if they don't respect women." Jesse pulled out a pack of cigarettes from his pocket. He tapped the top of the pack and a single cigarette gently fell out onto his fingers. He plucked a book of matches that were tucked inside the package wrapper. After lighting the cigarette, he inhaled a long drag, and blew out two smoke rings, which hung in the air. After admiring them for a few seconds, he spoke, "Those chauvinist pigs should add some women to the board, or else their wives should go on a sex strike."

Barney was listening intently. "A sex strike?"

"I mean a no-sex strike. Sooner or later, the men will tire of having sex by themselves."

I finally got the courage to engage Jesse in conversation, electing to call him by his formal name. "Dean, what are your plans for tonight?"

"You talkin' to me?" He looked offended.

"Yes, your name is Dean...correct?

"Nobody calls me Dean anymore...it's Jesse. So you want to know what I'm doing tonight, eh?" He thought for a few seconds. "Probably a little muff diving."

"Diving? Isn't the water a little cold for swimming now?"

"I'm not jumping into the river, fool. I'm plannin' to shoot some beaver."

"Where do you hunt beavers?"

"My favorite place is Beaver Island."

My Dad and I go fishing there all the time. I've seen a few beaver houses there. I didn't know shooting was allowed, though it's is a public park with picnic tables and kids' playgrounds."

"I'm not hunting an animal...I'm interested in another kind of fur." Jesse rolled his eyes and threw his cigarette butt on the ground.

Barney provided an excuse for my ignorance. "Jesse, Spike is a little naïve."

"No shit!"

I had no idea what Jesse really meant, although assumed it related to something sexual. I felt like crawling under the concrete slab but drifted away toward the trees. A few seconds later, I was surprised to hear Andy call my name. "Spykstra...you and Pfeiffer have caddie jobs. Move your butts and grab some coveralls."

Andy held an old green bag and handed it to me. "Spykstra, you can have Lou Sparks today. Pfeiffer, you take McAbre. They're playing with crazy Dr. Buffont and Dr. Afreudopolous.

"Barney, why did I get a job so early?"

"I told Andy you should partner with me today. Sparks will only take a C caddie and you'll be lucky if he gives you a tip. Andy calls this a poop loop."

"Do you know him?"

"He's an engineer and owns a firm that designs gauges and instruments for cars. He's a very dull guy, so his friends call him Sparky."

"Who's your golfer?"

"Mortimer McAbre. He's an undertaker and owns McAbre's Funeral Home. People are dying to see him and he never gets a peaceful rest...he can't decide whether it's better to play a golf course or to find a golfer corpse."

"Huh? Are the other two dentists or doctors?"

"No...they're a Greek and a geek." Barney chuckled. "Zorba Afreudopolous is a psychiatrist and his nickname is Bucky because of his prominent buck teeth. Fauntleroy Buffont is an astronomy professor, so everyone calls him Professor Orbit."

"Maybe I'll learn something from them."

"Yes, but nothing useful."

"Professor Orbit is married to Mrs. Buffoon."

"Really?"

As Barney and I patiently waited near the first tee, a tall, skinny golfer approached us, dressed in black from head to toe. He was very pale, as if he had been hibernating in a cave for years He cleared his throat and coughed into his right hand as he addressed Barney. "Son, are you my caddie today?"

"Yes, Mr. McAbre. My name is Tony Pfeiffer."

"How old are you?"

"Fourteen." Barney proudly replied.

"Hmmm…you fourteen year-olds are younger than the kids I grew up with when we were fourteen."

McAbre extended his arm to shake hands with Barney, who reluctantly reciprocated. As soon as McAbre turned away, Barney held his right hand up to his nose and took a sniff. He quickly wiped his hand off repeatedly with a golf towel. "Yikes! Touching McAbre's hand after he coughed in it was awful, much less imagining what he touched in his embalming room. He gives me the willies."

A golfer with a silver beard emerged from the men's locker room. He wore a green shirt, red and green plaid pants, white shoes, and a red cap with an oversized white bill. I shaded my eyes and squinted. "Barney, is that Sparks?"

"No, it's Santa Claus. He's a guest today from The North Pole Golf Club."

I thought I would offer something clever. "Barney, where's Vixen, Prancer, Dancer, Cupid and the rest of the reindeer then?"

"Vixen? I always wondered if Santa had a hot girlfriend."

"Barney, you can tell me your theory later. Is he Sparks?"

"Yup!"

Sparks walked right up to me and addressed me in a monotone. "Hello, my name is Lou Sparks. Are you my caddie?"

"Yes sir. My name is Scott. Nice to meet you, Mr. Sparks. Do you need your putter to practice?"

"Yes, I will putt, but first hand me the putting invention instrument which I've designed. It's in the right pocket of my bag." I unzipped the pocket and pulled out a foot-long instrument, which appeared to be a thick ruler. I inspected the miniature device, which looked similar to a carpenter's level. By tilting the little gauge, I could see it was a compass and also measured the angle to the ground in degrees. He picked two golf balls from the bag and ambled over to the practice green to putt. I studied his routine as he laid the instrument on the ground at several angles. Despite all of his effort, he missed badly at every attempt.

Two golfers neared the first tee, pulling carts behind them. One man was short and bald, attired in white shorts, an orange shirt, brown golf shoes, and white tube socks. His protruding buck teeth and puffy cheeks reminded me of a chipmunk, so I assumed he was Doctor Afreudopolous.

The other golfer had an old, creaky cart with a gigantic white bag highlighted by star patterns. He wore polka dot knickers, which hung a foot above his sandals, although he did not wear any stockings. He was overweight and displayed a strange haircut similar to a crew cut, but with a twisted clump of hair, jutting upward in front. His golf shirt had an image of a long telescope, pointed downward toward his crotch, so I concluded he was Professor Orbit.

Professor Orbit spoke first. "Good morning Morty and Sparky."

McAbre answered. "Good morning, Professor Orbit. What's with the hair style? Is that a crew cut?"

"Morty, a little experiment called a screw cut."

"And you have some cute pedal pushers on too!"

"They're called knickers. Old English and Scottish golfers wore those. An NBA team is even named after them...the Knickerbockers."

"What's the NBA?"

"The National Basketball Association!"

"Oh! Is that's the game where the players run around in their underwear and try to put an orange ball in a basket with a net?"

"Yep!"

P. A. Lloyd announced the foursome. "On the tee, the nine-twenty-four group; Morty McAbre, Fauntleroy Buffont, Lou Sparks and Zorba Afreudopolous. On deck, the nine-thirty-two group; Linus Mayer, Lars Dix, Del Casas and Dowd Jones, the fourth."

As Lars Dix walked past, I overheard his comment to Mayor Mayer. "We need to enforce some dress code rules here. These clowns on the tee are dressed like hobos. You need to rein in the caddies too. Did you hear what happened to Vicki last week?"

"Yeah, I heard about Vicki from the cops and the fire captain. We have a board meeting next week to discuss the dress code and the caddie program."

I was anxious to hear more, but needed to report to the tee, where Orbit was in command. "Let's tee off before we hit our mulligans!"

"Orbit, what order should we play today?"

"Morty, let's set our playing order by shoe length. Line up behind my club and let me size it up." Orbit dropped his driver on the ground and the four golfers placed their heels against the shaft. Orbit interpreted the line-up. "Morty, you have the biggest foot, so you're last. Sparky, you have the smallest feet, so you're second last. Bucky, you and I seem to be tied, but I'm wearing sandals, so I'll go first."

"Orbit, I don't understand how you picked the order."

"Bucky, I don't either, but let's play! What a nice morning. If there weren't clouds, the sun would be shining."

All of the golfers hit perfect drives, except for McAbre, who chopped a dribbler a few yards from the tee.

Orbit offered some advice. "Morty, go ahead and replay your first tee ball next."

McAbre grabbed another ball out of his bag, practiced his swing a few more times, and re-teed his ball. From the practice green, Mayer noticed the group was lollygagging. He walked over to check on the delay. "Guys, what's the holdup? We need to keep our tee times on schedule!"

Orbit explained. "Morty is rehearsing his swing since he spends too much time in his hearse." McAbre took another big cut. The clubface barely touched the ball, which caromed off the toe of the club."

Orbit offered more advice. "Morty, play your mulligan over again!"

Mayer was pissed. "What! You're allowing three tee shots without a ball out of bounds?"

Orbit explained further. "Our rule on the first hole is to hit until you're happy."

McAbre laced his third drive well down the fairway, when Mayer mumbled, "Well, I hope you're happy now!"

McAbre beamed. "Yes!"

As the group walked up the fairway, I whispered to Barney. "Professor Orbit seems to be in his own little world."

Orbit drove the conversation again. "Morty, what's cooking over at your funeral home?"

"Matilda Cooksie. We're trying out our new cremation equipment."

"You have a machine that makes cream?"

Morty tried to answer, but coughed repeatedly.

Orbit looked concerned. "Got a coughin' problem?

After managing to catch his breath, McAbre answered. "No, we have over twenty coffins in stock...plenty of models to choose from."

"Good, a corpse shouldn't have to wait for a coffin. What's with the all-black outfit, Morty? I wouldn't be caught dead in it!"

"Arthur Blackman died wearing these clothes. When we picked up his corpse yesterday, his wife told me that she didn't want them and I discovered that they fit me perfectly."

Everyone reached their drives. Sparks was the first to play and pulled the 7-iron. He circled his golf ball three times and finally lined himself up for the shot. Suddenly, he stepped away and took five practice swings. He rotated his cap, surveyed the fairway and lifted his finger in the air, apparently judging the wind. He took three more practice swings and adjusted his cap again. Then he checked his watch. He strode over to me, put the 7-iron back in the bag and pulled the 6-iron. He repeated the routine again.

"Sparky, take your time…you shouldn't rush your shot."

Sparks checked his watch again. "Orbit, I read in a science magazine that a person should concentrate at least five minutes on every job. A golf swing is a job too and it's been about five minutes now, so I'm ready to play."

"Why would a science magazine cover golf?"

"It doesn't, but it gave me an idea to shave the hair on my arms, reducing resistance to increase my swing speed." Sparks finally stepped up to the ball and swung hard. The ball hooked to the left, traveling over the fence and out of bounds.

"Nice shot Sparky, but the ball took a turn for the worse. The wind caused the ball to go left. Drop a ball next to the fence and just play your next shot from there. Those cheap bastards who built this course could have bought more land and then that ball would still be in play."

I checked the flag and the trees. It was perfectly calm. I glanced at Barney and shrugged my shoulders, attempting to understand Orbit's comment.

Orbit, Afreudopolous, and McAbre quickly launched their second shots, all of which landed on the green. They all walked together again when Orbit questioned Morty again. "Do you know who died last Saturday?"

"Elmer Fabricks...he was ninety-four. Elmer had an upholstery business and got sick, but never recovered. They read his will right after the funeral. It was a dead giveaway."

"Spike Jones died last Saturday too."

"Spike Jones? Did he own a nail company?"

"He was a famous band leader that no one has ever heard of. He improvised with sound effects on a lot of well-known songs."

"What songs?"

"I can't recall, but everybody knows them."

"Too bad that I wasn't asked to handle his funeral. I have a perfect casket for a musician. It plays music when you open the lid."

"A music box? What song?"

"A Roy Rogers song..."Don't Fence Me In"."

"I thought you were going to say "Happy Trails", which is a Roy Rogers' song too. Roy sings some great tunes. I'll make a recommendation to the board to pipe in some music on the driving range. Music would help everyone relax before they play. The first classic song they can play is "Home on the Range"."

"Yeah, they can also post signs of encouraging words to help build confidence too."

Sparks finally said something. "Gene Autry's songs are better. They should play "You Are My Sunshine" on the range too."

Orbit thought for a second. "Except on cloudy days."

I dropped Sparks' bag on the ground near the green and whispered in Barney's ear. "No wonder a guy who looks like Santa Claus likes Gene Autry, who sings all of those Christmas songs like "Here Comes Santa Claus," "Rudolph the Red-Nosed Reindeer," "Up on the Rooftop." and "Jingle, Jangle, Jingle"."

Spike, you're a baseball fan, but I bet you didn't know Gene Autry owns the California Angels Baseball Club."

"I thought the Catholic Church owned the Angels."

Barney looked over my shoulder. "You had better help Sparks. He's crawling under the barbed wire fence to get his ball."

I hustled over. "Mr. Sparks, let me retrieve your ball."

"Can you just lift the wire a bit?"

Sparks pants caught on a barb and his pants ripped. "Crap! At least I found my Shakespeare ball. That saved me a quarter." There was a six-inch tear down the seat of his slacks and his white boxer shorts were hanging out.

"Sparky, now you can sing Gene Autry's song "Here Comes Peter Cottontail". Your white cotton underwear is hanging out of your bunny tail."

"Not a problem, Orbit. My wife can stitch them up." Sparks measured two club-lengths from the fence marking the out-of-bounds line and dropped his golf ball on the ground. "I'm hitting my third shot now."

Orbit marched over. "You should have replayed your ball from the exact place where you struck your shot from the fairway." He displayed a book entitled *The Official Rules of Golf.* "See, the rule is written here on page four. Should I read it to you?"

"Don't bother, Orbit. You told me I can drop near the fence line."

"Oh yeah, I'm a forgetful guy. I always think two steps ahead. I also have a photographic memory, although it never developed properly."

"I'll play my fourth shot then." Sparks' pitch shot landed in the sand trap on the opposite side of the hole. He then took a huge swing, spraying a large swath of sand across the green, although the ball didn't move. Sparks swung again and caught the ball thin, screaming directly at Orbit. "FORE!" The ball struck Orbit's huge belly and landed on the green, ten feet from the hole. "Are you okay, Orbit?"

"Yes, I had a gut feeling you might strike me and for a second there, I thought the ball would lodge in my belly. I've seen a player hit a shot fat before, but not a shot that hit some fat. By the way, although you yelled fore, you are lying six because your fifth shot was the whiff."

"You're right, Orbit. I have six strokes now. Now, we're all on the green, but who's out?"

"You are, Sparky."

"I'm not sure." Sparks walked over to his bag and pulled out a tape measure. He asked me to hold the dumb end of the tape and attach the clip on the hole. Sparks explained, "I'm the smart one who gets to read the tape."

I bent over the hole and secured the tape hook on the edge of the cup. Sparks carefully pulled the tape tight over the end of his golf ball. "That's ten feet-three and one eighth inches. Now, I'll measure Morty's ball. "That's ten feet, three and one-half inches away. I was right! You're out, Morty."

I suddenly heard some screaming from the fairway. Linus Mayer drove his golf cart close to the green and shouted, "You guys are holding up the course!"

Orbit took a few steps toward them. "I didn't hear what you're saying!"

"Quit screwing around and get off the green, you numbskulls!"

Orbit lifted his middle finger to his mouth. "Shhhh! You need to be quiet while we're putting. Yelling while someone is putting is not good golf etiquette."

Mayer screamed, "Slow play is not good etiquette!"

Orbit then motioned downward with his hands, as if asking for silence. He turned and shuffled slowly toward the green. Mayer turned his cart around and drove back to where the others were standing on the fairway.

"What did he say, Orbit?"

"Doctor Bucky, he said that we're playing too slow. Everybody is in a hurry these days to play an 18-hole round in less than six hours. Golf is supposed to be relaxing."

Sparks had finished measuring the other distances for putting and McAbre lined up his putt as Orbit offered encouragement. "Bury it, Morty."

McAbre maneuvered his putt four inches from the hole. "I'll mark my ball." He meticulously placed a dime behind the golf ball.

Sparks now lined up his putt using the ruler device. He walked around the hole three times and dropped the device on four different spots. He then jotted a few numbers on a note pad. "I've got this figured out now." He lined up over his ball and squinted, closing his left eye. He brought his putter backwards in a herky-jerky motion and stubbed his putter behind the ball, taking a divot out of the green. "That was an accident. I didn't even touch the ball!" He tried to replace the turf, although the green was obviously damaged.

"Don't worry, Sparky. No one will even notice."

"Orbit, only if they're blind. Let's at least camouflage the spot." Morty bent over the trap and scooped up some sand, sprinkling it over the divot hole.

Sparks finally hit his putt four inches past the hole, dropping a penny behind his ball. He then placed another penny in front, a penny to the right and a fourth penny to the left of his golf ball before picking it up in his right hand.

"Why did you mark your ball so perfectly, Sparky?"

"Orbit, to be certain I replace my ball in the EXACT spot where it stopped. Now, I need to line my putt up and collect my senses."

"Why not? You might miss the putt and end up with a ten. I'll play now while you're checking." Orbit knocked his ball in for a birdie. He dropped his putter and skipped around the green while flapping his arms, as if he was a bird.

"Very clever! What do you do for a bogey? Pull a booger from your nose and eat it? And a booger from each nostril for a double bogey?"

"Morty, I don't have boogers, but I occasionally have dried nasal mucus. When I have an eagle; which I've never had, I glide around the green as if I was a hawk!"

McAbre now awkwardly putted his ball, shanking it a few inches to the right of the hole. As he bent to pick it up, Sparks stopped him. "Mark your ball so I can measure who putts first." Sparks pulled out the tape measure again. "I'm four inches away, Morty is five inches out, and Doctor Bucky is three inches, so Morty goes first."

Sparks' short putt rimmed the cup, finishing two inches away from the hole. He marked the ball again with his four pennies. Orbit pretended to sob. "Too bad Sparky...that putt would have gone in the hole if it hadn't."

McAbre and Afreudopolous tapped their balls into the hole, while Sparks lined up his two-inch putt. As he prepared to putt, I heard a ball whizz over our heads. It landed ten yards over the green. I gazed down the fairway, as Dix dropped an iron into his bag. Another golfer now swung and his ball glanced off the tree to the right of the green. Sparks finally guided his ball into the hole, like a hockey player handling a puck. "Give me a ten, Morty."

"Are you sure?"

Sparks deliberately counted every stroke. "I've lost count. Maybe it was a ten? Well, I had five putts, but I should have made the last one, so write down a nine for me."

As we left the green, Orbit saw Mayer's ball land in the greenside trap. Orbit walked into the bunker, and kicked sand over the golf ball until it was completely covered. He ordered me to rake his tracks, so there was no evidence where the ball was buried. Orbit hurried to meet the other players on the second tee, as Mayer's foursome rolled up in their carts. "Gentlemen, we're playing through."

"Playing through what?"

"Through your group. You're playing too slow. You guys took fifteen minutes to putt out on the first hole."

"Well, we play by the rules of golf."

"So, playing three balls off the first tee is allowed in the rules of golf? We make the rules around here. I'm the Club President and these guys are all are directors on the board. The rule requires slow groups must yield to golfers who keep a correct pace of play. Your group took forty minutes to play the first hole!"

"Show us the written policy in the Club rules."

"We don't have the MVCC policy manual with us."

By now, the next group following Mayer's foursome yelled and whistled. "Mayer, now your group is holding up the course!"

"What nonsense! Listen, after we putt out, we'll hit our drives, so get out of the way." Mayer's group hustled toward the first green.

"Orbit, what a bunch of know-it-alls? They act as if they're roosters who rule the henhouse. Someday, the roosters will come home to be roasted and we can lampoon them."

"Yeah, and we can harpoon them too!"

"You can say that again!"

"We can harpoon them too."

I peeked toward the first green. Mayer was searching in the trap for his golf ball and finally threw his hands in the air. He marched to the second tee box, where we were still standing. "What did you guys do with my golf ball? It rolled into the trap and the chubby guy picked it up."

"Who are you calling chubby?"

"You, Professor Tubby! What do you teach at the college…gastronomy?"

"Astronomy!"

"The study of asses, eh? Perfect!"

"I NEVER touched your ball!" Orbit led our group away from the tee. "Let's go! When they get past us, I'll hit into him, so he won't be the only one seeing stars! Mayer is a car dealer, isn't he? He probably never even graduated from high school and believes Mercury is the name of a car!"

"Orbit, Mercury IS the name of a car! Haven't you heard of the Mercury Comet? He owns the Mercury dealership here in La Crosse."

"I haven't, Morty. Wow…a car brand named after a planet and a model after an icy solar body too!"

"What model car do you drive, Orbit?"

"A 1952 Nash Rambler."

"If you could choose a car model name, what would you choose?"

Obit thought for a few moments. "Uranus."

"I understand car manufacturers build a lot a shitty cars now, but naming a car after a rectum would be too obvious."

"Bucky, you can't believe some of the stuff corpses have crammed up their asses. Last year, a dead guy farted a five-dollar bill out of his rectum. He was pretty old, so I assume he mistook it for toilet paper."

"How can a dead guy fart?"

"Until rigor mortis sets in, the body still has functions."

"What did you do then?"

"I took the poopy five bucks to buy a big box of toilet paper…it was an even exchange as far as I was concerned."

We had reached the tee shots, when we heard whistles from the second tee box. The Mayer foursome was ready to hit their drives, so Sparks and Afreudopolous hid behind a large oak tree. After Mayer's drive settled near us. Doctor Bucky kicked the ball up against the tree, where his next shot would be impaired.

When Mayer arrived, Afreudopolous pointed to the ball. "That's a tough break, Linus. I don't believe you have a shot there, except to punch the ball left-handed toward the middle of the fairway."

"Just my luck. I am penalized for a lost ball on the first hole and now I don't have a clear swing!" His cart partner, Lars Dix, suggested he declare an unplayable shot and accept a one-shot penalty.

"I don't need to take a penalty. I can make this shot. Watch out! I'm going to glance the ball off the tree out toward the fairway." He yanked a 4-wood from his bag.

Afreudopolous warned him. "You're hallucinating if you think you can play that shot."

"You're a head shrink, eh? Why don't you sing some magic words for me to execute this?"

"Okay, I'll sing the lyrics of the "Witch Doctor" song then." Doctor Bucky proceeded to sing two verses.

"Shut up, you chipmunk. You should have Dr. Dreiling repair your buck-teeth!"

Afreudopolous and Sparks moved aside, while I knelt down behind his bag. Mayer took a few practice shots, aborting his swing short of the tree trunk. He finally swung and the 4-wood smashed into the tree, breaking off the head, which landed across the fairway where Orbit was standing. I heard the ball ricochet off the branches above and saw it drop on Mayer's head. It finally came to rest on the same spot where it had initially landed.

"Linus, after my magic words, the ball binged around in the branches and banged on the top of your noggin. Did it hurt?"

"Yeah, it hurts!"

"This will hurt even more! You incurred a 2-shot penalty when the ball struck your body."

"I know that, you Greek geek! Lars, I'm picking up. Give me a 7X."
He inspected his broken club. "Where did the head on my 4-wood
go?"

I told him that it flew across the fairway near Dr. Buffont. Mayer
bolted toward Orbit, who handed the head of the 4-wood to him.
"The club head went farther than your golf ball."

Mayer was upset. "Damn it! I busted an expensive permission
wood!"

Orbit corrected him. "That's a persimmon wood...not a permission
wood! You knucklehead, if you had used your head and taken an
unplayable penalty, you wouldn't have broken your head and
wouldn't have gotten hit on the head. So why don't you head to the
next tee and move out of our way so we can play ahead. By the way,
golf rules state that you can't just pick up your ball. Should I show
you the 'Yousga' rule book? I have a copy in my bag."

"What's a 'Yousga' book?"

Orbit pulled out the book from his bag and threw it at Mayer, who
read the title. "This is the U.S.G.A. rules book...the United States
Golf Association. I don't need to read that...I know the rules! I can
pick up and take a triple bogey 7 for my handicap score."

"Your handicap is your ugly toupee. That cheap rug can easily
double as a floor mop."

"Shut up! I may enforce the dress code rule and order you off the
course for wearing pajamas. You need to wear socks and golf shoes
too."

"I can't bend over to put on my socks or ties my shoes, so I wear
sandals."

"Maybe you should go on a diet or find a valet who can dress you.
Your ass is so large, they can show movies on it. I'll bet you can't
even see your dick anymore with your huge gut."

Orbit was eager to wager. "You're on...ten bucks?"

"You're nuts!"

"Okay, let's bet another ten dollars that I can see my nuts too!"

"Good with me. So, twenty dollars that you can't see your dick or your nuts!"

Orbit pulled a mirror from his golf bag and held it out. "I can see my crotch perfectly. Should I pull down my pants too?" He held out his hand and rubbed his fingers together, a signal for Mayer to hand him the money.

"You need to see them without a prop, fatty. You owe ME twenty bucks! Right...Lars?

"From my legal perspective, Dr. Buffont is technically correct. However, as an independent judge, I would say he mislead you. Therefore, I rule there is no bet."

"Lars, Buffont thinks he's smarter than everyone because he has a FUD."

Orbit looked puzzled. "An FUD?"

"Whatever they call a doctor degree."

"A PhD?"

"Yeah, a PFD."

Dix intervened. "Did one of you guys take a big divot out of the first green? Someone dropped a lot of sand attempting to cover it up."

Orbit had an answer. "Maybe "Mr. Sandman" did it Do you remember that song by the Chordettes?"

"You guys are crazy! You should all be sent to a rubber room in a mental ward." Mayer and Dix sped off.

Our group quickly played out the hole and scampered to the third tee to hit into Mayer's group. Orbit gave instructions to McAbre. "Morty, they're still in range. Aim to the left and you'll be all right."

"I'm not sure. They can take legal action against me if I hit them on purpose. Dix is an ambulance chaser! He even filed a suit last year against his own father-in-law, Stitch Taylor, who is a tailor. Dix recently sued Taylor for using cheap fabric for his torn tuxedo that he tailored for him before Lars gained fifty pounds."

Orbit crushed a perfect drive arching through the air straight toward Mayer's cart, glancing off the side and rolled between Mayer's feet. Mayer looked back at us and stomped down on the ground repeatedly. He then jumped in the cart and was soon out of sight.

We walked along together on the fairway when Orbit started up again. "Guys, did you hear Dr. Dreiling married Ana Una?"

"Dreiling...the dentist? No, I haven't heard about it. Who is she?"

"She's a manicurist at Francine's Fashion & Beauty Shop. After their wedding, she got new name and a-dress. But I heard their marriage has problems already...they're fighting tooth and nail."

We came to the general area where Orbit's ball had stopped. "Where's my ball? It was right in the middle of the fairway! Wait a second...I see something white over there. Mayer mashed my ball into the mushy ground where the top was barely visible. I might need to use a mashie to hit my next shot." Orbit used a tee to dig out the golf ball and wiped it on the seat of his pants until it was clean. "Asswipes!" He threw the ball down and clubbed the next shot to the middle of the green. "I'm going to relax now. Doctor Bucky, did you happen to watch the Kentucky Derby last Saturday?"

"No...who won?"

"A horse named Lucky Derriere. He was an underdog, but was the favorite."

"A horse named after a buttocks?"

Sparks had read about the race. "Orbit, the horse's name was Lucky Debonair. Bucky, you have bigger choppers than that horse!"

"Sparky, I meant Lucky Debonair." He reflected for a moment. "Debonair...exactly like me...stylish, refined, and polished."

The players surveyed their putts, although Orbit's ball was clearly the closest to the pin. "I'm a yard from the hole. " He walked closer. "Well now, I'd say three feet." Orbit stood directly over the ball. "Maybe thirty-six inches after all."

"Sparky, your ball is just off the green, so you can play first...there's no reason to use the tape measure."

Sparks putted his ball, which bounced on every rotation, stopping two feet short of the cup. Sparks again marked the ball with four pennies and flipped it to me to clean. The other players finished holing out, leaving Sparks to putt out. Sparks sneezed on the ball, before diligently replacing it on the green. He lined up his putt with his device, consuming another five minutes. He finally stroked the ball, which bounced to the right of the hole. "It looked like the putt was good, but it'S NOT." He guided the ball into hole and examined it. "There's a big booger on it! No wonder the ball didn't roll straight."

Orbit proclaimed, "That's definitely a bogey then, but I would have given you the second putt if you had made it."

Afreudopolous noticed that the golfers on the fairway had been waiting for our group to finish putting. "Orbit, we better let the next group play through."

"That's Professor Parc's group. He's a science professor at La Crosse College too. Okay, but since we're waiting, did any of you happen to see the new Elvis movie?"

"Who is Elvis?"

"Doctor Bucky, you don't know who Elvis Presley is? He's my favorite singer! His latest movie, *Girl Happy,* just came out."

"Is the film about a gay girl?"

"No, Bucky. Elvis has a band at a Chicago nightclub, whose owner hires him to go to Fort Lauderdale to watch over his daughter, played by Shelley Fabares, on her spring break. She falls for Elvis, who is happy because he finally gets the girl."

"Does Shelley Fabares play the girl on *The Donna Reed Show* and sang "Johnny Angel"? If she fell for Elvis Presley, did she sing Elvis Angel in the movie?"

"No, Bucky. But Elvis sings a great song in the movie called "Do the Clam." The song recently got to number sixteen on the top singles list." He hummed for a few seconds and launched into his recollection of the lyrics.

"Dig in her clam…really"

"Yep."

The following group neared the tee. "Hello Professor Parc?"

"Hello Professor Orbit. The whole course is backed up…your group is suffering from golf constipation! We've only played three holes in an hour and a half. You need an enema."

"We already made enemies with Mayer's group. We let them play through even they were bumbling around with penalty shots, broken clubs, and making bets."

"Doesn't sound the way they normally play. We schedule our tee time right after them every Saturday morning, since we know they play fast. I can see them way ahead now on the 6th hole. Thanks for letting us play through."

"Don't rush, we're enjoying the clouds. Hey… speaking of constipation, how's your feces research going?"

"My students are overflowing me with samples…I might have to flush the entire project." Parc's group quickly hit their tee shots and walked down the fairway.

"Orbit, why are sub-par scores in golf all named after birds?"

"Good question, Doctor Bucky. You already know about a birdie and an eagle, but a double eagle is called an albatross and a condor is named for a hole-in-one on a par five. So, a par must be short for a parrot or a parakeet. There must be bird names for scores worse than par too. A bogey is likely called a cock, a double bogey a cockatoo, a triple bogey a peacock, a quadruple bogey a woodpecker, and a quintuple bogey is probably a nuthatch. Those names are scores for only men though."

"There are bird names for women's scores too?"

"Yeah...a swallow, a bushtit, a spotted shag, and a booby. Haven't you heard a women golfer say she had a booby, a tit, or a shag?"

"Um...yes."

Parc's group quickly played ahead and the fairway cleared. I walked alone with Sparks, as the other players hit shots on the other side of the fairway. I was taken aback when Sparks asked me a question. "Sonny, do you enjoy baseball?"

"I love baseball. My favorite team is the Chicago Cubs."

"Have you ever made it to a game at Wrigley Field?"

"No, it would be a dream though."

"I've been there many times. Wrigley is a beautiful ballpark with ivy on the walls and the stands that are close to the field. The ballpark is nestled in a residential neighborhood and most fans take the train to the game. There are no lights there, so all of their home games are played in the afternoon. And there are no advertising billboards in the stadium either. I sure hope it always remains that way...traditions are important to maintain."

"I've seen the Cubs on TV a few times, but we don't have a color television yet. I listen to the radio broadcasts every chance I get. The Cubs are ten and ten and tied with the Cardinals. They lost 5-to-4 to the Houston Astros yesterday. Ernie Banks blasted a three-run homer and George Altman also connected. Lew Burdette was the losing pitcher. Cal Koonce is pitching for the Cubs today."

"You seem to know your baseball. I played briefly in the minor leagues in the Pittsburgh Pirate organization when I was eighteen before I went to college."

"What team did you play for?"

"The Wichita Falls Spudders in the Texas League in 1921."

"You were born in 1903, so you must be sixty-two years old."

"Correct, you must be good in math, too. Maybe you should consider studying engineering in college. I went to Carnegie-Mellon in Pittsburgh and have a degree in Mechanical Engineering. I also grew up in Pittsburgh and went to Forbes Field often to see the Pirates play. Kiki Cuyler and Pie Traynor were their best players then."

"My Dad wants me to study engineering."

"What field are you interested in?"

"Civil engineering. I'm fascinated with building roads, bridges, and buildings. Was Pie Traynor an engineer too?"

"Not even close. Why?"

"I thought he was nicknamed after the numerical Pi...you know...3.1416."

"His name was spelled P-I-E because he just loved to eat pies. I once knew a guy nicknamed 'Pizza Pie' because he loved pizza."

"Why was Cuyler named Kiki?"

"Cuyler's first name was Hazen and his middle name was Shirley, so he surely needed a nickname. I once heard a story that his first nickname was Purple Hazen when he played in the Minors for the National Vols, whose uniform trim was purple. The name Kiki apparently stuck when he was a Pirate rookie. The veterans tricked him into looking for the key to the batter's box and a key to steal second base, so became known as Key-Key, which was later shortened to Kiki."

We arrived at the spot where Spark's drive had landed. He pulled a 3-iron from the bag and took another series of swings. He finally addressed the ball, which landed in the sand trap to the left of the green.

"Sir, what is your favorite team?"

"I became a Milwaukee Braves fan after the team relocated from Boston in 1953. They won the World Series in '57 and had another chance in '58 against the Yankees. They're moving to Atlanta after this season, so I won't follow them anymore, except for my favorite Braves' player, Lee Maye. Did you know that he sings in an Italian doo-wop group in the off-season?"

We reunited with the other players and Barney near the green. I handed the sand wedge to Sparks, who holed out from the trap.

Orbit was impressed. "Blasted...what a shot! Can you perform a birdie dance, Prancer?"

Sparks ignored him but tipped his cap. Orbit, McAbre, and Afreudopolous putted out and we strolled over to the 5th tee.

I rekindled the discussion on baseball. "What position did you play in the Texas League, Mr. Sparks?"

"Mostly a utility player...wherever they needed me, but I didn't play very much."

Orbit piped in. "I played a little baseball myself."

"What position did you play?"

"I was a catcher, Morty. I was already a little chunky and didn't even need a chest protector."

"They probably didn't have one big enough to fit 'ya."

"Yeah...and I didn't wear a mask or use a cup either."

"That explains why your nose is so crooked and why your voice is so high."

"My favorite team is the Minnesota Twins. They have two cats on their pitching staff...Jim and Muddy Grant. The players have weird names too, like Zorro Versales, Tony Olive, Herman Brewkiller, Julius Caesar, Earl Battery, and Minnie the Mincher. Based upon my telescopic memory, the stars for the Twins are aligning to win the American League pennant this year."

The 5th hole was a par 3 with a pond to the left, which appeared more golden in color than the normal blueish-green. Sparks was first to play, following his birdie, although Orbit burped in his backswing, causing him to hook the shot to the left.

McAbre shouted. "Go right...right...Goldwater...Goldwater."

The ball splashed in the middle of the golden pond, skipped three times, and disappeared.

Orbit shouted too late. "Skip...skip...skip...my darling Lou! I have a sinking feeling your ball is at the bottom of the pond. The ball needed another skip to make it to the other side. Otherwise, a sweet shot with a very nice concentric ripple pattern."

Sparks was not happy. "Morty, why did you cheer for my ball to land in the gold water?"

"I was yelling for it to go right, where Barry Goldwater stands!"

"Orbit... you pig...you distracted me with your untimely belch...and I can still smell it. Shucks, a ball lost that cost me a quarter! Why can't they make golf balls that float?"

"Sorry, Sparky...I can't control my digestive system. You should smell my farts if you think that's bad." Orbit burped again and paused, announcing an idea. "Maybe your caddie can wade in the pond and find your ball."

I started to sweat. "Ah...um...I can't swim very well."

"We'll throw you a life preserver."

"I can't catch very well either."

"The pond is only three or four feet deep anyway. You can't drown in a couple of feet of water!"

"He might sink into the mud and suffocate. If he does, I'll make sure he gets a nice funeral. We'll play Connie Francis' song "Drownin' My Sorrows" and the old spiritual "Wade in the Water.""

The players surrounded the pond, while I sat down to pull off my tennis shoes, socks, and coveralls. Sparks pointed to the spot where he thought the ball had completed its final skip, about five feet from the edge of the pond.

As I stepped in the pond, my right foot sunk into three inches of squishy mud. I put my left foot down and slid a few inches forward. After stepping on a ball, I scooped it from the muck. The old golf ball had a large cut with scummy green algae covering it. I threw the ball up on the bank.

Orbit motioned with his right hand. "Move three feet ahead and to your left and all will end well. You were playing a Shakespeare ball, right Sparky?" Sparks nodded. Shakespeare… Shakespeare…wherefore art thou Shakespeare?"

I slid over and was now standing in two feet of water. My left toe touched another ball and picked up a Shakespeare 1. "Here's your ball, Mr. Sparks."

"Thanks, sonny!"

Bucky Afreudopolous picked up the scummy ball and began to clean it. "The cut reminds me of a smile, so I'll play this ball now to feel happier." He started to hum "When You're Smiling," his buck teeth protruding even more with his wide grin.

I climbed out of the water, mud clinging up to my knees. Barney flipped me a towel, while I sat on the bank and scrubbed off the mud. The players were on the 6th tee, when I caught up with them. I threw the wet towel at Barney's head, splattering his face with mud.

"Boys, let's not argue over spilled mud!"

The clouds lifted and the sun appeared. "Here comes my sun. I knew he would come out if I smiled."

"I didn't know you were a father, Doctor Bucky. Where's your son?"

"Right there…Orbit", pointing to the sky. "You're an astronomy professor, so you should know what a sun is!"

221

"Oh, the sun. Yes, I have studied the solar system for my entire life. You know, ultraviolet light, which comes from the sun, is an electromagnetic form of radiation. Sunburn can happen due to over-exposure to the sun as well as a risk of skin cancer, although it might be much worse if not filtered out by the Earth's atmosphere and the ozone layer. There's no sun tan lotion in my golf bag, so I need to quit soon. I'm afraid of skin cancer, Bucky."

"I don't care if I contract skin cancer, but I sure don't want to get melanoma."

"Bucky, I arranged a funeral a few weeks ago for Allie Reptilian, who you might have known. She contracted melanoma when she was forty-seven years old, but her skin was tough and wrinkled, as if she were eighty-five. I told her husband to sell her skin to a company making alligator boots, although he discovered that he couldn't get much for it."

"Let's cut over to the 9th tee and get out of the sun as soon as possible. We can play down the edge of the fairway in the shade of the trees."

I couldn't believe I got another caddie job where I won't finish a full loop again. Barney was right. This was a poop loop and it wouldn't even be a loop."

Suddenly, all four golfers were in a rush. Afreudopolous and Orbit launched their shots simultaneously from opposite ends of the 9th tee box. Orbit slammed his club into the ground. "Damn, a perfect shot in the sun in the middle of the fairway! Bucky, I wanted to land my ball in the shade. Sometimes my brain doesn't do what I instruct it to do."

"Aim your next shot toward the tree line, Orbit."

"Yeah, but it's challenging to hit a good shot bad when you're trying to a play a bad shot good." After reaching his tee shot, Orbit aimed at a thirty degree angle toward the trees, although the ball caromed off a hickory tree and rolled into the center of the fairway again. "Damn!

Another bad spot in the middle of the fairway. I might even score another birdie, unless I keel over from sunstroke first."

The other golfers had all positioned themselves for their third shots to the green. Sparks was sweating profusely as perspiration dripped down his arms. As he swung, the club flew out of hands, hitting Orbit squarely on the back of his head. He instantly fell to the ground, as Sparks ran to his aid.

"Orbit, are you all right?"

"Sparky, my skull is numb. The more I understand, the less I know; and the more I know, the less I understand, but the future is coming."

"And the future will last a long time. I recall Mayer calling you a numbskull on the first hole. He must be a psychic. Is your cabeza okay?"

"I haven't ordered my beer yet, but I will in the clubhouse."

"I didn't say cerveza! How's your cabeza? You know…your head…how's your head, Orbit?"

"I think my head is still connected." He put his hands around his neck and rotated his head. "Yep, it's still there. Oh no! My arms are already turning pink from the ultraviolet rays!"

Sparks asked me about his shot. "I was watching the club hit Orbit and didn't watch my ball."

"You skulled the shot, sir! The ball rolled between the two ponds flanking the green and stopped ten feet from the hole."

Orbit was lucid enough to comment. "Holy cranium…two skulls on the same shot! There IS something very mystical about our round, Sparky."

"I'll buy you a Hamm's in the men's grill."

"I'll order a ham sandwich too…a ham and a Hamm's!"

"Quit hamming it up and play your shot. Don't you remember about sunburn?"

"Oh yes, the sun. If I could only find my stroke now." Orbit fired his shot on a line drive at the hole. The ball caromed off the top of the pin stick and bounced out of bounds.

"That's a clear message that I should quit. The shot was perfect and still went O-B!"

"Orbit, I noticed that you had a body order problem this morning, so it's only right that you're B-O!"

Angered by the bad bounce, Orbit intended to hurl his club down the fairway. At the last second, he awkwardly hung on to his club, which struck his right ankle. He crumpled to the ground like an imploded building. He rolled around and grabbed his ankle. "Ah...my ankle may be fractured."

"Orbit, let me check it. I've had some medical training."

"Morty, I don't need the kind of training you've received, but the pain is killing me."

"You're on the way to die then. Call me when you get there."

McAbre and Afreudopolous grabbed Orbit by his armpits and pulled him to his feet. "I can probably limp to the clubhouse by myself. I'll use the 8-iron as a cane to brace myself. I might as well start smoking that weed they call marijuana, since my round has gone to pot. Sparky, can you pull my cart to the bag room?"

"Sure, can I push it up the hill?"

"Absolutely not! A pull-cart must be pulled."

"Okay, I sure don't want any trouble with the cart patrol."

"See you guys in the bar."

"Orbit, should I drive you to the hospital for an x-ray?

"No, I've gotten enough radiation today from the sun already. My ankle is feeling better now. I'll start a tab in the bar. What's your number again, Sparky?"

"31416."

Sparks lugged Orbit's cart, while I walked beside him to the green. Sparks positioned Orbit's cart on the crest of a mound above the pond. As he walked away, the cart started rolling toward the water, turning over the bank into the lake. Most of the clubs fell out with a splash as they hit the water. "Oops, I hope Orbit doesn't mind. His clubs probably needed to be cleaned anyway."

"Sparky, the next time he shows up to play, he can put his scuba gear on to retrieve his clubs. It will be a new sport combining golf with swimming, called 'glug.' Maybe you should buy him a snorkel."

"Caddie, you're probably still wet from the last pond, so jump in and fetch Orbit's clubs out of the water. I'll make it worth your trouble!"

I removed my shoes and coveralls again and stepped in the water, which had a cement bottom. I turned the cart upright and counted the clubs. There are sixteen clubs here. That's two more than what the golf rules permit." I turned the bag upside down so all of the water emptied out and several items dropped from the pockets including tees, plastic ball markers, pencils, scorecards, a book of matches from Dizzy Izzy's Strip Club, a crumpled gum wrapper, and a packet stamped Trojan on it.

"Put the tees, pencils, and ball markers in the bag. Throw away the other stuff and the golf rules book too. I'll return the Trojan to Orbit."

Sparks, Afreudopolous, and McAbre all shook hands. Sparks handed me the putter and bent over to store a few items in his golf bag. "Thanks sonny. What's the rate for nine holes for a C caddie?"

"It's a dollar-fifty."

Sparks snagged a notebook from his bag and made a few calculations. "Here's a dollar twenty. That's a pro-rata fee for six holes and a twenty percent tip. I appreciate your help finding my ball in the water and pulling Orbit's bag out of the pond. I'm also awarding you my putting reader device. I've got a couple built in my shop, so it may be a real collector's item when it becomes commercialized."

"Thank you so much, Mr. Sparks."

"Please call me if you are interested in discussing an engineering degree. And one more thing, can you pull Professor Orbit's cart to the bag room?"

"Yes sir."

Barney and I trudged to the pro shop and bag room. Barney was pulling Afreudopolous's cart too. "How did you enjoy that round, Spike?"

"Great! I got drenched twice in the ponds and soaked again when Sparks paid me. What did you receive?"

"I got a buck seventy-five and a McAbre's Mortuary golf ball marker."

"Let me see it." I lifted it closer to my eyes. "Catchy ad here... *'AFTER YOU DIE, CALL US TO ARRANGE YOUR FUNERAL'.*"

"All printed on this little thing?"

I turned it over. "There's more...a phone number... *666-DEAD*. Their address is on there too... *666 TOMBSTONE WAY.*"

"I warned you of all of the crazy golfers here."

"Calling these guys crazy is an insult to the nuts in the Mendota Mental Hospital in Madison!"

We arrived at the pro shop where Bumgardner greeted us. "Howdy boys...Spykstra, you're a little wet. What happened...did you pee your pants?"

"I nearly did when Sparks ordered me to fish his ball out of the water on the 5th hole. Then I had to retrieve Orbit's cart in the pond on the 9th hole."

"Yeah, we saw the comedy from the pro shop and laughed our asses off for five minutes. What happened to the goofy professor?"

"Orbit hit himself in the ankle with his own club right after Sparks' club struck him in the head. He's goofy."

"Orbit is always a little spacey. He could be a cartoon character."

"Andy, he had sixteen clubs in his bag. I counted them after I recovered all the clubs from the pond."

"It's hard for me to believe that Orbit is a pretty good golfer. When he plays in the next match, I'll be sure to let his opponent know to check out the number of clubs in his bag after the round concludes, so Orbit forfeits."

"Andy, I always follow your caddie pledge of allegiance."

Andy thought for a Moment. "Spykstra, I might have a good job for you tomorrow. Can you get here by noon?"

"Sure."

Barney and I walked back to the caddie yard. "Barney, I'm curious why Andy asked me to come tomorrow."

"Who knows? Just be here on time."

"Do you know why Orbit had a balloon in that little packet that fell out of his golf bag?"

"Maybe he's planning to use it in his next erection project!"

"A missile launch related to his astronomy research?

"You might call it that. Spike, you need to enroll in a sex education course soon. Maybe by the end of the summer, you can get learn something here at the golf Club."

I was certainly anxious to learn about sex, but had no clue what Barney was talking about. My thoughts turned to Andy's request to report for duty the next day. The tone in his voice sounded suspicious.

227

Chapter 15

We were cruising on Highway 63 when I realized that the two glasses of milk from lunch had caught up to me. I knew Mom would lecture me about why I hadn't used the bathroom at the gas station in Ellsworth, so I shifted positions in the seat, hoping to stem the urgency. After ten minutes, I was reaching a desperate stage. I grimaced and squeezed again. "Dad, can you pull over soon? I need to go to the bathroom?"

Mom turned to glare at me. "Why didn't you go in the café or the filling station?"

"Well, I didn't need to go then."

Mom was irritated. "I should have reminded you. Milton…can you find a spot to pull over?"

"I'll look for a safe place, but there are two cars right on our tail."

After a mile, Dad slowed down, resulting in a series of honks from the driver following behind us. I twisted around, seeing through the rear window a DeSoto just a mere ten feet from our bumper.

Dad grumbled. "I hate tailgaters."

I heard Dad flick on the turn blinker with its steady clicking sound. He maneuvered the car onto the gravel shoulder, halting near a driveway entrance to a farm. The drivers of the blue DeSoto and the following white Chevy blared their horns as they passed.

Mom pointed to a grove of trees about thirty yards away. "Go quick before the people wonder why we're blocking their drive."

I sprung open the rear door and picked a path toward the trees through the overgrown brush. The prickly bushes scratched my bare legs and a few thorns dug in and became imbedded in my skin. I finally reached the trees, positioning myself away from the highway and unzipped the fly of my grey shorts. I had an immediate sense of euphoria as the steady stream gushed out. I carefully bent down to pluck the stickers from my shins and out of the corner of my eye, I saw something move in the grass below…a brown snake slithering between my tennis shoes. I screeched like a bat and jumped back several inches, urine splattering my shorts and streaming down my legs into my white tube socks. Regaining my wits, I moved a few feet to the right and forced out a few steams of pee until it reduced to a dribble. I zipped up the fly and stretched my tee shirt down, in an attempt to cover the pee stains. Fortunately, I had a hanky in my back pocket that I used to wipe my legs. I slowly made my way back to the car, hesitating with each step, and peering a few feet ahead for any more snakes. As I approached our car, I turned at an angle so that my parents were less likely to see my wet shorts.

Mom leaned out of the window. "What's taking you so long and why did you scream?"

"I was startled when I saw a snake."

"They're harmless. Now get in…we're in a hurry to get home."

Dad steered the car back on the highway and I could see on the speedometer that we were traveling again at fifty-five miles per hour. I pulled up my shirt and rolled down the back window so that the breeze directly hit the wet splotches on my shorts. It wasn't just snakes that I feared…talking to girls, speaking up in class, the transition to high school, punishments from Mom, lighting the High Mass candles in church, and being embarrassed in front of large groups of people to name a few. I thought back to the day at MVCC when I decided to take a huge risk, ignoring my trepidations and potentially detrimental repercussions, a decision that would end up changing my path as a caddie.

"Scotty. It's time to roll out of bed. I let you sleep too long."

"Mom, there's plenty of time, but I do need to be at church early to light the tall candles. I don't like the pressure with all the people watching me."

"They won't laugh at you. A server is a messenger of God."

I thought about telling Andy Bumgardner that... maybe it would ensure some heavenly loops for me.

As usual, the radio was tuned to WZZZ, which played symphony music on early Sunday mornings. I was familiar with a couple of songs, since Sister Seaxburh's Music Appreciation class featured composers such as Beethoven, Brahms, Mozart, and Chopin. However, last week, Sister Seaxburh played Leroy Anderson, who had some entertaining compositions like "Typewriter," "Bugler's Holiday," 'The "Syncopated Clock," and the theme for *I've Got a Secret*, "Plink, Plank, Plunk."

"Mom, I'm going to the golf course after Mass. The caddie master told me I would have a special job today."

"Your Dad needs help with the windows."

"But I promised the caddie master I would be there by noon."

"If your Father has a heart attack, you'll be to blame. Be home by six o'clock...I'm making a big supper tonight."

"If I don't get out on the course until one o'clock, I won't be home until six-thirty."

"Your Father has digestion problems and can't eat late. You tell the caddie master you need to be home by five-thirty."

"That's not the way it works there."

"You tell him, it's the way it works here."

I went to my room and dressed in a white shirt, tan trousers, and black shoes. As I returned to the kitchen, Newsman Hunter Chetley reported on the tornadoes in Minneapolis that killed thirteen people and injured seven hundred. La Crosse was known as God's Country, so I concluded that God must enjoy bitter cold weather in the winter;

stifling heat, overwhelming humidity, mosquito and fish fly infestations during the summer, as well as rampaging floods in the spring.

I arrived at the church early. After dressing in a comfortable cassock, I selected a scepter, pulled the wick out three inches, and bent it at a right angle for lighting the tall candles. In a drawer, I found a book of matches with Dizzy Izzy's Strip Club stamped on the book cover. I wondered if Father Rotsap snuck in there like he did in the Hollywood theatre. I struck a match and the wick ignited immediately. I walked out into the sanctuary, noticing the church was a quarter filled. I genuflected in front of the altar and peered at the six tall candles resting high above the altar, deciding to first tackle the three on the right. I dropped the flaming wick inside the top of the candle and started to pray. "Burn…baby…burn."

Perspiration streamed down my forehead and I wiped it with the sleeve of the cassock. I lifted the scepter and thanked God that the candle was finally lit. I proceeded to light the other two candles in sequence. I shuffled to the center of the altar, genuflected, and successfully lit the three candles on the left within seconds. As I was ready to leave the altar, I noticed the first candle flame had gone out. I initiated my counter-attack, patiently waiting for the candle to relight. I must have pulled the wick out five times, expecting success after each effort. By now, the church had nearly filled and I was certain that the parishioners were being entertained by my struggle to light the candle.

Gomer, my server partner that day, suddenly appeared at the altar, startling me. I turned suddenly and smacked the scepter against the base of the obstinate candle, which tumbled to the floor with a loud crash. Even worse, the bottom two feet of the candle snapped off. Gomer picked up the top part and jammed it back into the base holder. "What were you doing, Spike?"

"I can't believe my bad luck. That candle won't light!"

I handed the scepter to Gomer, who successfully lit the candle within four seconds. Thankfully, the rest of the service went smoothly without any hiccups. But immediately after the Mass concluded, Sister Moron stormed into the server room. "Mr. Spykstra, you owe money for a new candle."

"How much is it?"

"I'll tell you tomorrow at school."

"Thank you, Sister." I said as I stared down at the scuff marks on my shoes.

Sister Moron bolted away, slamming the door behind her.

"Why did you thank her, Spike? You should have told her to stick the candle up her butt!"

"I know."

I left the church and peddled my bike home, dreading what Mom would say. As I entered the house, I knew immediately she was upset.

"Scott, you are an embarrassment to our family. How could you be so careless to knock a candle over in front of the entire congregation?" She slapped me across the cheek. "Go to your room and don't come out until I tell you to."

Raising my level of guilt even higher, I couldn't look at her. I wondered how she could have forgotten about her earlier proclamation that I was a 'Messenger from God'.

I marched to my bedroom and quickly changed into my shorts and tee-shirt. I checked my watch…it was already eleven o'clock. I paced back and forth, waiting for Mom to release me. Another fifteen minutes passed and I finally heard Dad's voice outside my bedroom door. "Mom said you can go now."

I hurried past them without saying a word and quickly rode to the Club. I found Andy in the bag storage room. "Hi there, Spykstra. Why are you here so late?"

"You told me to be her by noon for a special caddie assignment…it's only eleven-thirty."

"Oh yeah, I remember now…glad to see you showed up. I might have something for you later.

"Who am I caddying for?"

"I haven't decided yet. Go down to the yard and I'll let you know soon."

Three caddies were playing poker, straddling a corner of the concrete slab. The Bunker twins and Jesse were sitting under a tree, listening to the radio. "Hi guys! Were there any jobs today?"

Tom responded. "Three guys got out earlier. We're hoping some couples might show up who need caddies. Why are you here so late?"

"I had to go to church. Yesterday, Andy told me he might have something for me around noon today. So, I'm waiting to see."

"Do you really believe that jerk?"

"Well…not really."

The Kinks' song "Tired of Waiting" was blasting from the radio. Jesse was puffing on a cigarette and singing along. "This song should be the caddie anthem. All we do is sit around waiting for a loop."

I was tempted to ask Jesse if his beaver hunt last night was successful but was afraid I would fall into another embarrassing trap. I decided to ask him about music instead. "What type of music do you enjoy, Jesse?"

He took a deep drag from the cigarette and blew the smoke out in my face, causing me to choke. "I'll tell you…ah…I can't recall your name?"

"Scott."

"Scott, I like some country-western tunes, although more cowboy oriented."

"Who are your favorite singers?"

"Johnny Cash and Marty Robbins."

The next radio song on the radio was "Wooly Bully" by Sam the Sham and the Pharaohs.

"I like this tune. The Pharaohs are cool...especially Sam,' Jesse added. "He wears a long robe and a turban on stage. I heard they tour in a 1952 Packard hearse with maroon velvet curtains."

"Weird lyrics though."

"I don't listen to the lyrics to most of the top one hundred songs. They're all pretty phony. Johnny Cash and Marty Robbins have real classic stories in their songs."

"What's your favorite song?"

Jesse drew another puff. "There's so many, but I like "Big Iron" by Marty Robbins. The song is about a shootout between the Arizona Rangers and an outlaw named Texas Red. It has a verse I use in the bars when I'm trying to picking up chicks, only I tell them that I have a big iron in my pants."

"You take a golf club with you to a bar?"

"I carry a different type of club. Oh...you're the kid who is so naïve about sex, right?"

I wanted to confess my ignorance but was too self-conscious. I redirected the conversation back to music. "Marty Robbins also sang "El Paso", didn't he?"

"Another good one."

KORN now played "Oh, Pretty Woman."

"Now that's a great tune, a Roy Orbison recording."

"How about Johnny Cash songs?"

"The best ones are "Ring of Fire" and "I Walk the Line", but my favorite is "In the Jailhouse Now", which pretty much sums up my last few years."

"Now you're in Andy's jailhouse."

"You're right. The vindictive judge gave me a bullshit sentence to suck up to these entitled egotistical golfers."

Our conversation was interrupted with an order from Andy. "Spykstra, come here now."

I bolted to the bag room. "Who am I caddying for?"

"I reffed a couple of your football games and recall that you're a pretty fast runner."

I was surprised that Andy remembered me from the football season and wondered how that could relate to a caddie loop. "Faster than most...why?"

"The troll, Vicki Dix, is sunbathing in her backyard right now. We need someone to pull off a prank. Come inside and I'll show you."

I followed Andy to the rear portion of the pro shop, which had three windows overlooking the lawns of the homes. PRO, Pags, and Robert Condor were each holding a pair of binoculars spying on Mrs. Dix, who was laying on a chaise lounge on her stomach, facing the pro shop. She was wearing a yellow bikini and the band, which normally held the top in place, was untied.

"Spykstra, see the sprinkler sitting a few feet from her? The water hose connects with the faucet on the side of the house. You need to hustle down there right now and turn it on. Unless you are completely careless, she will never see you."

"What?" I was panicked. "Will Mr. Dix or their kids see me?"

"Lars Dix is out playing golf and they don't have any kids."

"How about their neighbors?"

"That's a chance you will have to take. After you turn on the faucet, dart in the opposite direction and don't come back here until next week. Now, take your bike over to the gas station and leave it there. Tell Moe, the attendant, that you know me."

"This better not get me in trouble." I shuttered, imagining the punishment Mom would inflict if she discovered what I was up to.

"Not unless you goof up. Now, hurry before she changes positions."

I sped to the gas station and saw an attendant wearing a grease stained undershirt and shabby trousers. Holding a green gas hose nozzle, he studied the back and sides of a Corvair, searching for the gas cap cover. "Are you Moe?"

"Sure am. What you need?"

As I drew closer, I noted his grubby hands and long blackened fingernails. "Andy Bumgardner says you know him. I need to leave my bike here for a few minutes."

"Yeah, I know him at da golf course. Drop it in da back."

"Thanks, I'll be back in a few minutes. Oh…by the way…the gas cap lid is on the top of the left front side of the car." I had ridden in Gomer's family Corvair before and recalled his dad pointing out the gas cap cover to the attendant when we stopped to fill up.

Moe stepped around to the front of the car, futilely stretching the hose as far as it would reach, but an inch short of the lip. He released the nozzle prematurely, shooting gas on the side of the Corvair. The driver screamed at Moe, who managed to close the nozzle, but not before a stream of gas flowed into a nearby sewer grate.

Moe was an idiot, a complete dipstick. I wanted see what happened next but had to hustle to the Dix residence. I had no idea why I had committed to participate in this stunt for Andy and the PRO, but sprinted down La Crosse Boulevard for a half-block and turned right onto Golf Club Lane. A man was mowing his lawn, so I decided to walk the last thirty yards. I finally reached the Dix residence and crept along the side of the house, quickly locating the faucet. A few seconds would pass for the water to shoot through the hose before reaching the sprinkler, allowing time to retreat before Mrs. Dix could possibly see me. I took a deep breath and turned the knob three rotations and sprung away. Five second later, I heard her scream. I flew toward the edge of the golf course into a dense grove of trees. I raced a hundred yards north, cut down a gravel access road leading to the greenkeeper's storage barn, and loped back to the gas station.

Moe was now changing a tire on a car. "You out of breath…you okay?"

"Not really. I need to leave here fast."

"Rob somebody?"

"No, but hopefully some lady down the block lost her top."

"Her name Ethyl?"

"No…why?"

"A large lady Ethyl come by sometimes for me to pump her."

The only Ethyl I knew was Mrs. Buffoon, but not understanding his babbling, I made my exit. "I gotta go…thanks."

I jumped on my bike and started peddling feverishly, glancing down the street toward the pro shop. I didn't see any commotion, but prayed that Mrs. Dix hadn't called the police again. As I pulled into my driveway, I could see my shirt was completely soaked with perspiration and sweat was streaming off my forehead. I pulled to a stop near the garage, observing Mom planting flowers and Dad painting the trim on a screen.

"Why are you home so soon? I thought you had a caddie job."

I answered Mom. "I had a job, but it wasn't with a golfer."

"What did they ask you to do?"

"Tidy up the bag room and clean some golf clubs."

"Did they pay you?"

"Well, not exactly, at least not yet."

"You need to be paid for that. You could have done some other things here to help your Father. I'm finished planting flowers now, so I'm going to hunt for a four-leaf clover in the backyard."

Dad wasted no time and gave me an order. "Scott, go in the garage and bring out the screens and spray them before we put them on. Then go in the house and unlock the storm windows."

We worked the rest of the afternoon until all of the screens were hung and the storm windows were put away in the garage. Afterwards, I decided to practice some golf chip shots in the backyard until supper time.

On my third swing, Mom screamed through the window. "Don't take chunks out of the grass…they won't grow back! Your Dad has worked too hard on the lawn. Come in here and set the table for supper!"

I immediately replaced the sod, using my caddie training. I stumbled into the kitchen and sorted through the cupboard and silverware drawer to set the table, which took no more than a minute. Mom placed a tray of liver on the table after serving baked potatoes and kohlrabi onto the three plates. I hated her choice of food…she apparently was still be intent on punishing me. I kept my head down and tried to avoid eye contact with her. Dad wasn't talking either. Finally Mom spoke up. "*Bonanza* is on tonight. It's one of my favorite shows. Loren Greene is such a great actor."

"Elsie, his name is Lorne…L-O-R-N-E," he said deliberately enunciated the letters slowly.

"Milton, his last name is Greene…G-R-E-E-N-E and it is not the color." She spoke even slower.

"Elsie, I also want to watch *The Ed Sullivan Show*. Vaughn Monroe, Della Reece, and Juliet Prowse are scheduled to be on."

I decided to add to the conversation. "Maybe one of the British singing groups will be on too. Last week, Ed Sullivan had the Rolling Stones perform. Freddie and the Dreamers, and Gerry and the Pacemakers were on the past couple of weeks, too.

"I warned you not to watch those long-haired groups from England."

"But Mom, everyone I know listens to those bands and buy their records."

"Bands like Guy Lombardo and Benny Goodman will be popular with your friends someday."

"Ick, that's music for old fogies!"

"Are you saying your Dad and I are old?"

"Well, not really, but grandma is pretty old and she listens to those orchestras, like Lawrence Welk. Can I watch a little bit of *Walt Disney's Wonderful World of Color*? They're replaying an episode I missed."

"No! Your father is watching 'Sullivan'. Didn't you hear him? How would you enjoy some hot apple pie?"

"Yes, please cut me a big piece." I was thankful for something I liked.

Mom obliged and added some vanilla ice cream. I asked for seconds and thirds and surprisingly got them.

"Dad, I caddied for an engineer last week. Even though he was a baseball fan, if most engineers are as dull as he was, I'm no longer interested in that career. I'm sorry to disappoint you."

Dad frowned and Mom added, "You should consider a degree in business, so you can become a banker."

"Not likely. I also caddied in a group with two bankers, who were definitely strange."

"You have several years before you need to decide. Your Father didn't know what he would do either, until he found a job as a meter reader for the electric company."

"I was also in a group with a mortician, but that profession seems like a dead end career. The undertaker seemed pretty stiff, like he learned his social skills from his cadavers. The foursome included a college astronomy professor, who seemed to be on another planet, so being a teacher is out too. The other player was a psychiatrist, who would make a perfect character in an episode of *The Twilight Zone*."

I excused myself and went to my room to read a few chapters from my Geography book. We were studying Africa and I came to the chapter on Lake Titicaca. I paused, my mind distracted, trying to create other clever word combinations from the human anatomy.

I clicked on the radio to WPUK to hear The Duke of Puke. The first three songs, "Mrs. Brown, You've Got a Lovely Daughter," "Silhouettes," and "Can't You Hear My Heartbeat" comprised a triple spin by Herman's Hermits. My stomach was upset after eating too much apple pie, so I curled up in my bed to help ease the pains. After farting for nearly an hour, I decided to turn out the light after hearing "Cast Your Fate to the Wind,"…it seemed fitting. A few minutes later, Mom open the door to check on me and I heard a deep her sigh…the bad gas aroma was apparently still hanging around. Fortunately, I had turned off the radio and was facing away from the door, pretending to be asleep. After hearing the door quietly close, my thoughts shifted to the Mrs. Dix sprinkler caper. I was nervous about what I had done. Had anyone seen me run away? Were the cops called? Did the caddies get to see her topless? What reward would Andy have for me next Saturday? I played out dozens of scenarios in my head ranging from being arrested at the caddie yard, to PRO congratulating me. Eventually, my thoughts quieted and I was able to fall asleep.

Chapter 16

Barney intercepted me first thing on Monday morning as I was walking up the school steps to the third floor, where the 8th grade homerooms were located. I expected that he wanted to know about Andy's assignment, so I lied again, telling him that he needed me to sweep up the bag room and move some junk to the garbage containers. I couldn't admit my part in soaking Mrs. Dix, fearing Barney might leak it to someone who could get me fired or even arrested.

"Yeah, Andy had me doing crap for him last year until he finally got to know me."

"Andy seems to despise everyone, even his stooges." I quickly changed the conversation. "I can hardly wait until graduation on Friday."

"Me too!"

My buddies had already started the countdown to graduation months ago. Back in January, it seemed like it would be ages until we were out of St. Stephen's, but now we were in the final week. I felt unsettled, now that high school was only months away. There was a picnic scheduled for Thursday afternoon followed by playground games. Friday was designated as a half-day to clean out desks and lockers, as well as to receive report cards. The Friday graduation Mass was scheduled at four o'clock, followed by the diploma ceremony in the gymnasium. A dinner was planned afterwards at Steven's Supper Club with the expectation that all of the students' families would attend. I knew my parents would never consider joining, since Mom would be troubled with a crowded, smoke-filled restaurant.

We had little homework assigned for the final week, so I wanted to watch more television than normal. My favorite show on Monday night was *The Man from U.N.C.L.E.*, which aired at seven o'clock. My parents always watched *The Andy Williams Show*, where Eddie

Fisher and Wally Cox were the scheduled guests that night. I begged Mom to watch the entire *Alfred Hitchcock Hour*, which aired at 9 o'clock, but she still made me go to bed at nine-thirty.

I was having trouble concentrating in class on Tuesday. The hands on the wall clock seemed broken, as the minutes dragged by. Without a warning, Sister Moron spanked my left hand with a ruler. Her face was merely four inches from my head, staring at me with her bloodshot eyes. "I see you constantly watching the clock. Time will pass, but will you?"

I slumped down in my desk. "Sorry Sister, I can't seem to focus on class with only a few days left."

"Perhaps this will gain your attention, Mr. Spykstra. Write a five hundred word essay on what you learned in Civics class and deliver it to my desk on Thursday morning by nine o'clock!" I was stunned, feeling unlucky to be singled out. I looked around the classroom to see my friends all chuckling at my misfortune.

There now would be little time for watching TV the next two nights, although that evening, I viewed an old episode of *Mr. Novak* and part of *The Red Skelton Hour*. To my surprise, Skelton's show included an appearance by The Rolling Stones. Fortunately, Mom was washing dishes, so she wasn't aware of their performance. After they finished their set with "Satisfaction," I decided to retire to my room to try and formulate my essay. I couldn't concentrate, experiencing a high level of anxiety, so I decided to consult my Magic 8 Ball again.

"Magic 8 Ball, will I graduate on Friday?"

CONCENTRATE AND ASK AGAIN

"Will I graduate on Friday?"

CANNOT PREDICT NOW

"Will I be at St. Anthony's High School in September?"

OUTLOOK GOOD

I let out a sigh of relief. "Will I graduate from eighth grade?"

MOST LIKELY

I treated the answer as a definite confirmation. "Will I discover a girlfriend in high school?"

VERY DOUBTFUL

"Will I ever make the grade at the Mississippi Valley Country Club as a caddie?"

"BETTER NOT TELL YOU NOW

Figuring I had strained the Magic 8 Ball's predictive powers for the evening. I stashed it back in my desk drawer, evaluating whether I should request an Ouija Board for my birthday present as a more reliable prophesy mechanism. I opened the Civics textbook and my notebook and began to regurgitate the highlights of the semester that Sister Moron might appreciate.

The next morning, I saw OC walking down the hallway before class. "Hi OC. I haven't seen you around for a few days."

"I asked my sister to call the school for a medical excuse."

"What did you catch, a cold or a virus?"

"My brother and I caught a couple dozen sunfish, bluegills, and some crappies. Unfortunately, I got sunburned out in the boat, though."

Sister Moron suddenly appeared up the staircase and walked directly toward us. "Good morning, boys."

We greeted her in unison. "Good morning, Sister Maureen."

"Mr. Spykstra, how are you coming on your essay? Remember, I expect it to be on my desk first thing tomorrow morning."

"Sister, I nearly finished it last night. Only one more paragraph to add for five hundred words."

"I'm planning to count every word and all of the spelling had better be perfect. And now Mr. O'Connell, I understand you have been sick for a couple of days." She looked him up and down, paying particular attention to his reddish forearms. "Do you have sunburn?"

"Absolutely not, Sister Maureen."

"You wouldn't be playing hooky the last few days of school, now?"

"I have a rash from something I ate over the weekend. I believe my doctor called it hives."

"Mr. O'Connell, you may still be infected."

"Sister, I don't know, but I told my Mother I couldn't miss another day of school. You know, education is such an important part of my life. I missed your Civics class so much."

"I need to see a doctor's letter."

"Oh, I heard the doctor tell my Mother I was the last patient he would see before he took a trip to Antarctica?"

"To the South Pole?"

"Maybe he said South Poland. Well, wherever it is, he'll be gone for at least two weeks."

"I'm sure your doctor's office can write the letter based upon his medical notes."

"He gave everyone in his office a two week vacation since he was going on such a long trip."

"I'll call your home then and speak to your mother."

"My Mother went on vacation too, but you can speak with my older sister."

"But you just said that you talked to your mother about missing Civics class."

"Right...ah...ah...she called long distance to check on us and that's when I told her."

244

"Hmmm…so I will call your sister, Penny."

"No, she went with my Mother. I have another older sister now…I mean a step-sister. Her name is Maureen. What a nice name!"

"I didn't know your mother remarried. I'm so sorry. What happened to your father?"

"Nothing, he's still around to yell at me."

"Your father can call me then."

"My Father is on the same vacation with my Mother and Penny. They went to Florida."

"How can you have a step sister if your father and mother are still married?"

"Um, we kind of adapted her."

"You mean adopted?"

"Yeah, I meant adopted. Our family adopted her. She was an orphan and we got to name her, like one of those pagan babies."

"I haven't seen her in church with your family."

"She isn't a Catholic…she's Jewish. She wears a yam…I mean she wears a yarmulke. She doesn't feel comfortable in a Catholic Church yet."

"I need to meet her and see if she will consider converting to Catholicism."

"I forgot to tell you, she doesn't speak English."

"What does she speak? I am fluent in five languages."

"I told you she is Jewish, so she speaks Jewish."

"Jewish is not a language, Mr. O'Connell."

"I'll ask her later what language she speaks."

"How can you ask her anything if you don't know what language she speaks?"

"Sign language?"

"Mr. O'Connell, you're pulling my leg, aren't you?"

"No Sister, I would never touch you, especially your leg."

"Well, Mr. O'Connell, I assume you have sunburn from being out in the sun for the past two days. If I were you, I would be concerned about meeting our graduation requirements. I checked and you have missed thirty days. One more would be thirty-one and I would be obligated by the education policies of the Diocese to hold you back in eighth grade again next year."

"Thirty days? That doesn't seem right to me, that's an entire month!"

"Well, perhaps you have actually learned something, Mr. O'Connell. However, only four months in the calendar have thirty days. Don't you recall that old nursery rhyme?"

OC started to recite "Old Mother Hubbard", but Sister cut him off. "Not the one I had in mind, Mr. O'Connell."

"How about "Little Mrs. Muffet", the one where she had to go to the toilet?"

Sister interrupted again. "Not exactly…that's another nursery rhyme, but does not address the calendar, does it?"

"Well, how about "One, Two, Buckle my Shoe?" It certainly has some numbers.

"That nursery rhyme ends with 20, Mr. O'Connell."

"I can make up some lines…27…28, cut the bait, 29…30; I'm pretty dirty."

"Do you remember "Thirty Days Hath September"?"

"Oh yeah, that does sounds familiar. I'll be sure to remember that now."

I figured OC would try to keep the charade up for a while longer, but instead he held up his hands as if he had just been arrested. "Sister Maureen, I can't possibly repeat the eighth grade again! I give up and will confess. I didn't see a doctor and my parents aren't on vacation. I don't have a Jewish orphan half-sister and she doesn't wear a yam. I went fishing with my brother and I have sunburn. But I did have a case of hives, but sometime last year. What can I do to graduate? I can bring some fish we caught over to the convent for you to cook on Friday. Nuns can't eat meat on Friday, right?

"All Catholics must abstain from eating meat on Fridays. You can keep the fish though."

"Well, is there something I can do for some extra credit?"

"You will write an essay too. Since you seem to value education and appreciate my Civics class, write a thousand words on why education is the cornerstone of success and advancement in the United States."

"A thousand words? Why do I have so many while Scott only got five hundred?"

"You perpetrated a series of lies Mr. O'Connell. Do you want to repeat the eighth grade next year?"

"No Sister, thank you for your consideration. I will have the essay done by Friday morning."

As she walked away into her classroom, I started to clap. "That was a valiant effort. You even had me believing the story."

"I'm not sure where I went wrong."

"You should have worn a long sleeved shirt and used some of your mother's make-up to mask your sunburn."

"Any suggestions on the essay, Scott?"

"A thousand words is a lot to write, so use the words 'a' and 'the' as often as you can."

"I guess so. I need to call my sister right now to give her the topic for the essay. I need time to work on my graduation prank."

"What are you planning?"

"I can't tell."

Goober and Gomer had witnessed the hall discussion and were eager to find out what was said. "Your conversation seemed pretty intense with Sister Moron. What happened, OC?"

"I tried to recite a few nursery rhymes, but she interrupted me before I could say that "Old Mother Hubbard" wanted to give her dog a boner."

Goober roared. "Very funny!"

I didn't understand why they were laughing, but pretended to chuckle anyway.

OC continued. "I also mentioned the one about "Mrs. Muffet", who sat on a toilet, dropping her turds away. I also wanted to deliver my rendition of "Pee-Porridge Rot", but I guess she wasn't curious to hear more."

Goober reflected. "Have you ever smelled pee sitting in a toilet for a few days? It's awful. Let's get to class."

Thursday finally arrived. After morning Mass, I delivered my essay to Sister Moron. My class remained in our homeroom listening to the National Education Radio Network, which was piped in through the public address speaker. The topics included the Civil Rights movement, Malcom X, Vatican Council II, and the New York World's Fair. I scanned the classroom and most of the students were gazing out the windows or had their heads resting on their arms on the desks. Goober and Gomer were sleeping.

At noon, we were dismissed to change into tee shirts and shorts for the afternoon games and lunch on the school lawn. Mom packed a chicken sandwich, chips and a green apple in a brown sack. Gomer, Goober, Barney, and I gathered under a shade tree near the playground to eat and plan our afternoon activity.

"Let's organize a basketball game," Gomer suggested. Otherwise, we'll have to play kick-ball, four-square, or chalk a mural on the asphalt with the girls. We can't play softball because Sister Moron thinks someone will get clobbered with a ball on the other side of the playground."

We played basketball until three o'clock, rotating with two other teams. I tore my shirt, having fallen on the pavement twice, with blood stains on my shorts and shirt. When I got home, Mom yelled at me for an hour for the ruined clothes, yet failed to ask if I was hurt.

Graduation day finally arrived. I returned my textbooks, cleared out my locker, and scrubbed my desk with cleaning fluid. Sister Moron also asked Gomer and me to carry several boxes of books to the storage rooms in the basement. Later, the combined classes gathered for the graduation ceremony practice in the auditorium, where we were seated in alphabetical order. Goober confiscated a copy of the program and I scanned it, trying to estimate how long the ceremony would take. I noted that the names of the valedictorian and salutatorian would be announced by Father Rotsap at the conclusion of the ceremony.

After graduation practice, we returned to our classrooms. Sister Moron allowed four students with the highest grade points to bring in LP records, although they all had to be approved in advance. Mary Henderson brought in *The Romantic Strings of Andre Kostelanetz*. Bertha Knudson selected a Montovani album called *Folk Songs from Around the World*. Carrie Simpson chose a Leonard Bernstein record, *West Side Story*. Barney, who finished fourth in class ranking, asked Gomer to lend him his Beach Boys' album, which Sister Moron surprisingly approved, although she made certain there was not enough time to play it.

One by one, Sister Moron called each student to the front of the classroom to receive a report card. She frowned upon reading my name. "Your essay had three spelling errors and two punctuation mistakes. I should send you back to the fourth grade, Mr. Spykstra, but I won't. Please arrange to be a server at the graduation Mass."

"Yes, sister. Thank you."

I immediately checked the report card, which indicated my advancement to the 9th grade. After returning to my desk, I analyzed my grades. There were five A's, two B's and one C. I was crushed, when I saw the C was assigned by Sister Seaxburh for music class. I pondered whether she punished me for my possible hallway indiscretion and began to sweat at the thought. The letter grades converted to an aggregate number of ninety-three percent and hoped that Mom would be satisfied. Class was dismissed at noon, and as I walked out the front door of the school, my mind quickly shifted to the fall. The apprehension of high school began to trouble me again.

I was paired with Gomer as the altar boy team for the graduation mass, officiated by Father Rotsap. The girls were seated on the left side of the church and the boys in the first five pews on the right. The teachers sat behind the girls section, while the parents and relatives filled nearly half the church. As the Mass began, I spotted OC in the third pew, although a few minutes later, he was in the first row, having crawled under the pews. By the time for communion, OC had snuck back to the third.

As the communion service progressed, as usual, I carefully positioned the paten under each host that Father Rotsap picked from the chalice. OC now knelt in front of Father Rotsap. "Corpus Christi."

I looked down to see the phrase 'HI JESUS' stenciled on OC's tongue in black ink. Stunned to see the message, Father Rotsap lost his concentration and bumped his hand against OC's chin, causing the host to pop up in the air. OC leaned forward and caught it in his mouth like a hungry seal. Father Rotsap seemed confused, watching OC prance back to his pew. I cleared my throat twice before he regained his composure to resume the communion service.

After the Mass ended, I tore off my cassock and hustled to the school auditorium, where the graduation ceremony was scheduled to begin shortly. I spotted OC in the hallway, near the boy's lavatory. "OC, that was quite a performance and a nice catch too! Father Rotsap was in a trance when he saw your message. You're lucky Sister Moron was on the other side and didn't see it. You better hope he doesn't tell her. By the way, you still have ink stains on your tongue."

"I've been in the lavatory for the last ten minutes trying to scrub them off."

"I've got a couple of red licorice candies in my pocket that might help."

A few seconds later, Sister Moron stormed down the hallway, nearly running OC over. "Father Rotsap told me he saw words on your tongue when you received the Eucharist. If that's true, that's a mortal sin and you're not receiving your diploma. I don't care if your report card states your advancement to the ninth grade, you will not graduate!"

"His eyeglasses must have been crooked or something."

"I seriously doubt it, Mr. O'Connell. Let me see your tongue, NOW!"

"My tongue? Do you know what that signifies?"

"I don't care. Show me your tongue!" OC stuck out the very tip.

"The whole tongue, Mr. O'Connell."

OC took a deep breath, opened his mouth wide, and stuck his tongue out, but curled up in a U-shape.

"I need to see the flat part!" She was becoming more agitated, as her face was bright red, only three inches from his mouth. She adjusted her wire-rim glasses. "Your tongue is very red and your mouth smells of candy."

"I had a couple of candy licorice for dessert after receiving the Eucharist!"

"I still believe Father Rotsap. Now, Mr. Spykstra, you were helping Father administer communion, weren't you?" I sensed that she was planning to pressure me to rat on OC.

"Yes, I was holding the paten."

"What did you see on Mr. O'Connell's tongue?"

I paused for a second, deciding to lie one more time. "I was concentrating on holding the paten under every host that Father Rotsap pulled from the chalice, so I never saw his tongue."

"I know you are protecting Mr. O'Connell from receiving a proper punishment. God knows both of you are lying. That's a sin!"

I elected to lie again. "I'm not lying, Sister Maureen."

Still angry, she spun around, hustling down the hallway toward the auditorium. Our friends witnessed the entire confrontation from the end of the hall. Barney spoke first. "OC, I can't believe you stuck out your tongue at Sister Moron."

"She wanted to check if I had a case of tonsillitis. You know, like when a doctor asks you to say AHHHH."

Gomer checked the time. "We'd better be seated, the graduation ceremony is about to begin." They marched off, leaving OC and I in the hallway.

"Man, I owe you."

"Glad to help a buddy."

"Scott, let me give you an inside scoop. Don't shake Sister Moron's or Father Rotsap's hands when you receive your diploma. Pretend to sneeze or something, but don't ask me why."

I couldn't understand what OC's warning entailed, but began to rehearse my plan anyway. I took my seat in the last row of students, while OC was sitting directly ahead of me. Sister Moron began the ceremony, introducing Father Rotsap, who recited an opening prayer. Mary Henderson then read a poem she had written, followed by Sister Moron's commencement speech, which bored the restless students. Finally, the time arrived to present the diplomas, as the first two rows of graduates stood and lined up along the side of the stage. Sister Moron announced the student's name, handing a diploma to Father Rotsap, who presented it to each graduate, shaking their hand at the same time.

I noticed OC fidgeting in his seat. He stuck his right hand inside the back of his pants, appearing to wipe his butt repeatedly. OC winked at me as he stood up when his row was called. After Sister Moron announced OC's name, a few of his friends hooted and whistled. She surveyed the students trying to identify the culprits. OC stepped toward Sister Moron to shake her hand, the only student who elected to do so. Father Rotsap then presented OC the diploma and shook his hand for several seconds. I suddenly realized OC's intention when he turned to wave at the audience and bounced down the stairs back to his seat.

As I finally reached the stage, I noted the unsuspecting students ahead of me grasping Father Rotsap's hand. I nearly gagged when Sister Moron licked her fingers to get a better grip on the next diploma from the stack. As Sister Moron announced my name, Father Rotsap reached out his hand, extending the diploma toward me. I snapped it from his fingers and immediately covered my mouth with both hands, pretending to cough repeatedly. It seemed like an eternity until Sister Moron announced the next graduate's name. When I returned to my seat, I noticed a few students to OC's left, smelling their right palms.

I overheard OC mutter to Barney, "My hand smells like poop!"

Barney lifted his hand to his nose and sniffed. "Mine does too…ick!"

After the last graduate's name was announced, Sister Moron handed a manila folder to Father Rotsap. "And now, Father Rotsap will announce the names of the class salutatorian and valedictorian."

Father Rotsap cleared his throat. "I am pleased to announce the salutatorian of the 1965 graduation class of St. Stephen's is Bertha Knudson." Bertha slowly rose from her seat and strutted to the stage, where Father Rotsap handed her the award certificate. When the audience gave Bertha a round of applause, she curtsied, apparently trying to demonstrate her sophistication.

Father Rotsap coughed in his hand, and put it up to his nose. He had a strange look as he coughed a few more times, and then rubbed his right hand repeatedly on his sin fighter suit. He adjusted his glasses. "I am very pleased to announce the valedictorian of the 1965 graduation class of St. Stephen's is Matthew O. O'Connell."

OC sprung up, extended his hands high in the air, as if claiming victory. He awkwardly climbed over the students in his row and headed toward the stage. Most of the boys shouted, chanting in unison, "OC...OC...OC." I was stunned. How did he pull this one off... his grades were among the worst in the 8th grade?

Sister Moron yanked the microphone away from Father Rotsap. "There has been a terrible mistake. Mr. O'Connell is certainly NOT the valedictorian...Mary Henderson is. Mary, please come to the stage."

The boys booed loudly. OC stopped dead in his tracks and held up his hands in the air, questioning whether he had heard her proclamation correctly. OC slowly trudged back to his seat, shrugging his shoulders, signaling disbelief to what had just occurred.

Sister Moron concluded the ceremony by congratulating all of the students. The class cheered loudly as they filed out of the auditorium, while "Pomp and Circumstance" played over the loudspeakers. I glanced over toward my parents, as Mom nodded to me. I waved back.

Outside the school, my buddies gathered in a circle, as Barney took a poll on the graduation dinner attendance. "Is everyone going to Steven's Supper Club?"

I felt embarrassed to confess that I would not be in attendance. "I can't, my Mother has respiratory problems and can't deal with the cigarette smoke."

"Can't you come by yourself?"

"My Mom has a graduation dinner planned at home, so I can't disappoint her and my Dad. They're waiting for me in the parking lot."

I climbed in the backseat of the Plymouth and Mom spoke first. "What happened when Father presented the diploma to you?"

"Oh...I suddenly got a tickle in my throat and couldn't stop. You've always told me to cover my mouth not to spread germs, so I did."

"It still would have been good of you to shake his hand. The ceremony was nice, but why was there some confusion on the last award?"

"Father Rotsap has a problem remembering things sometimes. Are you pleased with my grades?"

"The ninety-three is okay, but that C spoils your entire report card."

"The C is in music, which is not an actual class."

"If you receive a C in any high school class next year, I will make you attend summer school!"

Whenever I accomplished something, Mom never seemed satisfied and Dad wouldn't ever overrule her either. I wasn't surprised at her reaction or Dad's silence, so I simply shut my eyes and tried to think about something more pleasant...OC's palm stunt.

Chapter 17

I was at the golf club by six-thirty and was number two on the C list. Jesse was propped up against his motorcycle and I reluctantly decided to engage him. "Jesse, did you caddie last Sunday?"

"Nope, only two A caddies were called. I was here all day, so at least I got credit for eight hours. The pro-shop needs to certify my time spent here as a condition for my probation. My sentence is two hundred-fifty hours and I've got thirty down now. Andy's shift was over at two and Benny made me wait until four o'clock. Andy won't sign my card, so I have to wait until he leaves or get one of the assistants to sign it. I even had to wait until six o'clock a few times. This is worse than busting rocks on a chain gang."

"You were on a chain gang?"

"Yep…at Waupun."

"Last week, we read a new novel called *Cool Hand Luke*. It's a story about a prison gang set in the early 50's."

"I'd like to read it…can you bring me your copy?"

"Sure…Sam Cooke sang a chain gang song a few years ago too."

"Yeah…they frequently played it in the joint." Jesse held a transistor radio turned to KORN, as Colonel Cobb played "Dream on Little Dreamer" by Perry Como. "Listen to these mushy lyrics…they're pathetic!"

As the song ended, Ham Radio read the weather forecast.

> *THE TEMPERATURE WILL CLIMB*
> *INTO THE MID-SEVENTIES TODAY*
> *WITH A FIFTY PERCENT CHANCE*
> *OF AN AFTERNOON*
> *THUNDERSTORM, SO TAKE ONE*
> *RAINBOOT WITH YOU. IF YOU*
> *HEAR SOME LIGHTNING, BE SURE*

*TO COUNT TO A THOUSAND
SEVERAL TIMES. WHEN YOU HER
THE RUMBLE, IT WILL TELL WHO
MANY MILES THE LIGHTNING
STRIKE HIT FROM WHERE YOU
ARE. EVERY THOUSAND COUNTS
AS A MILE. IF YOU SEE A CRACK
OF LIGHTNING AND NEVER HEAR
THUNDER, YOU'VE PROBABLY
BEEN STRUCK AND ARE LIKELY
DEAD, SO THERE'S NO REASON TO
KEEP COUNTING.*

"That radio clown has shit for brains! I heard he is the nephew of the radio station owner, which explains why he's still allowed on the air. At least that DJ, Cobb, has trimmed down his gaffes."

Ham Radio continued,

*AND HERE'S THE NEWS FOR
SATURDAY, MAY FIFTEENTH.
POLICE ARE INVESTIGATING AN
INCIDENT AT JEFFERSON HIGH
SCHOOL YESTERDAY. A
FRESHMAN REPORTED TO
SCHOOL OFFICIALS THAT HE
RECEIVED A WEDGIE IN ONE OF
THE BOYS' LAVATORIES. THE
CULPRITS ALLEGEDLY PULLED
THE FRESHMAN'S UNDERWEAR
OVER HIS PRIVATE PARTS UNTIL
IT RIPPED APART. THE
UNDERWEAR FRAGMENTS WERE
LATER FOUND FLYING ON THE
FLAG POLE IN FRONT OF THE
SCHOOL. THE POLICE ARE STILL
INVESTIGATING.*

*POLLY DUCKWORTH REPORTED
HER PARROT, QUACKERS, FLEW
OUT HER FRONT DOOR BETWEEN
EIGHT AND NINE O'CLOCK LAST
NIGHT IN THE NINE HUNDRED
BLOCK OF VULTURE LANE.
QUACKERS IS GREEN AND WILL
ANSWER TO THE NAME
QUACKERS. SO IF ANYONE SEES A
GREEN PARROT, PLEASE ASK IF IT
WANTS A CRACKER AND CALL
MRS. DUCKWORTH AT 272-2537.*

*FOR INTERNATIONAL NEWS,
THE...HMMM...K...K...K...KAN-NES
FILM FESTIVAL IS WRAPPING UP
TODAY IN K...K...K...KAN-NES.*

Radio gave up on the pronunciation of the word.

"Colonel, maybe they mean Kansas."

*"Ham, the name of the city is
pronounced 'Kan'...it's in France."*

*"They named a film festival after a
toilet?"*

*"It's a famous film festival, which
attracts the top movie people in the
world."*

ANYWAY...THE 'GRAND PRICKS
DU FESTIVAL INTERNATIONAL'
WAS AWARDED TO *THE K'NACK
AND HOW TO GET IT.*

Cobb stopped him suddenly.

*"Ham, it's pronounced Grand
'PREE', not Grand Pricks!"*

"Are you sure? The word on the sheet is spelled P-R-I-X."

"Believe me, the festival is pronounced Grand PREE and the movie title starts with 'nack'...the 'k' is silent."

WHATEVER IT'S CALLED, THE K'NACK IS A COMEDY. THREE GUYS VIE FOR A GIRL WHO MOVES TO LONDON. IT MUST BE LONDON, ENGLAND SINCE IT'S AN ENGLISH FILM.

AND NOW A WORD FROM A SPONSOR. ARE YOU HUNGRY FOR SOME FRESH MEAT? IF SO, MEET STARVING FRIENDS AT STEVEN'S SUPPER CLUB. THEY POUND THEIR MEAT UNTIL IT IS TENDER AND JUICY. MAYBE YOU'RE JUST HANKERING FOR A TASTY HAMBOOGER,. ALTHOUGH STEVEN'S ALSO HAS A WIDE SELECTION OF PORK SAUSAGES OF ANY SIZE. THE COMPLETE MEALS INCLUDE A BAKED PATATA WITH ALL OF YOUR FAVORITE TOPPINGS AND A CHOCE OF VETEGABLE. AND DON'T FORGET THE WIDE ASSORTMENT OF DESERTS...UH...I MEAN DESSERTS, NOT SAND...BUT LIKE PIES, CAKES AND SWEET STUFF. ON MONDAY, STEVEN'S FEATURES SURF AND TURF WHILE GRAZING ON THE GRASS AND LISTEN TO THE BEACH BOYS. HA...HA...HA...THAT'S A

*JOKE! SERIOUSLY, THEY HAVE A
WONDERFUL STEAK AND
SEAFOOD DINNER. COME ON BY
TODAY, THEY'RE ANXIOUS TO
COOK YOU...I MEAN COOK FOR
YOU.*

*"Ham, you said vetegable...it's
vegetable."*

*"Colonel, that's what I said. I wrote
the commercial myself, so I know all of
the words."*

*"Ham, I don't think it's a good idea to
write the scripts."*

*"Why not? My uncle approved it and
he owns the station."*

*NOW, HERE'S THE NEWS IN
SPORTS. IF YOU CALL GOLF A
SPORT, JACK NICKLAUS LEADS
THE NEW ORLEANS OPEN, WHICH
IS BEING PLAYED IN NEW
ORLEANS. HE HOLDS THE THIRTY-
SIX HOLE LEAD OVER FOUR
PLAYERS. THE WINNER RECEIVES
A CHECK FOR TWENTY THOUSAND
DOLLARS, WHICH IS A LOT OF
MONEY.*

Ham suspended the news broadcast again to chit chat
with Cobb.

"Colonel, have you played golf?"

*"Never...it's such a goofy game. They
hit a little white ball into a cup, right?"*

"Yep, but not in a glass cup or a coffee cup. It's a little round hole, that's cut on the green. I call the cup a can."

"Ham, why do the golfers all wear plaid or checked pants in those bright colors?"

"I don't know, but they're so out of style. Those wide white belts and white shoes are horrible too. They probably bought them in a half-off sale...you know...when the store manikins are only have half dressed."

"If I played golf, I would go barefoot and wear khaki army shorts and a tank top undershirt with clip-on suspenders."

"The only course that will let you play with that wardrobe is Pasture Golf Links near Westby. They have sand greens and some of the pins are missing, so they use broom sticks with rags attached for flags. They use a cow herd to keep the grass short, in what they call a fairway, but you need to steer clear of the cow pies. Colonel, do you know why golf tournaments are called an Open?"

"Why?"

"Because they don't play golf in a building. It's played in wide open spaces!"

"If they played a golf tournament in the Houston Astrodome, would they call it a closed?"

"Maybe if they could fit eighteen holes in there."

NOW A MESSAGE FROM ONE OF OUR FAVORITE SPONSORS, MAYER'S CHEVROLET. DROP ON BY AND DRIVE THE NEW CHEVY CORVAIR. IT HAS A NEW SLEEK BODY AND A COOL DASHBORAD THAT WILL TAKE YOUR BREATH AWAY.

A faint voice in the radio booth joked in the background.

"After you've stopped laughing at the ugly design."

There was a pause and Radio continued.

THE PLASTICE BUCKET SEATS WILL ALSO RESIST ANY ACCIDENTAL SPILLS.

The background voice was muffled, although the man laughed again.

"And the bucket seats will neatly collect your barf after you've given it a test drive."

After another long pause Radio rambled on.

MAYER'S CHEVROLET HAS A WIDE RANGE OF COLORS IN STOCK. MY FAVORITE IS CHARTREUSE, BUT THE CAR DOES COME IN GREEN. MAYER'S WILL ACCEPT YOUR TRADE –IN, AS LONG AS IT'S

ANOTHER CAR. MAYER'S ALSO
HAS A LAY-AWAY PLAN, SO YOU
CAN PLAN TO WAIT A LONG TIME
BEFORE YOU GET YOU CAR.
MAYER'S MERCURY IS LOCATED
ON MAYER ROAD, NEXT TO
MAYER'S USED CAR LOT, WHERE
THEY HAVE A LOT OF OLD CARS,
WHICH HAVE BEEN USED.

Cobb cued the next song.

HERE'S A NEW ONE BY IAN
WHITCOM CALLED "YOU REALLY
TURN ME ON." CALL ME RIGHT
NOW IF YOU LIKE THE TUNE. THE
LINES ARE OPEN AT POP-
KORN...767-5676.

As the song played, I heard a voice again in the background again, this time it was clearly Radio's.

"Have you seen the Corvair? Their
design engineers were drunk when they
decided to put the engine in the rear.
It's the biggest bomb since the Edsel."

Cobb broke in as soon as the song stopped playing.

THE NEW CORVAIR REALLY TURNS
ME ON. COME BY MAYER'S
CHEVROLET AND DRIVE ONE
TODAY

I commented to Jesse. "I bet that Ham Radio wrote that ad too. If Mayor Mayer heard that chatter, he'll have the dope fired, as well as the radio station engineer. You should have heard him chew out Professor Orbit last week."

"If you've seen the ads on TV for the Corvair, you know their design engineers are from another planet, called Detroit."

"Jesse, I know you own a motorcycle, bit if you had a car, what model would you buy?"

"A Porsche 550 Spider. James Dean raced that car," He said, as he lit up another cigarette.

I finally thought that I had broken through Jesse's shield, but our conversation was suddenly interrupted by Andy Bumgardner.

"SPYKSTRA...come here!"

I hustled to the bag room to intercept him. "Spykstra, did you hear what happened last Sunday? VD practically jumped a foot in the air when the sprinkler hit her and the top of her bikini top flew off, just like we planned. She didn't cover herself with the towel right away, so we had a great shot at her tits. PRO, Condor, and Pags were ecstatic. And do you know the best part? Her nipples are white!"

I wasn't exactly sure how to respond. "I'm happy the plan worked out."

"We appreciate what you did, so I'm making you a B caddie right now! You get a quarter raise! What's your first name again?"

"Scott."

"We give our best caddies a nickname. What does Pfeiffer call you?"

"Spike."

"Okay, Spike, you can call me Bum now and I'm assigning you to caddy for the mayor today. By the way, Ben Lipschitz dropped off an envelope for you in the pro shop. Tell Zero that Abe Goldman left one for him too."

While I was pleased that Andy seemed to be my buddy now, I worried about the loop with Linus Mayer, recalling the shouting matches between the foursomes last week and the caddie shack fire incident. I reluctantly picked up Mayer's bag and proceeded to the first tee, thrilled to see that Bing was assigned to Mr. Dix in my foursome. The other two golfers were riding in a golf cart.

The mayor was rambling to Dix near the first tee when I arrived. "Lars, did you hear those clowns on the radio? They butchered the commercial for the Corvair and left the microphone on during a song. I'm going to string that moron up by his nuts! I already called Maze Sweet, who owns KORN. He needs to give me free advertising for the rest of the year, and they're only using the scripts written by MY staff going forward."

"I heard the ad from my car. At least the disk jockey tried to make up for it using the song title. What was it again? "You Turn Me On?" Give him some credit, at least."

"The singer seemed like he was having a damn orgasm! Christ, where are the censors? I'm calling the FCC on Monday. Now, where's my caddie?"

I held up my hand. "Right here, sir. Do you need your putter?"

"Hell no. Hand me my driver!"

Mayer never bothered to introduce himself or even ask my name. I had a feeling that this golf round would result in a long day.

Dix was cordial to Bing. "I've had you in my group before. What's your name again?"

"Bobby Crosby, but they call me Bing."

"I remember now. Bing Crosby…right? My wife and I met Bing Crosby in Las Vegas once and she gave him a big smooch! He's a real crooner for a little squirt. Vicki bought every one of his albums as soon as we returned to La Crosse."

The other golfers, Del Casas and Dowd Jones IV, rolled up in their cart. "Linus, Dowd and I are truly honored to be playing with the Mayor of La Crosse and a car dealer tycoon too."

"Remind me to give you my autograph later. I'm currently negotiating on buying two more dealerships in Davenport, Iowa."

"How many now?"

"Good question, Dowd. Let me count them up…two in La Crosse, Eau Claire, Tomah, Moline, Burlington, Rochester, Winona, and Cedar Rapids. Those two will make eleven. Dad would be proud of me."

"Congratulations!"

"Just trying to get by. It seems everything costs more every day. Did you hear the details on the house we're building up on the bluff? The architect designed a living room with full-height windows overlooking the city. I'm letting Minnie plan the bathroom. She wants a bidet and a steam shower big enough for two people."

"Linus, what's a bidet?"

"Dowd, they're a French thing. I didn't know either until I saw one in Paris. It looks like a toilet, except it sprays a woman's box to wash away that tuna fish smell."

"Can men use a bidet too?"

"I tried it…kind of tickles your nuts though."

"Can it clean your hinder?"

"Maybe…probably could save on toilet paper too. Del, have you ever ordered a bidet for one of your houses?"

"Are you kidding? Some folks who tour our models have never even used an indoor toilet and don't even know how to flush. Have you guys seen the new homes we're building at Bluffview Estates?"

"I've seen your advertising in the paper but I haven't driven over to tour them yet. Vicki and I are very happy with our house, except for the damn caddies. What are your price ranges?"

"The Essex ranch model is only $13,995 and a buyer can close for only four hundred dollars down. The Aristocrat has a base price of $15,995 and The Cavalier is priced at $18,995 without the upgrades. We have some terrific new designs. Our premiere model, The Cavalier, is called a split-level. You enter on the main level, where you can have another bedroom, bathroom, or rumpus room. There is a set of six stairs leading up to the living room, dining area, and kitchen. Then there is a set of six steps leading to the bedroom areas. The garage is tucked under the upper level. We also have the typical ranch, as well as The Aristocrat raised ranch."

Jones looked bewildered. "Is the raised ranch built on stilts?"

"Dowd, we even sell them ladders to enter the door. The house is great for flood zones or swamps."

"Really?"

"No stupid! A raised ranch is another variation of the spilt-level, except the main level has the living room, kitchen, two bedrooms and one bath. The buyer can opt to have the lower level finished out with more bedroom and a bath, or they can leave as basement storage and upgrade later. The garage is detached if the buyer wants one. Our prices cater to a wider range of buyers and we have appliance packages in green, pink, or yellow. We can put in a dishwasher too."

"Del, a Chinaman? HO...HO!"

"Dowd, Chinamen wash clothes...not dishes and we don't offer washers or dryers. Seriously, the kitchen has laminated counter-tops with fruitwood cabinets. The bathroom and kitchen floors have vinyl-asbestos tile that's easy to clean. We can offer wool, nylon, or rayon carpeting in many colors. We have a new line of cotton carpet in a shag pattern too."

"Shag carpet? Like a woman's bush? Maybe you should change the name of your subdivision to Muffview Estates!"

"Speaking of muff, we have a knockout saleslady in our model office. Her name is Ada Mellon. She and her husband, Walt, are members here."

"I know Walt, but I've never met her."

"Linus, you're spending too much time working. Have you heard that Walt's clothing company is planning a line of see-through women's panties?"

"I'm getting more ass than a toilet seat, so those would be a waste of money for me."

"Dowd…that will be the day! I might buy a pair. Vicki and I need to spice things up a bit."

"Having a little problem at home, Lars?"

"Well, not really."

"Boys, I hate to change the conversation, but let's play some golf. What's the bet for today? How about a hundred dollar Nassau? Lars and I are partners and your handicaps nearly equal ours, so let's play even-up. Have you guys heard the story behind the Nassau bet?"

"Gambling in Nassau in the Bahamas?"

"No Lars, but a good guess. The Nassau Country Club on Long Island is one of the first golf courses built in the United States before nineteen hundred, when golf was primarily played by the privileged class…like us. The wealthy men from Manhattan rode the Long Island Railroad to the train station next to the Nassau Country Club. The scores of the eighteen-hole matches were published in the newspapers, so the rich golfers were embarrassed after they were drubbed by the local hustlers. So, they invented the three score Nassau bet. The front nine was one score, the back nine the second score, and the total eighteen result was the third. They would still typically lose 3-0, but didn't sound so bad compared to 16-2 or 17-1. Occasionally, the rich guy would win one nine-hole bet, so the score in the newspaper read 2-1."

"You're making up that story!"

"Of course not. I'm always truthful. Why do you think I was elected Mayor of La Crosse? Last year, I played at Nassau Country Club, where the story is chronicled in the men's locker room. There's a cemetery in the middle of the course too."

"Did the wealthy players kill their opponents and bury them right there on the course? You should tell McAbre, the mortician, about the cemetery. He would go to his grave to play there."

The group launched their drives and we made our way down the fairway. As Mayer reached his shot, I dropped the bag near the ball and tilted it toward him to help him select his club. I forgot Mayer was left-handed and stood on the wrong side of the ball. Mayer ranted, "You're a B caddie huh? What does B stand for…bumbles? See my clubs? They're hand crafted and the best set money can buy. See the shape of the head? They're left handed! Now, move out of my way and back up."

I felt like a fool, especially when Mayer proceeded to shank the ball at a forty-five degree angle on his next shot. "Damn it! The knucklehead caddie screwed me up!" Without a warning, Mayer threw the 4-iron, nailing me in the nuts. I tumbled over, rolling on the ground, screaming in pain. "Caddie, maybe you'll wake up now! Lars, can you believe he couldn't catch that club? He's retarded."

Bing rushed to my aid. "Spike, are you alright?"

I couldn't catch my breath to even answer.

"I'll carry your bag for a few minutes."

Mayer was still upset. "Bing, don't help that sissy!"

After a minute, I regained my strength and retrieved Mayer's bag from Bing. The rest of the front nine was uneventful, except Mayer threw three more clubs at me. When our group reached the ninth green, Mayer announced the golfers all needed beer from the clubhouse. "Dumb-shit, go get four beers from the men's grill and tell 'em to put it on my tab!"

Bing ambled over to me. "Have you ever had to order drinks from the bar between nines?"

"No, I have never even been past the 9th hole yet."

"There's a window on the side of the men's grill. Knock three times. Barry Keeper, the bartender, should be on duty. Ask him to draw four beers to go and put them on Mayer's tab. Meet us on the 10th tee and I'll carry Mayer's bag over for you."

"Can I order a drink? I'm thirsty!"

"Mayer didn't say you could, but there's a hose around the side of the clubhouse."

I found the bar window and knocked three times. A few seconds passed, so I knocked again and still no response. I tried knocking again and a man wearing a white dress shirt and a black bow tie finally opened the tiny wooden door. "What is it?"

"I'm a caddie. My name is Scott and I was sent by Mr. Mayer to order four beers to go."

"I can't help you. Go tell him he is over-extended on his credit at the club."

"I'm sorry. Do you mean you can't give me any beers?"

"Right! Go tell him right now that he is a deadbeat."

"A deadbeat?"

"Yep, he's overdue on his credit here."

"I should tell the Mayor of La Crosse he's a deadbeat?"

"Better yet, tell him he's a low-life scammer."

"I can't!"

"Congratulations kid! You passed the test."

"What test?"

"A-B-S-U!"

"ABS University?"

"A.B.S.U. is short for 'Always Be Sucking Up!' Your name is Spykstra, eh?"

"Yes, how do you know?"

"I'll let you in on a little secret. I was in the back of the pro shop last week when you turned the sprinkler on Vicki Dix. What a sight with her big bouncing boobs! Andy told me your name. I bet cheapskate Mayer didn't let you order a drink."

"No and I'm dying of thirst."

"Gulp this lemonade down while I draw the beers. Forget what I said regarding Mr. Mayor and A.B.S.U., okay?"

"Sure, thanks a lot."

Barry poured the beers in paper cups and positioned them in a paper sack with two handles, although there were no lids on the cups. The beers began to spill with each step I took. I delicately tried to hold the bag from beneath, but by the time I got to the 10th tee, nearly a quarter of each beer had disappeared. Unexpectedly, the bottom of the bag collapsed and one cup fell on the ground, beer running across the tee box.

Mayer was pissed. "Now I know for sure you're a bumbler. You owe me for one beer, so I'll skip any tip today for you. Hey guys, let's flip to see who doesn't get a beer."

"Linus, maybe you can slurp up some foam off the grass. Does anyone have a straw?"

I stuttered. "I'm sorry, the bartender filled them to the brim. I can go back."

"Don't blame the bartender, you're an uncoordinated spastic!"

"Linus, pour a little from the other three cups into the empty one. We'll have another round when we pass your tavern."

Bing tried to console me. "I should have told you to ask for a double sack. Balancing the beers is even trickier when you have to carry a golf bag."

"Lucky they didn't all fall through."

"Here's Mayer's bag. Forget what he said."

The group played on and occasionally the conversation got interesting with Mayer leading the conversation. "I can't believe some of the cheap screws we have here at the club. I heard that Sparks, one of the guy we played through last week, made his caddie jump into two ponds to retrieve his golf ball. In fact, I heard he often uses range balls when he's playing the course too."

I was tempted to announce that I was the caddie victim who got wet, but held my tongue.

"Linus, I saw him walking along the road one night near the fourth hole hunting for lost balls. He's trying to change the rules so that when he finds another golfer's lost ball, he should be rewarded with a two shot credit for his next round."

"Last week, I found Sparks' golf ball in the weeds that had a message written on it. It said 'IF FOUND, RETURN TO LOU SPARKS.'"

"That crazy Zorba, the Greek shrink doctor, plays golf balls with cuts in them. He feels the ball is smiling at him, which puts him in a happy mood.

"Have you seen the cars they drive? The fat astronomy professor has an old Nash Rambler covered with rust. I'm surprised the bumpers keep hanging on. Sparks drives a Volkswagen Beetle Bug with a little vinyl top he can pull it back, bragging about driving a convertible. The car doesn't even have a heater and the engine is in the rear!"

"Speaking of rears, when Professor Buffont walks down the hallway at the college, he should have a sign on his back saying 'CAUTION: WIDE LOAD AHEAD.' I bet he has an extra-large toilet seat in his bathroom."

"Maybe he actually sits on the toilet bowl. Del, do toilet seats come in different sizes?"

"Yes, but I order a standard size for the average ass. I can't waste money to inventory an assortment of toilet seats."

"Don't ever stand behind Sparks in a line either. His farts are disgusting. He was in the stall next to me last week and I nearly passed out. I even asked Jimmie for a clothes pin for my nose. We should post a no-smoking sign in the men's toilet. You never know what might ignite bad gas. Have you heard the song by Alfred E. Neuman called "It's a Gas?" The tune has a series of burps."

"Is Alfred E. Neuman that goofy looking character in *Mad Magazine?*"

"Yeah."

"Dowd, do you read *Mad?* They make a joke out of everything, especially politics. Their writers probably never had real jobs."

"I pick up the magazine occasionally when I'm visiting my brother. My nephew, Damien, has a subscription."

"Tell your brother he's raising a juvenile delinquent."

"Linus, he's the valedictorian of his graduating class at St. Anthony's High School. I would never label Damien a juvenile delinquent."

"What are his plans after he graduates?"

"He was awarded an academic scholarship to attend The University of Wisconsin in Madison in the fall."

"That figures…Madison is a hotbed for radical activities. They're demonstrating for civil rights, the end of nuclear warfare, the military draft, and a bunch of other meaningless shit. Our public university too…can you believe us taxpayers fund a base for revolutionaries? They have a lot of long-haired beatniks who lead the demonstrations…they're not even registered students."

"My nephew won't cause trouble. He studies constantly and has real short hair. He goes to bible study every week too."

"What major field of study is he planning?"

"Philosophy."

"He's a perfect candidate for radical brainwashing. The philosophy professors are some real left wingers who conduct teach-ins at Madison, Berkeley, and Columbia."

"Linus, what college did you attend?"

"I went to the school of hard knocks. I washed cars at my Dad's dealerships when I was in the sixth grade and then swept the floors and picked up the trash in the service garage. In high school, I got to change oil and rotate tires on cars."

"When did you sell your first car?"

"I was only twenty. I wore a double breasted suit and had a red bow-tie. The car was a 1946 Hudson Super four-door sedan. I knew then I could sell anything. How about you, Del?"

"I started at the bottom too. In high school, I worked for a roofing company. The obnoxious tar smell and the summer heat were unbearable. Then I worked on a crew nailing asphalt shingles on houses." He coughed for a couple of minutes and spit out some blood.

"Del, have you seen a doctor?"

"Are you kidding? I'm in great shape. Doctors don't know what they're doing. They might stick me in a hospital for a bunch of tests." He continued coughing for what seemed like a minute straight. "I built my first house in 1951 and we finished our two hundredth last week. We brought all of our subcontractors and suppliers to Dizzy Izzy's Strip Club for a big party. Sandy Easey, the nymph, and her friends took care of our guys in the back rooms."

"Dowd, I don't recall how you got into the stock brokerage business. Tell us again."

"Well Linus, I flunked out after one year at the University of Iowa. I was in a fraternity and all I did was party and play poker. My uncle was a pretty senior guy at Dean Witter and convinced them to give me a shot. I nailed the personality tests...one of the highest scores ever. I aced the broker exam too, although I have to admit, a friend stole a copy of the test. I got eighty percent right! At Dean Witter, I partied as if I was back in my college fraternity with a lot of drinking, schmoozing with clients, and gambling on stocks. We had a good research department, which helped a lot. Then Bache offered me a signing bonus in 1962, and I've been doing pretty well. Based on your monthly statements, you should be happy."

"Not bad, Dowd. Now, can you two caddies jog down the fairway to spot our drives?"

I really needed to confide in Bing. "Isn't a nymph a mythological beautiful maiden? What has that to do with that lady at the strip club?"

"Nymph is short for nymphomaniac."

"What is a nymphomaniac?"

"A woman who has an insatiable desire for sex...you know...fornication."

I must have looked puzzled so he clarified himself. "Fornication is another name for intercourse. Where have you been?"

"Well, I don't have any older brothers and my Dad would never discuss sex. Knowing my parents, I'm not sure how I could have ever been conceived. Maybe I was adopted. I'm struggling to piece all of this together."

"When a guy and a woman have sex, it's called screwing. A guy inserts his penis into a woman's vagina."

"OC and Jesse must have been trying to give me some hints about that."

"I'm not sure what they told you, but you can learn a lot more from Jesse."

"OC said a guy can put his penis into a woman's butt-hole."

"Don't believe everything that Zero tells you."

The golfers all reached their shots and Del Casas engaged Mayer in some official community business. "Linus, I'm going to need your influence to arrange condemnation proceedings on a property over on 29th Street. I need a wider frontage for access into an exclusive subdivision I'm planning. I acquired some parcels along Oakwood

275

Forest and have options on forty more acres, but an old couple won't talk to me about selling their old family farmstead for sentimental reasons. I even offered them a fair price for a change."

"What's their name?"

"Stitch and Julia Taylor. They must be at least eighty years old."

"I don't know them. Do they have a lawyer?"

"Not that I know of."

Dix overheard the end of the conversation and drove his cart closer. "The Taylors contacted me a couple of weeks ago to represent them. I wouldn't worry, if you know what I mean." He winked twice.

Mayer put his finger in Casas' face. "Del, you need to have some back-up insurance, I have two International Harvester pick-ups on my lot that need your company name painted on the doors."

"I was just telling my CFO yesterday we needed a couple of new trucks for our fleet."

"You should also arrange some cash to lend to a few influential councilmen for a vacation trip next winter!"

"If you recall, I made loans to the council members five years ago for their trip to Hawaii, when I needed planning approval and subsidies for the cost of the utility lines for the Bluffview Estates. After the vote, I forgave the loan repayment and interest, right Lars?"

"Vicki and I really enjoyed that trip to Honolulu."

"I also had the problem with the street near the Synagogue a few years ago."

"That was before I became the mayor. Dowd, you were on the council then. How were you able to finesse Del's request on that one?"

"I was the senior member of the council then. There were only nine councilmen, so we only needed five votes. I knew four of them were avid golfers, so I set up a trip to the Masters Golf Tournament in

Augusta. Then we played a few rounds at some great courses in Georgia, including Callaway Gardens and East Lake Golf Club, where Bobby Jones was a member. Del got his project approved pretty quickly."

"I sure received a lot of threatening telephone calls from the Heebs. The new street cut off some of the parking for their synagogue. Most of them walk to their Shabbat service, so we convinced the council they didn't need as many parking spaces. We also had the city auditors put a little pressure on reporting their sales tax collections from their businesses, so that shut them up pretty fast."

"Dowd, didn't you risk some stock brokerage business by offending the Jew boys?"

"The Heebs don't buy stock. They only buy real estate, like the buildings which house their businesses. I tried to sell them stock years ago and every time, they tried to jew my commission down. I finally was able to open an account with Abe Goldman. He bought one share of stock, but as soon as the price went down, he called me every hour for three days to take the stock back at his cost and refund the commission. He called the office manager repeatedly, until we finally relented. Obviously, we closed his account."

Apparently, no one had lectured Jones about using the word jew as a verb.

"The Heebs complain every month when they receive their club statements, even though it's typically only a couple of bucks. I have no idea why we allow them to stay."

"Linus, you should know that the club needs the dues. Del, are you winning at pocket pool? You're a scratch golfer, so quit playing with your nuts and hit your golf ball!"

"My balls itch...I can't quit scratching them. I forgot to ask if you guys are interested to play again tomorrow morning. Lars, can you?"

"I can't. I always watch *Meet the Press*."

"Dowd?"

"I can't play either. I plan to stay in bed and have my girlfriend press my meat."

"Linus, how about you?"

"Del, you should remember that I always attend Methodist church services at 10 o'clock. There are quite a few influential members who attend that I need to impress and demonstrate my evangelical beliefs, even though I really fake it. I am a generous church contributor, so we have a reserved seat in the front row and a special parking space.

They stood on the 15th tee. "Linus, I forgot our Nassau bet. How do we stand?"

"Lars and I won the front nine by one and we're up by one on the back nine now. Do you want to press us?"

"Sure."

"Duly noted, Del."

"Dowd, do you have any hot stock tips?"

"Bache is recommending the airlines stocks and Eastern Airlines is our top pick. You might check out Curtis Publishing Company, which is not on a Bache list, but I love the company. They publish *The Saturday Evening Post, The Ladies' Home Journal,* and a few other magazines. I also am recommending Studebaker. They have the Avanti II rolling out, which will really return them to profitability."

"Dowd, you've got to be shitting me! Avanti is one of the ugliest cars I've ever seen. I had a chance to buy the Studebaker dealership in Madison last year, but their sales were nosediving."

"Linus, that's why their stock price is such a bargain."

"Studebaker is like a bug looking for a windshield! But you can buy ten shares of that publishing company for me on Monday. Minnie reads those magazines, so it must be a decent company."

"I'll make a note right now." Jones pulled a notepad from his bag and repeated the order aloud as he scribbled on the paper. "Buy twenty-five shares of Curtis Publishing for Linus Mayer."

"Lars, are you interested in buying any stock?"

"You can buy five shares of that Eastern Airline stock, although I've never been on one of their planes. We flew TWA for our trip to Hawaii and I've only flown Ozark or North Central Airlines out of La Crosse."

"Dowd, no stock for me. I've got too much cash tied up on all of my land deals."

The 15th hole was a par 3, situated on the edge of a public street. For some reason, a small tavern was nestled among a line of modest houses across the road from the tee. The tavern was called Clyde's Bar and was operated by Mayer's brother, Clyde. It appeared to have been a former house converted to a commercial use.

"Aren't you guys happy I orchestrated the zoning change, allowing the house to be converted to a bar? We don't have to wait to drink until the 19th hole now. My brother and I bought the house for a bargain and the change in use sailed through the planning department like butter. The neighbors were a little upset, but who cares about them?

I studied the row of nicely kept bungalows. The tavern seemed out of place. There were only four parking spaces in front of the bar, so I assumed the customers parked in front of the adjacent houses during peak hours.

"Linus, you are one crafty guy! Bing, go over to Clyde's and order four beers and whatever you want to drink. Here's a five dollar bill."

"Can I order something for Scott?"

"Sure, as long as he pays for the drink himself."

I shook my head.

"I'm sorry, Scott Can you carry my bag to the green while I run over to the tavern?"

"No problem...take your time and don't spill the beers."

By the time I anchored the flagstick in the cup, Bing returned with the beverages.

"Bing, I hope you did better than Bumbles and didn't spill any beer. I'm running a little low on alcohol. I only got half of my normal amount on the 10th hole."

"Mr. Mayer, they're full to the brim."

Mayer chugged his beer quickly, as we walked over to the 16th tee. The course ranger, John Reid, raced up in his silver cart to intercept us. He appeared to be at least seventy-five years old and wore a white cowboy hat and dark sunglasses that masked his eyes. He was bent over at a thirty degree angle as he limped to the tee box.

"Howdy, Lone Ranger...where's Tonto?"

"Tonto's getting new silver heals on his shoes. Mr. Mayer, the National Weather Service has issued a severe thunderstorm and tornado warning, so everyone needs to get off the course."

"Aw, we have enough time to finish our round. We have a big match going."

"Well, don't blame me if you get struck by lightning!" John excreted a juicy tobacco wad, which landed on Mayer's golf shoes, looking like they were covered in puke.

"You old fart...look what you did! Get a towel and clean these off!"

"Sorry, Mr. Mayer...my aim wasn't quite up to snuff." He hobbled back to his cart and returned with a towel and wiped the shoes.

"Why do put that crap in your mouth? Man, your teeth couldn't be browner unless you use shit for toothpaste."

"I've been chewing since I was fourteen, so it's a little late to quit. I carry around this tin cup that I spit in." As he rested it on the front of his cart, a gust of wind spilled the cup on the tee box.

"Real nice! Clean that up too or it will kill the grass."

"Right-o Kemo-sabe! Hi-yo Silver...away!" Reid drove down the fairway.

"The old man is senile."

"Like George Palmer said, he played football too long without a helmet."

The wind picked up suddenly, as a low line of storm clouds gathered to the west. Mayer set up for his tee shot, when a squall knocked off his golf cap. The wind lifted the edges of his toupee, which now clung to his head by one piece of glue. He wrestled the toupee back in place, although it was crooked. I quickly recovered his cap, which Mayer pulled on immediately. I glanced over at Lars Dix. The wind gust had conquered his complex comb-over, now resembling long strings of spaghetti standing on end. He grappled with his hair, trying to bring it under control. Bing instantly located a golf cap in the side panel of the bag. Dix snagged it and tucked his hair underneath.

Mayer's empty beer cup had flown all the way to the 15th green, while Bing was still holding Dix's beer. Casas' and Jones' cups tipped over on the tee box. "Look...the wind is forming white caps from the beer foam. Shit, I hate wind," Mayer barked.

"A big storm is brewing. We need to hustle. Linus, should we just quit and head in?"

"Del, you pressed us, so we need to finish unless you want to forfeit right now."

"You always insist on playing everything out, don't you?"

"Why not? What fun would life be without a little adventure?"

"So, Linus...why not buy some Studebaker stock then?"

"Dowd, I didn't say life would be fun with a little stupidity."

The group quickly played the 16th hole. Ominous, black clouds had gathered closer as they reached the 17th tee. Lightning flashed intensely, followed by explosive thunder that shook the ground. I recalled Ham Radio's count-off I had heard earlier on the KORN broadcast. The center of the storm was no more than two or three miles away.

Bing tapped my arm. "Spike, find a club cover in Mayer's bag. Attach it to the bag with the snaps and make sure all of the clubs are protected. Open Mayer's umbrella and hang the towel from the sprockets. When you walk down the fairway, hold it over Mayer's head, so he doesn't get wet."

Mayer wavered over his tee shot on the 17th tee, waiting for the wind to calm down. He took a quick, choppy swing, as we watched his drive land near the out of bounds stakes.

"Linus, you should hit a provisional shot…that ball looks like it's out of bounds," Casas observed as he squinted toward the white markers.

"I don't think so, Del. I had a good eye on it."

As we walked off the tee, I managed to cover the clubs as the rain fell more progressively, although I struggled in the wind to hold the umbrella steady over Mayer's head. Suddenly, a violent gust pulled the umbrella away and the towel brushed against Mayer's head.

"Give me the damned bumbershoot, Bumbles. Hand me that thing!" Mayer seized the umbrella, causing the prongs to knock his cap off. His toupee flopped around again, until he got his cap back in position. "What in hell gave Andy the idea to assign you to me today? Christ, the caddie program has really hit rock bottom."

I wanted to blame the wind gusts, but decided to stay silent. When we reached his tee shot, I could clearly see that his ball was at least three feet out of bounds. Mayer peered across the fairway, watching the other players closely.

"Drop my bag right here," directing me to a spot five feet closer to the fairway. He waited a few seconds until another bolt of lightning pierced the black sky. "Guys, look at that one," signaling to the other players as he pointed upward. Out of the corner of my eye, I saw a golf ball roll off the top of his shoe, nestling perfectly on a mowed section of the rough, two feet in bounds. He had dropped a ball down his pant leg from his pocket and used the golf bag for cover just in case his opponents were watching. On top of that, he distracted them with his lightning bolt observation when they looked away.

"Hey guys, my eyes are perfect...my ball IS in play." Mayer yelled to the golfers, so they could easily hear him. He played his next shot to the green and mumbled to himself, "Boy, am I a great player or what?"

I thought that it might be a rhetorical question, but decided to respond just in case. "Yes, sir...that was unbelievable!"

"Caddie, after you replace my divot, go retrieve my tee ball over there, but don't be too obvious so those guys don't see you pick it up."

"Yes sir...I understand."

I dawdled to replace the divot, making sure that the other players had advanced up the fairway before I picked up his golf ball.

The lightning bolts became more intense, followed instantly by loud thunder claps. When I caught up with Mayer at the green, he studied the sky, "Guys, there's a little utility shed that will shelter us while the storm blows over. You caddies need to fend for yourselves, but don't let our bags get wet!"

Bing motioned to me. "Let's stand under the oak trees."

"Bing, we were taught at camp to stay away from big trees in a thunderstorm."

Hail stones suddenly pelted down. "Go wherever you want, but the hail stones are getting intense!" I followed Bing, taking cover under a tall oak tree. A blinding flash of lightning blistered a limb above us and the thunder blast threw me to the ground. A blue flame shot from the tree, which split in half, falling four feet from the spot where I was laying on the grass. Mayer's golf bag flipped over and a three clubs flew out. As I rose to my knee, my heart seemed like it was racing two hundred beats a minute. "Bing, do you know how close we were to dying?"

"From the lightning strike or the falling limb?"

"Either one, although Mayer might kill me anyway if I screw up one more time."

The storm passed quickly, but the tornado warning siren from the nearby fire station was still blaring. Mayer and Dix strode over to us. "Lars, they look all right to me."

"The caddies?"

"Hell no...our clubs!" Mayer lifted it to the sky and peered down the shaft. "Wait...my 7-iron might be bent!" Caddie, you may need to pay me for a new club!"

"Linus, let's tee off before the storm returns."

Mayer's tee shot landed under a pine tree in the 18th hole rough. As Mayer addressed the ball, his swing was clearly obstructed by the branches.

"Bumbles, back up slowly and lean back against the branches so I can hit the shot."

I instinctively questioned Mayer if he was violating a golf rule, ignoring one of Andy's commandments. "Isn't there a penalty for holding back branches to assist a player?"

"Shut up! The branches are restricting my swing! They should have been cut back by the ground's crew. I'll bet that idiot, Mole, forgot about it."

Mayer's 5-iron shot landed in the front bunker, buried in the wet sand under a ledge. Jones and Casas flew their approach shots on the green, but far from the pin. Dix's second shot landed ten feet from the hole. "I have a decent shot at a birdie and our opponents need to roll good lag putts just to save par."

Mayer peered into the trap. "Lars, what bad luck on a perfect shot. The damp air must have held up the ball flight. Bumbles, wipe the sand wedge grip and pass me the club. I can knock the ball close to the hole, even though the shot seems impossible."

"Linus, you can't go straight at the hole. The ledge of the trap will knock the ball down. You should aim your shot toward the side of the green and try to one-putt from there."

"Naw, I can make this!" The bottom edge of Mayer's club touched the sand before his ferocious backswing. Large clumps of mud and dirt followed his golf ball on to the wet green. The ball skipped three times on the green and nestled into the hole for a birdie 3. "HOO-HAH! I called that!"

"Linus, one of the most incredible bunker plays I've ever seen!"

Casas stood on the far side of the green, stunned to see the ball go in the hole. "Lucky shot, Mayer. Dowd, one of us needs to make our putt to tie now, but the green has indentations from the hail. Lars, this isn't fair that we have to putt."

"Play it as it lies, as they say...that's the rub of the green. Linus played his shot with the hail divots."

"Lars, I'm not certain the official rule for a damaged green. We'll putt under protest and ask Palmer for a ruling later."

Jones' and Casas' birdie putts wobbled off course, obviously impacted with the hail stone perforations. Dix's putt was also pushed away by the dents in the green. After the players shook hands, Mayer flipped the wedge at me. "Make sure you clean all of the dirt out of the grooves. I don't need any crud left on them for my next round."

"Yes sir. I'll be sure the grooves are perfectly clean."

"Boys, Lars and I will meet you in the men's grill to collect our bet. I need to go to the pro shop to pay my bumbling caddie. Shit, he should pay me for the great exhibition I just put on to win the match and the press."

I accompanied Mayer to the pro shop, where Andy intercepted us. "How did go out there Mr. Mayer. Did you survive the storm?"

"The storm was a humdinger! We camped out in that little shed near the 18th tee while the storm blew over. The lightning struck a huge oak tree near where we were and the limb split after fire shot out. I nearly shit my pants!"

"Hopefully no one was hurt. We had reports of some minor damage on the course."

"My 7-iron might be bent though. Lars and I won our match on the last hole, so all is good. I shot a 74."

"You're a stud!"

"Why did you give me a loser caddie today? I told you to never give me anyone except an A. He's apparently a B caddie, but it was an F caddie performance, so you should fire him. Did he receive any training at all? Christ, he nearly took out my eyeball when he was holding the umbrella." He sighed. "Well, since Lars and I won four hundred bucks apiece, I'm in a good mood, so give the kid a quarter tip. Put it on my tab in the pro shop."

"Sure thing and I'll personally take him out for more training."

"I'm not sure he's worth your time…seems like a complete loser. Oh well, just another dud in the world. Now I need to speak with George on a ruling for hail damage on a green and to ask him to measure my 7-iron."

"Have a nice afternoon, Mr. Mayer!"

Andy now turned to address Bing and I. "Spykstra, we give you a good job and you screwed up. And Bing, you're supposed to help rookie caddies."

"Bum, you know what an asshole Mayer can be. He threw a few clubs at Scott on the front nine and bitched when he spilled some beer after the turn. The wind blew up on the last couple of holes and the scene was hilarious. Mayer's cap blew off and his toupee was flapping around in the wind…twice! Dix's comb-over was a joke too. It looked like his hair was under a linguini attack! I had trouble holding the umbrella for Dix too and Mayer got stabbed when he jerked the umbrella from Spike's hand."

"Spike, what's the story?"

"Bum, the round was worse than that war movie, *The Longest Day.*"

"All right, go in the pro shop and pick up your money."

Bing and I strolled toward the bag room.

"Spike, did you see Mayer cheat on his last shot? He grounded his club in the sand trap, which is a two shot penalty. Dix saw the infraction too and didn't say a word and the other guys were too far away to see. Golf is considered a gentleman's game, so Mayer or Dix should have called a penalty. Dix made a par, so the match would have all ended in a tie anyway. It shows how desperate Mayer is to win at all costs. He's in the pro shop right now telling PRO about the hail damage on the green. I don't know what the USGA rule is, but you can bet that Palmer will side with Mayer."

"Mayer ordered me to hold the pine tree branches on his approach shot on the last hole and didn't call a penalty either. I can now see how the game is played around here. But remember A.B.S.U."

"Yep, how did you know?"

"Barry Keeper told me."

"See you later, Spike."

"So long, Bing."

Looking back on that day, I discovered that business deals were often transacted on the golf course. Over the summer, most of it appeared legitimate, although some seemed shady, especially when it involved the government. I also discovered that some men would compromise their moral principles when it involved a bet.

Chapter 18

I expected to be assigned to caddie for a lady at some point and I got my chance on the first ladies' day event of the season. Very few women normally took caddies, although I heard that there would be several jobs for opening day for the MVCC Women's Golf Organization. There were eighteen foursomes registered for the nine-hole event.

When I arrived at the club, Barney and OC were sitting on the corner of the concrete slab. "Barney, how did the graduation dinner go last week?"

"Pretty boring. Some mother decided to invite Sister Sexy, Sister Wizard, and Sister Moron, who had the brilliant idea to have Mary Henderson read poetry, and the girls' choir sing a few hymns. Goober's father was planning to tell a few jokes, probably some dirty ones, although the nuns' presence certainly killed that idea. The party broke up before eight-thirty."

"OC, did you go?"

"Are you kidding me…with Sister Moron there? She's still planning to retract my diploma because of the valedictorian fiasco, but it's too late and she doesn't have any proof I inserted my name on the award certificate."

"How did you pull off the prank?"

"Simple…I saw Mrs. Buffoon deliver the diplomas to the school office and put them in a drawer in an unlocked file cabinet. I told her there was a sick child in the first grade, and when she left, I rifled through the drawer, discovering the achievement awards under the diploma stack. I took the valedictorian certificate to my cousin's print shop and he reproduced an exact copy with my name. On Friday morning, I snuck in the office and inserted my award beneath Bertha's. Mary Henderson's award certificate was still below mine, I just stuck a piece of paper in between."

"It was the highlight of the graduation ceremony. I thought Sister Moron was going to have a heart attack and Mary Henderson actually cried for a few seconds. The graduation address from Sister Moron was awful…the whole ceremony stunk."

"Yeah, in more ways than one. Right OC?"

"Right!"

"OC, did you pick up the envelope Goldman left in the Pro Shop for you?"

"He left three bucks, but no Dizzy Izzy passes. Benny is a liar."

"Three bucks for three holes is unbelievable! I got the same from Lipschitz…very generous!" I concluded that all Jews may not be as frugal as what most people had told me.

"Are you set to caddie for some ladies today, OC?"

"Barney, will I need to get a supply of sanitary napkins?"

"Forget about women's hygiene. Menstruation isn't your problem…PERIOD!"

"What else do I need to know?"

"A few ladies will have golf bags, but most of them have pull carts with bags, so pull the thing, walk behind the lady, and watch her shots."

"Barney, let me get this straight. I need to caddie for some old bag, watch her behind, and pull my thing?"

"You know what I meant and speaking of sanitary, watch your language. Women don't seem to laugh at the stuff men feel is funny."

"When do we find out what groups we're assigned to?

"Buddy has a list." He turned to address him. "Hey Buddy, can we see the caddie assignments?"

I peered over Barney's shoulder, scanning the sheet, finally spotting my name. I was assigned to a group including Vicki Dix, Ethyl

Buffont, Ada Mellon, and the lady pro, Sally Van Dyke. I looked more closely to see that I was assigned to Vicki Dix.

OC grabbed the sheet from Barney's hands and searched for his name. "I can't believe I'm caddying for Mrs. Buffoon. Geez, if I stay behind her, I won't be able to see where I'm going. There's no way she can waddle nine holes on those tree trunks of hers. I couldn't possibly carry her if she collapses, although we could her on her side and sing "Roll out the Barrel.""

Buddy scanned the assignments and made an observation. "Hey, James…you're gonna be happy."

"Yeah, I'm tuning in for the big fight tonight between Muhammad Ali and Sonny Liston from Lewiston, Maine. What else could make me happier?"

"You're getting your wish for a big tipper today. You'll notice our foursome is stacked today and I don't mean by golf talent. If our gals were playing for a trophy called the Chest Cup, they would win by several inches. We've got VD and Sally Van Dyke in our group. Hey…I just realized Sally's initials are also VD, so we have two VD's in our group today! Jesse, you're assigned to caddie for Ada Mellon, who is also built."

"There is a shotgun start at nine o'clock."

"Barney, they're using guns today?"

"OC, shotgun is a golf term meaning each group begins on a different hole at the same time. They usually blow a horn from the pro shop, although they may use a starter's pistol."

Jesse leaned in. "If they need a pistol, my NAACO Brigadier forty-five caliber semi-automatic handgun is locked in my motorcycle storage compartment."

Barney looked shocked. "You have a gun?"

"Sure, you never know when you need a pistol."

I automatically knew one. "Like when you go beaver hunting…right Jesse?"

"Not exactly, but you never know when someone messes with you. When I pull out my pistol, they always run away scared."

"Aren't you afraid you might shoot someone by accident?"

"Pfeiffer, are you kidding me? I have a firearm permit and the Second Amendment to the United States Constitution grants people the right to bear arms."

OC had an idea. "Maybe the Founding Fathers just wanted to give folks the right to wear short sleeve shirts."

"Shut-up, wise ass. What do you know about the Bill of Rights?"

"Nothing, but I've been read the Last Rites."

"Jesse, the Founding Fathers never contemplated automatic weapons when they wrote the Constitution. There are too many murders using those types of guns. Did you know there were over nine thousand murders in the United States last year? I'm all for the Constitutional rights to have guns, as long as the guns are the same types used when the Second Amendment was passed into law."

"Pfeiffer, do you mean muskets? What kind of doll do you sleep with, pumpkin? Shit, do you still use a nipple and suck your thumb?"

Barney was speechless. The silence was broken as Andy walked over to address all of the caddies. "All of you retards have jobs this morning. I posted the assignments on the board. Put your gear on, find your player's bag or cart, and hurry to the hole your group is assigned to. And I don't need to hear any complaints from the bitches this year, so watch your language."

I scanned the list again, noting our group was starting on the 1st hole. Andy came over to speak with me. "I assigned you to caddie for VD today, which should give you a chance to peek at her tits too. She's wearing a loose fitting top, so you might be in luck."

Vicki Dix, the president of the women's golf group, now addressed the women, who had gathered in a circle around the pro shop. "Welcome to the opening day at the Mississippi Valley Country Club. I am delighted to see so many women and several new faces. Our committee has many unique events planned over the summer with lunches following every round, so we're hoping you will be able to join each week and form new friendships. The pro shop will set up the foursomes randomly as we feel those pairings are the best way to socialize."

Ethyl Buffont raised her hand. "Can we set up our own group?"

"No, we need to be more adventuresome this season and we'll also have some fun games. In addition to our golf scores today, we have a contest, called the 'Telephone Game'. Every group will match the best individual net score on each hole to the letters on a telephone dial. The group that makes up the most unique word or word combinations will win a special prize. Here's a cheat sheet with phone numbers and the letters. Your caddies can help you too."

Ethyl Buffont raised her hand again. "Mrs. Dix, what's for lunch today?"

"Pulled pork."

OC fired back under his breath, "Can I be on the menu?"

"What do you mean?" I asked, puzzled by his question.

"Never mind."

VD continued, "Please hurry to your starting hole, so we can all begin at nine sharp. The pro shop will blow the horn signaling you can tee off."

Andy pulled Jesse aside. "Convict, I can't afford to have these witches freaking out when they see the tattoos on your arms, so keep your long-sleeve shirt on all day."

"But it will be hot."

"I don't give a shit if you sweat your ass off."

"The Second Amendment to the U.S. Constitution allows me to bare my arms."

"What! You have to be joking…doesn't that deal with guns?"

"I didn't know you were a constitutional scholar!"

"Leave your sleeves down or you'll find yourself back in jail."

Buddy was irritated. "Andy, why did you give me three rookie caddies to work with?" He turned to glare at us and shot back an annoyed look at Andy. "I can't possibly tell them all what to do for nine holes. The women are going to be pissed and I won't get a tip."

"I wanted to give you an opportunity to return Vicki's pink slipper."

"Oh yeah, her shoe is buried in the cart room under some junk." Buddy ran to the cart room and returned in less than a minute with a brown paper sack. He then sprinted across the parking lot and went into the dark toilet cavern. After he returned, I saw him stash the sack in a side pocket in VD's golf bag.

We congregated on the first tee to await the women. Within two minutes, Vicki Dix strolled up to me, accompanied by a very attractive lady. "Boy, since you're holding my bag, I assume you're my caddie."

I was nervous, fearing she knew that I had pulled off the sprinkler incident. My voice was trembling. "Yes ma'am."

"Do you have a name?"

"Yes."

"Well, what it is?"

My knees couldn't stop shaking. "Scott…Scott… Scott…Spy… Spy…Spykstra."

"Do you have a stuttering problem? If you do, I'll demand another caddie."

"No, I don't stutter. I had something caught in my throat for a second there."

"Hmmm…I know a Steven Spykstra, who's a real estate banker in Milwaukee. Is he related?"

"No. I don't know him."

The attractive lady addressed Jesse. "Good morning young man. My name is Ada Mellon and you must be my caddie."

"Yes, my name is Dean James, but my friends call me Jesse. Would you mind if I smoked?"

"Absolutely not. I smoke Virginia Slims. I've come along way, baby…all the way from New York! Can you light me up too?"

Jesse pulled out a match and lit her cigarette. VD also reached for a pack and motioned to Jesse to light her cigarette as well. "Ada, I used to smoke Old Gold, but I loved the Silva's ads, 'Cigarettes are like women…the best are rich and thin'."

"Jesse, I haven't had a caddie for a long time, so you can remind me what to do."

"Ada, he works for YOU, so order him to do anything you need."

"Okay, Vicki. I need to work on putting, so I'll be back to the tee soon."

I noticed Mrs. Buffoon using a set of steps to descend to the tee area, needing to place both feet on each step. I contemplated how my home scale would respond to a person weighing more than the two hundred-fifty pounds. Would it automatically freeze at two-fifty, roll over to a new number, or simply break?

As she neared the tee, I could see that she was breathing heavily. She suddenly turned away, apparently hoping no one noticed her viciously scratch her crotch area.

VD apparently saw it. "Are you alright?"

"I'll be fine. Please give me a couple of seconds."

"We haven't played together. I'm Vicki Dix and my husband, Lars, is on the Board."

"Nice to meet you, Vicki. I'm Ethyl Buffont. I am an algebra teacher and school nurse at St. Stephen's Grade School."

"We belong to St. Stephen's, so I'm surprised we've never met."

"Did you have kids in school there?"

"Heavens no. We've never even had time for kids, even though Lars and I practiced nearly every day...well, not as often anymore. What's your husband's name?"

"He's a professor at La Crosse College."

"Professor Buffont?"

"Yes, he teaches astronomy."

"You're married to that Orbit guy, eh? Lars has mentioned him."

"What does Lars do for a living?"

"Larson graduated from Harvard Law School at the top of his class. He's an attorney."

"We should have dinner sometime. Our favorite restaurant is French's Buffet. They offer an all-you-can-eat special on Sunday and Tuesday nights. We love the broasted chicken and the chicken fried steak."

"I bet you go there often. I mean, do you go there often?"

"At least once every week."

Sally was the last to join the group. "Ethyl, have you met Sally, our new lady assistant pro? She's playing with us today."

"Hello Ethyl."

"Sally, I didn't know there were lady assistant golf professionals."

"They're a few of us out there. I met George Palmer in Miami at the golf trade show in January and he offered me the job right there on the spot. It's been hard to adjust to the cold weather, since I've lived in Florida my whole life."

Buddy whispered to me. "It wouldn't take me too long to become HARD with her in any temperature."

Since he emphasized the word hard, I assume that he was referring to an erection. I guess I wasn't naïve about everything after all.

"Sally, you will enjoy meeting the ladies here. Perhaps you can show us a couple of tips today."

Buddy whispered again. "Her tips are already showing."

"Vicki, a golf professional cannot give instructions when playing in a tournament."

"We won't tell anyone."

"I really can't. I'm sorry."

Ada Mellon strutted over to the group. She had shed her jacket, revealing a perfect set of knockers, enhanced by her thin waist. Her blonde hair was pinned in a ponytail and she wore a short blue skirt. She gestured toward Sally. "Good morning…you must be Sally. My name is Ada Mellon and I'm so pleased we were matched up to play together. I haven't had much time for golf, although I'm planning to make it a priority this summer."

"Why haven't you played?"

"I'm a realtor and part-time interior decorator, so it's a challenge to juggle the jobs with golf."

Buddy snickered as whispered to me again. "I want a job juggling her melons and decorating her interior."

"Shhhh! I'm trying to hear what they're saying, Buddy." I pleaded.

"Do you sell houses? I thought only men were realtors."

"Vicki, I've been selling houses for several years now. I am marketing new model homes in Bluffview Estates for Del Casas Homes. We have such beautiful houses, which include split levels and raised ranches with great appliances packages and wall-to-wall shag carpeting. A few homes are upgraded with a natural fireplace. You should come by and see the latest in our bathroom fixtures."

Buddy was relentless. "She is the actual model. What I would give to see her shag carpet! She can raise my fixture before I dive into her fireplace."

"Shhhh!"

"Ada, what does your husband do for a living?" VD asked.

"He's the CEO of MellonMade Enterprises. He's a graduate of Notre Dame University and was a star football player there."

"They have the most beautiful dresses and women's apparel. I can't wait to see their new fall lineups."

"Yes, they have a lot of returning lettermen and expecting a winning season."

"I'm not talking about football. I was commenting on their fall fashion lines, which should include the mini-skirt, recently promoted in several London fashion shows. Say, I would love to arrange a dinner with you and our husbands. There is a new French restaurant downtown next to the Stoddard Hotel we've wanted to try. What is your schedule next week?"

"I'll have to check Walt's calendar since he is on the road so much. You know…all of the fashion shows in New York, Chicago, Milan, and Paris. He also spends a lot of time in Phoenix for some reason."

"I'm sure he is a busy man."

Mrs. Buffoon joined the conversation. "I've read a review on the restaurant too. What's the name again…Brassiere 38? Let's all go together."

"Ethyl, it's an upscale restaurant compared to the French place you frequent and the name is actually Brasserie 38! A LARGE party may have trouble getting a reservation and I doubt they serve chicken fried steak," VD retorted.

Ignoring VD's rude remark, Mrs. Buffoon changed the conversation back to clothes. "Ada, does your husband's firm design clothing for full-size women?"

Ada quickly studied Ethyl's dimensions. "No, but Walt has mentioned a specialty store in New York called Jumbo's Fashions."

Sally seemed agitated. "Can we discuss golf? There are prizes today for the lowest scores and I want to win."

"Me too!" VD added. "I have many trophies and another one will look great on my rack."

Buddy seemed intent on providing me and OC more feedback. "VD's rack looks full already. I would guess she wears a DD. OC, why would someone name a restaurant after a bra?"

"It's a clever name for a restaurant where all the waitresses wear only thirty-eight size bras."

Our side conversation was interrupted by Mrs. Buffoon. "I didn't even notice you standing over there, Mr. O'Connell. I didn't know you were a caddie."

"Mrs. Buffont, my parents demand that I make some money to help pay for high school. I was relying on a scholarship from St. Anthony's, but I needed to be the eighth grade class valedictorian or salutatorian. As you may have seen at the graduation ceremony, I was robbed of the award."

"I wasn't there. What happened?"

"Father Rotsap announced my name as the valedictorian and then Sister Moron intervened, saying Mary Henderson got the award."

"Who is Sister Moron?"

"Oh, I meant Sister Maureen of course."

Fortunately for OC, the horn sounded to start the round, distracting Mrs. Buffoon.

"Ladies, we can tee off now. Ethyl can go first, Ada second, Vicki third, and I'll bring up the rear."

"The rear? Now we're talking!" I didn't need to turn to guess who was talking again.

Mrs. Buffoon wobbled over to the tee, bent over, and tried to put her tee into the ground. A loud fart exploded from her butt.

"Ethyl, we need to get off to a roaring start, but I didn't have that in mind," VD snarled.

Mrs. Buffoon dropped to one knee to help secure her tee, but was having trouble pulling herself up on her feet. She motioned OC over and held her hand out. OC reluctantly clasped it, but lost his balance, as Mrs. Buffoon pulled him on top of her. He quickly rolled over and jumped to his feet.

"I'm sorry, Mrs. Buffont. I wasn't prepared to play wrecker."

"Can one of you other caddies please help me? I can't get up."

Jesse and Buddy ignored her plea, so I reluctantly stepped forward and clasped her sweaty left hand tightly. OC secured her right hand, while I braced myself. She nearly pulled me over too, but I locked my left knee. She grunted, stood up, and grabbed her thigh. "I have cramps."

Buddy laughed as he drew OC and me aside. "I'll bet she meant to say she has crabs! Didn't you see Mrs. Buffoon scratching her snatch?"

"Crabs? She has seafood in her pants?"

"Yeah, Zero…seafood improves her eyesight!"

"When I fell on her, I thought I landed in a bucket of pudding."

Mrs. Buffoon cut another fart, but boomed her drive well down the fairway "Sally, I got all of that one!"

"You sure did. For a second there, I thought he pro shop fired another shot to start the event. I haven't played with a lady using flatulence for power, but you may have something there.

"Sally, a loud fart doesn't smell as much as a silent one, because there is less air to dilute the hydrogen sulfide. Fart gas travels at ten feet per second and you should also know the average person farts fourteen times per day."

"You probably bring up the average," Sally joked. "So gas travels at ten feet per second, eh? The smell must have reached the group on the next tee, because they're all holding their noses!"

Ada was next to hit her drive. As she bent over to secure her tee, Buddy and OC bumped one another vying for a perfect angle. She concentrated and swung with perfect tempo. The golf ball launched off the tee like a rocket and landed only twenty yards short of Mrs. Buffoon's ball.

"Ada, that's one of the most beautiful natural swings I've ever seen."

"Sally, my father was the head golf pro at a country club in New York where I grew up. We lived a block from the course, so I got to play or practice every day."

VD was next to play. Although she appeared to be in her late-forties, she still had a shapely hour-glass figure. OC and Buddy knelt for a better view of her hinder.

Buddy gestured to me. "We're on the wrong side to see her cleavage with that low cut blouse."

VD lifted a perfect drive and Sally was impressed. "My goodness, we have a real talented foursome the pro shop assembled. Vicki, you've had some lessons too."

"Yes, George Palmer has worked on me for several years."

Buddy thrust his fist in the air. "I heard PRO has been pumping her for a long time."

I murmured back. "I'm not sure about that. He was as anxious as the other guys to check out her boobs."

"What?"

"Ah…something Andy mentioned the other day."

Sally was last to drive. She wore a tight pink golf shirt and her nipples were clearly visible through her bra. I sensed tightness in my shorts, so I pulled VD's bag closer.

Buddy had another comment as we left the tee. "We have three beautiful bodies and a blimp. Does anyone have some helium to launch Mrs. Balloon into orbit so we can get a substitute?"

As the group walked down the fairway, VD motioned toward Buddy. "I've only seen one of you caddies before. Isn't your name Buddy?"

"Yeah, I've been here for five years now. I graduated from Lincoln High School last week."

"What are your plans now?"

"I plan to caddie for Ms. Van Dyke today."

"I meant, what are your plans after high school?"

"To be a master mechanic. My Dad has a repair shop on Logan Avenue. My specialty is lube jobs, especially for women."

"Well, I assume engines need to be tuned up often, but my husband takes care of my motor."

"Yes, but you never know when the rods need to be changed. The bolts and nuts might be worn out too."

"How would I know if my engine needs a tune up?"

"If your motor sputters, you should change the spark plugs. If you have a bumpy ride, your body may be out of alignment. You can come in for a check-up and we'll inspect everything."

"Maybe I will. What's the name of your shop?"

"Discovery Body & Repair."

"So, are you other three caddies new here?"

OC spoke first. "Yes, we have been out on a few rounds, but we're looking forward to caddying for a few years, hopefully. My friend Scott and I are going into high school in the fall."

"Dean, you seem a little older than the other caddies."

"Yup...I'm twenty-one, Mrs. Dix."

"Why are you only starting to caddie? There can't be much money in it."

"I'm doing a research project for a sociology professor to find out how wealthy people live."

"Could my husband and I be part of your research? Lars and I are pretty rich, although we certainly want more."

"Good...you've already helped me."

VD and Ada smothered their second shots, and after blowing out another fart, Mrs. Buffoon bombed her three wood shot straight up the fairway.

Sally was curious, "Ethyl, what did you eat for breakfast?"

"Three fried eggs...no four, a stack of pancakes with maple syrup, a few strips of bacon, six pork sausages, and four pieces of buttered white toast."

"Is that all?"

"Oh, I forgot...three powdered donuts from Grandma's Donut Shop."

"Whatever you ate, you're cooking with gas."

VD and I strolled to the spot where her ball had landed. I handed her a pitching wedge and stepped two feet backwards, lifting my toes to improve my sight angle to her cleavage. When she bent over to pick up a leaf, her yellow blouse opened to expose her pink breasts, and for a brief second, I saw her white nipples. My weenie got stiff again, so I pulled the golf bag closer. After VD rolled her shot to the green, she buttoned up her blouse.

Buddy circled the green. "Spykstra, I heard VD ask for a wedge, so I was checking from behind to see if her underwear was riding up her butt. She has one of the roundest asses I've ever seen. Except for Mrs. Buffoon, they all have nice butts! We must be in hinder heaven. Do you know where heaven REALLY is?"

"Up in the sky somewhere?"

"Hell no...heaven is between their legs!"

"Why?"

"You may discover that someday if you're lucky."

Buddy and OC took positions directly behind Sally, VD, and Ada as they squatted to line up their putts. I tended the flag stick, as Jesse was preoccupied lighting another cigarette. After everyone had putted out, VD was eager to record the results. "I'll write our scores and telephone letters today. Ada and Ethyl each had a stroke, so we all tied with net 4s, so the phone number 4 matches up with G, H, or I."

Buddy whispered to me, "I wish they would stroke me, except for Mrs. Buffoon...her grip would surely strangle my cock."

Mrs. Buffoon manufactured another super-dooper, as her second drive exploded. As the foursome trudged down the fairway, Mrs. Buffoon continued to scratch herself, but queried Ada. "I'm considering redecorating our living room. Do you suggest the carpet and the drapes are the same color? We have brown carpet and brown curtains now."

"Not necessarily, carpeting typically comes in standard stock colors, so it's easier to blend the shading of the drapes. For example, I have black carpet at home and off-white drapes...actually more blonde in color."

"Thanks...I might ask you to help me some time."

"I'd love to."

The players were set to strike their second shots. VD topped her ball, while Ada pulled her ball into the left rough. Sally connected with her 4-wood to within one hundred yards of the green. Mrs. Buffoon flinched, causing her shot to flare into the trees. She grunted and swore. "Damn it, Sally...my itch won't stop."

"Did your itch cause the twitch? I've not heard of a cure for a crab louse, although trimming your pubic hair might help."

"What makes you think I have crab louse?"

"Because you hit a lousy shot and are getting crabby. You're scratching your crotch so vigorously, you'll tear your pedal pushers!"

Buddy heard their conversation. "I had never heard of a woman pruning her pubic hair, but it sure sounds intriguing."

As Mrs. Buffoon tromped up the fairway, I wondered if ants or worms were terrified as she took each step, as if an earthquake was erupting. My thoughts were suddenly interrupted when VD screamed after hacking another grounder. "Darn! What am I doing wrong today?"

I decided to offer her encouragement. "At least your ball went straight at the hole and not in the trees."

She stared at me with a frown. "I wasn't speaking to you, so shut up and keep your thoughts to yourself."

I tried to apologize. "Sorry." As she briskly walked away, Buddy offered a suggestion. "I'll tell you what's wrong with her. She's on the rag...ask her if she needs a sanitary napkin."

I ignored him and trotted to catch up with her, as she approached her ball that was awkwardly sitting between two grass mounds. After several practice swings, VD surveyed the lie. "These big humps are making this challenging."

OC now joined in. "With her big tits, every swing should be challenging!"

Sally took an inventory of the other player's shots. "What's everyone's score? I'm laying four now."

Buddy seemed excited. "She's gonna lay all four of us in the woods!"

Ada proclaimed, "I'm laying five!"

"She must be a nymphomaniac too!" Buddy beamed with excitement.

I corrected Buddy. "They're just counting their shots." But Buddy shook his head, rejecting my theory.

When they completed the hole, VD confirmed the best team score was a six, relating to M, N, or O. "Our telephone word will need to begin with HO, GO, IM, IN, or IO, since the other combinations don't seem to make sense."

The ladies and caddies now gathered on the 3rd tee, waiting for the fairway to clear, when VD initiated a discussion. "Lars and I just bought a Zenith Space Command 600 remote control for our color television. We can change cable and control the sound without leaving our chairs."

Mrs. Buffoon interrupted. "You never know what they will invent next. I need a remote device that controls my husband. There will be a button to take out the trash, another for mowing the lawn, one for helping set the table, and the best of all, a button for the bedroom."

"And what would the bedroom button do, Ethyl?"

"Stop him from snoring, of course."

"My bedroom button would have a different function...HA... HA...HA."

Ada and VD cackled while Sally glared at them.

Mrs. Buffoon's face became red after a slight smile. "Vicki, you have a color TV? We only have a black and white one and we only get one channel, WIZZ, with our rabbit ears."

"Ethyl, our cable television system has seven stations and there's no reason to use an antenna. They plugged a cable into my TV box."

Sally suggested that the caddies walk down the fairway to track their drives. OC turned to Buddy. "I bet you were begging to say you would love to plug your cable into VD's box."

"Zero, you have such a dirty mind! What I was contemplating is to have a remote control for women. The control would have a button for strip, one for spread your legs, another for kiss my dick, and one more for bend over."

Jesse finally decided to offer his opinion. "Buddy, you'll need a button for 'moan', since your little unit couldn't possibly induce an orgasm. And you'll need another button for 'quiet,' when she laughs at the size of your tiny pecker."

"Hey asshole, I'd pull my cock out here right now, but the ladies will fight to see who will ride it first."

"Dream on…you would take an hour to find your dick in your pants, much less pull it out. Is it true you need to take a piss sitting down?"

"At least I have dick."

"Have you heard of the TV show *Have Gun Will Travel*?"

"Sure, the main character is Wire Paladin."

"Wire is not his first name…it's just Paladin. Anyway, the point is I have a HUGE gun, which has travelled far and wide."

I recalled that he carried his big iron in his pants at bars, so that seemed to make sense.

"We can compare the size of our dicks later. Let's watch their drives now."

Except for Sally, the three women were now playing poorly. VD squarely connected with her second shot toward the pin, but the ball rolled between the front traps, across the green, and disappeared in the pond.

"Not fair, that was a perfect shot!"

I was tempted to make another comment but bit my tongue at the last second. VD tossed the club at me, but already having plenty of practice with the Mayor, I easily snagged the club mid-air. Sally shanked her ball into the trees, when Mrs. Buffoon simultaneously hit her in the foot with an errant shot. Meanwhile, I accompanied VD to the pond and spotted her golf ball two feet in the water. Recalling my prior accident, I carefully retrieved the ball and cleaned it carefully. She dropped the ball at her feet, nudging it an inch with her foot to improve her lie. "Hand me the sand wedge...I need to knock this shot in for a par."

"Should I pull the pin?"

"I'll tell you when I want the pin pulled. Now, move out of my view, so you don't distract me." VD bladed the ball over the green into a trap and flung the club in the water. "I told you not to move in my backswing, Go fish the club out, boy!"

I hadn't even taken a breath while she swung, and wanted to protest her accusation, but immediately pulled off my sneakers, rolled up my coveralls, and waded in the pond. I quickly located her sand wedge. By the time I dried myself off and slipped my shoes on, the group was assembled on the 4th tee.

VD cursed. "Hell, we didn't score well again, although Sally fortunately dropped her putt for a bogey five, so that's a J, K, or L. Now we have HOL, GOL, HOJ, GOJ, HOK, GOK, IMK, IMJ, IML, INK, INJ, or INL."

The next hole was par 4, although the women's tees were placed a hundred yards in front of the men's tees, making it only two hundred yards. The right fairway was flanked by a pond. Mrs. Buffoon paused to comment, "Look at all those cute geese swimming on the lake."

Buddy launched a comment instantly, pointing at the women. "Yep, look at those honkers!"

The ladies all propelled their tee shots within thirty yards of the green. As VD reached inside a pouch in her bag for a divot tool, she discovered the paper sack with a pink slipper inside. VD immediately snatched the shoe and closely inspected it. "This may be my lost slipper," as she tore off her stocking and golf shoe, gliding her bare foot into it to be sure. Suddenly, she had a strange expression on her face and quickly pulled her foot out of the slipper. Her toes were covered in a thick brown paste. "This looks like poop!" VD held the slipper to her nose to get a good whiff. "Oh my God…it IS poop!" She dropped the slipper on the grass and quickly ran to the edge of the pond, dipping her foot in the water, desperate to wash off the crap. "Caddie, clean my foot with your towel NOW!"

I bent down on one knee and rubbed the top of her foot and then the bottom. "Between my toes!" I carefully used the towel to scrub between her toes, reminding me of the dental floss procedure Dr. Dreiling used on my teeth. "Wash the slipper in the water too. Does anyone have some antiseptic in their bag? I could contract tetanus!"

Mrs. Buffoon shouted, "I have antiseptic in a first aid kit stored in my bag."

"You are a saint! Can you clean the shoe with the disinfectant too?"

While Mrs. Buffoon applied the antiseptic to VD's foot, I scrubbed her slipper.

"I don't understand how my slipper got into my golf bag. The evil caddies or bag room attendants must be involved. Boy, what do you know about it?"

"I have no idea, Mrs. Dix. I just picked up the bag from the bag room this morning."

"There must be an investigation. Boy, go collect some pieces of the poop from the water to be used as evidence. Stool samples need to be taken from every caddie and the bag room attendants. I need to find the perpetrator and have him arrested!"

"Vicki, what would be the charge?"

OC had an idea. "A dump in a pump? You'll need to call the pooper troopers."

"Shut up! Did you plant the poop there?"

"No ma'am. I'm sorry to be making jokes."

Mrs. Buffoon had finished using the antiseptic. "You will need a scientist to study the stool samples."

"I'll hire a scientist then. Do you know one?"

"My husband knows a college professor who teaches scatology."

"S...cat...ology? Why would I hire someone who studies cats?"

"Scatology is the study of feces?"

"What's his name?"

"Professor Kaka?" OC jested again, but this time loud enough so only the caddies could hear.

"His name is Professor Parc...he's also a member here."

"I've heard of him, but Lars said he doesn't know 'Shit from Shinola'."

"Vicki, he doesn't. Professor Parc told us the saga of his PhD exam one night at French's Buffet. Apparently in the seventeenth century, farmers in Chinola, a small Chinese province, bred a pig and a cow, and called it a 'Sowacowa'. They discovered it produced a unique form of manure and when burned, created a storm, which is where the term 'shit-storm' came from. The Chinola story was an on a PhD oral exam, although Parc had forgotten the story and failed the test, so he's always admitted that he did not know 'Shit from Chinola'."

"Can you ask the professor if he can help with stool samples?"

"Sure, I know he is interested in more research. I've seen the feces photo book he's working on. He's naming each pattern and color and implementing a scratch and sniff concept."

OC cracked another joke. "I can smell a best seller there or maybe just a best smeller."

Meanwhile, I didn't know how to procure the turd samples out of the pond without using my hand, but finally pulled the umbrella from the

VD's bag sleeve and with the pointed edges, snagged four nicely shaped turds. I placed them in the towel and fluffed them to drain off the water."

"You contaminated my umbrella scooping out the turds! You should have used your fingers. Oh well, there should be enough evidence. Make sure you don't lose them and put the slipper in a pocket in my bag. And Ethyl, can you spray some antiseptic around the prongs of my umbrella."

OC whispered to me, "You can tell her the bumbershoot is now a bumber-shit!"

I rolled up the towel and managed to tie the ends to resemble a diaper and delicately inserted it into VD's bag.

Sally was distraught. "Can we please concentrate on our tournament now? We're holding up the group behind us."

Sally made a birdie 3, so VD advised everyone that the letters D, E, or F were now added. "Let's see if any of the letters make a word. Several combinations don't work now, although there are four obvious words...HOLD, HOLE, GOLD, and GOLF. This seems promising. We can also use a combination of letters to make a clever phrase. My committee made the rules, so we can be a little flexible."

"Ladies, let's concentrate on our score and not the letters. Golf is a serious game and you're turning our round into a joke. We're already over par using our handicaps."

"I can play better if I didn't have my nasty itch."

"Ethyl, do you have something in your first-aid kit to help beside the antiseptic?"

"No."

Ada spoke up. "I have a can of mosquito spray in my bag left from last summer."

Mrs. Buffoon read the instructions printed on the side of the can. "Ada, I don't know if insect repellant is a good idea."

"What do you have to lose? At least the mosquitos and flies will stay away from you."

"I'm not so sure," OC whispered.

Mrs. Buffoon stood behind a grove of trees and turned away, unbuttoning her pedal pushers. "WOO! The spray is cold and it stings!" She slowly wandered back to the tee. "Thanks, Ada."

The group had to wait for the green to clear, so Mrs. Buffoon and Ada sat down on the bench while Vicki stood behind, watching Sally practice her swing. I knelt on one knee on the left side of the tee, while the others caddies lined up next to VD. I glanced back toward the bench, focusing on Ada's legs, which grew wider apart. I expected to see her underpants, but blinked repeatedly when I saw a patch of black pubic hair. I tried not to stare, but could not take my eyes away. Suddenly, she crossed her legs. I shut my eyes, fixating on the heavenly image I had just observed, wondering if she had purposely exposed herself to tease me.

Ada stood up. "Walt and I were having dinner at the Club last night and Curly, my kitty, escaped from our car. Did any of you see my pussy this morning?"

I hadn't seen a stray cat around the caddie yard, so I kept quiet.

"Sorry Ada, I didn't see it in our backyard this morning."

With my head still spinning, I hadn't paid any attention to any of the women's shots. I followed VD by three paces, pretending I knew where her ball landed. She circled the trap and surveyed her ball, which was half-buried under the lip of the trap. I handed her a sand wedge as she kicked the sand. "What else will go wrong today?" She swung and the ball didn't move. She swung again, this time the ball clipping the trap ledge and rolling back into an adjoining deeper sand trap. On her third attempt, she managed to land the ball on the putting surface. "These bunkers are just too big."

The other women had hit errant shots as well. Ada and Jesse searched for her ball in the bushes to the right of the green. Mrs. Buffoon had launched her shot thirty feet over the green and was stymied by two large oak trees, while Sally's ball was sitting in a depression off the back of the green.

"Ada, do you have a bush there?"

"Yes, Sally. It's thick and I also have a shaggy lie."

"Try to clip it tight, so the ball gets on the green. Ethyl, do you have an opening?"

"No, these huge limbs are blocking the way to the hole."

"Ethyl, I'm in a strange position too. I'll have to kiss this off the fringe and suck it up to the hole."

By the time all four players had putted out, the best score was a 4. VD configured the new letters of G, H, and I. "I'm not sure what we have now, but let's see what letters we collect on the remaining holes."

"Vicki, we're three over par after only five holes, so let's make some birdies. The pro shop stacked our group and we're a big bust so far. We need to stop all of the meaningless chit-chat."

"Sally, we should attempt to win the telephone game, since we're not going to win with our score. Some groups will shoot under par using their handicaps, but no one will be as clever as we are to link a few letters together."

"Vicki, my career is based upon improving golf scores, so I'm not purposely rigging a score for a magic letter to win your stupid little game. You should be ashamed."

On the 6th tee, I heard VD whisper to Ada to purposely arrange the proper telephone letters for the balance of the holes and sabotage Sally when necessary.

Mrs. Buffoon was complaining again. "Something is burning me. I can't seem to find my rhythm."

"Maybe you need more food. We haven't heard any farts for several holes now," Sally said, offering an explanation. "What's wrong with YOU, Ada?"

She moaned. "My rhythm feels good but I can't putt. It's always stiff and too long. It reminds me of MY husband's bobber. What about you, Vicki?"

"I'm having putting problems too. It's always soft and too short. It reminds me of my husband's bobber too."

"Vicki, you are only interested in discussing the size of your husband's equipment, your cable box, or your television remote control."

Ada seemed puzzled, "We just bought a touch tone phone, so no more dialing. They just started manufacturing them and my husband has a good connection to purchase one."

"Really? We need to buy one soon. My fat fingers get stuck in the rotary holes all the time and I keep dialing the wrong number. Last week, I called McAbre's Funeral Home instead of Fern's Furniture Store. When I asked them if they had beds with lifetime guarantees, they told me their beds last for an eternity and they've never had a complaint. I finally realized I dialed the mortuary by mistake after they mentioned their selection of coffins."

Sally bolted to the tee and smashed a long drive toward the trees on the edge of the dogleg and VD crushed a solid drive the same direction. While we walked up the fairway, VD asked Buddy what type of golf ball Sally was playing.

"A Dunlop 2."

She then asked me to drop her bag and rummaged through the pocket where the golf balls were kept. "A-hah...here's one."

We approached the area where their drives landed, although none of the balls were in sight. We all searched for Sally's ball, when VD spotted the Dunlop 2 under some long grass. When everyone else moved away, she cleverly picked up Sally's ball, replacing it with her Dunlop ball, which had MVCC imprinted on one side. Vicki carefully placed it with the stamp facing the ground. "Sally, we found your ball."

"Thanks Vicki." Sally then addressed the ball and hit it nicely toward the green.

Several feet ahead, I located VD's ball, although she clunked a tree on her next shot with her 3-wood. "Where did my ball go?"

"Sorry Mrs. Dix, but I didn't see the direction after it struck the branches."

"What are you here for? Were you even watching? Did any of you others see my ball?"

"No, Vicki…the ball didn't come our way."

We scoured the trees and rough areas, but to no avail. "I'll have to declare a lost ball and drop a penalty shot from where I played the last one." She decided to use a 4-wood, and her ball ricocheted off several more trees. "Did you happen to see where THAT one landed?"

"No Mrs. Dix, I have no idea."

"Boy, you are totally clueless." She made a token effort to search for her ball and finally threw her hands up in the air. "Sorry partners, I'm hitting the woods great, but I can't seem to get out of them. I'm out of the hole."

Meanwhile, VD and I joined Mrs. Buffoon and OC to search for her second shot, which had also landed in the trees. OC finally discovered her ball wedged between a large stone and an oak tree. "I'd say you're between a rock and a hard place."

"Yes, Mr. O'Connell…with the rock in the way, I'll have to roll my 9-iron over and play it backwards like a rock and roll hit." Mrs. Buffoon grunted as she swung, but the ball landed in the branch of an evergreen tree, five feet off the ground. "I'll pretend that I'm a baseball player and knock my ball out to the fairway. Mr. O'Connell, hand me the driver, which has the biggest face." She took a few swings, resembling Babe Ruth taking batting practice. As she took a huge cut, the ball clipped the club hosel, striking her on the nose.

"Ethyl, you were right regarding having contact with the largest face. You sure have a nose for the game!"

"Vicki, let's face it…that decision was a mistake."

"No kidding, plus you have a penalty for the ball striking you. I'd say you're out of the hole too."

"Yes, I call 'Uncle'."

OC looked around. "You're calling your uncle?"

"It's a figure of speech, Mr. O'Connell."

The group now turned to watch Sally play her third shot, which was forty yards short of the green. She bent over and inspected her golf ball. "Vicki, this Dunlop 2 golf ball has a MVCC stamp on it. I can't believe I hit the wrong ball, which is a 2-shot penalty."

VD spoke up quickly. "What a shame!"

I wonder where my first drive went. I had a lost ball and hit the wrong ball, so I have no idea how many shots to declare. I'll just drop out." She yelled at Ada, who was across the fairway…"Ada how many shots have you taken?"

Ada screamed back, "FOUR!"

OC instantly dove to the ground.

Mrs. Buffoon reached down to see if he had fainted. "Are you hurt?"

OC rolled over. "No…but Mrs. Mellon yelled FORE, so I thought a golf ball might hit me. Andy told us that the first day!"

Sally seemed irritated, "Get up…you idiot. She was just letting us know how many strokes she has. Ada, this hole is all on your shoulders now."

The group surrounded the green as studied the putt for several seconds and stroked the ball, which began to curl too soon. "Stay up…stay up!"

Mrs. Buffoon shouted, "That's what I yell to my husband…but it NEVER works. He always falls asleep at nine o'clock!"

The ball stopped short of the hole and to the right.

"Ada, the putt just petered out."

"Would you stop, Vicki? Enough!" Sally sounded exhausted.

Ada tapped in for a double bogey net 6 and another M, N, or O. Vicki winked at Ada, happy that she had rigged the score.

Sally killed her drive on the seventh hole, while Ada and VD topped their shots less than thirty yards each. Mrs. Buffoon took a big wallop and whiffed, although the ball fell off the tee. OC ran over and teed the ball up for her again. She swung even harder and her club buried into the turf creating a giant divot, while the ball spun backwards.

"Ethyl, I've never seen anyone hit a shot backwards before. I guess the angle of the swing produces backspin on the ball at a high velocity."

"I can't catch my breath. I need to quit."

The other women continued their anemic efforts, spraying their shots in every direction. Sally's ball landed in a divot, causing more problems and the group ended with a double-bogey 6 score again, generated an M, N, or O for the telephone game. On the eighth hole, a best score of 6 resulted in the same letters.

They reached the ninth hole, where VD and Ada received a stroke. VD tried encouraging the players. "We need to par this hole for sure to get a net 3 and an E for the telephone game."

VD and Ada cranked perfect drives, while Sally crushed her tee shot nearly two hundred yards, caroming off a sprinkler head in the fairway, veering toward a pond. We spotted Sally's ball imbedded in the mud. "I can't play from this squishy muck. I'll have to measure and drop a ball near the red stake, where it entered the hazard area. Caddie, I want the woody with the longest shaft for the best angle."

Buddy whispered to me. "I can't believe she just said that!"

"She wants the longest wooden club for her ball drop from the hazard line to get the best possible lie." Buddy shook his head again in bewilderment.

After the other women had played out for net fours, it all came down to Vicki's par putt to record a net 3, with her ball two feet from the cup. "My putt is a 'gimme', since the ball is within the leather."

"Vicki, you need to putt. 'Gimmes' are only excuses between golfers who are bad putters. Do I have to remind you again we're in a tournament?"

"Come on, Sally! I always make short putts."

"Okay, then jam it in."

She sized up the angle of the green with her putter. "This bends six inches according to my plumb."

Buddy raised his eyebrows three times and winked at me.

As VD hovered over the putt for several seconds, I heard a plop sound. A bird had dropped a load on the back of VD's golf shirt.

"What was that?"

"Vicky, a bird just got a free drop on your back!" Ada smirked.

"Oh my God...I can't believe it! I get my foot in shit and now a bird poops on me!"

"Vicki, call the poop squad to capture all the sparrows in the city so you can find the perpetrator?"

"Shut up, Ada." VD scowled at me. "Boy...rub that crap off me with your wet towel."

I carefully wiped the spot as best as I could, but the green stains were still there.

VD tried to pull her shirt forward, so she could see the damage, but couldn't stretch it that far. "What else can happen to me today?"

Sally pointed toward the cup. "How about making that putt for a net birdie?"

"Oh, yes." VD collected her bearings before stroking the ball gently, which curved sharply, rimmed off the top part of the hole, spun around two times and dropped in. "That makes 4 and a net 3, which gives us an E and spells out 'HOLE-IN-ONE! No one can possibly match our word!"

"Well done, Vicki…a Jayne Mansfield putt for sure."

"Jayne Mansfield?"

"You really used the full cup!"

Sally hung her head in disappointment. "Our team has a net score of seven over par…that's terrible!"

"But Sally, we got a HOLE-IN-ONE for our telephone game!"

"Good for you, Vicki. Go call the number and see who answers. "Now Ethyl, I'm glad to meet you, but perhaps the pro shop should have scratched you for opening day."

"Ada and Vicki, I'll call you next week to set up a dinner with our husbands." Mrs. Buffoon offered eagerly.

"Ethyl, we can wait!" Ada replied as she and VD walked toward the clubhouse, leaving Mrs. Buffoon, who had sent OC for a gas cart.

As we headed to the bag room, Buddy couldn't restrain himself. "I can't believe how many hints they made for having sex with us!"

"Buddy, you have a one track mind, you Putz! Don't run out of lubricant from polishing your rod too much in your repair shop." Jesse rolled up his sleeves and pumped his biceps to display his tattoos. He sauntered over to his motorcycle and sped off.

"I would have taken him on, except he has that gun. Let's go see what the bimbos paid us. Did you guys create any vulgar letter combinations?"

OC raised his hand. "I had 'IN-LEG-MOOD', but that's a stretch."

I wasn't too creative either. "I have 'GOLF-IN-ONE' or 'GOLD-I'M-ONE'."

"Those aren't very original. All I came up with is 'HOLD-IN-ONE'. Damn, I was hoping for something dirty."

OC corrected him. "The ladies' 'HOLE-IN-ONE' slogan IS dirty. That's why people use toilet paper! Don't you recall our horrible initiation contest?"

I was still confused with the apparent sexual connotations that Buddy whispered to me on the course. I was more curious why Mrs. Mellon had blonde hair on her head, yet her pubic hair was black…the same as our neighbor, June Morgan. Whatever the pattern, I certainly had a brief glimpse of heaven on the 5th tee and decided to keep it a secret.

Chapter 19

For weeks, I noticed a poster on the pro shop window and an ad in the newspaper promoting a charity celebrity golf tournament as a fundraiser for St. Luke's Hospital at MVCC. The celebrities included Fuzzy Thurston, Henry Jordan, and Lionel Aldridge from the Green Bay Packers, as well as Gene Oliver and Lee Maye from the Milwaukee Braves. With his Notre Dame connection, Walt Mellon had invited Johnny Lujack and Leon Hart, who were Heisman Award winners in 1947 and 1949, respectively. Local radio and television announcers, as well as golf professionals from the area, were also expected to participate. Each group would be assigned one caddie, although the players would ride in gas carts accompanied with their bags. I was anxious to see which group that I would be assigned to.

The rookie caddies lounged on the grass, listening to KORN on OC's transistor radio, when Colonel Cobb announced the next song.

> NEXT UP IS "CONCRETE AND
> CLAY." I HOPE ALL OF THE
> TENNIS PLAYERS OUT THERE
> LOVE THIS ONE.

The song ended and Cobb was back on the microphone.

> THAT TUNE WAS RECORDED BY
> UNIT 4 +2. THAT IS NOT A TYPICAL
> NAME FOR A BAND...WHY NOT
> SIMPLY NAME THE GROUP UNIT
> 6? AND NOW, LET'S TAKE "A WALK
> IN THE BLACK FOREST" WITH
> HORSE JANKOWSKI.

A minute into the song, OC proclaimed, "Who would buy this record...there's no lyrics?"

"Make up some lines, OC."

"Okay." He thought for a moment and launched in. "The Black Forest is where I start...it's so dark...I love to fart...so many trees...lots of places to take a pee."

"OC, call the radio station and let 'em know you found the words."

"Scott, I didn't know they lost them. Speaking of calls, last night I tried dialing the HOLE-IN-ONE number from the telephone game that the ladies made up last week. I couldn't seem to get a connection or else maybe the phone number was out of order, just like those stupid women golfers."

"That contains nine numbers, so no wonder the line was dead. Local calls have seven numbers and long distance calls have ten when you add in the three digit area code. You could go insane trying to repeatedly make a nine digit telephone call and expect to get a connection. Hey...that could make a great script for an episode of *The Outer Limits* though."

Colonel Cobb queued up the next tune.

> *"THEN I'LL COUNT AGAIN" IS*
> *NUMBER SEVERTY-SIX ON THE*
> *CHARTS THIS WEEK FROM*
> *JOHNNY TILLOTSON.*

When the song ended, Ham Radio read the news.

> *EARLIER TODAY, ED WHITE*
> *BECAME AMERICA'S FIRST*
> *ASTRONAUT TO WALK IN SPACE.*
> *HE WAS TETHERED TO THE SPACE*
> *CAPSULE, FLOATING FREE FOR*
> *TWENTY MINUTES. THE FLIGHT*
> *WAS LAUNCHED THIS MORNING*
> *FROM CAPE CANAVERAL IN*
> *FLORIDA AND IS EXPECTED TO*
> *ORBIT THE EARTH SIXTY-SIX*
> *TIMES OVER THE NEXT THREE*
> *DAYS.*

Radio stopped reading.

> *"Colonel, I bet they will be pretty dizzy after sixty-six orbits. I'd like to float in space for free too. It sounds like a real bargain. How can I become an astronaut?"*

> *"The Ringling Brothers Circus shoots a guy from the cannon, so it may be a place to audition, Ham."*

> *"I'll give them a ring-a-ling."*

Radio chuckled for a few seconds.

> *BACK TO THE REAL NEWS...BODIES ARE STILL BEING DISCOVERED FROM TUESDAY'S COAL MINE EXPLOSION NEAR FUKUOKA, JAPAN.*

Radio apparently checked his news script.

> *"Colonel, is that the actual pronunciation?"*

> *"Ham, you shouldn't say the 'F' word on the air."*

> *"I just said it on the air...maybe the Gemini astronauts picked up our broadcast coming around in their orbit."*

Cobb didn't respond, so Radio continued.

> *OH WELL...TWO HUNDRED BODIES HAVE BEEN FOUND SO FAR AND THREE DOZEN MRE ARE MISSING.*

Radio decided to comment to Cobb again.

"Colonel, if I were a miner in there, I would rather be missing than dead."

"Ham, if you were missing, I don't think that anyone would be searching for you."

Radio refocused his attention.

BACK TO THE LOCAL NEWS...THE POLICE ARE CLOSE TO MAKING AN ARREST IN CONJUNCTION WITH THE EPISODE TWO WEEKS AGO WHERE A KID LOST HIS UNDERWEAR IN A WEDGIE INCIDENT.

"Colonel, I've been hanging on by the seat of my underpants until those perpetrators are caught.

NOW, HERE'S THE MAJOR LEAGUE BASEBALL SCORES...4 TO 3, 8 TO 4, 10 TO 6; AND IN A REAL BARN-BURNER...11 TO 10.

Cobb stopped him again.

"Ham, tell the listeners who won the games?"

"The winning team won every game."

"Okay...can you just read the weather report?"

THE TEMPERATURE WILL REACH A HIGH OF SEVENTY-SEVEN WITH A CHANCE OF A FEW SCATTERED THUNDERSTORMS TONIGHT. THE LOW WILL BE IN THE MID-FIFTIES. THE HUMIDITY IS SIXTY-THREE

*PERCENT, AND THE BAROMETER
IS FALLING.*

"Colonel, someone should quickly catch the barometer before it hits the ground and breaks. A tavern would be difficult to find with a broken barometer."

"Yep!"

*NOW A WORD FROM FIRST
INTERCONTINENTAL BANK. F.I.B.
NOW OFFERS FREE CHECKING
ACCOUNTS WITH A MINIMUM
DEPOSIT OF TWENTY-FIVE
DOLLARS AND ALSO HAS TIME
DEPOSIT ACCOUNTS FOR UP TO
FIVE YEARS. SET UP A SANTA
CLAUS FUND TODAY FOR YOUR
FAMILY'S CHRISTMAS PRESENTS.
WE OFFER A CONVENIENT DRIVE-
THROUGH WINDOW AT OUR NEW
LOCATION. DO YOU NEED A LOAN
FOR YOUR CAR OR HOME
PURCHASE? REMEMBER, YOU ARE
NUMBER ONE AT THE F.I.B.*

There was a long pause and Radio continued.

"Colonel, FIB has the perfect initials for that bank."

Colonel Cobb immediately countered Ham's blunder, apparently improving his on-air awareness.

*FIRST INTERCONTINENTAL IS
NUMBER ONE AND WILL EMBRACE
YOUR FINANCIAL NEEDS. HERE'S
THE NUMBER ONE SONG ON THE*

CHARTS, "BACK IN YOUR ARMS AGAIN" BY THE SUPREMES.

Their voices could still be heard over the record.

> *"Ham, you shouldn't say that just because they rejected your car loan application."*
>
> *"They're a bunch of bait and switch bastards."*
>
> *"They may have rejected you because of job security. I know your uncle owns the station, but I heard some advertisers have campaigned to have you fired. You can't make up your own comments to the news and the sponsor ads."*
>
> *"Fired? My audience begs to hear my folksy comments."*

Andy interrupted, holding the celebrity assignment list. I finally spotted my name matched with Ralph Upchuck, my favorite disk jockey. The other players in the group were Dr. Paul Yurren, Dr. Dihn Dong, and Dr. Colin Oskopie. They were starting on the 5th tee and Colonel Cobb's group was assigned to the 4th hole. I noticed that Linus Mayer, Lars Dix, Dowd Jones, Walt Mellon, Hank Kerchev, and Del Casas were all playing in groups with the celebrity athletes.

I couldn't contain my excitement. "I'm in a group with The Duke of Puke. WOW! Jesse, who did you get?"

"They stuck me with Ham Radio, the dimwit."

OC cut in, "I have Colonel Cobb. Pfeiffer, whose group are you in?"

"I'm caddying for PRO."

Lance had Hunter Chetley, while Tom Bunker was stuck with the sleepy WZZZ weather guy, Sonny Cloud. Ron Bunker was in the group with Cy Clone, the WIZZ weatherman. Rusty Steele was assigned to Richard Bore, the dull morning host on WZZZ.

"Bing, whose group are you in?"

"Andy assigned me to Lee Maye from the Braves. He gave Moose Lionel Aldridge, supposedly because their names matched. Andy decided to caddie and took Henry Jordan and the other senior caddies all got the pro athletes.

Jesse corrected Bing. "Let's be honest. You and Moose were assigned to the only two Negro athletes, since Andy and his buddies are bigots."

Our exchange was interrupted as the celebrities emerged from the clubhouse, escorted by the Club Board of Directors. I slowly passed the table where Lee Maye and Lionel Aldridge were signing autographs. My eyes were glued to their faces and arms, having never seen a Negro in person. Their skin was much darker than they appeared on our black and white TV set at home.

Although I had never seen a photo of Ralph Upchuck, I thought I could spot him based upon his attire. Even though the Club's dress code had been relaxed, I assumed Ralph would still dress inappropriately. I saw a barefoot dwarf wearing khaki army shorts, a tank top undershirt, and clip-on suspenders, wondering if he was The Duke.

OC tapped me on the shoulder. "The midget without shoes is Colonel Cobb and the dude next to him is Ham Radio." Cobb was short, no more than four foot-six inches tall and was as bald as a cue ball. He appeared to be around thirty years old if I had to make a guess. Ham Radio was nearly six feet tall and a bit younger. His face was dominated by a thick red mustache and a giant nose. He wore plaid golf slacks, a bright red golf shirt, a white belt, red and white golf shoes, and a newsboy flat cap that matched his pants.

Andy instructed us to report to the driving range and assist the players in our groups. The names of the celebrities were posted on signs, along with the number of the hole where they were starting the golf round. I hustled to the range. Three guys, resembling triplets, stood by the Hole 5 sign. They each dressed in baggy orange shorts, pink golf shirts, tan tennis shoes, and black stockings, pulled up to their knees. As I approached them, I read the emblem MEDICAL INSTITUTE OF AMERICA on their wrinkled shirts. Their faded red caps were decorated with white sweat stains and displayed the initials M.I.A. I recognized Dihn Dong, the doctor who had rushed to aid Abe Goldman, after he was struck by Ezra Epstein's golf ball.

I introduced myself to the doctors, "Good afternoon doctors, my name is Scott and I'm caddying for your group today."

The oldest doctor, who had a closely trimmed grey mustache, responded instantly. "I'm Dr. Paul Yurren from St. Luke's Hospital. My partners are Dr. Dong and Dr. Oskopie."

Dong and Oskopie grumbled in a very low pitch, ignoring my attempted handshake. After watching the doctors try to execute a few practice shots, I could see they were all hacks. Although The Duke had not shown up yet, there were more spectators gathered behind his range sign than where any of the professional athletes were stationed. I noticed a tall, bearded, man sauntering toward me, walking bow-legged. He wore only a leather vest, a skimpy orange bathing suit, and red cowboy boots. He also sported a white cowboy hat with a rotating propeller on top. This strange character had to be Ralph Upchuck.

The spectators, mostly younger fans, started chanting loudly..."Puke...Duke...Puke!"

Ralph didn't disappoint them..."RRRRRR...AAAAAA...LLLLL...FF!" The spectators cheered as he neared us. "What's up docs?"

Yurren addressed him. "Did you just come from a swim meet, a carnival, or a rodeo?

"A rodeo! In case you haven't heard, I broadcasted from atop a mechanical pony in front of Woolworth's for the past thirty-six hours. My fans must have dumped over four thousand nickels in the slot that I got concerned that the pony might collapse from fatigue. I raised over four hundred smackers for Roy Rogers' horse, Trigger, who is gravely ill. If Trigger dies, the funds will be directed toward his preservation, so he won't be sent to the glue factory. I haven't slept in two days and my legs are killing me. Yippee ki-yay!"

"We are doctors at St. Luke's. I'm Paul Yurren and practice urology."

"What your middle name?"

"Phillip."

"So, PP Yurren, eh? Did you ever read the novel *Yellow Trickle* by I.P. Daley?"

"I haven't, but meet Dr. Oskopie, a proctologist, and Dr. Dong, another urologist."

Ralph bent over and blew out a loud fart. The audience hooted and applauded again. "Docs, did you specialize in your medical fields based upon your last names or is that just a coincidence?" The doctors looked at each other and shrugged, apparently not understanding the question.

I reluctantly introduced myself to The Duke. "Hello, Duke. I listen to your show every night. My name is Scott Spykstra and I will be your caddie today, but I won't be toting the bags though. I'll be a fore caddie to watch the drives, help with the pin, rake the traps, keep score, and assist in anything else you might need."

"I'll need a cold beer every hole and a hot waitress to serve me."

"Some of the volunteer hospital nurses are serving food and drinks on the course."

"I need a beer right now, so find me one, kid!"

I sprinted to the clubhouse and hammered on the bar window. Barry Keeper was manning the men's grill and quickly poured two beers for me. I briskly returned to the range, handing The Duke one beer cup. He chugged it down without taking a breath, erupting in a violent belch. The fans cheered again. I held the other beer in case he needed another one right away.

Mayer Mayor had been observing The Duke's antics from the other end of the range. He scampered over to confront The Duke and Cobb. "We decided to slightly amend the dress code today, but you two bumpkins are taking this to an extreme. Cobb, I'll let your play barefoot, but you need to wear a shirt."

"I'm wearing a shirt!"

"That's an undershirt" He pointed at OC, "Caddie, run to the men's locker room and ask that dim attendant for a golf shirt. There's a bunch in the lost and found. Now, as for you Upchuck, you need a shirt and a pair of shorts, and there are no boots allowed on the course."

"Chief, they told me I'd begin on the range, so I wore cowboy boots and my leather vest. I just came from a horsey ride for the last two days, so I figured I'd fit right in." He burped again.

"Fool, you look like a carnie. In case you don't know, I'm President of the Club and the Mayor of La Crosse."

"OOOOOO!" Duke wiggled his fingers at Mayer, as if putting a hex on him.

"Laugh now, joker, but I'm going to wipe you off the air by an executive order, no matter how popular you may be with your demented followers. But if you plan to play golf here today, you WILL wear Bermuda shorts and a golf shirt. And just as I told Cobb, you can play in your bare feet, but take off those ugly boots!"

"Sure, I can chuck em' off." The Duke collapsed on the grass and began to struggle taking his boots off. He looked desperate as he pointed at me. "Hey kid, help me pull these off."

I secured the heel of his right boot, and leaned backward, putting all my weight behind it. The boot shot off his foot and I fell backwards, landing on my rear end. The fans roared in laughter. I jumped up instantly and extended my hands in the air, pretending it was a prearranged gag. The Duke held out his left leg, although I kept my balance as the boot released. I peered down at his dirty white socks, which had large holes in the toe area, revealing a gross purple fungus on both of his big toes.

Mayer now turned to me. "Bumbles, why are you still caddying here. I told Bumgardner to fire you. Oh well, get your ass over to the locker room...pronto. Ask that goof, Jimmie, for a shirt and some shorts for Hopalong Cassidy here."

I sprinted to the locker room and caught up with OC. "Jimmie, OC and I have the two crazy DJ's in our groups and Mayer ordered them to wear golf shirts from the Lost and Found. The Duke of Puke needs some golf shorts too."

"Check the closet, there's plenty to select from." OC picked a faded purple shirt for Cobb. I rummaged through the pile and found a pair of orange shorts and a pink golf shirt to match the doctors' wardrobes. "Thanks Jimmie. By the way, Mayer called you a goofy dimwit."

"I'll have to cook up a little surprise for him. Maybe a little touch of wintergreen in the crotch of his jock will work. Did you know he wear a supporter when he plays golf? Apparently his nuts hang down so low that they interfere with his swing."

I hurried back to the range and offered Ralph his clothes.

"These rags almost match the doctors, but they dress like they're attending a costume party for circus clowns." The Duke walked across the practice green to join the rest of the foursome. "You guys are MDs, huh? MD must stand for mental defects! If I hang around with you all day, I expect to get an honorary degree!"

The horn sounded, signaling it was time for the players to drive to their starting hole. The Duke hopped in the driver's seat of Yurren's cart and popped the clutch, vaulting the front end of the cart in the air. He slammed his foot on the gas pedal and suddenly braked, launching Yurren up and over the front of the cart. He rolled in a summersault like an acrobat over the cart path. The Duke's golf bag fell off the cart too, smacking the faces of the clubs against the hard asphalt.

"Nice roll, PP. Now, I know for sure that you're from the circus!"

Yurren staggered to his feet. "Let me drive!"

"No, but you can drive when we get to the tee!" Yurren reluctantly started to lift himself back into the passenger seat just as The Duke accelerated. It took a few seconds for Yurren to awkwardly pull his body into the cart as he clung to the side. I picked up The Duke's golf bag, anchoring it around my right shoulder, and hopped on the back of Dr. Oskopie's cart. I delicately balanced The Duke's second cup of beer in my left hand and gripped my right hand on the seat rail to secure my body. As we trailed The Duke's cart, I observed his path through three sand traps and across the second green. He then drove over the third green, snagged the flagstick and turned his cart around, taking dead aim at Colonel Cobb's cart on the fairway. Using the pin as a lance as if in a jousting contest, The Duke forced Cobb to swerve, tipping his cart over into a shallow pond. The Duke screamed, "Cobb's program ratings are sinking and so is he! HEE-HAW!"

We finally caught up to The Duke and Dr. Yurren on the 5th tee. The Duke gestured toward his golf cart, "Boy, these things are awfully slow and sure do bounce when driving through those beaches, but the ride is pretty smooth over those green carpets."

As I secured The Duke's golf bag to his cart, I alerted him of his lost clubs on the range. "I picked up your clubs when they fell off your cart on the driving range."

"What are those for?"

Dr. Yurren pointed to his clubs. "Golfers hit a golf ball with them."

"Oh, I thought the bag was a portable urinal and the clubs were weapons that I could use on that idiot car dealer's automobile inventory."

A refreshment stand was located adjacent the 5th tee. An older nurse was arranging the drinks and snacks as The Duke screamed at her. "Hey miss, can I have a kiss?" He bent over and pulled down the back of his shorts and swim suit.

"You should be ashamed of yourself!" The nurse exclaimed in disgust, pointing her finger at him.

"Why, did I forget to wipe?"

"You are a degenerate, sir!"

"Okay then…you can just clean the jam between my toes then." He lifted one foot exhibiting his deformed toes.

"You're a cad!"

"No, I'm not a part time caddie. Now, pour me a beer!"

"You're already drunk, so no more alcohol for you!"

"No thanks, but my caddie is holding another beer for me." I handed the cup to The Duke and he immediately chugged the entire beer again, The Duke's fans quickly gathered around the tee and cheered more vocally. "Puke…Duke…Puke." He stuck his finger down his throat, and threw up right on the tee box. He wiped his mouth on the back of his arm and shouted at the nurse again. "Miss, do they call you a nurse since you work in this nursery? Nice bush you have there!" She turned to glance at the shrubs behind her.

The doctors were shocked with The Duke's behavior, but Yurren seemed pleased to see the spectators lined up to purchase beer to aid the hospital. "The hospital makes a quarter on every beer sold today. Boys, we should tee off now. Ralph, this hole is a par 3 with a pond to the right of the green."

"PP, there's a flock of geese camped out there on the green carpet. Let's see if we can bag a few!"

"Ralph, let's wait until they fly away…geese lives matter."

"Yeah, if we kill one, they may have a shit-in on the green carpet and poop there all day!"

The geese must have anticipated an attack, as they all suddenly flew away. The doctors hit their shots toward the green, with The Duke last to play. Ignoring the iron I suggested, he opted to use a putter, managing to hit his ball fifty yards down the hill. The doctors each took three more plays to land their balls on the green, while The Duke purposely threw his putter and ball into the pond on his next turn. He took off his shirt and golf shorts and dove in the water. A young female spectator stripped to her bra and underwear and joined him in the pond, as well as ten guys who followed her lead. The doctors putted out, ignoring the pool party that had spontaneously broken out.

The Duke doggy paddled to shore, crawled out of the pond on his stomach, and staggered into his cart. The gear was in reverse, so he backed the cart into some fans, who actually prevented the vehicle from rolling into the pond. Somehow, he managed to drive over to the tee without hitting a tree. He slurred, "How did we do, PP?"

"We managed a triple bogey 6 for our best ball."

"Is that all? We should have scored at least an 8! Say, PP, how do you enjoy examining peckers all day?

"I never discuss my medical practice."

"Can you take a peek at my pecker?" He was now peeing on the tee box, shielding himself from the spectators between the golf carts. "How about telling me a few stories about bearded clams?"

"I don't discuss my medical practice."

"Oskopie, you're pretty quiet. You must love looking up asses all day long. Do you have a mining degree too?"

Oskopie ignored him.

The Duke anchored his index fingers on each side of his eyes and turned them up facing Dr. Dong. "Hey slope eyes, what's your name again?"

"Dr. Dihn Dong."

"You must be smart to be a doctor. Why are you called a ding-dong?"

"My first name is Dihn…D-I-H-N."

"So, how often do you ring a lady's bell when you examine them?"

"I never discuss patients."

"Ah so, then tell me how you got your last name."

"My family name is Vietnamese."

"I recently met your brother Wang."

"I don't have a brother."

The insults ended when one of The Duke's fans ran over and gave him another beer. He chugged it again, crushing the cup after he finished, then immediately fell to the ground, and passed out. Dr. Yurren ran to take his pulse to verify he was still breathing. "If he hasn't slept in over thirty-six hours, it's no surprise that he passed out. He's so despicable, maybe we should let him lie here and let the geese eat him."

Oskopie replied, "No…that would be cruelty to the geese. Let's get an ambulance."

Yurren shouted to the crowd, "Can one of you run to the clubhouse and call an ambulance? Doctors, I'll wait until the medics arrive and will catch up later. I wish we had been matched with another celebrity. Oh well, at least our entry fee is going to a good cause."

I was disappointed. The Duke's behavior was outright obnoxious. While I loved his radio show antics, his deplorable actions in person were rude. His devoted fans circled him on the tee, hoping he would awake to continue the golf round. Standing on the 6th green I could see Duke was still unconscious. A few minutes later, an ambulance weaved through the course.

Yurren rejoined our group on the 7th hole. "Upchuck was still passed out when the ambulance arrived. He should be fine when he sobers up."

"I've never met a stranger person. Perhaps I would find his brain in his rectum if I performed a colonoscopy on him."

The rest of the round was dreary and all of Duke's fans instantly abandoned our group. The doctors very rarely talked to each other and never spoke to me, even to say thank you when I handed them their putters, raked the traps, or handled the pin. The doctors were odd, so at least they had something in common with The Duke of Puke. The players finished around six o'clock and the caddies gathered around the yard to compare their stories.

Barney reported that PRO shot a seventy-five and played with some nice Onalaska businessmen, who paid him ten bucks."

OC described his round. "Cobb was a joke. He finally dried off after landing in the pond, although used that as an excuse for his horrible play. We quit counting his strokes, after he got to two hundred. The other players in our group were pharmacists, and they were almost as bad as Cobb. I assumed they drugged themselves before the round. They paid me two-fifty, all in quarters, along with a ten cent coupon for a bottle of aspirin."

"How about your round, Jesse?" I queried.

"Radio lived up to his reputation as a complete idiot, talking nonsense for the entire eighteen holes. Professor Orbit, Doctor Afreudopolous and the mortician, Morty McAbre, were in his group. Those morons made Radio appear smarter than he really is."

Rusty Steele was standing next to Jesse, and continued the conversation, following in a counter-clockwise order around the circle of caddies. "Bore was real dull, so he was actually perfectly matched with the bankers from First Intercontinental Bank. Jerry Misor told me I was receiving three dollars, but he inserted the bills directly into the hospital money box and told me it was my gift to the hospital fund. I protested but they wouldn't listen!"

Tom Bunker was next to report. "Sonny Cloud talked meteorology the whole round. He played with some roofing contractors, who were so frustrated with his incessant weather rambling that, I thought they were going to nail him to the bench on the last hole. I got nothing! Ron and I switched groups in the middle of the round and they didn't even know it. Ron, what was Cy Clone like?"

"He only discussed his women fans. What an egomaniac! He doesn't know anything about predicting the weather. He said that he was a meteorologist, but he didn't know anything about meteors. And he must have smoked two cartons of cigarettes during the round! There were butts all over the place, not to mention the three lawyers in his group. They all lied on their scores and stiffed me too!"

Moose interrupted, "Lionel Aldridge was a great guy...very smart. After his football career is over, he plans to be a TV broadcaster. Three members of the St. Luke's Hospital Board played with him and they gave me ten dollars too. Bing, how did you make out?"

"Lee Maye was a real interesting guy. Last year, he led the National League in doubles with 44 and hit .304. However, I discovered he is an accomplished tenor and also sings in falsetto. Early in his music career he sang doo-wop with future members of the Platters, the Penguins, and the Coasters. He also had several recordings with Richard Berry and the Crowns. He's struggling to balance his musical career with baseball, though. Some of the other hospital board members played in his group and they paid me eight bucks."

Buddy wandered into the caddie yard. "I had his teammate, Gene Oliver...what a comedian! He had us in stitches all day. Dowd Jones...I mean 'Dowdy Doody', and a couple of his clients joined him. Jones kept trying to sell everyone stock, until Oliver finally told him to shut up. They only paid me three dollars, but I had a great time."

Rutt stood next to Buddy. "Fuzzy Thurston was hilarious too. I found out he initially had a basketball scholarship at Valparaiso University and didn't play football there until his junior year. He and Max McGee are partners in the Left Guard Restaurants across Wisconsin. They've been considering one in La Crosse, but haven't decided yet. Del Casas brought two of his subcontractors, who got pretty drunk. They didn't pay me anything, but all the laughs were worth it."

I finally decided to provide the details of my group. "The Duke of Puke chugged three beers and passed out on our second hole. Didn't you see the ambulance that had to come and pick him up? He was crazy, but we had at least a hundred fans following him. The other players were doctors who had no personality and rarely spoke. It was torture to caddie for them. They only gave me two bucks and shamed me into donating the money to the hospital fund."

Andy joined us in the caddie yard and announced that he and his stooges were going to stay and play some poker. It was getting late, and I knew better than to play with those cheats, so I said my goodbyes and headed out. As I approached the parking lot, I noticed Lee Maye and Gene Oliver walking to their car. I decided to catch up with them and ask for their autographs. They could not have been more cordial, as they happily signed an extra scorecard I had in my back pocket and asked a few questions about myself. I was proud to have even decided to approach them. I was anxious to tell my parents that I had met two stars from the Milwaukee Braves baseball team, one of whom was the first black person that I had ever met, so I hopped on my bike and sped home.

When I entered the house at six forty-five, I knew immediately that Mom was mad, as she gave me the silent treatment. Dad had apparently eaten supper and was watching *The Virginian*. She threw the dinner on the table and stormed into the living room. When I finished eating, I joined them. "I met two players from the Milwaukee Braves...Gene Oliver and Lee Maye, and got their autographs. They were very nice."

"I've heard of them." Dad mumbled.

Mom maintained her silence.

"A disk jockey from WPUQ was in our group and there were lots of people following us."

"Uh-huh."

"Well, I'm going to my room now. I'm pretty tired."

"Milton, let's watch *The Dick Van Dyke Show*."

I was depressed that I couldn't share my stories from the day with them. I shut my bedroom door and slipped into my pajamas. I hopped into bed and turned on the radio in an attempt to improve my mood. I was stunned that The Duke of Puke was in the studio, concluding he had a speedy recovery from this afternoon's episode. I listened to his program for nearly three hours, waiting for him to make mention of the golf outing, but The Duke seemed too busy bragging about his drugstore pony ride fundraiser for Trigger. Maybe he couldn't even remember being at the golf course.

I punched my pillows a few times to form a comfortable headrest and thought about the celebrity tournament. I had always been intrigued by celebrities from television and radio, expecting most of them had engaging personalities. However, observing The Duke and Colonel Cobb in person and hearing the stories about the other broadcasters from the caddies, certainly changed my opinion. Was everyone in the TV and radio business like them? The professional athletes, on the other hand, seemed to be sincere...much more genuine. I was surprised Mom hadn't yelled at me to go to sleep yet...she was really taking this silent treatment seriously. I shut off the light and radio and rolled over to fall asleep.

Chapter 20

The MVCC caddies were allowed to play the golf course on the first Monday morning of every month. Our first opportunity was in June and I had arranged to play with OC and Barney. Like most situations involving OC, it was eventful day, so say the least.

In preparation of our caddie round, I practiced hitting Dad's old golf balls around the open field near my house with a set of four irons I received as a Christmas present. I worked on my putting using three golf balls I found on the course, aiming into a glass laid sideways on the carpet in the hallway. For my first official golf round at an exclusive country club, I decided to dress like a professional golfer. I picked out a pair of khaki pants and a green golf shirt, but had to play in my sneakers, since Mom and Dad wouldn't spend the money on a pair of golf spikes. Dad had an old golf bag stashed in the basement, and with his permission, I fashioned a rope onto the strap to make it easier to carry. I heaved it over my shoulder, jumped on my bike, and headed to the Club, hoping to play my first eighteen hole round ever.

Monday morning was also the regular Junior Golf Day for the members' children. When I arrived at the course, a dozen young kids surrounded the first tee as Buddy, Rutt, Bronco, and Moose hit their drives. All of the junior golfers seemed to be dressed in matching uniforms…khaki shorts and white collared shirts, and carried similar red, white, and blue checked golf bags.

Barney instructed us, "Let's line up behind the A caddies. The pro shop won't open until noon and no one is policing the tee times, so anything goes." Immediately after Moose launched the final drive, Barney put a ball on a tee, crowding out a group of ten year-old girls. "Honey, we're going next because we work here."

"My Mom said we are next to tee off after those caddies. We've been waiting here for thirty minutes."

OC stepped forward to block them. "We don't care if you've been here all night. Too bad…so sad. We're going ahead of you. Besides, we're only a threesome, so we'll play faster."

The girls began to cry and one of them ran to the clubhouse.

"Crap!" Barney exclaimed. "That girl was Mayer's daughter, Molly. Let's hit right away before her mother kicks us off."

Without any warm-up, Barney clubbed a decent drive, while I chopped a dribbler with my 3-iron. OC swung and missed twice, before slicing his ball far to the right.

"OC, what a huge badnana ball!" I joked, recalling Andy's description of a bad slice. Your shot was so far off-course, your golf ball may have nailed some monkeys in South America. You had better take a compass and a map with you, so you can find your way back to the fairway."

OC countered, "Scott, you look like a bozo with those long pants. And I see you only have four irons and a putter in your shitty old bag. If it's too heavy for you to carry, let me know."

I ignored him, glancing back toward to the clubhouse where a group of women were pointing at us. I hurriedly played my second shot and surveyed the fairway. The senior caddies were already on the first green, although there were three groups of junior golfers lined up about every hundred yards apart. Buddy and the boys must have quickly played through all of them.

Barney yelled, "Out of our way kiddies…we're playing through!"

I smacked my next shot, barely missing a boy's head and OC's ball ricocheted off a girl's golf bag, landing in the fairway. The girl bawled as she inspected the bag, finding a round hole in the side panel. She addressed OC, sobbing between each word. "You hit my bag and left a hole."

"Sorry, I yelled FORE! Now you have a holy bag. Praise the Lord!"

Barney ignored her and studied the fairway, "We're almost through the little munchkins now, so let's make time."

I bombed my next shot into a trap, but my next shot was a new adventure, since the municipal course did not have any sand bunkers. After two chunky shots, I struck the ball thin, soaring out of bounds. I started to jump the fence to retrieve my ball, when Barney screamed at me. "What are you doing? Take a ten and let's go!"

"That's my best golf ball."

"Forget it! Take a ball from your player's bag on your next caddy job. Your player will never miss it."

"That would be stealing, a violation of the Seventh Commandment!"

OC interrupted, "Big deal...my goal is to break all Ten Commandments! I've got seven down and three to go. I may have to enlist in the army and head over to Vietnam to knock off the fifth one though." He broke his train of thought and pointed in my direction. "Hey, there's a grass snake over by the trap."

I immediately jumped and ran to the other side of the green, believing that it was a safe enough distance.

"I've got a great idea," OC said with a mischievous grin. "I'm going to stuff the little critter in the hole as a present to that whiney girl behind us." He scooped up the eight-inch grass snake with both hands and made his way onto the green, where he jammed the snake into the cup. When OC scampered to catch up with us on the 2nd tee, we gazed down the fairway, where all of the sprinklers were engaged.

"How do they expect us to play through those?"

Barney advised, "OC, just wait until the spray moves past your ball and then sprint to play your shot."

After OC hit his drive, he patiently waited for the stream to pass and raced to his ball. The grass was saturated, causing him to slip, sweeping his feet out from under him. He splashed into a small pool of water. "Shit...I'm soaked. I'm going to turn all of the damn sprinklers off."

"Don't do it! Sod Greenman will be pissed."

"I don't care. I can't focus with the water bearing down on me every swing." He skipped his next shot off the grass, creating a jet of water, simulating the wake of a motor boat. "Crap, at least I won't have to clean my ball!"

I heard screams erupt from the direction of the first green and assumed the girls had discovered OC's slithering surprise. As the squeals subsided, I turned to concentrate on my shot. I decided my ball was outside the range of the longest water shoot and gingerly approached my ball. Unfortunately, the circulation was wider and coming much faster than I had judged. I futilely tried to avoid it, but the wave blasted me with cold water, soaking me, my bag, and my clubs.

After a few more shots, we finally made it to the second green, clear of the sprinklers. I noticed a guy from the grounds crew was methodically turning off each sprinkler back in the fairway. As he drove his utility cart past the green, Barney shouted out, "Hey Mole...stop!"

"Nope, they need me water 3 fairway. Sod-man yells at me."

"Can't you pause for a few minutes? We'll play fast!"

"Nope."

He sped off to set the sprinklers on the 3rd tee and in the fairway. I now recognized him as the attendant at the filling station, where I had left my bike the day of the sprinkler prank.

"Barney, does that guy work at the gas station, too?"

"Yeah, but just on weekends."

"I thought that his name was Moe."

"It is, but we call him Mole, since he smells like he lives in hole." Barney beamed, apparently proud of the rhyme he just created.

With terrible luck, we managed to hit our balls in the line of almost every single sprinkler head on holes 3 and 4, looking like we had been caught in a rainstorm by the time we reached number 5. We caught up with Mole, who was cutting the green. Barney screamed at him to watch out, but the drone of the mower was too loud to hear.

"Barney, let's hit anyway. He seems as dumb as a doorknob…if we nail him in the head, it will only help."

OC's shot careened off Mole's utility cart, rolled onto the green, and hit the lawn mower. He kicked the ball off the green into the trap and continued mowing.

As we advanced to the green, Mole gave us the 'Love Potion Number 1' signal. "You tryyna' hit me on purpose?"

"We were screaming, but you didn't hear us."

"Why you not wait? I need to mow."

"Mow a different green, doofus."

Mole pointed at OC, "How you know my last name?"

"That's your real name?"

"Yeah, Moe Doufuss. I got work to do." He loaded the mower in his cart and drove away, as rain droplets began to pepper the green.

"Boy, he stinks. I wonder when he had his last bath."

"OC, he lives in the back room of the gas station. I doubt there's any plumbing in there, except a sink and a toilet."

I had seen the 'Love Potion' sign a few times recently, but the signal didn't seem to follow OC's explanation from last year.

"OC, you told me that the middle finger gesture was a romantic message. Mole just shot up his middle finger at us. What's so romantic about cutting a green?"

"Ah…ah…well, I was wrong. It really means 'go to hell,' at least that's what my brother told me."

"Thanks a lot!"

"Sure…anytime, Scott."

I began to sweat, recalling my stupid gesture extended toward Carrie Simpson. No wonder why was she looked upset and avoided me afterwards, along with her friends? I knew I couldn't trust OC.

Rain began to fall steadily, so we sat down on a wooden bench covered by the roof of a restroom shelter. "Let's wait here until the rain stops. Barney, have you heard about the new movie, *What's New Pussycat?* They've been advertising it for weeks, so I went to the first showing yesterday. I assumed there would be some good sex scenes with the word pussy in the title and an actor with a name of Peter and O'Toole."

"Did it, OC"

"Not exactly. Several sexy women were in the movie, but I wasted fifty whole cents!"

I didn't want to admit my ignorance again, so changed the conversation. "OC, what happened to the junior kids? Maybe they quit when they saw the snake."

"I don't know, but I have another brilliant idea. I'm going to take a big dump in the women's toilet and stuff a lot of paper on top. It's Women's Day tomorrow, so some lady will have a nice surprise waiting for her."

He skipped around the back and returned several minutes later with a big grin. "Perfect, I wish I could be here to see the first lady who uses that toilet."

"Why don't you contact *Candid Camera* and tell them about your prank?"

"What's *Candid Camera?*"

"OC, it's a TV show. You've never seen it? They set up hidden cameras and film people doing stupid stuff. You can't believe people can be so gullible. The members here would be perfect actors for their show."

Mole soon returned and parked his cart under the eaves of the shelter.

"Mole, I thought you had a lot of work to do."

"I ain't gonna do nuthin' in the rain."

"You should take a shower...you stink."

"I ain't got no soap."

"There's some soap in the can."

He peered around the area. "I no see no pop can."

"Not a pop can...the bathroom can! There's soap in the women's bathroom."

"I ain't no girl, so I no go in there."

"I'll get the soap for you."

OC was back in a few seconds and flipped a soap bar to Mole. He stripped down to his underpants, which were covered in yellow and brown stains. He held up his undies with his left hand, as the elastic band was so worn, it could no longer hold them in place. Mole planted himself under a broken section of the eaves trough where the rain was pouring down and lathered up. He then went into the men's bathroom, exiting with a handful of paper towels to dry off.

"Mole, you need a new pair of underwear."

"No, I just change them around." He pulled his briefs down, exposing his boney hinder. He turned his skivvies inside out and pulled them back on, so the fly fold was now over his rear end. "See?"

"You're a genius."

He pulled his overalls on and reclined on the cart.

"Mole, how long have you worked here?"

"Three or five years, but I pump gas over der." He pointed in the general direction of the filling station.

Sod Greenman suddenly appeared from the behind the trees, driving a tractor. "Mole, why are you sitting around?"

"Dryin' off from shower."

"There's plenty of work to do. Get your ass to the barn and clean some of the equipment." Mole obediently drove off again through the course.

"Hello boys, are you caddies?" Sod, the greenskeeper, asked.

"Yes we are."

"Well, I hope you are replacing your divots and keeping the course in good condition."

OC responded. "Oh, yes…absolutely!"

Sod stared at OC, detecting something was up. He climbed down from the tractor and headed toward the women's restroom, as OC sprinted to intercept him. "Can I help you with anything, mister groundskeeper?"

"Just checking the light bulbs, the toilet paper supply, and see if the sinks and toilets are working."

OC returned to the bench and squirmed in his seat as Sod went into the women's restroom. "I put the seat cover down, so maybe he won't check."

After a few minutes, Sod emerged, muttering something under his breath that I couldn't quite make out. He stood under the eaves where Mole had taken his shower, holding out his work boots to wash them off. "Damn it, the mad lady shitter struck again. We had the same problem last Tuesday with the women's can on the 14th hole. There's crap all over the floor in there. We'll have to use a plunger and flush out all the paper. Did you caddies see anyone ahead of your group go in there?"

"There were some older caddies playing ahead of us."

"We've had some problems with those delinquents over the years. I would love to catch the perpetrator. I'd shove their head in the toilet until they couldn't breathe. I'll have to send Mole back here to clean this up."

Barney waited for Sod to depart before inspecting the damage. "The water keeps flowing over the rim. The toilet must be broken. Man, it stinks in there. What did you eat, OC?"

"I haven't shit for a few days. My butt just exploded, but I feel real cleaned out now though."

The rain continued and ten minutes later, Mole returned.

"Mole, you're back here so soon. What's up?"

"Sod-man said I need to fix lady shitter."

"Yeah, the toilet is overflowing in there."

"A lady stuck?"

"Nobody is in there, so you can go in."

Mole cautiously approached the door, slowly opening it a few inches. He peeked in, taking a deep whiff of the pungent air. "Lots of poop on floor!" He carried a snow shovel and broom into the restroom, propping the door open to let the air clear. He scraped the remnants of OC's turds and shreds of toilet paper into a pile, shoveling the mixture into a large trash can that he loaded onto the back of his cart. As Mole drove away, the clouds broke up and the rain subsided.

"Guys, we need to be off the course by noon, so we can't play many more holes. We must have been sitting here for ninety minutes."

We quickly teed off and played the next three holes in a record twenty minutes. As we studied the 9th fairway from the tee box, we saw a group of four girls talking, apparently unaware that the hole was open in front of them. "Aren't those the same girls who we skipped in front of on the first tee?"

"Yeah, they are. How did they jump in front of us?"

"They cut in, so let's hit into them…they're just yacking anyway."

"Not so fast, OC. Don't you remember that one of them is the Mayor's daughter, Molly."

"Barney...even better! C'mon, if we hurry, we'll have time to play a few holes on the back nine."

OC smashed his ball, nearly hitting the girls. A few seconds later he yelled "FORE" as loudly as he could.

Barney elected not to hit. "The last thing I need is to have old lady Mayer screaming at me for hitting her kid."

I followed Barney's lead and also elected not to play. We walked briskly up the fairway and reached the girls. Molly spoke up, "You tried to hurt us. I'm going to tell my mother on you...and my father too! He's the Mayor and the President of the Club."

OC quickly defended himself. "I wasn't trying to hurt you. The ball went farther than any shot I made today and it was barely rolling. I yelled fore too!

"You are only a caddie and my Dad says caddies shouldn't be allowed to play golf here."

"YOU are the ones who are bad. You cut in front of us and are holding us up by just talking. Look… there's no one in front of you!"

"My Dad says that we can go wherever we want to play, so there!"

"Well, you shouldn't play in the rain."

"It's not raining anymore."

"Just wait a few seconds." OC turned the spigot of a nearby sprinkler, which instantly erupted, soaking the girls as they frantically ran toward the pro shop.

"OC, why did you do that? We're in deep trouble now."

"Barney, they're probably still wet from the rainstorm anyway. Let's head over to the back nine."

After playing the 10th, 11th and 12th holes, Barney started to panic. It's after twelve o'clock and we're probably in trouble already...let's quit."

OC objected, "No, I'm playing great now. I got a double bogey on the last hole!"

Barney and I convinced OC to return to the caddie yard. As we approached the pro shop, I saw VD, Mrs. Mayer, and Molly Mayer gathered around Andy. When we got closer, the girl pointed at OC, "He's the one who tried to hit us and got us all wet."

OC countered, "They were holding us up by just talking in the middle of the fairway, so we decided to play through them."

"You cut in front of my daughter and her friends on the first tee too!"

"Don't caddies have tee time preferences on Monday mornings?"

VD now joined the debate. "There is no such rule. You're just beating around the bush to avoid a punishment."

"Oh, how do you like beating around the bush?"

"I beg your pardon. What on earth do you mean?"

"I heard that you love to masturbate! You know, beat around your bush! You admitted it in the confessional."

Mrs. Mayer gasped, slapped OC across the face, and covered Molly's ears. My jaw dropped as my eyes darted back and forth between OC and the women, wondering what would happen next. I couldn't believe what just unfolded and that OC dared to admit to hearing a confession. I looked at Barney, who had buried his face in his hands in disbelief as well. Andy was dumbfounded and stood frozen, mouth agape, watching the exchange.

VD shouted, "You should be ashamed of yourself! Get off the premises now before I call the police!" She took a swing at OC, and lost her balance, falling awkwardly to the ground. Mrs. Mayer pulled her up and escorted her toward the clubhouse. VD turned to glare at us and delivered a forceful 'Love Potion Number 1' sign again.

Andy thawed and stepped forward, "O'Connell...you're FIRED! Come into the pro shop for your work permit!"

In another act of defiance, OC sprinted to the caddie yard and rode away quickly.

I recollected OC's story of his confessional experience, and put two and two together, just realizing that the lady who thought OC was Father Rotsap was Vicki Dix.

Andy was astonished at what had just occurred. "Pfeiffer, you have a real nice classmate there. I always knew that Zero was the perfect name for him. Why did you allow him to hassle those girls?"

"I told him not to hit at them, but he went ahead anyway. Scott and I didn't even play the ninth hole."

"Bum, he's right." I added.

"We are all going to catch hell. We'll be lucky to keep the caddie program going. Jesus, the Mayor's daughter too! And what's this story involving VD masturbating?"

I decided to divulge OC's confessional story. "Mrs. Dix apparently told OC that she kissed other women and masturbated...it's apparently related to bating fish."

Andy rolled his eyes. "Why would she tell Zero that?"

"He was sleeping in the priest's compartment in the confessional at St. Stephen's Church one morning and VD apparently thought he was the priest. She blurted out her sins for OC to hear, including cheating at golf."

"I hope that he gave her a severe punishment for lying about her golf scores."

"He got nervous about being discovered, so he didn't have time."

"I can't wait to tell PRO and Pags. But for your punishment, you two are prohibited from ever playing golf here again. Now scram!"

"Spike, let's hope the worst is behind us. I really don't care if we get suspended from golfing here anymore."

"I do! I hate that municipal golf course."

The bike ride home felt long and arduous, as I had a pit in my stomach from the confrontation outside the pro shop. I was concerned that the Mayor could have me arrested for being a party to an assault on his daughter, although I feared Mom and Dad's punishment would be far worse. Once again, OC had caused trouble for me. Since I shared VD's juicy confessional details with Andy, I held out hope that he might defend me when PRO heard about the incident.

Chapter 21

The blazing heat, coupled with the stifling humidity, created many unbearable days during July and August. Our house was not equipped with air conditioning, so I spent more time in the basement, which also served as a shelter from Mom's constant surveillance. The basement was slightly cooler, although had an extreme musty odor, even with a dehumidifier running constantly. I even tried experimenting by piling ice cubes in front of a fan, although the test failed miserably.

I went to the club every day and my vigilance began to pay off. Andy assigned me to more courteous male golfers, who were more engaging, compared to the players I was paired with early in the season. They consistently played eighteen holes and paid fifty cent tips. Some caddies went away on family vacations, while some of the older caddies quit coming entirely, so I got a loop every day.

In addition to the oppressive heat, mayflies had invaded the city. The nasty creatures had only a twenty-four hour lifespan, although the infestation lasted two weeks. On at least five evenings, Mayor Mayer dispatched a fleet of snow plows to remove the dead insects from the downtown streets, where the pests were addicted to the bright lights. The plows were also used to clear the Linus Mayer Bridge, formerly the Mississippi River Bridge. The City council had recently approved the name change after Mayer's intense lobbying efforts. Three inches of dead mayflies were piled outside the pro shop every morning, so Andy ordered Jesse to sweep up the insects and deliver them to the caddie slab, where the senior caddies created a crackling sound by stomping on them. I speculated why no one had been smart enough to turn off the lights overnight.

On Saturday, a perspective new caddie candidate showed up. After the traditional tee digging ritual, the senior caddies dumped a handful of mayflies into the kid's underwear before Andy even had a chance to welcome him. He didn't last long. Buddy and Rutt were intent on having someone eat the dead mayflies, so they decided to pick on

Moose, stuffing a handful into his mouth until he started to choke. Jesse came to Moose's rescue by pounding on his back repeatedly. I felt guilty that I hadn't helped Moose, but was still afraid of retributions from Buddy and Rutt. Barney had observed the entire incident, but froze in place too. Moose left immediately after the hazing without saying a word.

"Barney, do you think Moose will ever come back here?"

"I doubt it, Spike. He's going off to college soon. He received an academic scholarship from Marquette University as a pre-med major."

"Do you know what the other senior caddies are planning when summer is over?

"Buddy is pursuing that apprenticeship in his Dad's auto repair shop and Rutt is moving to Kenosha to work in the American Motors automobile plant. Bing enrolled at La Crosse College to become an elementary school teacher. Bronco enlisted in the Navy and you probably know already that Andy is headed to the Marine Base at Camp Pendleton in California. Moose and Bing will get college deferments for the military draft, but I wonder how long it will take for the Selective Service to catch up with Rutt and Buddy?"

"Maybe someone should tip them off." I had never gotten over their bullying.

Barney brought his transistor radio to the caddie yard after OC's firing. The Rolling Stones latest song, "Satisfaction" started spinning as Colonel Cobb introduced the tune.

> *THIS SONG IS NUMBER TWO ON THE TOP HUNDRED LIST. THE TITLE IS ACTUALLY "I CAN'T GET NO SATISFACTION," BUT THEY SHOULD TAKE AN ENGLISH CLASS AND RENAME IT "I CAN'T GET ANY SATISFACTION"!*

Ham Radio butted in,

"*Colonel, I thought the Rolling Stones were British, so they should know proper English.*"

"*They are English. Have you listened closely to the lyrics? There's a phrase written especially for you, so why don't you give our audience some useless sports news?*"

Radio took the prompt and returned to his script.

CAROL MANN WON THE TWENTIETH WOMEN'S U.S. OPEN.

Radio abruptly stopped reading.

"*Colonel, someone needs to tell me how a man can win a women's golf tournament?*"

"*Ham, the golfer's first name is Carol...that's a lady's name.*"

"*I've heard of men named Carroll, like Carroll Hardy, the baseball player, or Carroll O'Connor, the actor, and Carroll Dale, the football player... right?*"

"*Who is Carroll Dale?*"

"*A wide receiver, who was traded to the Packers by the Los Angeles Rams in April.*"

"*A pro football player with two ladies' names...Carroll and Dale? Dale can also be a man's name too, eh?*"

"*Well, parents can give a boy a woman's name or a man's name to a girl. Do you think a woman could ever become a man or could a man change into a woman?"*

There were a few seconds of dead air until Radio continued with the news.

THE WORLD IS STILL MOURNING THE DEATH OF TRIGGER, THE WORLD'S MOST FAMOUS HORSE, WHO ROY ROGERS RODE WHILE AT HOME ON THE RANGE. TRIGGER DIED SATURDAY AT THE RIPE YOUNG AGE OF TWENTY-ONE.

Radio paused again.

"Boy, I'm still in mourning. Trigger was my pal and he was a palomino too. Colonel, did you know Trigger's original name was Golden Cloud? Maybe he produced yellow vapors when he farted. He'll probably be sent to the glue factory now."

"Ham, I'll check for his name on the next container I buy. I thought you were delivering sports news."

"Trigger probably ran in a horse race sometime."

THE BASEBALL WORLD IS STILL DISCUSSING THE FIST FIGHT BETWEEN RICHIE ALLEN AND FRANK THOMAS ON SATURDAY. NO, THEY DIDN'T ENGAGE IN A PRIZE FIGHT...ALLEN AND THOMAS ARE TEAMMATES ON THE

*PHILADELPHIA PHILLES
BASEBALL CLUB AND THE
ALTERCATION TOOK PLACE
BEFORE THE GAME DURING
WARMUPS.*

Colonel Cobb now interrupted.

"Ham, why did they punch each other?"

"Thomas may have called him Dick."

There was another few seconds of dead air until Radio continued.

*IN CASE YOU HAVEN'T HEARD
THE RESULTS FROM THE
WIMBLEDON TENNIS
TOURNAMENT, ROY EMERSON
BEAT FRED STOLLE 6-2, 6-4, AND
6-4 IN THE GENTLEMEN'S
SINGLE'S FINALS IN LONDON.*

Ham Radio added more commentary.

"Hmmm, Gentlemen's singles? Colonel, did they play in white tuxedos? I heard that all of their clothes have to be white."

"Tennis is such a stinky game...what weird scoring! When you have no points, you have love."

"Well then, when I go out on the town tonight, I'll wear a shirt with a zero on the front and a zero on the back. That should bring some success looking for a girlfriend."

"You need all the help you can get with your big schnoz. And when you have a

tie in tennis at 40-40 and beyond, you have 'deuce.'"

"Number two?"

"Like I said, tennis is a crappy sport."

Radio refocused on reading more sports news.

> *YESTERDAY, IN MAJOR LEAGUE BASEBALL, THE PATHETIC LAST PLACE NEW YORK METS AND THE CHICAGO CUBS MET UP IN A DOUBLEHEADER IN THE BIG APPLE. THE FRATERNAL MINNESOTA TWINS SOCKED BOSTON IN A TWIN BILL IN THE TWIN CITIES. THE MILWAUKEE BRAVES WERE ROCKETED BY THE HOUSTON ASTROS 5 TO 4 AFTER A BLASTOFF HOMERUN. THE BRAVES AND THE CUBS ARE IDLE TODAY, ALTHOUGH BASED UPON THEIR HORRIBLE RECORD, THE CUBS SEEM TO BE IDLE EVERY DAY, EVEN WHEN THEY PLAY. FIRST PLACE MINNESOTA PLAYS THE RED HOSE AGAIN TONIGHT WITH MR. MUD, THAT COOL CAT, PITCHING FOR THE TWINKIES.*

Cobb cut in again.

"Ham, who are the Red Hose?"

"Colonel, the Red Hose is a nickname for red stockings, like red socks...the Boston Red Sox. I guess Red Hose could also apply to the original Cincinnati Red Stockings, who

shortened their name to the Reds in 1890. However, in 1953, Cincinnati changed their name to the Redlegs, because communism became associated with the name Reds, but they reinstated it in 1961, so communism must have gone away then."

"Ham, once again, you've given the audience more useless information. And here's a song dedicated to you."

FOLKS, IT'S BRAND NEW ON THE TOP HUNDRED, AT NUMBER EIGHTY-SEVEN, FROM DINO, DESI, AND BILLY CALLED "I'M A FOOL."

"Barney, I can't believe that corn-ball is still a broadcaster."

"Me too, but they won't let him read commercials anymore. Spike, my brother found a key for a door leading to a back staircase which leads to the attic in the clubhouse. He told me that you can peek into the women's locker room through the floor. I'm sneaking up there later…are you in?"

"Sure, as long as we won't get caught."

"Jimmie said no one knows about the stairs."

"When are you going?"

"Right after our loops. I asked Andy to assign us to an early group." He turned up the volume on the radio. "Listen, they're playing this song every hour. It's called "I'm Henry the VIII, I Am"…very catchy lyrics."

"It's the same verse over and over again. People will be sick of it real fast."

Andy now stood in the caddie yard. "Spykstra, I assigned you to caddie for Ada Mellon today. Can you handle her? You're the only caddie in her group."

"Sure."

I tried to imagine how I would handle a romance with her. Should I begin with a kiss on the back of her palm or on her cheek? I hoped she would be wearing a short skirt again for another peek at what Buddy called heaven. After meeting her on the first tee, I was disappointed to see that Mrs. Mellon was wearing shorts, and even more disturbed that she did not remember me from the lady's day event. The women's group did not generate any interesting conversations, at least when I was close enough to hear. Ada paid me a fifty cent tip, the most I had gotten all summer from a woman golfer. When I was done with the loop, I grabbed the sack lunch Mom had prepared, which contained a chicken sandwich and a McIntosh apple. I also computed the number of potato chips that Mom had rationed for my lunch. I counted eleven.

Ten minutes later, Barney joined me on the caddie slab. "Spike, are you ready to go to the attic before the women have a chance to change clothes?" He wiped the sweat from his brow. "Man, is it hot? It must be a hundred degrees!"

"I'm set to go."

To get to the service door of the clubhouse and avoid detection, we snuck around several cars in the parking lot. We found Jimmie, who was carrying a load of towels to the men's locker room. "Hi guys...I'll unlock the stairwell door for you. When you reach the attic, be careful to stay near the beams, because the wood floor is real creaky. You'll see a few gaps over the ceiling fans to view the women's locker room."

"Jimmie, how long can we stay up there?"

"All afternoon if you can stand it, Bro, but I bet you won't last an hour with the heat. Here, take a few towels with you."

Jimmie cautiously slipped a key into the rusty latch and opened the old wooden door. The heat instantly emanated down the narrow staircase and with each step, the temperature seemed to increase by a degree. We reached the second floor and pivoted at a ninety degree angle to ascend the next flight of steps. The passage was only two feet wide, making me feel claustrophobic. We discovered a wood paneled door at the top of the stairs, where a crudely painted sign was inscribed, *'DANGER-KEEP OUT'*. I shrugged my shoulders, wondering if we should proceed. Barney twisted the black doorknob to the right and pushed. The door wouldn't budge. "Is it nailed shut?"

"Let me try." I twisted the wobbly knob left and heard the latch release. I meticulously pressed the door open inch by inch, avoiding even a slight noise. All of a sudden, the top hinge broke off slamming the heavy door against the wall. Barney awkwardly grasped it, tilting it so it seemed secure. The angle allowed a stream of light to shine into the dark attic for us to see the wooden planks. Taking Jimmie's advice, I crept along one of the beams, until I saw a few slivers of light through cracks in the floor. I knelt down to gather a perspective on the room below. There were two lines of white lockers, a few benches, and a small sofa. I moved a few feet to the right for another angle, although could only see a chair in front of a make-up table with a mirror. I glanced over at Barney, who was apparently content with his viewpoint. "Barney, what do you see?"

"Some lockers and a couple chairs."

"Me too…this doesn't seem very promising."

Sweat was pouring off my forehead and my shirt was already completely soaked. Barney pointed down, noticing someone had entered the locker room. I hurriedly returned to my original spot, pressing my head against the floor to achieve the widest view. A short woman, wearing a red bathrobe, strutted past the lockers and disappeared. Mrs. Mayer now arrived at her locker, stopping directly below my vantage point. She rotated the dial on the padlock of her locker door, kicked off her pink golf shoes, and threw her white socks into the locker. She lifted her arms above her head, swiping her armpits with each hand, and sniffed both of her palms. Apparently satisfied, Mrs. Mayer slipped on her orange sandals, closed the locker door, and shuffled away.

I spotted Ada Mellon enter the room and my heart raced. She rested on the bench in front of her locker for a moment and opened the locker door, which partially obstructed my view. As she unbuckled her shorts, I pushed my forehead to the floor until it hurt. She wore short pink panties, exposing an inch of her butt-cheeks. She grabbed a yellow skirt from the locker and secured it around her waist. Then she removed her panties, stuck them in her purse and left. I was crushed.

I patted the pool of sweat which had collected on the floor, using one of the cotton towels, and pressed my face to the floor again. A tall, young lady wearing a short robe strolled by. I twisted my head to follow her path, but it was useless. A large lady, wearing a towel like a turban around her head, now entered the room, bumping into the side of the lockers. As she rounded the corner, I realized it was Mrs. Buffoon. As she plodded away toward the shower room, I could see that the bath towel was too small to wrap completely around her midsection, exposing her flabby buttocks. I rolled over on my back and rubbed my eyes, attempting to strike the vision from my mind.

"Barney, did you see that?"

"Yes, unfortunately."

I returned to my position, crossing my fingers for luck. I tried to check my watch using the dim light, although the humidity had caused steam to collect under the face. I grabbed a towel and swabbed my arms, head, and legs again. Several minutes passed, with no activity, but then, a divine vision appeared. It was Sally Van Dyke. A few seconds later, Vicki Dix slipped in the lounge, checking between the rows of lockers. VD then drew near Sally, staring into her eyes. They embraced and kissed on the lips. Barney moved slightly and the floor creaked, causing the women to peer up to the ceiling. Sally whispered into VD's ear and then took her hand, leading her into another section of the locker room, instantly out of my range.

"Barney, I can't stand being up here another minute. I'm dizzy from dehydration. Let's go."

"Good idea."

We stumbled toward the light, leaving the door ajar and carefully descended the stairs. I could not wait to ask Barney about what we had witnessed. When we reached the hallway, Jimmy intercepted us. "How did it go, Tony? You guys are so wet, it looks like you went through a carwash."

"It was a steam bath up there. We didn't see anything, except for Mrs. Buffont's big fat hind end. Can we try again next week?"

"Maybe, I'll let you know if I'm working. I'll see you at home tonight. Remember, don't tell a soul."

"Our lips are sealed."

We left the building through the service door again. Barney opened the door slowly and peeked around to be sure no one saw us exit. When we got outside, I finally had the chance to question Barney. "Barney, do you remember that VD confessed to OC that she kissed other women? Why would two beautiful women do that? Maybe they were celebrating winning the women's day event?"

"I doubt it, but Jimmie told me a story he read somewhere about women who are romantically attracted to other women. The next time you go the public library, check out the art history books. There are tons of pictures of famous paintings of partially clothed women or completely naked ones, embracing each other."

Andy intercepted us. "Where have you guys been? You're all wet! You better not have been using the Club's swimming pool."

"Andy, we went the snack shack to buy an ice cream cone. There's a new hot chick working behind the counter."

"Pfeiffer, I needed a couple of caddies for Mr. and Mrs. Dix for nine holes. Where were you?"

"We just saw Mrs. Dix. Ah…ah…she was at the snack shack too."

"Her husband called. They're playing together at three-thirty."

"Oh, we thought she was playing with someone else."

"What are you saying, Pfeiffer?"

"Oh, nothing. So, she's playing another round then?"

"Yeah, they're teeing off soon. I had to assign them to the Bunker twins. You two can hang around in case someone else needs a caddie."

Barney and I returned to the caddie yard. "Barney, you nearly spilled the beans."

"I know, sorry, I think my brain got scrambled from the heat."

I still did not comprehend what I had seen, or Barney's explanation either. My mind dialed back to Mrs. Mellon's pink panties. I wondered if they were the edible style Walt Mellon had described earlier in the year.

Chapter 22

Weeks drifted by and the end of summer vacation was unfortunately in sight. I recalled waking up on Monday, August sixteenth, studying the calendar on my bedroom desk. It was the last week for caddying, as my parents planned a weekend vacation at Balsam Lake in northern Wisconsin. Football practice was scheduled to begin on the following Monday, a week before the official start of classes. Eight freshman football games were scheduled every Saturday, so I could only caddie on Sundays for the rest of the season.

I normally arranged an activity with my grade school buddies every Monday, but nobody was around that day. Goober left for a family vacation in Door County, while Gomer was visiting his grandparents on their farm near Sparta, and Barney had to help his father and Jimmie paint their house. With no plans on the docket, Mom decided it would be the ideal time to head downtown and buy new school clothes, an annual pilgrimage that I dreaded every year.

Since Mom did not have a driver's license, we had to ride the noisy municipal bus, which travelled a circuitous route to and from downtown. Mom and I walked one block to the bus stop, and as usual, the bus was several minutes behind schedule. As it finally pulled in, Mom stepped on the bus first, depositing two dimes and two nickels into the collection device, creating a clinking sound as the coins trickled through it. The bus driver wore an official uniform with the name Earl stenciled on his pocket. "Good morning ma'am, are you riding all the way downtown?"

"Yes, we're going shopping for school clothes for my son"

"What school does he attend?"

"He will be at St. Anthony's next week."

"The Ants, eh?"

"No, they're called the Saints!"

"I call 'em the Ants. Can you take your seat now? I can't drive unless everyone is seated."

Mom led me to a seat facing the aisle, near the rear of the bus. The blackened plastic seat had a large rip, which had been taped over. As the bus pulled away, the nauseating smell of diesel fuel permeated the section where we were seated. At every bump in the street, the bus shook violently, vaulting me an inch in the air. Most of the older passengers had to cling to the hand rails to avoid being shaken out of their seats.

After a few blocks, the bus stopped where three girls were waiting. I cringed, recognizing my classmates Carrie Simpson, Jane Miller, and Linda Allen. Embarrassed to be seen with my mother, I reversed positions with her and slumped down in the seat, hoping she would shield me from their view. Fortunately, they took seats in the front row of the bus.

"Scotty, why did you move?"

"I was sitting on a crack in the seat…it was bothering me."

"Aren't those girls in your class?"

"What girls?"

"They're sitting in the first row."

"I can't tell from here."

"After we're done shopping for your clothes, let's stop at Woolworth's and I'll buy you a chocolate sundae."

The driver brought the bus to a halt at every stop, regardless if there were any waiting passengers or not. I heard the driver ask every boarding passenger about the weather, even though the sky was perfectly clear. No wonder why the bus was always behind schedule. We pulled into the Main Street staging point, as I glanced down at my watch, ten minutes late. My classmates exited at the last stop, so I dawdled a few seconds, hoping the girls would scatter without noticing me. Mom stood on the sidewalk, while I lingered on the bus.

"C'mon Scotty dear, what are you waiting for?"

I pretended to search the seat. "I dropped a dime between the seat cushions."

I peeked both directions out of the bus door, making sure the girls were out of sight. I finally took two steps down and leapt onto the sidewalk. Mom grabbed my hand, as we waited for the stop light to change before crossing Main Street, for the short stroll to Doerflinger's Department Store. Upon entering the ancient three-story brick building, we passed the women's department, featuring lady manikins outfitted in only bras and panties. I was taking an inventory of the underwear displays when Mom noticed. She firmly placed her hand on the top of my head and swiveled it forward. "I saw you ogling the manikins. Shame on you! Let's head to the basement to the children's area. Perhaps they might have something on sale in your size."

"Mom, we tried that last year and didn't find any."

"It doesn't hurt to look again."

Mom spied a table marked as a close-out sale. There were five layers of trousers haphazardly piled up, without regard to any logical order or size. She rummaged through the pants. "Scotty, look through the stack over there." I complied and discovered a maroon pair marked 'XL.' Hating the color, I buried them underneath the counter, so Mom wouldn't discover them.

"Scotty, here's a green pair that might fit. Slip them on in the dressing room."

"I hate green. Everyone will think I've enlisted in the army."

"See if they fit and I'll keep searching for another color."

The dressing room curtain wasn't wide enough to completely cover the opening, but after adjusting it slightly, I undressed. I struggled to pull on the trousers, knowing immediately it was a futile effort. I took a deep breath, sucked in my belly, and managed to snap the waste button in place. The bottom of the pant legs were four inches above my ankles. I exited the dressing area and modeled the trousers for Mom. "Scotty, they don't look bad. Maybe you can pull them down a couple of inches. They're on sale for only ninety-nine cents."

I checked the full length mirror to verify the length. "I can hardly squeeze into this pair. Look, I'm practically busting the waist seam."

"All right, but I found a pair of maroon pants under the counter. Try them on."

I rolled my eyes. "I'm not wearing that color and besides, they're the same waist size as these ugly green ones."

"Very well, let's go up to the men's department on the second floor."

Mom decided to take the elevator, which took several minutes to arrive on the basement level. The elevator operator was a feeble woman, who was at least eighty years old. She barely managed to close the gate in the cab. "What floor, folks?"

"Second floor men's department...please."

"Going up...second floor...please hang on to the handrail." She pushed the button for the second floor, although the elevator did not move for several seconds. The cab shook and finally started to climb, stopping a few seconds later.

"First floor...women's apparel and jewelry."

The door opened and my three girl classmates were standing at the elevator platform. I had nowhere to hide, feeling my face turning red, as perspiration dripped from my armpits.

Linda Allen greeted me. "Hi Scott."

"Hello." I was very uncomfortable.

Mom seemed eager to speak with them. "Are you girls shopping for school clothes too?"

"Yes, Mrs. Spykstra. We're going to the third floor young women's department."

The elevator operator interrupted, "Going up...please hold on to the handrail."

"Mrs. Spykstra, are you headed to the second floor?"

"Yes, we're shopping for trousers for Scotty to wear next week when high school classes begin."

I wanted to crawl in a hole.

"That's so nice of you to help him pick out his clothes."

Thankfully, the elevator operator interrupted again. "Second floor...men's department."

I couldn't wait until I got out of the elevator.

"Bye Scotty. I'll see you in school soon."

"See ya." I was struggling to say anything. On top of the embarrassment of being seen with my mother, she referred to me as Scotty.

"Those girls were very polite. Why didn't you talk to them?"

"Because you were talking to them."

"Let's go over there to the young men's area."

An older lady sales clerk approached us immediately. Her name tag read Hilda. She reeked of perfume and had horned-rimmed glasses, with ties strung around her ears. "Can I help you?"

"Hilda, we need school pants for Scotty. He might need a thirty-two waist size and a thirty-one inch length."

"Let's be sure, so I'll measure him." She produced a yellow measuring ribbon from her pocket and stood behind me. "Please stand still while I put the tape around your waist."

I was nearly choking from the obnoxious odor of her perfume. As she reached around my chest to secure the measurement, her floppy boobs brushed against my back. "You were right, he has a thirty-two inch waist. Now, let me measure his length." The lady rested the back of her hand against my groin area and dropped the yellow tape ribbon down. As she got down on her knee to read the end of the tape, her glasses slipped down her nose and her knuckles bumped my left testicle. "The length is between thirty-one and thirty-two inches."

"Hilda, do you have any trousers on sale?"

"Not now."

"Let's see what you have in stock anyway."

"Young man, do you have any color in mind?"

"I prefer tan, brown, or grey."

"Here's the pile with your size. We have all three colors in stock. Here, slip on the brown pair in the dressing room."

Mom grabbed another pair, hunting for the price tag. "They're listed at six dollars."

"Right, although if you buy three pairs, I can let you have them for five dollars each."

I cautiously opened the door to the men's dressing closet, sat down on the chair, and undressed. Suddenly, the door flew open and Mom threw another pair of trousers at me. The clerk stared directly at my boxer underwear.

"Scotty, I found a grey pair on another counter marked as a close-out sale from last year. They're only two bucks. The trousers are size thirty-four waist with a thirty-five inch length, but you'll grow into them."

I put on the brown pants and emerged from the dressing room to model for Hilda. "They're a perfect fit. Turn around so I can see the back."

I pivoted, observing myself in the three-angled mirror. "They feel great."

"Scotty, put the grey pair on now."

I returned to the dressing room and upon donning the grey slacks, I immediately hated them. I couldn't keep them from falling down, so held the waist band with my hand, while the cuffs dragged along the floor.

"Scotty, they look fine to me. You can use your belt to tighten the waist and roll them up on the bottom.

"Mom, the waist is way too loose and they're too baggy. If I roll them up, my friends will call me a farmer."

Mom seemed exasperated. "Oh well, we're just starting to shop, so we may return later."

"Can I help with anything else? Do you need socks, shirts, or shoes?"

"No thanks."

"Let us know if we can do anything else to assist you. Thanks for coming in."

Escaping from Hilda's perfume, I could breathe again. I steered Mom toward the stairs, avoiding another elevator encounter with the girls. "Mom, let's walk down the stairs. The elevator takes forever."

"Scotty, let's head over to Monkey Wards. They usually have a better selection."

"Why didn't you buy the brown pair I tried on?"

"They would have cost over six dollars with the tax. I've never paid that much before."

We marched two blocks south, crossing Fifth Avenue, where Mom took my hand again. We entered the Montgomery Ward's store through the revolving door. As we strolled through the women's section, I couldn't help but gawk at the women's manikins again. Mom slapped the back of my head. "Why are you looking again? You need to go to confession on Saturday!"

I would never go to confession again after hearing OC's story. In the future, I decided to simply say five 'Our Fathers' and five 'Hail Marys' every week on my own to cover everything, the normal pattern for my penances from Father Rotsap.

The store had an escalator, which we rode to the second floor. I scanned the women's shoe department below, realizing a shoe salesman would have ample opportunity to see between the legs of any woman wearing a dress as they tried on shoes. Lost in thought, I stumbled off the escalator when reaching the top.

"Scotty, are you all right? Weren't you watching the steps? You might have gotten hurt. That's why I still need to hold your hand."

A younger sales clerk headed directly at us. "Good afternoon, my name is Duane. How can I be of assistance?"

"My son needs some new britches for high school. Do you have any on sale?"

"What school are you attending?"

"He's starting at St. Anthony's in a few days."

"I have a few friends who went there too. I graduated from Lincoln three years ago."

Mom was in a talkative mood. "How nice! How long have you worked here?"

"I've been here full time since graduation and part time during high school. I was in the boys department initially but have been in the young men's area for two years now. I meet such interesting teenagers nowadays."

He seemed to study my body as his eyes moved up and down the length of me. "You're very muscular. Do you work out?"

What a weird comment to make, I thought, so I hesitated to respond immediately. "I have a set of weights at home I pump most days."

"If you need a partner to work out with, I'm at the city recreation center nearly every day. We can spot each other."

"What a nice invitation. Scotty, have you ever been down there?"

"No, but Gomer's little brother has gone there for swimming lessons."

"Yes, the pool is very nice. They limit the pool to men only on Tuesday and Thursday nights and everyone swims in the nude. It's very exhilarating!"

"I don't really enjoy swimming that much."

"You don't know what you're missing. So, your name is Scott? I love that name...so masculine. Well, can I measure your size?"

Thankfully, Mom reacted instantly. "A sales lady measured him at Doerflinger's. He needs a thirty-two waist and a length of thirty-one or thirty-two."

"Good, let's step over here. These trousers are on sale and the next table has the latest shipment we received last week. What color do you want?"

"Tan, brown, or grey."

"I only have a white pair on clearance sale. I prefer white myself, since they tend to highlight the shape of a young man's back side, you know?"

"I won't wear white pants. Someone will think I work in a hospital."

"You are so particular, Scotty. I can't understand why you will not wear white. Duane loves them, so you should too." Mom continued rifling through the stack. All right then, how much are the others? I can't seem to find a price tag."

"Hmmm...I don't see one either. The stock room must not have marked them yet. I'll have to check." He left to find a supervisor.

"Duane is so helpful. I hope the price is low enough, so we can give him the sale."

"Uh huh." I mumbled in response, although I didn't share the same opinion. Duane seemed overly friendly and made me feel uncomfortable.

He returned shortly. "The department manager told me they are five ninety-nine."

"We can't spend that much."

"I can throw in a free pair of socks with each trouser you purchase today."

"Scotty has enough socks as long as I can keep sewing up the holes."

"I can go ask the manager for a discount on our briefs. We are carrying a new line which firms up a man's crotch area."

"Scotty prefers loose fitting boxer underwear." She was embarrassing me again.

"He doesn't know what he's missing. Is he interested in trying a pair on?"

"Not today, but do you have any shirts on sale?" I breathed a sigh of relief.

"Long sleeves or short sleeves?"

"Either one."

"Come with me over to the rack. What size does he need?"

"Good question." I could have kicked her in the shins.

"I'll just measure him?"

Duane pulled out his yellow tape and positioned his body tightly against my back, immediately detecting his nauseating cologne. As he draped the tape around my chest, I sensed something pushing against my hinder. Duane lost his grip on the measurement tape and needed to go for a second attempt. "I want this to be perfect." I felt the pressure on my rear again.

"I'm sure he needs a medium size."

"Duane, don't the shirts have a neck or chest size?"

"No, only small, medium, large, and extra-large."

I could not understand why he even needed to measure me. Mom yanked two shirts off the rack and held them against my chest. One shirt was a short-sleeved blue and yellow checked. "Perfect…and it's your school colors too!"

"I prefer long sleeve shirts this year."

"Scotty dear, here's one with long sleeves." She displayed the shirt, which had small curled chords on the front, while the back pattern had sections of solid colors.

"My friends will call me a rodeo cowboy if I wear that western shirt."

"Duane, what do you think?"

"The shirt is very manly…like Rock Hudson and everyone knows how handsome he is. Maybe everyone will call you Rock when you wear it."

"Duane, we'll take both shirts."

"Excellent! Is there anything else? Are you sure you won't try our underwear or a buy a pair of dress shoes?"

"Not today. Thank you so much for your time."

Duane led us to the check out and punched a few buttons on the cash register. "That comes to three dollars and thirty-seven cents including sales tax. Will you be paying in cash or by check?"

"Cash." Mom dug into her purse and laid three single dollar bills on the counter. Duane waited patiently while she found a fifty-cent piece that she dropped on top of the bills. He reached for several coins in the cash register and placed a dime and three pennies in her palm.

"I'll write my name and my phone number on this paper in case you come back to buy anything else. And Rock, I mean Scott, don't forget my invitation to come down to the city recreation center. I'm usually there in the morning on the weekends and nights when they assign me the early shift. We could really have some fun."

I was desperate for an excuse to reject his invitation. "I'm playing football at St. Anthony's, so will be busy with practice every day."

"That's too bad. Maybe after your season ends."

"Let's go Scotty, we still need to find you some trousers."

As we left the store, I crumpled Duane's note and threw it into the first trash receptacle that we passed. The next stop was BML Mart, housed in an old stone building near the river. As we navigated Fifth Avenue, Mom held my hand again, just as the three girl classmates crossed in the opposite direction. "Hello again Scotty and Mrs. Spykstra. It's so nice of your son to help you across the busy street."

"Oh, it's an old habit of mine to hold his hand since he was three years old."

"Oh, I see." Carrie said, trying to suppress laughter. I spotted a nearby manhole cover and thought about climbing down inside. How could Mom be so oblivious?

A minute later, we strolled past Goldy's Diamond Store. Abe Goldman was inside at the counter with a customer. I pointed at him. "Mom, I caddied in a group with that guy early in the season."

"He's Jewish, huh? Did he even pay you?"

"No."

"That figures."

"Well, I wasn't his caddie, but he paid a generous rate to my friend OC."

"Oh, that's very surprising from what I've heard about Jews."

"That day, I had a double with Mr. Lipschitz, who owns BML Mart. He paid me three bucks for only three holes."

"Hmmm…all in pennies?"

I stared at her in annoyance. "NO!"

BML Mart specialized in heavily discounted general merchandise, and the store was organized in a haphazard manner. The biggest bargains were situated in the rear of the store, requiring shoppers to pass through the entire floor area. Every five minutes, a loudspeaker blasted an announcement of a limited price buster sale on one item.

It took several minutes to locate a table of boys' slacks, where a large red sign read 'FIRE DAMAGED SALE'. A heavy set male clerk, who had a horrific body odor, approached. "What do you need?"

"Schools clothes, do you have trousers on sale?"

"The table right here." He gestured to a table to his right. "Yesterday, we got a shipment from a fire in a clothing factory in Los Angeles. They're a great bargain if you don't mind a little smoke odor."

I kept my distance, as the clerk's stench was overwhelming. A little smoke smell couldn't possibly be as bad as his 'B-O'. I began to sweat too, as the dated structure was not equipped with air conditioning or fans.

"You should be able to find several pairs in any color. Let me know when you decide to buy anything. I'll be over in the tire area."

"Sir, the sign says two dollars each pair, correct?"

"Right."

"Do you have a changing room?"

"No, but he can probably slip in some behind the refrigerators."

"Are there any shirts on sale too?"

"Yes, they're a buck each...from the same fire. They're hanging on a rack over there by the mattresses." As he held up his arm pointing in the general direction, I saw huge sweat stains under his armpit.

"Can you show us where?"

The clerk impatiently checked his watch. "Okay, but be quick." He led us around a long line of beds and mattresses. "I'll check back with you later."

Mom dug through the pile. "Most are small or extra-large sizes, but here are two mediums." She held an orange and a pink shirt in the air.

"Too ugly!"

"Scotty, here's one with yellow with black stripes."

"I'll look like a bumble bee, no thanks."

Mom quickly ripped through the rest of the shirts on the rack. "This one is mismarked. It's a plain dark blue one."

"Let's buy it."

"Scotty, don't you want to try it on?"

"No."

"Let's check the trousers now." After twenty minutes of sorting through dozens of pants, I found a tan and grey pair with my exact size. I didn't like the cut, but was tired of this pants adventure. We hunted for the stinky clerk, finding him in the tool area. "We found what we needed." The clerk then led us on a circuitous route through the back of the building to a checkout counter at the entrance.

"Can I have a bag to carry the clothes in?"

The clerk sneered at her. "That costs a nickel."

"I have to pay for a bag? No thanks, I'll just carry the clothes."

It was ninety degrees outside, but it felt refreshing to leave the stifling hot box building. We trudged on down the street toward Woolworths. "Would you like a hot fudge sundae now?"

"Sure, as soon as I cool down."

We entered the old dime store on Main Street. The oak floors were worn down from frequent sanding and creaked as we headed to the lunch counter. We took seats on the round, faded red padded stools. A middle-age man with a white waist coat and white paper cap immediately came to wait on us. "Do you need to see a menu?"

"No, but I'll have cup of coffee and he will have a hot fudge sundae."

"Coming right up! Do you need sugar or cream for your java?"

"I ordered black coffee, not java, and no cream or sugar…just black."

The waiter carefully poured coffee from the pot and placed the cup on a saucer, positioning it in front of Mom. "Would you care for a warm piece of apple or cherry pie?"

"No thanks." Mom's loquaciousness had clearly dissipated as the day had worn on.

I carefully studied the waiter as he prepared the sundae. He reached into a freezer compartment and dropped four scoops of vanilla ice cream into a tall clear glass. At the end of the counter he pulled out a ladle from a black pot and scooped three servings of chocolate topping. He opened a refrigerator, procuring a container of whipped cream, dropping a spoonful on top of the sundae, and topping it off with a bright red cherry. "Sonny, here's a spoon too to go with the sundae. More coffee...ma'am?"

"Sure, fill 'er up."

"Anything else?"

"Just the check please."

The waiter grabbed a green tablet, took a pencil from behind his ear and scribbled a few things on the pad, placing the check face down on the counter. I picked up the check and scanned the paper...fifteen cents for the coffee and thirty cents for the sundae. Mom searched her purse for change and dropped forty-five cents on the counter.

We walked two blocks to the main bus stop and sat down on the wooden bench. Painted on the back was an advertisement from Mayer's Mercury. "Mom, see this sign? I caddied for Linus Mayer this summer, too."

"I hate his silly commercials. He seems so insincere. Dad will never buy a car from him."

"I wanted to tell her that he was a terrible person, but recalled Andy's tenth commandment."

The bus lingered in a staging area a block away for several minutes, finally pulling to a stop in front of the bench. Earl, the same bus driver, opened the folding door. "Hello again! Did you have a pleasant shopping trip?"

"Oh yes, we found what he needed."

"Think it rain later?"

"Maybe it will and maybe it won't."

"That's what I'm-a thinkin' too."

"I'm glad we agree on something."

"Me too."

Mom escorted me to the same seats we had sat in on the morning trip. "Did you ever find the dime you were hunting for under the seat?"

"No."

"What a shame. I know how diligent you've been with the caddie job. People don't appreciate what a dime can buy now compared to when I was your age."

"Mom...ah...next year, I want to shop for my own clothes by myself. I'll use the earnings from my caddie jobs to pay for them. Okay?"

"I'll talk to Dad, but I'll miss going downtown with you. Will you still go to Woolworth's to buy a sundae?"

"Probably."

I didn't feel like talking further. I slumped down in the seat and closed my eyes, pretending to be asleep. I felt like it was the first step in what would be a hundred miles of bad road to establish my independence, but at least it was a start.

Chapter 23

I slammed the snooze button down as the alarm sounded off at the usual six o'clock. I pulled the sheets over my head in protest, refusing to believe that it was time to get up. It felt like I had only been sleeping for five minutes. The anticipation of the upcoming caddie football game and my most important caddie assignment of the season resulted in a restless night.

Since April, the rookies had lobbied to play the A caddies in a game of touch football, primarily as a way to try and even the score from the initiation, but also to let out some built-up aggression towards the guys who had been giving us crap all summer. There had been endless trash talking leading up to the game and Buddy even proposed wagering five dollars for every player, an idea we instantly rejected. The older guys insisted that Andy referee the game, but we demanded that he play instead…payback was due.

We agreed to play in the morning before golfers would show up for their regular rounds. Later, I was set up to caddie in a big money game with PRO, Dowd 'Dowdy Doody' Jones, Walter Mellon, better known to the caddies as 'Water', and Linus Mayer. Over the summer, I had observed several money games amongst the members. They varied, but I'd never seen anyone play for more than twenty bucks. Betting that much money seemed foolhardy, but when I heard the wager for today's match were a hundred dollars a hole, I was shocked. I had never dreamed that anyone would play for stakes that high as it nearly equaled my Dad's annual salary, but these guys were big shots, or at least they thought they were. I was assigned to caddie for Jones, known to be most generous tipper at the Club, on the rare occasions when he took a caddie. Bing was directed to caddie for the Mayor, Buddy had PRO's bag, and Rutt would tote 'Water' Mellon's clubs. Being the least experienced and having never caddied in a group with PRO before made me nervous for the match.

The second alarm buzzed. I accepted my fate and crawled out of bed. I shuffled over to the closet to retrieve my jockstrap out of my gym bag that was nestled in its usual spot on the floor in the left back corner. I hadn't used it since the infamous hazing incident, but thankfully I remembered to throw it in the wash afterwards. The football rules were limited to two-hand touch, but I grabbed my cup just in case, knowing how the older caddies tended to bend the rules. We named our team the 'Super Loopers' and decided to wear the same color shirt in solidarity, but also to aid in finding each other on the field. I rifled through my dresser drawer and pulled out a blue t-shirt at the bottom of the pile.

I brushed my teeth quickly and closely inspected my chin and cheeks. There was more evidence of peach-fuzz growing on sections of my face, so I decided to remove it. I hadn't shaved yet, although occasionally, had used a scissors to trim longer strands of hair. However, that seemed futile, now that more whiskers appeared. For years, Dad had used a razor with shaving cream, although I detested touching the watery soap. I opted to use his old electric razor, which buzzed loudly. As I moved the razor head across my right cheek, it pulled the hair with sharp, painful tugs, no matter what angle I tried. Exasperated, I decided to try his safety razor, but chose to forgo shaving cream. I scraped the blade over three pimples, which began to bleed profusely. I grabbed some toilet paper and pressed on the wounds repeatedly, but the blood continued to ooze out. Mom came into the hallway and noticed my predicament.

"Scotty, are you shaving? Milton, come here! Scotty cut himself and he's bleeding."

"Son, have you tried to shave before? I should have showed you how."

"The electric razor kept pulling my whiskers, so I decided to use the blade."

"Without shaving cream?"

"Ick, I hate that stuff."

"Milton, don't you have a styptic pencil to stop the blood?"

"There's one here in the medicine cabinet." He fetched it from the shelf and pressed on the cuts until my skin burned. "Press hard with the washcloth."

I followed his instructions and a few minutes later, the bleeding stopped.

"Scotty, if you had let me pick your pimples, you wouldn't have scraped them off. I made some French toast, so come and eat."

I stacked three slices of French toast on my plate and drowned them with runny maple syrup. I sliced the stacks in quarters and finished the hefty portions in just four bites, quickly washing them down the breakfast with a tall glass of grape juice. Mom frowned, disapproving how I managed to shovel breakfast down in just seconds, but I figured she was most disappointed at a missed opportunity to have an audience for her radio news commentary. I carried my dishes to the sink and hurried out the door.

By the time I arrived at MVCC, all of my caddie teammates were there. Rusty Steele had been self-appointed as our team captain and copied a few play diagrams onto mimeograph paper that he distributed to each of us. I held the sheet up to my nose and took a whiff...the pungent odor was addicting.

Rusty then announced our positions. "Each team will have five players on the field. I'll be the quarterback and Jesse will be our primary receiver. We'll confuse them by alternating the Bunker twins as wide-outs on offense and as pass defenders on defense. Scott, you'll be my blocking back when I run the ball and a safety valve for passes. Lance, you are our designated rusher on defense and the center when we have the ball. Scott, on defense, you will blitz the quarterback or fall back into pass coverage. Jesse and I will also be pass defenders. Scott, you are the kicker too."

"Do we know what positions the senior caddies are playing?"

"I heard Andy will be their quarterback, Bronco the center, and Jake the blocking back, so that leaves Buddy and Rutt as their receivers.

We will have more speed, but Bronco and Jake will be tough to fight through. Let's practice a few plays before the senior caddies arrive."

We ran over to the open field near the caddie yard and worked on our plays for twenty minutes until Rutt and Buddy showed up. "Practice won't help you losers. You might as well forfeit right now and save yourselves the embarrassment. You can still change your team name to the Loser Loopers!"

"Ruttledge, what's your team name?" Jesse asked as he moved toward Rutt.

"We call ourselves the A-Squad."

"Ass Squad?"

"No, the Aaaaa-Squad." He said, putting emphasis on the long 'A.' "James, we're going to kick YOUR ass! It might be a good idea to have an ambulance standing by."

Jesse and Rutt were nose to nose when Buddy moved in to separate them. Rutt and Buddy returned to the couches, while the Super Loopers sat on the corners of the concrete slab.

I wanted to engage Jesse, but didn't want to end up embarrassing myself in front of him again. Since I knew a good amount of sports trivia, I decided to ask him about the upcoming football season. "Jesse, how do you think the Packers' season will go this year?"

"They need to improve from their eight and five record last year. The loss to St. Louis in the ridiculous Playoff Bowl game must have really pissed Lombardi off. The Colts and the Bears will be tough to beat."

"Lombardi didn't care about that meaningless runner-up game. I'm surprised that he didn't forfeit by not showing up. The '65 preseason actually started last week with the All-Star game in Chicago. The Cleveland Browns beat the college all-stars twenty-four to sixteen. Do you remember when the Packers lost to the college players two years ago?"

"Lombardi must have really been ashamed of that game."

"The collegians have actually won eight times going back to 1934 and the time it happened was in 1958 against the Detroit Lions."

"No kidding?"

Just then, Andy drove up and jumped out of the car, signaling me to come over. "I heard this is your last week caddying."

"Yeah, my parents are taking me on vacation tomorrow and football practice kicks off on Monday. Our first scrimmage is next Saturday against Jefferson, but I still may be able to come out on Sundays."

"I have to report to the Marine Base in California next Friday, so I won't see you again."

"Maybe next spring?"

"Most Marines are sent to Vietnam after basic training, so perhaps in two years." He led me around to the back of his car and lowered his voice so no one would overhear. "I wanted to let you know about an annual event that's going on tonight. After dark, a few of the members invite some naked gals out on the 12th green for a little golf game called 'Muff from the Rough.' I thought you might want to join me, Rutt, and Buddy after ten o'clock."

"My parents won't let me stay out that late."

"Tell them you're sleeping over at Pfeiffer's house. He's one of your buddies, right? Hell, you can invite him too, but don't tell anyone else. We can only involve a pretty small group. There's no way the men can know we're spying on their little game. Be at the pro shop by nine-thirty."

"Can I ask his brother, Jimmie? He's trustworthy. He may have already heard about the plan anyway."

"Man, I hate to allow another person. We'll have a crowd."

"Please?"

"Just once I'll give you a favor, but tell him he owes me one. Let's get going on this football game.

Bronco and Jake drove up in Bronco's old pick-up truck, and Andy addressed them. "Boys, I need to go and open the bag room, so I'll be right back. Benny's covering for me until nine o'clock. We have ten minutes, so go tell Rutt, and Bronco to warm up. They're probably sleeping over there on the couches."

When Andy returned, we all gathered out on the field. The A caddies surrounded the Super Looper squad as Buddy outlined the rules. "Okay meatballs, the first team to score four touchdowns will win and there's no extra points. After a two-hand touch, the play is dead. We set some yellow and red flags for the field boundaries and the goal lines. The field is about sixty yards long, so there can be some first downs. If neither team has scored four touchdowns by nine o'clock, the game will end based upon who is winning then."

"What if we're tied at nine o'clock?" I asked Buddy.

"We win in a tie."

"Why?"

"We make up the rules on our home field!"

Jesse went after Rutt again. "Ruttledge, do you have enough hankies to wipe away the tears when we win?"

"Jailbird, you won't even be around to see the end of the game. What hospital do you prefer?"

Andy came in to break up the verbal assaults. "We'll flip a coin to see who kicks off and Buddy will make the call. Ready?" Andy quickly flipped it high up in the air.

"Heads!" Buddy shouted clearly.

The coin landed on the ground and rotated at the last second. The head was clearly visible as Andy immediately picked up the coin. "HEADS! You guys kick off to us and to be fair, we'll let you pick the side of the field you want to defend."

"We'll take the west end. So, when we have the ball, we go east, right?"

"Right!"

"You kick off from the end zone line. You can either punt or kick off the ground."

Rutt flipped the ball to me, and I motioned for the Super Loopers to gather toward the west end zone. I told Rusty that I had observed that both sides of the coin were heads.

"I saw that too. At least we got to pick the direction when we have the ball. Their receivers will have to look into the sun."

I elected to punt the ball, which spiraled far down the right sideline. Andy caught the ball and his momentum carried him out of bounds around the twenty yard line. Jesse was first downfield and knocked Buddy over with a forearm shiver, even though the play was over. Buddy was clearly pissed and jumped up immediately. "So that's the way you want to play?"

"Did you get an owie...little baby?"

Buddy shot the 'Love Potion' signal at Jesse as he retreated to the A-Squad huddle.

Andy assembled his team and then set up their alignment for their first play. He anchored himself in the quarterback position, five yards back from Bronco, who got set to hike the ball. Lance and I set up three yards to the left and right of Bronco.

Andy yelled out, "Ready...set...hike!" Bronco hurled the ball five feet over Andy's head. As the football rolled toward the end line, Andy lunged for the ball and slipped on the wet grass, falling to the ground. I easily sidestepped Bronco and Jake, scooped up the ball, and dashed ten yards into the end zone for a touchdown. As our team celebrated, Andy screamed at Bronco. "What the hell were you doing?"

"Sorry, we should have practiced the center hike a few times."

"Don't center between your legs next time. Stand to the side of the ball and flip it to me. Now, let's get serious."

Jesse taunted the A-Squad. "One touchdown and only three to go."

"You're just lucky! Now go kick to us again."

I elected to kick off the turf, resting the ball flat on the ground. The pigskin spun like a knuckleball and deflected off Jake's hand, bounding toward the end zone, landing out of bounds three yards from the goal line.

Andy shoved Jake. "Jake, why did you try to catch that?"

"I thought I could snag it and run up-field quickly for a better field position."

"Well, you didn't...you nincompoop!" Andy was visibly upset. He gathered his team in the huddle and yelled at them again. They lined up in a similar formation to their first play as Bronco bent over, holding the football upright on the ground. He peeked at Andy, who held his hands out as a target. "Ready...set!"

Bronco abruptly slung the ball to Andy, who was unprepared to catch it. As Andy tried to scoop up the fumble, I shoved him to the ground. The ball took a weird bounce and ended up in Lance's hands, who walked over the goal line for another touchdown.

Andy argued the outcome. "I had the ball in control when Spykstra touched me, so they play was dead."

I disagreed. "You never had the ball under control...we have two TDs now!"

"Unfortunately, he's correct." Jake confirmed the ruling. "That wasn't even close, Andy."

"Whose side are you on, Jake? Can you center the ball?"

"Sure, I played center in high school."

"Why in the hell didn't you tell me before we started?"

"You never asked me."

"Am I supposed to know everything?"

"You sure act like you do."

"Let's get our shit together and catch up. They haven't even had the ball yet for Christ's sake. Let me handle the next kick-off."

The Super Loopers gathered one more time at the end zone line at the west end of the field. I created an artificial tee, digging my heel into the turf. I slid after taking five long strides, nicking the top of the ball, which wobbled over the grass, coming to a stop where Bronco was positioned. He held his arms out, as if blocking everyone away from the ball. I slipped past him and picked up the pigskin as Buddy raced up the field to touch me. But Jesse held out his foot and tripped him, causing him to fall face down in the damp grass. "You're a dirty player, jailbird... I ought to punch your lights out!"

"Greco, I'd punch your lights out but they're already pretty dim. Bronco never downed the ball, so that's an on-side kick...we're on offense!"

Andy grabbed the football. "There's no onside kick in touch football, James!" Andy was really pissed. "Bronco, you dumb shit, why didn't you pick the ball up and run? We would have gotten at least ten more yards."

Bronco pointed at Andy. "Because YOU told us that YOU would handle the kick-off."

"Yeah, but I was standing down near our end zone, you dope."

Jake defended Bronco. "Well, we all heard your orders Andy."

"Forget it! Let's score a touchdown. We're only thirty yards from the end zone. Let's huddle up."

The A-Squad altered their formation. Jake was now the center and successfully hiked the ball to Andy, who faked a pass and sprinted to his left, where the field was clear. Jesse raced to intercept him and crashed into Andy, sending him flying out of bounds against a large oak tree. The collision left Andy sprawled on the ground, grasping for his air. Rutt rushed to his aid. "Andy, are you all right?

Andy nodded his head, struggling to breathe, as Rutt and Buddy helped him to his feet. "Did I cross the goal line for a touchdown?

"He knocked you out of bounds a few yards short, but we have a first down."

"Damn it, let's score on the next play." Andy shouted as he limped to the huddle. On the next play, the Super Looper defenders lined up directly opposite the three A-Squad receivers, planning to block them at the snap of the ball. I got a good jump after the center snap, forcing Andy to immediately pass the ball to Buddy, who squinted directly into the sun. The ball careened off his chest directly into Jesse's hands. He easily juked past Andy and sprinted down the field for another touchdown.

I ran to congratulate Jesse. "I had no idea you were so fast."

"I got a lot of practice running from the police, but I was also a sprinter and hurdler for the two years I was in high school."

I passed Andy, returning from our end zone. "Andy, we have three touchdowns…one more TD and we win!"

"I can count! We're going to score four in a row to still beat you."

"You only have one first down so far. Maybe you should forfeit before you get hurt again."

"Spykstra, don't be a wise-ass. I still hand out caddie jobs here. I don't care if you're a B caddie, so watch yourself. Kick again, but we're trading ends of the field now."

"No way!" I instinctively responded "You won the coin flip and chose to receive first. We got the choice of the goal we were defending."

"Not for the entire game. We're changing directions on the field now!"

I was upset at his arbitrary decision. "You can't change the rules in the middle of a game."

"I AM changing the rules."

"Then we're changing the rules too. We've decided three touchdowns win the game. Let's go Super Loopers." We marched off the field.

"You can't quit. You didn't score four touchdowns! Come back here now." Rutt protested.

Buddy seconded the motion. "Quitters never win. Come back here you losers."

"We want a rematch!"

"Shut up, Bronco! You're implying that they won!" Andy shouted at him, angrily.

Jake was more conciliatory. "Andy, you can't keep changing the rules."

"Rules are meant to be changed."

"Right, I'm sure you can change the Marine training when you arrive there next week. Your drill sergeant must be anxious to meet you."

"Christ, I can't play anyway. My ankle is killing me...I can barely walk." Andy turned and started to follow us off the field. "I'll tell you what, if I change any rules, I'll start with the silly rules of golf. The Scots invented the game...you know...from Scotland. The only good idea they had was how many holes a standard golf course would be based upon how long it would take to consume a jug of Scotch Whiskey. Supposedly, St. Andrews originally had twenty-two holes, where half of them were played going away from the clubhouse and the same holes back. It must have made for some interesting rounds with two groups playing the same hole simultaneously, especially after downing a few rounds of Scotch."

Jake added more commentary. "Some courses in Scotland had only six or seven holes, so those golfers must have drank swiftly or used whiskey jugs that were much smaller."

Jesse had been listening intently. "Do you know what the Scots did in the fifteenth century?"

Bronco had a guess. "Invented the bagpipe?"

Jesse shook his head. "I don't think so, but in 1470, their King James III condemned golf and football in favor of archery. I read about it in a book in prison."

"I can understand condemning golf, but why would anyone cancel football?"

"Rugby was called football in those days, Broncovich. Maybe we should have played your team in a game of rugby today and beat you at that too." Jesse turned and walked away.

I felt proud to lead the resistance of Andy's arbitrary rule interpretation, as well as declaring victory for the Super Loopers. The A-Squad retreated to their couches after the game. I could smell the smoke from their cigarettes and heard them bickering about losing.

Bing drove into the club and parked at the far end of the lot. He got out of his white Volkswagen Beetle and trotted to the caddie yard. "Spike, what happened in the football game?"

We scored three quick touchdowns without even running an offensive play. Andy then tried to change the rules, so we walked off the field, declaring ourselves the victors. He even rigged the coin toss."

"Andy must be pissed."

"Probably...he got his wind knocked out and sprained an ankle when Jesse tackled him."

"I'll bet none of you gets a loop today, he's so vindictive. Andy would rather tell the golfers that there are no caddies available, rather than give you jobs. He'll make a great Marine. I bet he can't wait to kill the VC...the Vietcong."

"Say, if the Vietcong are called the VC, should we refer to VD as a Vietdong?" Rusty joked, haven taken OC's place as the caddie clown.

Jesse groaned. "Rusty, you're a dong!"

Andy called Bronco, Jake, Buddy, Rutt, and Bing for caddie jobs for five women players and announced there wouldn't be any caddie requests until the Men's Day tee times, which started at noon. I wondered if I still had the caddie assignment for Dowd Jones or if the invitation to attend the late night men's event was still valid, but I wanted to give Andy a little more time to cool off before I asked.

"Barney, I need to ask you something." We walked fifty feet away, where none of the other caddies could hear us. "Andy told me about an annual ritual that some men have scheduled tonight. They bring naked women on the course!"

"Oh yeah…Jimmie told me yesterday."

"Are you going?"

"Yeah, and so is Jimmie."

"How can you leave your house so late?"

"My older sister is watching us while my parents are out of town. She won't care as long as we're home by eleven."

"Can I stay over tonight? I need to give my parents a reason for not sleeping at home."

"Sure, but we'll have to sleep in our backyard in a tent."

"Good! I'll be over after dinner if my parents let me go at all."

We returned to the caddie yard, where Jesse corralled me. "Hey Spykstra, Andy talks to you for some reason. Can you go ask him if we will have jobs today? I only have three more days to fulfill my community service requirements and I don't want to suck up to these creeps any longer than I have to."

"You don't like the golfers here?" Barney commented sarcastically.

"From what I've learned about golf, it's a game based upon honor, but I've observed plenty of cheating here and Linus Mayer is the biggest offender of all. Look, I've made plenty of mistakes in my life and picked the wrong guys to hang around with, but I've read a lot of books during my jail time and believe that without law and justice, there would be anarchy. The judge who sentence me to caddie for community service believed that interaction with rich folks would help with my social skills, but this summer I've certainly seen a lot of hypocrisy…believe me."

"So you aren't in it for the money?" Barney laughed.

Jesse lit up a cigarette, took a long drag, and blew the smoke at Barney. "I sure am! Where else can you average less than fifteen cents an hour? I didn't know slavery was still legal in the United States! Hell, they paid me that much for making license plates in the state pen."

Barney coughed from the smoke, trying to wave it away. "But we're all being rewarded from the education and inspiration the members have bestowed on us."

Jesse laughed. "Oh yeah, especially the valuable insight Mayer gave me about his life the one time I caddied for him. All he did was brag about his success in business and knowledge of world affairs. He ripped me up and down for my lack of caddie skills, even though he shot a 72 for the round. AND, he didn't give me a tip because he said I cost him twenty bucks…only because I handed him a 9-iron, instead of the 6-iron that he asked for on the last hole. I made one simple mistake, but Mayer chewed me out more than my probation officer. I'd love to run into him somewhere outside of the Club to have a little heart to heart discussion."

Bing interjected, "I heard he hangs out at the Fireside Lounge late on most Thursday nights…you know, the place out on Highway 61."

"The Fireside Lounge, eh? I've been there a couple of times. Now, Spykstra, will you go talk to Bumgardner for us?"

I was now concerned that I had made a hasty decision by antagonizing Andy. I trudged up to the bag room and found Andy taping his ankle. "Bum, do I still have the job with Jones at two o'clock?"

"Maybe."

"Bing told us you probably wouldn't give out jobs to the rookie caddies today. If that's the case, Jesse doesn't want to hang around if there are no more jobs."

"Tell the jailbird that I'll ruin his probation for sure if he takes off. But, I'll be honest with you…it's so hot today that many of the golfers who pull their carts will want to ride, so we'll run out of gas carts, and they'll want a bag toter. So, tell your football buddies they might get lucky."

"Am I still invited to the men's deal late tonight?"

"Yeah."

"Pfeiffer and his brother too?"

"Jesus, all right, I must be getting soft with all of my pain." He hesitated for a few seconds. "Spike, I'll have to admit, I admire your spunk to challenge me during the football game." I couldn't believe that Andy complimented me. Although his favorable tone didn't last long, as he immediately went back into drill-sergeant mode. "Now get out of my office!"

I returned to the caddie yard and found Jesse. "Andy said to hang around or he'll void your probation, but he admitted that we would probably have loops later when it gets hotter."

"What an asshole!"

"He's taping his sprained ankle, so you can at least relish that."

"Maybe we should kidnap him right now. We can use the tape to gag him and bind his hands and feet." He turned his head to yelp at Barney. "Pfeiffer, did you bring your transistor radio with you today? We need some entertainment."

"Yeah, I left it in the saddle bag pockets on my bike."

"Saddle bags, really? Maybe you should attach a little basket on the front handlebars, like little girls have. Have you taken off the training wheels yet, buckaroo?"

"I never had training wheels."

"Okay, Dale Evans, fetch your transistor radio from your saddle-bag…I want to listen to KORN."

As Barney adjusted the dial for the perfect signal, "Down in The Boondocks" was nearly finished playing. Colonel Cobb then introduced a new record, debuting at number sixty-five, called "We Gotta Get Out of the This Place" by The Animals.

"Billy Joe Royal and Eric Burdon must have caddied here…two songs in a row about being stuck at this shithole golf Club!"

"Jesse, I recall a Rick Burton who caddied here a couple times last year."

"Pfeiffer, Eric Burdon is the lead singer for the Animals."

"Never heard of 'em."

"Haven't you heard "House of the Rising Sun"?"

"Is that the one about the Tokyo Imperial Palace?"

Colonel Cobb now introduced the next tune.

> *AND NOW, HERE'S A NEW SONG*
> *CALLED "EVE OF DESTRUCTION,"*
> *RECORDED BY BARRY MCGUIRE.*
> *THE STATION MANAGEMENT IS*
> *PLANNING TO BAN THE SONG*
> *FROM THE AIRWAVES, SO THIS*
> *MAY BE THE LAST TIME YOU HEAR*
> *IT.*

"Now shut up and listen closely to these lyrics." Jesse commanded as he pointed to all of us.

We didn't dare say a word. I concentrated on the lyrics and tried to interpret what they meant. After the song ended, Jesse stared at us. "That's a protest song drawing attention to the obliteration of the world through war. What do you think?"

"I enjoyed the beat and the rhymes were good." Barney observed.

Rusty added, "I dug the rhythm too."

"Did you idiots even listen to the lyrics?"

"Jesse, where is the Jordan River?"

"Steele, it forms the boundary between Israel, Syria and Jordan...didn't you take a geography class? Maybe Andy's right, you guys are a bunch of morons. Look...there's injustice happening in all parts of the world. People are killing one another based upon hatred and radical religious beliefs. The leaders in Washington are escalating a war in Vietnam, sending young men to die for no reason. And we have sparred with the Russians on the edge of a nuclear holocaust several times."

"Jesse, my Dad even built a fall-out shelter in our basement."

"Pfeiffer, that's probably not a bad idea."

Their conversation was interrupted by a commercial jingle.

> *GRANDMA'S DONUTS ARE SO*
> *GREAT...YOU CAN'T EVER COUNT*
> *HOW MANY YOU ATE...COME ON*
> *DOWN AND HAVE SOME*
> *FUN...GRANDMA'S DONUTS ARE*
> *NUMBER ONE.*

"The song "Eve of Destruction" sends a very serious message, and then the station played a silly jingle to promote a donut shop." Jesse seemed irritated.

"What's wrong with Grandma's Donut Shop? I love their glazed ones."

"The commercial conveys a happy theme, despite so much hatred in the world, like in the Middle-East."

"Jesse, no one hates Grandma's Donuts."

"I'm not referring to some stupid donut shop! I've seen the rough side of life, so believe me. Listen to the silly tune they're playing now."

*THAT'S "SUNSHINE, LOLLIPOPS,
AND RAINBOWS," THE LATEST HIT
FROM LESLIE GORE AT NUMBER
THIRTY-TWO AFTER NINE WEEKS
ON THE CHARTS. NOW, HERE'S
ANOTHER MESSAGE FROM
GRANDMA'S DONUT SHOP.*

"What's wrong with a happy life?"

"Pfeiffer, a happy life is just a fantasy. You're all being treated as if you are sheep!"

"Baa…baa…baa." Barney laughed.

Jesse rolled his eyes and shook his head.

*AFTER THREE WEEKS ON THE
CHART, THIS TUNE WAS WRITTEN
AND SUNG BY THE TROUBADOUR
POET FROM MINNESOTA…BOB
DYLAN. THE SONG IS CALLED
"LIKE A ROLLING STONE."*

Jesse raised his arm and gestured toward the radio, "Fellas, pay close attention to this one."

We listened intently for the entirety of the song that seemed to go on forever, when Jesse asked our opinion. "Well?"

Barney responded again. "That guy has a bad voice, the song is way too long, and the words don't make any sense." I agreed with Barney, questioning mostly why they would ever play a song of that length on the radio, but decided to keep quiet.

"Bob Dylan has written some pretty powerful songs. You gotta know "Mr. Tambourine Man," right?"

"Jesse, I thought the Byrds recorded it." I recalled.

"They did, Spykstra, but the song was written by Bob Dylan. His real name is Robert Allen Zimmerman and he was born in Duluth, right up Highway 61 from La Crosse. He went to the University of Minnesota and dropped out to go to New York City. He lived in Greenwich Village, which is where a lot of folksingers like him congregated in the early sixties."

My Dad had an album of folk songs in his collection and I had read the back cover which had some historical background. "Jesse, Dylan was influenced by singers like Hank Williams, Woody Guthrie and Pete Seeger…right?"

"Yup…Dylan wrote a lot of protest songs starting with the Civil Rights Movement and other themes dealing with adversity in society and politics. You might have heard of "Blowin' in the Wind," "It Ain't Me Babe," "Maggie's Farm," and "The Times They Are a-Changin'." I have all of his record albums."

Barney blurted out, "I remember "Blowin' in the Wind". The radio weather guy, Ham Radio, played the song last week when there was a tornado warning."

I tried to impress Jesse again, "Barney…Peter, Paul, and Mary recorded that song and made it famous."

"Spykstra, you seem to know your music." Jesse complimented.

> THE SKIRTS ARE UP FOR THE
> BEACH BOYS WITH "CALIFORNIA
> GIRLS" AT NUMBER FOUR.

"Jesse, do you like this song…it's a pretty happy one."

"I especially love girls from California."

The volume waned and then the radio went silent. Barney frantically pushed the on-off switch repeatedly and banged the radio several times. "The batteries must have run out of power."

"I'm taking my motorcycle over to Burger Shack. They have a cool waitress over there who wants to keep me warm at night. If Andy needs to know where I went, tell him I'll be back by noon." Jesse gunned his motorcycle a few times and rode off.

"Barney, I'm going to eat my lunch under the shade over by the trees. Andy told me I still have a job caddying for Dowd Jones at one o'clock."

"Dowdy Doody? Lucky you!"

A few minutes later, I heard Andy screaming for me as he stumbled into the caddie yard. "Spykstra, where are you?"

"Right here, Andy," I shouted, coming out from behind the trees.

"Robert Condor needs to work on his game. He's qualifying for the Carling World Open in Massachusetts next week. Here's the shag bag...sprint over to the practice range, hurry!"

I dashed to the range, where Condor was pacing back and forth. He wore bright yellow pants, a dark blue shirt, white golf shoes, and a white belt. Like always, his sandy-blonde hair was meticulously greased back with a part in the middle.

"Good afternoon, Mr. Condor. My name is Scott Spykstra."

"Yeah, I remember you now. Where have you been?"

"I ran over here as soon as Andy gave me the shag bag."

"Well then, you're all warmed up for a little more exercise then."

I dropped about fifty balls on the tee area and ran out onto the range. Condor chipped the first few shots only twenty-five yards, so I decided to retrieve them on the trip back in. Condor then struck some high wedge shots, which I decided to catch directly into the shag bag. I gathered eight in a row before Condor aimed fifteen yards to the left and then fifteen yards to the right, alternating each shot. After a few minutes of testing my skills and quickness, Condor selected another club from his golf bag. The next shot had a much lower trajectory and whistled forty yards over my head. I crisscrossed the range even more and soon, I was dripping with sweat, as the heat was overwhelming, boiling up from the ground. After exhausting all of the practice balls, Condor waved me in. "Not bad, pal. I want to hit a few drives now, so get way out there by the fence."

I emptied the shag bag and sprinted at least two hundred yards out. Condor teed up the first ball, propelling a low liner directly at me. The speed of the ball was deceptive, smacking the upper part of my right leg. I winced in pain and fell to the ground. Condor motioned for me to stand up before he launched the next drive, which hooked severely. I slowly got to my feet and retrieved the ball, which had bounced off the metal fence marking the border of the range. Condor then cranked a wicked slice, which bounded over the opposite fence into a neighboring yard, where I encountered a vicious pit bull. As I tried to reach for the ball, the dog stuck its head through a hole in the fence and bit my left ankle. I crumpled to the ground, blood seeping through my sock. I staggered to my feet and tried to kick the dog in the teeth.

An old man flew out of the house. "Why are trying to hurt my dog?"

"The mutt just bit me."

"Good… maybe you'll stop hitting golf balls into my garden? I've told you guys, I'm not tolerating this anymore! You're destroying my tomatoes, so I'm calling the police this time."

"I didn't hit the golf ball here, sir."

"I don't care who struck it. You work for the club, don't you?"

"Well, sort of."

"What's your name?"

"I'm only a caddie, sir."

"I'm not asking you again. WHAT'S YOUR NAME?"

"Scott."

"Scott, who?"

"Scott Spykstra." I muttered sheepishly, immediately regretting not coming up with a fake name instead.

"God-damn golf course! I've lived here for sixty years...before the course was even built! Who is going to pay for my broken tomato plants?"

"Sorry, sir, I just started working as a caddie here a few months ago. The ass pro struck the ball."

"Ass pro? What's that?"

"The Assistant Golf Professional...he's a jackass!" I could now hear Condor screaming, observing him waving me to come in.

"What's the holdup, idiot? I didn't have anyone to use as a target."

"You smacked a ball over the fence in a guy's yard and he's calling the cops. You broke his tomato plants and his nasty dog bit me."

"It's lunch time, so you probably needed a bite anyway...HA...HA. You should have been fast enough to catch it on the fly." He smirked.

"Well, I had to run all the way over from the other fence line...nearly sixty yards."

"I asked for an experienced caddie and Bumgardner gave me a retarded cripple."

"I ran as fast as I could...I'm sorry."

"Go back to the shop and tell Bumgardner I need a real caddie out here."

I hustled to the pro shop and found Andy, who looked irritated. "The grumpy old fart neighbor called the pro shop complaining you kicked his dog."

"His pit bull bit me on the ankle first. Condor blasted a ball over the fence into his garden and the old timer asked for my name to report me to the police."

"He's a pain in the ass, always calling to complain. Why are you back here so soon?"

"Condor wants another caddie to shag balls for him. He said I was too slow."

"I'll have Jesse James run a few laps out there for him. That should be interesting. You need to grab Dowdy Doody's clubs from his Jaguar XK150 that he left in the No Parking Zone."

As I got closer, I eyed Jones' license plate, which read '*BIGBUKS-65*'. I opened the trunk, lifting his bulky professional size black golf bag, which had Dowd Jones IV imprinted in white italic lettering on the side. I lugged the heavy load to the first tee and joined the other caddies and golfers. Mayer was dressed in orange slacks and a black shirt, black belt with white and orange two-toned shoes. PRO, maintaining his stylish image, sported red slacks, a white shirt, a black belt and black shoes. 'Water' Mellon dressed the most conservative with light brown trousers, a green shirt, a brown belt and brown shoes.

Bing noted the sweat running off the bill of my cap. "Spike, it looks like Condor put you through a nice work-out."

"Yeah, he was knocking shots all across the range and his first drive hit me in the leg. He banged one over the fence into an old geezer's garden and broke some tomato plants. His dog took a bite out of my ankle, too." I showed Bing the welt on my leg, which was growing larger and turning purple, the dimple pattern of the golf ball clearly stamped against my skin. I then rolled down my bloody sock, showing the dog's teeth marks imbedded in my right ankle.

"Condor loves to play his silly game with caddies to chase down his shots. He's a real piece of shit."

Dowd Jones, who was dressed in bright yellow slacks and purple shirt, stalked me down. "I've been waiting for you for over five minutes! Do you know what five minutes can mean in the stock trading business?"

"You might miss buying a herd of cows?" I guessed.

"I trade common stocks, not livestock. I might lose a few hundred dollars for a client if I can't make a trade within seconds. I lead a life on the edge every moment of the day."

"I don't understand the stock market, sir."

"Well, if you're a good caddie today, I might give you a big tip and I'm not talking the size of my penis. I lead a clean life too. I don't smoke, I don't drink, and I don't swear. Now, hand me the putter!" He paused for a few seconds to search his pockets. "God-damn it, I left my cigarettes in the bar!"

I followed Jones over to the putting green where Mayer was discussing politics. "The worst thing was that damn Lyndon Johnson crushing Barry Goldwater in the presidential election last year. I thought there was an opening after Kennedy got knocked off in Dallas, but LBJ is bound and determined to implement JFK's wasteful spending agenda to provide welfare for the dumb shits who are too lazy to hold a job. He's also championing a voting rights law, as if the darkies can even read a ballot." I shouldn't have been surprised, but I was a little shocked that the Mayor of La Crosse could be such a bigot. The other golfers carried on, so I assumed that they must either think the same, or perhaps just didn't hear him. Mayer continued, "Do you know what LBJ stands for?"

"Lyndon Baines Johnson." PRO answered with confidence.

"No George...Lying Bullshit Jackass."

Mellon had another suggestion. "How about Loose Bucks Jackoff?"

"Johnson is a bleeding heart liberal all right. That's hard to believe from a Texan. At least he's keeping Goldwater's mission alive on beating communism, by ordering more soldiers to Vietnam every day. He recently announced they were increasing the troop count to one hundred twenty-five thousand soldiers. Walter Cronkite reported last night that marines destroyed a Vietcong base in the first major ground battle there. Last week, helicopters dropped in a platoon that killed a lot of those Charlies. There's also been a few air battles where we cleaned up too and our B-52 bombers are obliterating the gooks on the ground. LBJ is doubling the draft to thirty-five thousand poor slobs every month."

"You have a kid who is seventeen years old, right?" PRO questioned Mayer.

"Yeah, he'll be a senior in high school his fall."

"After he graduates next year, won't he be eligible for the draft?"

"George, we don't worry. He'll have an academic deferment for attending college. He's applying to Harvard, Princeton, and Yale...all Ivy League schools."

"I thought you believe in the school of hard knocks. Didn't you say that college is a joke?"

"Not when there's a threat to being drafted and getting killed. Even if the student deferment doesn't work, I've spoken to a few congressmen, who can pull a few strings in Washington."

"You must know all the right folks."

"Just in case, the head of the local draft board is a close friend too. He received a good deal on his car purchase." He winked, "if you know what I mean."

"Linus," PRO queried, "did you know that in 1954, the US signed a treaty prohibiting an invasion of a Southeast Asian country without the support of all of the members. It's called SEATO."

Jones entered the conversation. "SEATO? Sounds like a treaty promising to put the toilet seat down after taking a leak. HO...HO!"

Mellon ignored Jones' joke and challenged PRO. "George, I didn't know you were a historian."

"Walt, I read a lot of history. I even researched the records at Notre Dame and discovered you never played in a football game. From what you've been saying all these years, I thought by now they would have renamed the stadium Mellon Field, given all of the heroics on the gridiron you've bragged about."

"George, my real heroics involved dating all of the coeds. There's a lot more to college than being on the football team."

"There sure is!" Jones added excitedly, "I got drunk every night from what I can remember, which ain't that much!"

"George, forgot about that worthless SEATO deal. We had the right to send troops to Vietnam without the support of those weak treaty members after the North Vietnamese fired on our ships last year in the Gulf of Tonkin. That was an outright act of war, just like the Pearl Harbor attack and the Lusitania sinking in World War I!"

"Linus, that lying bean counter, Robert McNamara, poured gasoline on the fire with his gross exaggerations, and congress passed the Gulf of Tonkin Resolution which gave Johnson unlimited war powers.

"Who is Robert McNamara?"

"Dowd, he's the Secretary of Defense in Washington. You've heard of the Defense Department, haven't you?"

"Sure, George."

"Listen guys, the government is treating people as if they're a bunch of mushrooms."

Dowd look bewildered. "Mushrooms?"

"Dowd, mushrooms are fed a lot of manure and kept in the dark, just like Washington treats the public with their bullshit! Their lies are even worse than the scores you brag about."

Mellon commented, "I know we're wasting a lot of money and lives in a war we'll never win in the damn jungle and rice paddies. We should drop the A-bomb on Hanoi right now and end the war quickly, right Linus?"

"Walt, the USA will never lose a war. General Westmoreland, the overall commander in Vietnam, predicts the Vietcong will run out of body bags soon and it's only a matter of time before they'll surrender. God is on our side too."

Jones interjected, "Speaking of being on the right side, we have stock recommendations for several defense companies who will be big winners in a long war."

"Dowd, the stock market is rigged, so I put my money in acquiring private companies, where I can see all of the records."

Mayer agreed with Mellon. "The same way I evaluate car dealerships."

"Dowd, don't bother to send me your stock ideas. I can't afford to buy stocks on my puny golf professional salary, right Linus?"

"George, we have the topic of your compensation and your contract extension on the agenda at the next board meeting. If you win some money today, maybe you can buy a couple shares of stock."

"My watch shows it's almost one o'clock, so let's tee off. I assume we're playing with the usual partners...me and Dowd?"

"Right, George...and our stakes are a hundred bucks a hole for the best ball with carry-overs."

"But so we're perfectly clear, a hundred dollars per man."

"Right, Linus, but you need to pay up one of these days. You owe me two thousand bucks from the last couple of rounds."

"How about double or nothing?"

"Sure, just our side bet though."

"You're on. I shot a 72 last week. It should have been a 71, except that outlaw caddie handed me a 9-iron instead of a 6-iron and my shot came up forty yards short on 18. I really gave him shit. I'm calling the Chief of Police right after this round to inform him that the jailbird violated his probation. I'm calling the judge tomorrow too...that'll teach that derelict!"

"Linus, you can't tell the difference between a 9-iron and a 6-iron when you set up for the shot?"

"I never pay attention to the club face. I always concentrate on the ball."

"All right then…double or nothing for two thousand straight up and no shots, as well as a hundred bucks a man for our team bet."

Mayer agreed with PRO and added. "I see we have that pokey foursome in front of us again today…the strange professor, the shrink, the crazy engineer and the dead guy."

"Dead guy?"

"The mortician…we played through them on the second fairway months ago. They tried to hit into us a couple holes later, so maybe we can use them for target practice today to get even."

"Linus. I won't allow any of that. With our big stakes, Dowd may take an hour to play every hole anyway. Dowd, we don't have to worry that you'll run off to a pay phone to make a stock trade, will we?"

"I've got my secretary, Doris, covering for me. The market closes at three o'clock central time, so there's only two hours left in the trading day."

"Can she make a stock trade for a client?

"No, but she can take down the order, which I'll execute in the morning."

"I thought I just heard you tell your caddie that a trade needs to be made within minutes, since you live on the edge."

"Oh, yeah…well, the client never knows when the trade is actually executed. It's all based upon trust, anyway. They all know I'm looking out for their best interests."

"I heard that Doris is pretty hot!"

"She sure is, Linus. We play a little game, called exchange trading, in the back room at the end of the day."

"With your tiny cock? Are you sure it isn't called short selling?" Mayer had a wide grin, as he stuck out his tongue and wiggled it.

All four players smashed perfect drives and they continued their political discussion walking together down the first fairway. I wanted to hear everything they said, so I trailed a little closer than usual.

"Walt, Johnson is doling out more of my tax dollars to all those welfare beggars every day."

"But Linus, if the government shells out enough money to all those losers, they won't protest and disrupt everything. With the Voting Rights Act, they can cast more votes for candidates who promise even more giveaways."

"Then why are the spooks burning down buildings in the Watts section in Los Angeles? Christ, I'm in the seventy percent tax bracket and my hard-earned money is being doled out to the gravy sucking bums and welfare junkies!"

"Linus, you can't possibly be paying a seventy percent marginal tax rate. Don't you have some clever tax consultants advising you to take advantage of the write-offs and deductions?"

"Walt, my marginal tax rate is actually lower than ten percent, but I don't want anyone to know."

PRO had been listening intently. "Guys, the Watts riots have a lot to do with housing discrimination, high unemployment, and police brutality."

"No it's not, George. Those darkies protest when they're evicted from their apartments after skipping out on their rent and when their cars are repossessed. The lazy bastards don't want to work when they can collect public assistance. Those community agitators, like that muslin Malcolm X, was one of 'em and got what he deserved."

"Linus, you should obtain your information from a wider array of news sources. I sure hope you don't listen to the bumbling announcer on KORN. Malcolm X was actually a minister and was assassinated by another Muslim faction. By the way, it's Muslim…not muslin!"

"George, are you certain of that? Why did he have the last name of X anyway...it doesn't even have a vowel."

Jones interjected, "Maybe it was the Roman numeral ten, so he was Malcolm Ten. The English have Roman numerals after king's names and the French too. Maybe his father was Malcolm Nine and his grandfather Malcolm Eight. The muslins have secret code words too. Isn't their religion called Islamb? What the hell is that... a fanatical group whose symbol is a lamb?"

PRO laughed. "Dowd, the religion is Islam, I-S-L-A-M, and has nothing to do with an animal. And again, it's pronounced Muslim, with an M at the end, not N."

Mayer had more background information to contribute. "Dowd, have you heard that Cassius Clay recently converted to Islamb and changed his name to Muhammad Ali. His name is still mud as far as I'm concerned. Shit, I lost a lot of money when Sonny Liston took the dive in that fight in Maine because the bout was fixed. Wait until loud mouth Ali is drafted for Vietnam...the Army will teach him a thing or too and maybe his drill sergeant will challenge him to a fistfight.

"Linus, Ali brags that he floats like a butterfly and stings like a bee, but if I went a couple of rounds with him, he would float like a rock and smell like a stinky sock."

"Dowd, he would be dead drunk if he had two rounds of drinks with me. But he copied me when he proclaimed himself the greatest and the king of the world."

"Linus, Ali said he was pretty too, but it sure doesn't apply to your ugly mug."

"Who are you calling ugly, Jones?"

"You, but I'm pretty!"

"Dowd, you're pretty all right...a pretty pathetic golfer."

The group waited several minutes for the Orbit foursome to clear the green before they played their next shots. After their balls landed on the green, Dowd Jones continued the discussion. "Ali hangs around with that other bigmouth, Howard Cosell…they're buddies."

"You're right, no wonder they get along so well."

"Linus, you and Cosell have a few things in common too. You both talk too much, seem to be an expert on everything, and wear bad toupees."

"Walt, you might go bald one day and will need a new 'do' too. Now, let's get back to discuss LBJ's war on poverty. I heard he signed Medicare and Medicaid into law a couple of weeks ago. The programs are socialistic insurance policies for old folks and low income people like us have to pay for."

"Linus, do you know anyone who is poor or disabled and need assistance?"

"Not offhand, George. I only hang around rich and successful people."

"Linus, there's a new successful music group from England called The Beatles. How would you like to hang out with them?"

"That band from England with the long-hair? Hell, that's another thing wrong with kids these days. The band played before sixty thousand screaming fans at Shea Stadium in New York on Sunday. Christ, the fans were screaming so loud they couldn't even hear the songs. Mark my words, in two years, when someone mentions the beetles, they will only describe an insect crawling along the ground."

PRO chuckled. "Linus, the Beatles chose their name after Buddy Holly and the Crickets, who were popular in Britain. They inserted an A for an E, so it described the music beat. The Beatles' original name was The Quarrymen."

Mayer pointed his right index finger in PRO's face. "That proves they have rocks in their heads, George."

The group reached the green. Everyone missed their birdie putts, so they tied with par. They went to the second tee and had to wait again.

"Linus, does your son listen to the Beatles?"

"His favorite band is the Beach Boys. They're a clean cut all-American group from California. But my daughter, Molly, loves the Beatles, especially John Lennon. She cried when I forbid her to watch them when they appeared on the *Ed Sullivan Show*. I also took away the radio in her room, so she can't listen to their songs in our house."

"Linus, why don't you issue a proclamation as the Mayor to prohibit the radio stations in La Crosse from playing Beatles' songs?"

"Good idea, Dowd. I'll issue an executive order tomorrow."

"What authority do you have to regulate the airwaves? The FCC governs the radio."

"Because I'm the Mayor, George! I can't wait until those eighteen-year old Beatles' fans are drafted and sent to Vietnam. The military will straighten 'em out right after they lose their long hair at basic training. Have you heard that new song called "Eve of Destruction"? I called Maze Sweet and ordered him to stop playing that song on the air. Have you listened to the lyrics? If the eighteen year-old kids are ever allowed to vote, we'll return to the dark ages in no time."

PRO seemed to be getting upset. "Linus, do you realize that eighteen kids can be drafted, but can't vote?"

"But George, we lowered the drinking age in La Crosse to eighteen, so that's a good tradeoff, as far as I'm concerned. We even offer a free beer night at Clyde's Bar. Of course, it's only between six and seven on Mondays and we only have one bartender on duty, so we don't give too much away."

Jones presented another opinion. "If the younger kids vote, I can legally sell them stock. That might not sound so bad to me."

PRO smirked. "Do you really think that those youngsters will have any money to buy stock?"

"You never know."

"Those traitors who burn their draft cards to protest the war should be arrested and thrown in jail for treason."

"Linus, Congress recently passed a law defining draft card burning as a crime."

"Great! Hey, maybe the Secret Service Commission can draft those Beatles into military service too."

"No they can't, Linus. Conscription is administered by the Selective Service Commission, not the Secret Service Commission.

"Conscription? I'm talking about the draft."

"Linus, you certainly won't have to worry about seeking a higher office."

"My office is on the third floor in a three-story building, so I can't go any higher unless I move up to the roof."

"You just proved my point!"

Mayer now prepared to hit his drive. I concluded that most of the dialogue had completely gone over his head. The players launched perfect shots again and all walked abreast down the fairway.

"Linus, you mentioned the Secret Service. They guard the President, but did you know they were initially created to catch counterfeiters?"

"Walt we've had a couple of customers use counterfeit money to buy cars over the years, but we've never been contacted by the Secret Service. We just called the local police department to arrest the crooks. Maybe they brought in the Secret Service, which is their secret."

"The Secret Service should investigate the U.S. Treasury Department. They're running a huge fiscal deficit and printing counterfeit money to fund LBJ's Great Society and the damn war."

"The Secret Service didn't do too good of a job protecting Jack Kennedy in Dallas, did they?"

"Linus, a lot of their agents were out late drinking and entertaining hookers the night before the assassination. To use a military term, they were AWOL. Most of our Senators and Congressmen are guilty of desertion too. Our country is going off on the wrong track."

"Walt, our Senator Proxmire isn't one of them. He is a democrat but a fiscal conservative and fights all of the ridiculous spending bills that Congress attempts to pass. He is strictly opposed to campaign funding too. He doesn't even spend a dime to run for office. In fact, he sends donations back to his constituents and uses his own money to buy the stamps. The lobbyists in Washington are bribing politicians to vote for any interest that they represent."

"Who cares, George? We're all making good money and enjoying the country club lifestyle!"

"Dowd, I agree with you. George, I send a lot of money to the lobbyists to help my businesses, which employ a lot of folks in La Crosse."

"Walt, lobbying should be outlawed. Where money is involved, congressmen will always be captive."

"George, I trust you enjoy your position as the head golf professional at Mississippi Valley Country Club, don't you?"

"Of course, Walt."

"Then, I'd be more careful what you say publicly. We're all friends here, but a few influential people at this club wouldn't agree with you."

"Understood. I go along and pay my bills and taxes as all fools do."

"I hate to disappoint you George, but I've decided to place one of my companies under bankruptcy protection."

"Aren't you worried with the repercussions of your bankers and the negative stigma if the story is reported in the newspapers?"

"The bankers are lining up at my door for our business. Jerry Misor, the President of First Intercontinental Bank, was practically drooling on me when we played together a few months ago. However, Harry Ott, his Chief Credit Officer, got pissed when we were taking his money in our bet. Ott was so anxious about our wager, I thought he was having a nervous breakdown.

"Walt, his eighteenth nervous breakdown?"

"Maybe his nineteenth, Dowd…and then I told him our plan for edible women's panties and he refused to associate with a company with questionable moral issues. They walked off the course in the middle of the round and never paid us for the bets."

"Walt, are you taking that company public? I would have thousands of buy orders if my clients heard about a company selling edible panties."

"We're still in our testing stage on that, but we need to lower the price a bit…they're a little expensive for wearing only once. We're finding women don't buy them and men typically don't shop in women's lingerie departments."

"Maybe you should have a mail order business and ship them out."

"That's part of our research. We've placed strategic ads in the typical men's magazines for the past several weeks, but won't know for another six months."

"Somebody told me you were making see-through women's underwear too. Are you having any success?"

"Much better, Dowd, but we still don't know if we can generate a decent profit."

"What company is having financial problems?"

"I own a plastic injection molding company that produces plastic toys and little gadgets. The competitive manufacturers in Hong Kong are undercutting our prices and our distributors don't seem to mind who they are buying their products from. That doesn't make any sense to me. We're fighting the communists in Vietnam, supported by Hong Kong China. The distributors should be more loyal to buy American products."

"But Walt, Hong Kong is a separate country. They're not part of China anymore."

"They're still all Chinamen to me."

Mayer raised his voice. "Some crooked Japanese companies are attempting to build automobile dealership networks in the United States. They are trying to convince us that the Datsun is a quality car, but I told them that it's a tin can. Our car engineers in Detroit are designing vehicles that the Japs will never measure up to. They wanted me to open a Datsun dealership in Minneapolis. I told them we beat them in World War II and we would beat them in the car business too."

"Linus, German cars are being sold here as well."

I could see that Mayer was getting more frustrated. "Yes, George. They're attaining a small foothold with their silly beetle car, which has the engine in the rear! Their engineers must have their brains in their asses too."

"But Linus, you're selling Corvairs at your Chevy dealerships…that car has the engine in the rear too."

"It does?" He coughed a few times, collecting his thoughts. "Well…it's a better rear engine design than the Germans have. They also called and asked me to open a dealership right here in La Crosse. I lectured those Krauts why no one in the U.S. would buy their cars either."

"The German VW Beetles and the British Beatles seem to be ganging up on you, Linus."

"George, you're right. They're not playing fair! We need higher tariffs on the foreign car companies and the record companies, so the U. S. bands, like the Beach Boys, can prosper and stop the British music invasion."

Dowd Jones expressed his thoughts. "I can understand why kids are buying British records, since they were on our side in the world wars, although we need to remind them of the reasons behind the American Revolution."

"But Dowd…you drive a Jaguar…that's a British car!" PRO quickly countered.

"Hmmm… I didn't know that. Well, I guess that the Brits are okay then."

"Linus, I can give you a list of lobbyists in Washington if you need some help with tariffs."

"Thanks Walt, but I can't understand why our citizens would ever buy cars from companies in countries that tried to destroy us twenty-five years ago? Who knows, maybe the Koreans will emerge in the car or TV production business next. For all I know, the Chinese are planning to roll out a new rickshaw or upscale skateboards."

"Linus, you may have to go back and sell buggies. You won't have too much competition there and maybe another division to mass produce buggy whips."

"George, you're distracting me so you guys can win our match. My balls have been burning since the first hole and something smells like mint!"

I now recalled Jimmie's threat to sabotage Mayer's jock strap and chuckled quietly to myself, shielding my mouth with my hands so the players wouldn't notice.

The golf game dragged on until six-thirty. The conversations went from politics, to baseball, to football and finally, to an assessment of most of the women members. PRO and Dowd took turns monitoring Mayer's shots, knowing his tendency to cheat. PRO and Jones won eight hundred dollars each and Mayer lost his double or nothing bet, so he now owed PRO forty-eight hundred dollars. Jones was so excited for his winnings, and he gave me a dollar bonus and a hot tip to buy G. Heileman Brewing Company stock.

On my ride home, I reflected on the stories I heard on the golf course that day. I had never thought much about politics in Washington,

D.C., although Mom could chatter for hours reflecting her opinions. Except for the sports section and the comics, I rarely read the newspaper, so did not have a grasp on current events either, other than what I occasionally heard on the radio broadcasts or the evening television news on WIZZ. I vaguely recalled hearing about the assassination of Malcolm X several months ago, although dismissed it as some random event that did not connect in any way with my daily life. The Watts riots had been the top story on the current evening news, but Los Angeles was a long way away from La Crosse, so I quickly dismissed it. There also seemed to be multiple stories about the military escalation in Vietnam. I recalled Mom saying that two of my second cousins had recently been sent there. A Volkswagen Beetle passed me on La Crosse Boulevard. Bing drove one and I had seen a few more around town, but knew that Dad would always be loyal to U.S. auto manufacturers.

My thoughts reverted to my Dad's boring occupation as a meter reader, comparing it to the dynamic businesses the golfers were engaged in. Mellon, Mayer, Jones and PRO appeared to lead exciting lifestyles based upon the entertaining stories and jokes that they spun on the golf course. I wondered if they were as happy as they appeared to be. When I got home, I considered consulting my Magic 8 Ball on my future career path, but decided to leave it to fate for now.

Chapter 24

As I glided my bike up the driveway, Mom poked her head out the back door. "Hurry up! I've been holding dinner. The meat is drying out." I quickly parked my bike in the garage and hurried up the steps and through the screen door into the kitchen. "Where have you been?" Mom barked impatiently, as she was now seated at the table next to Dad, already halfway finished with his plate.

"My caddie job ended late and I had to clean up my player's clubs. I got a dollar tip because my guy won eight hundred dollars!"

"Uff-Da! You have to be mistaken. No one plays for that much money. Bup-bup-bup…march right over to the sink and wash your hands, mister. Your poor Dad barely earns that much in two months from his job!"

"They were playing for a hundred bucks a hole and the head golf pro was playing for another two thousand dollars against another golfer."

"No wonder the world is going crazy. You must never gamble…it's a sin. A gambler can quickly lose all of his money. Those golfers probably can't afford to buy shoes for their kids."

I sat down at the table across from Mom, who was adding more meat to my plate and a large spoonful of mashed potatoes. I could feel her intense stare without even having to make eye contact. "I don't bet, Mom, even though most of the caddies play poker every day."

"So your golfer won eight hundred bucks and all he gave you was one dollar for a tip?"

"Yep, he's a stockbroker. But he did give me a stock tip."

"Your father has never bought one share of stock…we keep all of our money safe in a passbook account at the bank. We keep our Christmas fund there too, so we can have a few nice presents each year. And how do you suppose we can go on vacation this weekend?" She didn't pause for an answer. "Lots of diligent saving, that's how…no frivolous gambling on the stock market."

418

"Mom, can I sleep over at Barney's house tonight?" I interrupted, desperately trying to veer off course from another lecture about being modest with money. "His family is going on vacation next week, so tonight is the last time we can have some fun before school begins."

"I don't know. What does his mother say?"

"She's fine with it. We'll sleep out in his backyard in a tent."

Dad surprisingly entered the conversation, since it didn't even seem like he was paying attention, "We have to leave for Balsam Lake by seven, so you won't have much time."

"That's right, your father has a long drive tomorrow and we have to leave early to beat the traffic."

"I promise to be home on time. I'll take my portable alarm clock and set it for six-thirty."

"What do you say, Milton?"

"If he promises to be here on time, he can spend the night at his friend's house."

"Okay, but you had better be here no later than six forty-five and have your packing done tonight."

I gave myself an imaginary victory pat on the back. "Thanks, can I have another helping of mashed potatoes and beef roast?"

"I made a little extra because I thought you would be hungry."

After finishing my last bite, I brought the dishes to the sink, where Mom was meticulously cleaning. "I need to take a shower. It was so hot on the golf course today."

"Don't use too much hot water. I've got another load of clothes to wash."

Heeding her warning, I took a one minute shower, leaving the water temperature more cold than warm. I ruffled through my dresser drawers and tossed enough items to make it through three days into my duffle bag. I grabbed my sleeping bag and headed for the door.

"Mom, I'm all packed. I gotta go now. I'll be home by quarter to seven."

"You better be! Do you have your toothbrush?"

I jumped on my bike and charted the quickest route to Barney's house. I made it there within six minutes and found Barney and Jimmie waiting on the front lawn. "Barney, is your sister still on board with our plan?"

"Yeah, I told her that we're going to a year-end party for the caddies at the Club."

"I'll throw my sleeping bag in the tent. My Mother might call to check on us, so can you go tell your sister we'll be playing Monopoly in the tent?"

Barney went into the house and returned a few minutes later. "She understands everything. I might have to buy her a present, but it's all set.

"Let's go to the Club," Jimmie said as he guided his bike out of the driveway onto the sidewalk. "I heard that they have two strippers from Dizzy Izzy's and a couple bar maids from the Club coming."

I was excited. We started peddling our bikes, as dusk shrouded the city, and I flipped my handle bar flashlight on. As we neared the pro shop, I could see Andy surrounded by several sets of golf clubs. "Bum...we're here."

"No kidding! Spykstra, I need you to clean the rest of these clubs. The last groups came in all at once and I couldn't keep up. I also have to gas up the carts for tomorrow and park them in the garage."

"Andy, when will the men bring the women out to the course?"

"Around ten o'clock, Pfeiffer, but we need to be positioned in the bushes before the entourage arrives so they don't see us."

Jimmie announced his plan. "Let's hide in the bushes to the right of the green to be close enough to see some muff."

"Why don't you go camouflage yourself as a fir tree and plant yourself right next to the green?"

"Hmmm…not a bad idea."

I started cleaning the irons from one of the bags. Barney jumped in to help, while Jimmie ran to the men's locker room to see if he could sniff out any more details. I heard the roar of Rutt's old truck as it sped into the parking lot. The rusted heap came to an abrupt stop as the breaks squealed and the tires skidded on the pavement. Buddy and Rutt jumped out to meet Andy in the cart garage. A few minutes later, Buddy emerged through the bag room door. "Rookies, nice of you to come back tonight and help Bum clean the clubs."

Barney piped up. "We're here to check out the strippers. Andy invited us."

"Bum must be losing it…maybe he got a concussion in the football game." Andy ran out of the bag room, seemingly in a hurry to get out on the course.

"Bum, what the hell…you invited a rookie caddie?"

"It's none of your business, Buddy. Do you guys have the rest of the clubs cleaned yet?"

I looked around. "Only two more sets to go."

"When you're done, put 'em in the bag room. There's a number on the bag and a map legend for the bag room on the wall where pull carts are stored. Spykstra, can you figure out the layout?"

"I got straight A's in geography this year." I checked the tag, noting it was Professor Buffont's pull-cart, designated for stall C-009. I had a sudden need to pee and decided to use Orbit's bag as a urinal, feeling pretty creative. As I zipped up my fly, Andy came around the corner. "What in the hell have you been doing? We're waiting for you to go out on the course."

"I had to find the correct stall for Buffont's cart."

"It should be stored in the C section…you baby! You're in the B section. I thought you could read a map."

"Oh, this was the first 009 I saw and the stall was open, so I assumed I was in the right place."

"When you get to high school, you'll need a guide dog to find the classrooms. Let's go now. I'll grab a flashlight."

As we left the bag room, I spotted Jimmie jogging back from the clubhouse and asked him, "Did you hear anything more?"

"I overheard Dowd Jones mutter that they were nearly set to head out on the course. He must have been drinking for hours because he was pissing in the sink. They're waiting for the gals from the strip club. They were supposed to be here by ten."

Andy assembled everyone in front of the pro shop. "This damn flashlight won't work…the batteries must be dead. Shit…flashlights are just a place to hold old batteries."

We trailed closely behind Andy, Buddy, and Rutt as they charted a course to the 12th green. Rutt hadn't realized that we were right behind them, overhearing his braggadocio. "Guys, did ever tell you how I killed a green parrot one day with my pellet gun? It must have been someone's pet. That was almost as fun as when Bronco and I ripped a kid's underpants off in the boy's lavatory and strung the shreds up on the school flag pole…HEE…HEE…HEE."

Jimmie scratched his head, "I remember those news reports months ago. What a shame if someone squealed on Rutt?"

Andy directed us when we reached the 12th green. "Let's split up. Buddy, Rutt and I will take cover behind the evergreens to the right side of the green. You other guys can lay down over there behind the low shrubs."

"Andy, that's nearly twenty-five yards away. We may not be able to see anything unless we stand up."

"Pfeiffer, if you don't like it, go home! But whatever you do, don't stand up and remember to keep your mouth shut…don't even breathe and stay put until they're gone."

I heard the boisterous laughter of several men and the sound of women cackling. The entourage, consisting of two women and six men, arrived at the edge of the green. I could clearly hear Dowd Jones and Walt Mellon's loud voices, their words slurred.

Jones tripped on a rake and fell into a trap. "Who put the bunker there? It wasn't there this afternoon. Shit, I got sand in my underwear and my shoes, Walt!"

"Take 'em off, Dowd."

Jones sat on the ground, took off his shoes and socks, and pulled his pants down to his ankles. He stood up and fell over into another trap as the men collectively had a good laugh.

"Boys…nice of them to put a beach right here. Hey, Rhonda, help me get out of this trap!"

Barney whispered to me. "Rhonda is a barmaid in the men's grill room.

I now recognized Pag's voice. "Annie, moon me!"

"What did you say, Pags?"

"Show me your fanny!"

"Very clever, Pags. I heard two new songs on the radio today. The Kingsmen just recorded "Annie Fanny" and Toby Bennett has a new tune called "Fly Me to the Moon"."

Barney whispered to me again. "Annie is the other waitress, but where are the strippers?"

Pags shouted, "Walt, where are the strippers?"

"They're not coming, even though we told them we would pay them a hundred bucks each plus some bonus money for personal services."

"Barney, what services is Mellon talking about?"

"Shhhh!"

Jones ordered the girls to strip. "Annie, sit down on the green and straddle the hole with your legs apart, so you form a V...a V for vagina. I want to see some muff."

Rhonda raised her hand. "What should I do?"

Mellon instructed her, "Honey, you have bigger knockers than Annie, so you can help in our next contest."

Solid clouds now covered the moon, so I couldn't see the women clearly, even when Jones shown his flashlight on them. I had a brief view of Annie's hinder before she sat on the green and got a brief glimpse of Rhonda's silhouette when the light hit her body. I rubbed my eyes, attempting to focus, even though she was thirty yards away. "Barney, can you see them?"

"Shhhh!"

Mellon shouted. "We're ready to play Muff from the Rough. Boys, you each have three tries to chip the ball into Annie's snatch."

The men were so drunk they could barely stand up, much less swing a club. Jones took the three hacks and buried the clubface into the ground without touching the ball each time. Mellon shanked the ball with his first two tries and whiffed on his third attempt. "I tried to hit the skank, not hit a shank."

The men wailed in laughter. Pags was next to play and rolled two shots between Annie's legs and into the cup. Everyone cheered. The other guys missed wildly or whiffed. One ball came into the bushes and nearly struck me.

"Next challenge! Rhonda, lower yourself on the green facing Annie and touch your boobs to the ground."

Rhonda knelt on her knees and thrust her arms down. "This way?"

"Perfect! Your boobies form a tunnel, so we can run the balls through them toward Annie."

"You can line up your shots with the crack in my ass. Don't swing too hard now, I don't want to call a plumber to extract a ball out."

"Classy...very classy!" Mellon chuckled.

Jones slurred, "Rhonda, your butt isn't all it's cracked up to be."

Annie blocked my view of Rhonda. I desperately needed to move a few feet to the left or right, where Barney and Jimmie were positioned, so I edged myself a few inches to the right.

"Stay put, Spike. You're making too much noise... Shhhh!"

"I can't see a thing!"

"Shhhh! Stay where you were."

"Dowd, you go first. Imagine you're hitting between two mountain peaks turned upside down. Now set the flashlight down on the ground so it shines right at Rhonda's rear...it can be our guiding light."

Rhonda turned. "I watch *The Guiding Light* soap opera every afternoon."

"Rhonda, maybe you can sing a little soap opera music to help with our concentration."

"Mr. Mellon, I can't sing opera, but I know another song, "I've Got a Tiger by the Tail."" She said, and then launched into the first two verses.

Jones continued his spasmodic shots, whacking the ball sideways. "Shit, I missed all of them. Give me another chance!"

"Dowd, you had your turn...now move out of my way." Mellon took a few practice shots and lined up, peering down the line marked by the flashlight. "What a view!" His first shot hit Rhonda in her left foot and the second shot in her right foot. The third shot was on line, but hit her right breast. "Shit, the ball was a tit right."

The other players tried in vain but the boob gap was apparently too small. Pags was the last to play. On his second shot, the ball rolled straight through Rhonda's boobs, but stopped an inch short of the cup. "I was robbed, my chip was in the hole all the way." Pags bent down to survey the line, gathering his concentration. He took a slow backswing and nudged the ball, which went through Rhonda's tits, and crept closer to the hole. It hit Annie's thigh and nestled perfectly into the cup.

The guys screamed and congratulated Pags. "Pags, you win the trophy for the 1965 Muff from the Rough Championship."

"A trophy?"

"We'll engrave your name on an actual golf cup and we glue a bunch of curly black hair from Fred's Barbershop around the rim."

"Walt, I can't wait to hold it."

Annie was still straddling the hole. "Are we done yet, Mr. Jones?"

"We're done with our game, but the night is young. Let me show you where the sex green is…I mean the 6th green. I've got another pin stick to show you there."

"Lead the way!"

Rhonda was still hovering over the green. "What about me?"

Mellon pulled her up. "I've got another club I'd like you to hold. C'mon, my car is in the parking lot."

The group disbursed. Barney, Jimmie, and I waited until they were out of sight and finally stood up, as Andy, Buddy, and Rutt emerged from the evergreens. "Well, did you guys enjoy the show?"

"I barely saw a thing."

"Spykstra, like I mentioned before, you need a seeing-eye dog!"

"I can see fine but I was too far away. Besides, Annie was facing the other direction and she was blocking my view of Rhonda."

"Spykstra, maybe you can find a better spot next year. Good luck in high school."

"Good luck in the Marines, Bum."

Andy, Rutt, and Buddy headed toward the 6th green to follow Jones and Annie.

"Barney, we'd better get to your house now. It's nearly eleven o'clock and I need to be up early."

I was disappointed that another promising plan had fallen short of my expectations. I wanted to join Andy, but I was already risking an arrest for curfew violation. Barney suggested that we take the back streets to his house to avoid the police. We had only ridden three blocks, when a car light suddenly reflected off a nearby street sign. I swiveled to see a bubble on top of a sedan that had just turned onto 27th Street. Jimmie shouted. "It's the cops! Yikes, we'll be arrested for curfew! Let's step on it and cut down the alley to the right!"

I was standing straight up on the pedals, trying to move them faster. The alley was layered in gravel, sending vibrations up through my arms and across the rest of my body as I struggled to control my bike. The police car stopped at the entrance to the alley and slowly turned in, about forty yards behind us. Jimmie screamed more instructions. "Left on King Street and then left down the next alley!"

I was dripping sweat and my heart was pounding, ready to explode in my chest. After turning into the next alley, Jimmie spotted a narrow path between two garages, surrounded by dense bushes. "Hurry...we can hide in here!"

I glided my bike into the yard, stomped on the breaks, and skidded on the grass, tipping over. Jimmie peeked back around the corner of the garage. "I think we lost him. I just saw the cop car roll past the alley. Scott, shut off that light on your bike!"

My hands were shaking as I desperately tried to find the switch on the flashlight. The sweat, pouring down my forearms and hands, made the simple task seem impossible. After three swipes, I finally succeeded.

"Scott, get rid of that reflector on your bike too." Jimmie suddenly kicked it, shattering it into several pieces.

"Thanks a lot, Jimmie!"

"We'll need to wait here for at least ten minutes, so the cop gives up on us."

A porch lamp on the nearby house switched on, abruptly flooding the yard in bright light. A man's voice shouted. "Who's there?"

"Let's scram!" Jimmie led us on the streets we had just travelled, assuming the cop wouldn't guess that we would return in that direction. The street lights provided a guide to the route, although bands of gnats and flies swirled under the lamps. The bugs occasionally hit my face and one flew into my mouth. I tried to spit it out, but ultimately swallowed it. I clomped down on my lips, breathing in the moist air through my nose. I suddenly realized that we had just entered the Club's parking lot.

Jimmie directed us to stop near the clubhouse. "I have an idea. We can sleep in the men's locker room. I don't want to take a chance to go home tonight."

"Good idea, Jimmie. I'll call our sister and tell her that we need to stay here because of the curfew. She'll understand."

I was stunned. "I need to be home by six forty-five."

"Spike, you can leave at six-thirty and be home in time. There will be light, so you won't need to worry. If a cop stops you, just tell him that you have a morning paper route."

"Yeah, but I won't have any papers."

"You can leave right now if you want."

"No, I don't want to risk it." I couldn't believe I had gotten myself into this predicament.

I checked my watch. It was already a few minutes past midnight. There were five cars still parked near the clubhouse and one had the overhead light on. A lady opened the rear door and as we drew closer, I identified Rhonda, who was only wearing a bra and panties. Mellon escorted her toward the clubhouse.

"Look at that! Mellon must be taking her into the men's locker room. We'll have to use the service entrance. Let's park our bikes in back of the clubhouse."

Barney and I hung back in the laundry area, while Jimmie crept into the locker room. I could hear women's laughter which sounded like Annie's and Rhonda's voices.

Jimmie quickly returned. "Mellon and Jones are in the showers with the women. We can't possibly stay in the locker room as long as they're here. Let's go up the back stairs to the attic and sleep there until they leave."

"Jimmie, it's still boiling up there."

"Tony, do you have a better idea other than sleep in the grass with all of the bugs?"

"Jimmie, how about the women's locker room?" I didn't like his suggestion, it seemed risky.

"Hmmm...that's not a bad idea." Jimmie led us down a corridor to the entrance door to the women's locker room. He turned on the lights and we ascended the stairs. I recalled the layout of the lounge from the spying incident and picked out a davenport under my former perch, while Jimmie and Barney found couches in the other aisles. Jimmie turned out the lights, except for one in the bathroom area. My heart was pumping, knowing it would be difficult to sleep, even though I was exhausted. I closed my eyes and attempted to relax in the cool air-conditioned room.

Within a few minutes, I was aroused by a light shining from the stairs. I heard the voices of two women, who I immediately recognized as Sally Van Dyke and Vicki Dix.

Jimmie jumped from his spot and whispered to me. "Get into an empty locker...NOW!"

I lifted the latch on a locker next to my couch. It was empty, except for some hangers. Although the locker was nearly six foot in height, it had a twelve-inch high shelf on the top and a six-inch high ledge on the bottom, where shoes are stored. Somehow, I squeezed into the cubbyhole, banging my head against the shelf. I carefully pulled the door shut and turned the latch as the ladies entered the room. Except for my hands, I couldn't move. It reminded me of the straightjacket feeling I had the morning at Church when I donned the tiny cassock.

Sally and VD passed by, apparently on the way to the bathroom area. The next sound I heard were showers flowing. Seconds later, Jimmie tapped on the lockers. "Scott, where are you? 'We gotta get out of this place' while we have a chance. The gals are taking a shower together."

Recalling The Animals song in my head, I managed to flip the latch and opened the locker door as we made our escape. Jimmie held out his hand and pulled me out. We flew down the stairs and the corridor toward the men's locker room. Jimmie surveyed the area, surprised that Mellon and Jones had cleared out, along with the barmaids. "Everyone is gone, so we can bed down here now."

I checked my watch again. It was nearly one AM. I grabbed some towels for a pillow, found a leather chair, and snuggled to find a comfortable position. I closed my eyes and fell asleep immediately.

Chapter 25

That was one of the worst night's sleep I ever had. The anxiety of getting caught sleeping in the locker room and the fear I'd be late to meet my parents had me waking up every hour...2:11...3:08...4:17...5:03...6:14.My brain inspired alarm clock buzzed in my ear a minute later and I shifted to get out of the upright chair, peeling the skin on the back of my legs away from the leather, like slowly removing a bandage. I gazed over the armrest and saw Barney curled up on a bench, covered with two jackets. My eyes burned and I rubbed them repeatedly as I got up to leave. I opened the service door and peered outside. Dawn was breaking and a heavy fog had enveloped the parking lot. I wiped my eyes again, and began peddling to Barney's house down the same streets where the police car had chased us just a few hours earlier. I swiftly made my way, making the fifteen minute trip feel more like five, and when I got to Barney's house, I sprinted to the backyard to grab my unrolled sleeping bag from the empty tent and raced toward home.

As I turned into our driveway, Dad was loading the car trunk with fishing gear and a small suitcase. "Good morning, Scott. Did you have a nice time? Your mother is making sandwiches and loading some other food for the cooler." He glanced down at the back of my bike as I wheeled it into the garage. "What happened to the reflector? It's broken."

"I don't know...maybe someone broke it at the caddie yard yesterday."

"I'll get you a new one when we get back."

I stumbled into the kitchen where Mom was scurrying around. "We bought some pop last night, so let me know what kind I should pack. We have grape, orange, root beer, lemon-lime, and cream soda."

"Two of each, except the cream soda."

431

"I only have room for three cans in the cooler and you can only have one pop a day, anyway…that's the rule."

"Fine…one grape, orange, and a root beer. What kind of sandwiches are you making?"

"Peanut butter, egg salad, and tuna fish. Which one do you want?"

"None of them. Can't we stop at a Burger Shack in Eau Claire or Chippewa Falls for lunch? There must be one along the highway."

"All they sell are hamburgers. Remember, Catholics can't eat meat on Friday."

"Can we just pretend that it's Saturday?"

"Shame on you!"

"I'll take peanut butter. Can we at least go out for a walleye fish fry tonight for dinner?"

"Your Dad is planning to go fishing with you after we get there. I'll fry up some fish for dinner in our cabin. Milton, do you have everything packed up?"

"I've got everything in the trunk except for the cooler. Let's go…we're already five minutes behind schedule. I'll lock up the house."

"Honey, be extra careful driving with these foggy conditions."

I climbed in the back seat and closed my eyes, eager to sleep on the five hour drive. Dad cautiously backed the car out of the driveway and we headed toward the highway. Mom turned the radio to WZZZ just as Hunter Chetley recited some agricultural commodities prices, the river stage levels at several Mississippi River locks, and the closing stock prices of a few local publicly traded companies. I had no interest in the cost of a bushel of wheat or soybeans, nor did I care about how the river levels impacted the fishermen, however, I recognized the name of a couple of the companies that Dowd Jones had pitched during the golf round yesterday.

Richard Bore, the monotone music host, played an old song called "Papa Loves Mambo" by Perry Como. When he followed with Andy Williams' "Moon River," I couldn't forget the vision of Annie's hinder from only a few hours ago.

I dozed off before we reached the highway when a news bulletin from Hunter Chetley, pierced my slumber.

> *A FEW MINUTES AGO, WE*
> *LEARNED OF A SHOOTING THAT*
> *OCCURRED OVERNIGHT AT THE*
> *FIRESIDE LOUNGE ON HIGHWAY*
> *61. ACCORDING TO AN*
> *EYEWITNESS, AN UNIDENTIFIED*
> *MALE WAS SHOT WITH A*
> *HANDGUN AFTER A*
> *CONFRONTATION WITH ANOTHER*
> *CUSTOMER INSIDE THE BAR*
> *AROUND ONE A.M. THE VICTIM*
> *SUFFERED A WOUND TO THE*
> *CHEST AND WAS TAKEN IN AN*
> *AMBULANCE TO ST. LUKE'S*
> *HOSPITAL. WE HAVE DISPATCHED*
> *A REPORTER TO LEARN THE*
> *IDENTITY AND CONDITION OF*
> *THE GUNSHOT VICTIM. WE WILL*
> *UPDATE YOU WITH MORE*
> *DETAILS AS SOON AS THEY*
> *BECOME AVAILABLE. SONNY*
> *CLOUD WILL NOW UPDATE YOU*
> *ON THE LATEST LA CROSSE*
> *WEATHER.*
>
> *THE WEATHER CONDITIONS WILL*
> *BE MOSTLY SUNNY TODAY WITH*
> *EXPECTED HIGHS AROUND*
> *NINETY DEGREES. IT WILL BE*
> *MUGGY WITH THE HUMIDITY*

*NEAR EIGHTY PERCENT. THE
AIRPORT REPORTS SEVENTY-SIX
DEGREES WITH ONE-HUNDRED
PERCENT HUMIDITY AND THE
WIND IS CALM. THE FOG WILL BE
CLEARING AROUND NINE
O'CLOCK. NOW WE HAVE A WORD
FROM ONE OF OUR ADVERTISERS,
GRANDMA'S DONUT SHOP.*

*GRANDMA'S DONUTS ARE FUN TO
EAT...COME ON DOWN FOR A
REAL TREAT...FRESH BAKED ALL
DAY LONG...LOTS OF
TOPPINGS...YOU JUST CAN'T GO
WRONG.*

My thoughts quickly shifted away from the grim news story as the catchy jingle played, and I immediately recalled Jesse's explanation of the silly commercial, depicting life's charade.

Hunter Chetley resumed the broadcast with additional local and world news.

*FROM VIETNAM, FIVE THOUSAND
MARINES DESTROYED A VIET
CONG STRONGHOLD ON THE
TUONG PENINSULA IN QUANG
NGAI PROVINCE. THE
COMMANDER HAILED
'OPERATION STARLIGHT' AS THE
FIRST MAJOR AMERICAN GROUND
BATTLE VICTORY OF THE WAR.
THE VIET CONG CASUALTIES
NUMBERED OVER SIX-HUNDRED
KILLS.*

*AT THE NAZI TRIALS IN
FRANKFORT, GERMANY, SIXTY-SIX*

*FORMER SS SOLDIERS RECEIVED
LIFE SENTENCES FOR ATROCITIES
COMMITTED AT THE AUSCHWITZ
CONCENTRATION CAMP, WHERE
OVER ONE MILLION PEOPLE
WERE KILLED.*

*THE PUBLIC WORKS DEPARTMENT
ANNOUNCED THEY WILL OPEN
FIRE HYDRANTS BETWEEN TWO
AND THREE P.M. ON 23RD STREET
BETWEEN ADAMS STREET AND
STATE STREET. PLEASE REFRAIN
FROM DRIVING THROUGH THE
AREA UNLESS YOUR CAR NEEDS A
WASH.*

*THE ALTAR SOCIETY FROM ST.
STEPHEN'S IS HOLDING A BAKE
SALE IN THE SCHOOL GYM TODAY
AND TOMORROW BETWEEN EIGHT
A.M. AND NOON. THE SCHOOL IS
LOCATED AT 2340 WEST STREET.
THAT'S THE NEWS AT SEVEN
O'CLOCK. SO LONG FOR NOW.*

Richard Bore chimed in to announce the next tune.

*HERE IS A SONG RECORDED IN
1960 BY ROSEMARY CLOONEY
CALLED "HEY LOOK ME OVER"*

"Milton, I sent over some cookies to the Altar Society
for the bake sale." Mom paused to listen to the chorus
of the song. "Rosemary Clooney is one of my favorite
singers, don't you agree?"

"Oh yes, she has a great voice."

*AND NOW, HERE IS ONE OF THE
OLD TIME CLASSICS SUNG BY
BING CROSBY. YOU CAN SING
ALONG AT HOME. IT'S CALLED
"DANNY BOY"*

My eyes were heavy, but Mom's loud screeching, as she sang along, kept me awake. Thankfully, she stopped singing after the second verse. As I finally started to doze off again, Hunter Chetley suddenly interrupted the song.

*WE HAVE AN UPDATE ON THE
SHOOTING AT THE FIRESIDE
LOUNGE. OUR REPORTER, KENT
CLARK, HAS CONFIRMED FROM
AN EYEWITNESS THAT THE VICTIM
IS LINUS MAYER, THE MAYOR OF
LA CROSSE. THE WITNESS TOLD
KENT THAT A YOUNG MAN FIRED
A LARGE PISTOL AT POINT BLANK
RANGE TO MAYER'S CHEST,
FOLLOWING A BRIEF ARGUMENT.
MAYER COLLAPSED AND THE
ASSAILANT SAT DOWN AT A
NEARBY TABLE, WHEN HE WAS
SUBDUED BY THE BAR PATRONS
UNTIL THE POLICE ARRIVED A
FEW MINUTES LATER. WAIT...I AM
HEARING FROM MY PRODUCER
THAT KENT CLARK IS AT THE LA
CROSSE POLICE HEADQUARTERS
AND IS CALLING IN WITH THE
LATEST INFORMATION. PLEASE
STAND BY.*

"Uff-da...the Mayor. I can't believe what I'm hearing, Milton!"

A few seconds passed, while the WZZZ engineer tried to connect the call from the reporter with Chetley.

> *ONE MORE MOMENT UNTIL WE*
> *ARRANGE THE CONNECTION.*
> *KENT, CAN YOU HEAR ME?*
>
> *YES, HUNTER.*
>
> *KENT, WE UNDERSTAND YOU*
> *HAVE BREAKING NEWS ON THE*
> *MAYOR'S SHOOTING.*
>
> *YES, WE HAVE LEARNED THAT A*
> *MAN HAS JUST BEEN CHARGED*
> *WITH SHOOTING MAYOR LINUS*
> *MAYER. THE SUSPECT'S NAME IS*
> *DEAN JAMES, WHO HAS AN*
> *ADDRESS IN LA CROSSE.*

I sprang up in my seat, as if a bolt of lightning had just shot down my spine.

> *THE ASSAILANT, WHO IS TWENTY-*
> *ONE YEARS OLD, HAS BEEN*
> *COOPERATING WITH THE POLICE.*
> *ALLEDGEDLY, HE TOLD THE*
> *DETECTIVES THAT THE GUN*
> *ACCIDENTALLY DISCHARGED*
> *FOLLOWING AN ARGUMENT WITH*
> *MAYER AT THE FIRESIDE LOUNGE.*
> *THE CHIEF OF POLICE INFORMED*
> *ME THAT JAMES HAS AN*
> *EXTENSIVE JUVENILE RECORD*
> *AND WAS WELL KNOWN BY THE*
> *DEPARTMENT. IN FACT, THE DUTY*
> *OFFICER MENTIONED THAT HE*
> *RECEIVED AN ANONYMOUS*
> *MESSAGE EARLY LAST EVENING*

*THAT JAMES HAD VIOLATED THE
TERMS OF HIS CURRENT
PROBATION. THE ALLEGED
WEAPON WAS A NAACO
BRIGADIER, A FORTY-FIVE SEMI-
AUTOMATIC HANDGUN,
REGISTERED IN JAMES' NAME.*

*THANK YOU, KENT. PLEASE
INFORM US ON WHAT ELSE YOU
LEARN. NOW, MY PRODUCER IS
TELLING ME THAT WE ARE
RECEIVING AN UPDATE FROM
THOMAS LOWELL, OUR REPORTER
WHO IS STANDNG BY AT ST.
LUKE'S HOSPITAL. LISTENERS,
PLEASE STAND BY WHILE WE
PATCH HIM IN.*

*THIS IS THOMAS LOWELL
REPORTING FROM ST. LUKE'S
HOSPITAL. A MEDICAL
SPOKESMAN HAS JUST INFORMED
US THAT THE VICTIM IN THE
EARLY MORNING SHOOTING IS
DECEASED. HE CONFIRMED THE
IDENTITY OF THE VICTIM AS
LINUS MAYER, AGE FIFTY-SEVEN
AND IS THE MAYOR OF LA
CROSSE. WE WILL REPORT ANY
FURTHER BREAKING NEWS
IMMEDIATELY. THOMAS LOWELL
SIGNING OFF.*

Chetley choked, apparently trying to collect his thoughts.

*THIS IS SHOCKING NEWS TO
DELIVER. TO SUMMARIZE, THE*

*MAYOR OF LA CROSSE, LINUS
MAYER, HAS BEEN PRONOUNCED
DEAD FROM A GUNSHOT WOUND
AFTER AN ALTERCATION THAT
OCCURRED EARLY THIS MORNING
AROUND ONE A.M. THE SHOOTING
OCCURRED AT THE FORESIDE
LOUNGE LOCATED ON HIGHWAY
61. THE AUTHORITIES HAVE
ARRESTED DEAN JAMES, A
TWENTY-ONE YEAR OLD LA
CROSSE RESIDENT, WHO
APPARENTLY WILL NOW BE
CHARGED WITH MURDER. MAYER
IS ALSO KNOWN FOR HIS
FLAMBOYANT TELEVISION AND
RADIO ADVERTISEMENTS AS THE
OWNER OF SEVERAL
AUTOMOBILE DEALERSHIPS
THROUGHOUT THE MIDWEST. WE
WILL HAVE MORE NEWS AT THE
TOP OF THE HOUR. AND NOW, WE
WILL HAVE A WORD FROM OUR
SPONSOR, GRANDMA'S DONUT
SHOP.*

"Milton, we should have stopped at Grandma's to pick up a few powdered donuts for our trip."

Richard Bore announced another tune.

*LET'S KICK OFF THE NEXT
SEQUENCE WITH GENE PITNEY,
WHO SINGS "THE MAN WHO SHOT
LIBERTY VALANCE" FOLLOWED
BY PATTI PAGE WITH "HOW MUCH
IS THAT DOGGIE IN THE
WINDOW?"*

"Scotty, your Dad and I are talking about getting a dog. Would you help take care of it?"

I was in a daze.

Mom raised her voice. "Scott, I'm asking you a question! Answer me!"

"Ah…I'm sorry. I know Dean James. He's a caddie at the Club. His nickname is Jesse James."

"Like the outlaw? Isn't he a little old to be a caddie?"

"He was in trouble for some criminal behavior, so a judge sentenced him to do community service as a caddie at the golf course. I think he's twenty-one years old."

"Heavens, you hung around this delinquent felon?"

"He's a good guy, Mom."

"A good guy with a criminal record? Now he will be charged as a murderer. Isn't that ironic?"

"He told us he carried a forty-five-caliber gun that he locked in his motorcycle."

"A handgun? I don't know anyone who carries a gun except policemen. Why on earth would anyone need a gun?"

"Jesse said that the Second Amendment to the Constitution gives everyone the right to protect themselves with rifles and handguns. The law states that a well-regulated militia has the right to bear arms."

"A regulated militia? Was he a member of the Auxiliary Police or the National Guard?"

"I don't think so."

"Your caddie friend had a motorcycle too? Was he a member of the Hell's Angels? Milton, do you remember the movie with Marlon Brando, where he played the leader of a biker gang?"

"Sure. It was *The Wild One*. We saw the movie at the show ten years ago."

Frank Sinatra's "The Best is Yet to Come" was playing in the background and started to fade in and out as we were losing the signal from WZZZ.

"Milton, we must be out of range. I'll find another station." She slowly turned the dial until we heard a disk jockey with a strong signal.

THAT WAS PATSY CLINE SINGING
"I GO TO PIECES." WE'RE ALL
COUTRY KOOP-780. AND NOW,
HERE'S JOHNNY CASH WITH "I
WALK THE LINE."

"I can't stand Western Country music. I'll search for another station."

I instinctively yelled at her. "Leave that on! "Walk the Line" is one of Jesse's favorite songs."

But Mom ignored my plea, and turned the knob on the dial to the next station that came in clearly. I buried my head in the pillow I had brought along for the trip. I didn't care to hear another song or any more commentary from my parents. My head was spinning, but fatigue quickly set in and I dropped into a deep sleep. I didn't wake up until I felt the car lurch forward as we came to a stop in a gravel parking space next to a tiny wooden cabin on Balsam Lake.

Chapter 26

As I expected, the weekend at Balsam Lake was boring. The schedule was not all that different from home, except it was replaced with long, boring hours of fishing with Dad and playing cribbage with my parents at night.

When we arrived in the early afternoon, I helped Dad unload the car and brought everything inside for Mom to sort and unpack. She settled in and got straight to work scouring the entire cottage. I was sure that the place was clean, but Mom worked diligently to scrub the kitchen counter, utensils and dishes, swept the floors, and made up the beds with sheets, pillows, and blankets that were packed at home. In addition to not trusting the cleanliness of the cabin, Mom didn't feel comfortable using the bedding that the resort provided.

The cottage was small, but cozy, with just one bedroom, along with a sparse living area with a two seater sofa and a small cot, generously undersized, that was situated in the corner. A compact kitchenette was adjacent to the living room, housing a two burner stove and tiny oven, along with a square table and four old wooden chairs. Mom and Dad slept in the bedroom and I got the cot, where I curled up with my pillow and thin blanket as my feet hung over the end.

Within an hour of our arrival, Dad had gone around back to the wooden dock to locate the row boat that was included in the cottage rental. After strapping on our life vests, we were out on the lake with our rods in tow. I had always hated to fish, although it was Dad's favorite pastime. He had recruited me to be his angling partner ever since I could remember and I had become pretty proficient at casting. We didn't own a boat, so it was always more of a challenge to catch fish from a bank than floating on a lake or on the Mississippi River backwaters. Trout streams were Dad's preferred venue, where he could work magic with a fly rod, often using flies that he tied himself. He had the patience of Job, a trait that I certainly did not inherit. I wished that he had the same passion for golf that he had for fishing. Golf, to me at least, was a sport that seemed to require much more skill than patience.

I provided the power for our old wooden boat, rowing it a hundred yards from the dock to a spot, that Dad felt was lucky. He opened his silver tackle box, which was meticulously organized, selecting a multi-colored lure that was shaped like a minnow.

"I'm going to cast for walleyes and northern pike...I heard the lake was stocked with them this spring." He handed me a red pole and a cardboard container. "I bought some worms on the drive up when you were sleeping. Bait the hook on this pole and maybe you'll catch some bluegills or perch."

I pulled the cardboard container top open, seeing a couple dozen worms wriggling in some moist dirt. They reminded me of baby snakes, so I instantly looked away. This was always the worst part of fishing trips with Dad. I detested touching the worms, especially the plump purple ones, and even more, hated driving a hook through their squirming bodies. I took a deep breath and in one fell swoop, grabbed one the slimy ones and drove the hook in, as the blood began to ooze onto my fingers. "Yuck!" I exclaimed and instinctively plunged my hand into the cool blue water and swished it around making sure all of the worm guts were washed away.

Regaining my bearings, I cast the bait about ten feet from the boat, observing the red top of the white bobber standing straight up on the water. After every five minutes, I reeled in the line and alternated throwing it on the left and right sides of the boat. Dad was busy casting the lure about forty feet in front, slowly turning the crank on the spinning reel.

Other than Dad's occasional casts and the faint sounds of birds chirping along the shore, there was complete silence out on the water. I stared at the motionless bobber as it floated on the surface of the lake and began thinking about the past several months.

It seemed surreal that the summer had come to an end so quickly and that I would be starting classes at St. Anthony's in ten days and football practice in just three. My thoughts bounced back to April, when Barney first told me about caddying. From his initial description of the job, I never would have expected how much would have come from my time at the Club. Thankfully, I had Barney there to show me the ropes and warn me about the older caddies and some of the members. I grew closer to with him and his brother, Jimmie, and we would be forever bonded after last night's adventure that resulted in us sleeping in the Men's Locker Room. I forged new relationships with the Bunker twins, Rusty, and Lance, who were all attending the two public high schools, but I knew that we would meet up shortly on the gridiron. I missed having OC around in the later summer months after his altercation with VD and Minnie Mayer. His non-stop entertainment had me and the other guys constantly laughing.

The senior guys were another story. I had encountered a bully in my neighborhood who would pepper me with crab apples or snowballs on my bike ride back and forth from St. Stephens, eventually having to detour three blocks out of my normal route to avoid him. But Buddy, Rutt, and Bronco were, by far, the most hostile individuals I had ever come across. After hearing about Rutt's dad and the other guy's stories, I was intrigued with how their wretched upbringing were to blame for their viciousness, as well as a lack of empathy and remorse for their vile behavior. The initiations and constant insults from them were unsettling and certainly traumatic at first, but looking back, they were challenges I had to overcome in order to survive in the caddie yard. Poor Franny, among a few other newbies, didn't even last one whole day.

"Scott...Scott...SCOTT!"

Startled out of my daze, I looked at Dad and started reeling in my line.

"It's been over an hour with no bites, so let's head over there," he said, pointing to a section near the shore where a few dead trees had fallen into the lake.

With my cautious rowing strokes, I strategically positioned the boat about twenty feet from the logs, coasting the last few feet so the fish wouldn't detect us. Before we resumed our casting routine, Dad ordered me to place a fresh worm on the hook. I resisted at first, but ultimately followed his command. With the flick of my wrist, I plunked the line three feet from a moss covered log, a perfect spot I thought. In a few seconds, my heart skipped a beat as the bobber moved slightly up and down, then sideways, and finally totally under the surface of the water. I yanked the pole up and felt the strong tug on the end of the line.

"Start reeling it in," Dad instructed.

Within a few turns of the reel, I could see a yellowish colored fish desperately churning underwater to break free of the hook."

"Looks like a sunfish...a six incher," Dad observed. "Pull it up into the boat."

The sunfish flopped on the wooden planks and Dad scooped it up with his left hand, as blood slowly dripped from its mouth. He stuck his fingers inside and tore the hook out, causing more blood to gush out onto the floor of the boat. He filled a small bucket with lake water and plopped the sunfish inside, turning the water into a pinkish hue.

"Now we're cooking, way to go, Scott! Now, catch another one!"

I hadn't seen Dad that excited, since he triumphantly killed a mouse that had invaded our house back in March. Reluctantly, I reached into the worm container again, wondering what happened to the last sacrificial victim. I snagged a thick one, took a deep breath, and punctured its body twice. "Ugh!" I yelped and stuck my left hand in the lake again.

I cast the line in the same spot and stared at the bobber intently, eagerly awaiting my next prey. A long five minutes passes without a nibble, so I recast about five feet to the left...nothing. Back to my original spot...nothing. Close to the shoreline...nothing. I repeated this sequence two more times before the excitement of the first catch finally wore off and I went back to reflecting on my summer at the MVCC.

Andy was terrible in the beginning too, probably even more cruel than the senior caddies at first. It wasn't until the sprinkler incident with VD that he even started to warm up to me. I still can't believe I had the nerve to follow through with it and shudder to think what would have happened to me had I gotten caught...or worse, what would have happened if I had wimped out. I know I would never be a close pal of Andy's, but I think I may have finally earned his respect that day on the football field. I stood up to him and the senior caddies, emerging as a leader for the rookies. I didn't realize it at the time, but that established a level of self-confidence that I never knew I had before. They weren't intimidating to me anymore, nor were girls, teachers, or my parents. Suddenly, the thought of high school didn't seem so threatening. I was actually looking forward to it.

The memory of my first day at the Club came rushing back. It was out on the second green when I had just received the second verbal insult from Andy after nicking the edge of the cup as I tried to pull the pin out. A simple mistake, no doubt, yet he followed through with the callous attack. I was planning my escape and started my retreat when Jesse, of all people, stopped me and convinced me to stay with just a few brief words. What if he hadn't been there to stop me? My first caddy season was certainly no picnic yet the thought of not having that experience seemed unsettling. I had met so many different people, and learned so many things about life and myself, none of which would have happened if it hadn't been for Jesse. But now, I felt depressed...Jesse James, the caddie who unknowingly had provided the greatest impression on me, was sitting in a jail cell, charged with murder.

Dad suddenly interrupted, "Scott, you seem lost in thought."

"Just thinking about the caddie who shot the Mayor...I still can't believe it."

"Yeah...murders are pretty rare in La Crosse. I can't even remember the last one."

"I can't believe that Jesse would purposely shoot the Mayor…it had to be an accident. What do you think will happen to him?"

"I suppose there will be a funeral and a burial in the cemetery."

I looked at him strangely. "I meant the caddie."

"It depends on how the district attorney will try the case. But if a repeat offender kills a high profile person, like a Mayor, it could lead to the death penalty. It all depends on a jury's verdict and the judge's sentence."

"Death penalty?" I said, shocked. "Have you ever been on a jury, Dad?"

"Only once…it involved a robbery, but the defendant was a habitual criminal, so it was easy to find him guilty."

I was even more disheartened than before. I reeled in the line and dropped the hook just two feet from the boat. To my surprise, the bobber was pulled under in just a few seconds. I reeled the short line in and pulled another sunfish into the boat, except I felt no joy this time. Dad excitedly grabbed the fish, extracted the hook again and threw it into the pail, as the water turned a murkier red.

Two more dull hours passed without any more bites. I glanced down at my watch and it was already after six o'clock.

"We had better head in…Mom will be wondering where we are. There's only two fish to eat, so one of us will need to have something else."

"Don't worry, Dad…I'll just have the other half of my peanut butter sandwich that Mom made for lunch."

I was somewhat relieved. Pan fried fish wasn't a favorite of mine, especially eating one that I had just caught.

My stomach was already growling after I finished my half sandwich back at the cottage, but I only had to suffer until morning when Mom would make plenty of eggs, bacon, and pancakes for breakfast to relieve my hunger pains.

The cabin didn't have a television, so after supper, I played three handed cribbage for an hour or so with my parents. By the time eight-thirty rolled around, I couldn't keep my eyes open any longer. I crashed on the cot in the corner of the living room, while Mom and Dad went to bed.

The next morning, Mom didn't disappoint me, making a breakfast fit for a lumberjack. The news broadcast sounded from a transistor radio that Mom packed, set on the windowsill above the sink. We were too far from La Crosse, to get a signal from WZZZ, but Mom found a local station that played forties classics speckled with a short hourly news report, which included a brief comment on Mayor Mayer's murder, but no further details. Like clockwork, right after the last bite of breakfast, Dad had us shuffling out the door for a full day of fishing on the lake. Not wanting to miss an opportunity to catch a fish, Dad insisted we bring lunch with us to eat on the boat...a fried egg sandwich and a few potato chips that Mom packed into two brown paper bags.

Saturday was a nearly a repeat of Friday afternoon, except neither Dad nor I caught a fish after eight hours on the boat. We quit in the late afternoon around four o'clock and headed back to the cabin. Dad took a nap, leaving an hour to myself, which I spent outside walking around the shoreline, skipping rocks across the rippled blue water. Dad and I played cribbage until supper was ready, although he won all three games with his crafty pegging. While Dad was disappointed not to catch any fish that day, it was good news for me was because Mom made hamburgers and hot dogs instead. After she was done cleaning up, Mom joined us for a few more games of cribbage before she decided it was time for all of us to go to bed.

After breakfast on Sunday morning, we left for an early Mass at the tiny Catholic Church in the Town of Balsam Lake. The Church was packed and despite arriving ten minutes before the service started, there was standing room only. Afterwards, we headed back to the cabin, packed up the car, and left around ten o'clock for the five hour drive back to La Crosse.

Chapter 27

I was awoken abruptly as our car crossed over a deep chuckhole on the pavement that shook the backseat. Dad was not happy. "Why can't Minnesota keep their roads repaired like they do in Wisconsin? That tire better not be damaged!"

Looking out my window, we passed a route shield displaying 61 in thick black numbers, followed by a highway distance sign indicating that we were only-five miles from La Crosse. I shifted my glance forward, noting dark clouds stretched out across the horizon creating a thick blanket of grey. The main channel for the Mississippi River was again in sight through the windshield, as rain drops began to collect on the glass.

A flashing neon sign caught my eye across the road, and as we got closer, I was able to make out the words lit up in bright red letters...THE FIRESIDE LOUNGE. I sprang across the backseat to get a better view. The parking lot was empty except for two police cars that were parked near the front entrance. The door had been cordoned off with yellow police tape in a big X, so it was safe to say that the joint was closed for business.

My brain started whirling, trying to reconstruct all of the events leading up to the fateful incident that occurred inside that building in the wee hours of Friday morning. Mayer had reprimanded Jesse during his recent caddy assignment, prompting my recollection of Mayer's threat to intervene with the judge who presided over Jesse's probation. One of the news reports had mentioned that the police had received an anonymous call about Jesse's probation violation a few hours before the shooting. It had to have been Mayer, I concluded, probably making that call shortly after completing his golf round. One of the other caddies must have tipped off Jesse about Mayer's threat...likely Rutt or Buddy, knowing of Jesse's short fuse. They were always plotting to get Jesse in trouble, although I would never thought it would go this far. Following the conversation where Jesse told us about Mayer's lambasting, a caddie had mentioned that

Mayer hung out at The Fireside Lounge on Thursday nights. Everything started to fit together, especially Jesse's forewarning about packing a handgun in his motorcycle to frighten challengers.

The lounge began to fade as I gazed out the back window until I could no longer see it in the distance. I slumped down in the seat and thought of Jesse sitting alone in his prison cell at the police station. My stomach clenched, feeling as if it was tied up in knots as I thought about his fate. I recalled my conversation with Dad out on the lake...the possibility of the judge sentencing him to the death penalty based upon Jesse's criminal history. I wanted to puke. Sure, Jesse had a record, but there was more to him than that.

I traced back to my memories of Jesse as they unfolded at the Club. The morning of the tee digging, he demonstrated a hot temper and violent aggression when he punched out Rutt. His toughness came out again during the football game, when he got physical with the senior caddies and slammed Andy against the tree. Jesse's stories describing prison life and his time spent prizefighting were intoxicating. And his tattoos, loud motorcycle, handgun, and cigarette habit, signified his independence to me. Mom barely let me cross the street without holding her hand, so the thought of driving a motorcycle would terrify her, probably sending her straight to the hospital with worry. And if I ever got caught with a tattoo or smoking a cigarette, I'd be banished to my room for life.

Jesse was certainly intimidating, but was also incredibly perceptive. Once you got past the bruiser façade, there was so much more intelligent reflection. During the humiliating caddie training lesson, after Andy and the senior caddies mocked me, I wanted to quit. But it was Jesse who told me to stay, imparting the wisdom that those guys were all talk. It's embarrassing to think back to our first conversation and my naïve probe about beaver hunting and muff diving, but Jesse never gave me a hard time about it. A few weeks later, he started to open up and we had an interesting discussion about his favorite singers and tunes. I recalled his carnal fascination with women, yet his opinion was that lady golfers at MVCC should have more privileges. And just a few days ago, he attempted to provide a sobering lesson on the direction of government and society to us unsuspecting caddies, lecturing us on the meaning of song lyrics played over Barney's transistor radio. Jesse had a broad knowledge of the world, having been a voracious reader while in prison. He was much wiser than anyone I had ever met. He clearly understood the country club dynamics and could see through the phoniness of some of the members and did not tolerate fools, yet, was always polite to them, even Linus Mayer. He talked about reading psychology books to explain his perception of the members of the MVCC. Finally, I recalled his debate with Barney about gun rights...how ironic that it now apparently came back to haunt him. My hunch was that Jesse pulled out his pistol to confront Mayer and something tragically went wrong in the tavern.

From my position in the back seat, I studied my parents. Elsie babbled about her flower garden and how her rose bushes hadn't produced enough blooms, while Dad ignored her, focused on the road in the steady rain. After these past five months, it had become blindly apparent that my parents had established a very sheltered environment for me. Their vivid memories of the Great Depression had created a passion for saving money and living simply, a notion that they attempted to drill down into my psyche at every opportune moment. While money had never been an important element in my life before I began to caddie, the wealth of the Club members had opened my eyes.

Like Jesse, I studied the behavior of every player I caddied for, as well as the other golfers in the group. Deciphering the personality traits of the golfers was intriguing. The most honest and cordial members I encountered were primarily high school graduates, who had worked their way up the ladder of success through hard work. However, many of the members were bombastic and arrogant, flaunting their possessions and vacation trips, while constantly berating the club staff and the caddies.

Most of the caddies and the male golfers had fantasies regarding women, so I was not abnormal after all. The heavenly image of Ada Mellon was still etched in my mind, as well as VD's white nipples and the opaque figures of the two naked barmaids on the 12th green on Thursday night. I was still puzzled about observations from the women's locker room between Sally Van Dyke and Vicki Dix. There were so many missing pieces and hopefully, I would learn more about sex at high school or at the golf Club next year.

I had never particularly tuned into politics and world events, although the dialogue of the golfers had broadened my consciousness. I would now pay more attention to the news on the radio or TV, and keenly listen to song lyrics, based upon Jesse's advice. Based upon Mom's commentaries over the years, she now seemed extremely myopic, reflecting her very narrow perspective on life. Although I now was more prepared to question her opinions, that challenge will be daunting.

I was appreciative of Mom and Dad's lessons on the value of hard work and respect for elders. I probably wouldn't have gotten very far in school in school or as a caddie without those moral pillars. My parents and teachers had formed my core values, so I could never compromise honesty and ethics to cut corners for advancement, even though I had told a few more innocent lies than usual lately, having observed lairs and cheaters in the caddie yard and even more on the golf course. But most of my small fabrications seemed harmless, so I started to justify them as acceptable to reconcile a conflict. I had even fibbed to Mom, telling her that I had gone to confession and that one REALLY seemed justifiable.

Despite my fear of negative consequences from my parents and authority figures, I found myself in a few risky predicaments over the summer. Following Andy's orders, but ignoring sound judgment, I turned the sprinkler on VD. It was a dicey move, but resulted in establishing a rapport with Andy, which created more opportunities for me. The eventful night of spying on the women, running from the police, and hiding in the Women's Locker Room, was fraught with danger, but thrilling none-the-less. And the afternoon spent in the hot attic over the Women's Locker Room was yet another gamble. I was never much of a risk taker before, but I was learning that the potential rewards could be worth it.

Dad turned the car off Highway 61 towards The Linus Mayer Bridge. For a brief moment, I thought of the Mayor, his corpse probably now stored in a vault or in a casket at McAbre's Funeral Home. I quickly changed my attention to the St. Anthony freshman football team orientation at nine o'clock, where I would see Goober and Barney. Afterwards, I could buzz downtown to pay for a professional haircut, buy the pants that I tried on last week at Doerflinger's Department Store, and then ride to the bank to make a deposit into my savings' account for the balance of the one hundred sixty-seven dollars accumulated from my summer earnings. The next mission will be to send two dollars to the Chicago Cubs Baseball Club for a 1965 yearbook.

My thoughts drifted to the future. How would the Vietnam War end? Would LBJ's Great Society be a long lasting success? How about Lou Sparks' putting invention? Would Japanese or German automobiles ever successfully compete with domestic manufacturers? Would stockbrokers be replaced by machines? Is it possible for politicians to become honest and transparent? Would the United States Government restore fiscal conservatism? But most importantly, would the Chicago Cubs ever appear in the World Series, much less, actually win it?

I shifted positions, observing myself in the rear view mirror. I peered through the window into the mist as we crossed the river, envisioning its circuitous course to the Gulf of Mexico. I closed my eyes, pondering what path the future would bring for me too.

CPSIA information can be obtained
at www.ICGtesting.com
Printed in the USA
FSHW020601230219
55870FS